ORPHANS

A.V. PARKS

To Bill, of course

Excerpt from
The Science of the Mysteries . . .

The *Introim*

Disembodied spirits emanating from the Grand Aeons, sent to Earth to help and enlighten Mankind.

The Saturni: Those *Introim* who became embodied and sought to maintain their power and satisfy their appetites by eating every living thing.

The *Lwas*: The Introim who refused to join the Saturni, exiled to the fringes of society and the enslaved peoples of the world.

The Skin Eaters: Creations of the Saturni, human in origin but endowed with supernatural powers and enchained by their addictions.

The Great Saturni: The four great powers of wealth, glamor, rationality, and faith, which rule our current world.

The Four Gifts: The four great *Lwas* who are said to offset the Great Saturni.

The *Jumbies*: Those children who, chosen to be Skin Eaters, fail in their initiation.

The Mounts: Those children who are said to be uniquely receptive to being possessed by the Lwas and giving them human form.

Excerpt from
Daedalus: A Tradition of Service . . .

. . . the Daedalus School occupies the former Livaudais Mansion in the historic Garden District of New Orleans, once the home of Francois and Niobe Livaudais. Niobe Livaudais, nee de Marigny, was descended from one of the oldest families in New Orleans; her brother, Bernard de Marigny, once owned vast tracts of land south of the Vieux Carre; and her sister, Agatha de Marigny, once presided over the city's glittering salons . . .

Content Advisory

This is a work of dark fantasy and Southern Gothic fiction.
It contains ritualistic violence and morally ambiguous behavior,
and scenes that may be upsetting to some readers.
Reader discretion is advised.

Introim

In the beginning of the world, the desert was covered with a sea of grass. There were tides of wind over the sea, and the grass waved like water. There were animals there—some dangerous, some good to eat—and there was fresh water and berries and leaves. And there were the people.

They traveled in a group, for protection and for company. Nobody wanted to be too far from anyone else. That way, when trouble came, there was always somebody you could ask for help. And at night, when the world was large and dark and there were too many lights in the sky, the people huddled together for protection from less specific fears—fears without teeth or claws, but fears nonetheless, which made them shiver and feel like their heads were thin and porous and the mysteries of the world were coming through.

That all changed when the dreams started. Suddenly, they knew their purpose. They were there to build stone circles. The labor was hard. They felled trees with flint axes and used the logs to drag the stones forward. The night when it happened, they were all lying together by the fire. When the noise started, a glorious, ringing, golden sound seemed to be shimmering all around them, unlike anything they'd ever heard before. It was as if the wind and all the birds in the world and all the animals in the world and all the thunder in the world had started blowing and singing and roaring and rolling all at once, all around them.

A shining shower of lighted globes began to descend from the sky, like beautiful round worlds coming into their bodies. And they heard the voices of the Saturni.

"We are the Saturni. The locust ones. Gods of the belly, who eat and are never filled. This is our rank breath, clotted with old blood. These are our teeth, that bite continually. This is our power: destruction. This is our goal: annihilation. Let us live inside of you, and you will be as gods. Let us command you, and you will rule the earth. We need you to feel, to touch, to taste, to experience life, and to give us a time and a place to sate our hunger. We are the beasts as pitiless as stones, and we will never rest so long as anything on earth remains alive."

Chapter One

Daneel woke in pitch-black darkness and stifling heat.

What had seemed like a good idea at the time, climbing into the attic of his grandmother's house to escape the rising flood waters, had left him, in sleep, with the sensation of being adrift in a floating coffin. The attic, really no more than a crawl space, pressed down on him like a bad dream of being smothered alive, and the heat made him feel like he was being roasted. It was worse than anything he'd ever experienced in his entire twelve years of life, which was saying something, especially if you came up in the Lower Ninth Ward in New Orleans.

His sweat had soaked and dried and soaked again into his T-shirt and jeans, and now, however many hours later, his clothes felt stiff as cardboard. His throat was parched, and ... he wondered if he might be hallucinating, if the creepy bugs on his skin were real. He shivered, imagining roaches and spiders. He hauled himself up and crawled over to the trap door in the roof, beating on it with his fists until the swollen wood finally gave way.

He began to push the door all the way open but stopped himself. He could hear water sloshing outside, and he debated whether opening the door was a good idea. Had the water already risen up high enough to cover the house, and was he going to let it in? Was he going to drown, just when he was trying to breathe?

He couldn't stay another minute in the attic—he knew that much for sure. He shoved the trap door all the way open. The lapping waves he'd heard were somewhere below him. Otherwise, it was quiet. And dark—so dark it seemed as if he'd gone blind. He crawled to the edge of the roof, feet dangling, trying to get his bearings. The street, the houses, everything around him was underwater, and up above him stretched a sky so empty it made him dizzy.

So much space. The moon was rising, and he watched as its rays stretched out in long, silvery bands across the shimmering surface of the oily lake, which was what had become of his street, his front yard, his everything. There was an eerie sound of timbers creaking and debris washing somewhere here and there. He wondered if there were bodies. Did everybody die? Did everybody get out except him, passed out with heat in his cramped hiding space?

He remembered his Nani saying she was going for help, sloshing out in water up to her waist in the direction of Claiborne Avenue, which was the last time he'd seen her. The water had been coming in fast then, and he had no idea what might have happened. Did she die? Did she return to look for him? Was she swept away? He forced himself to take a deep breath and tried to keep from bawling like a little kid, pressing his fist against his mouth as he looked around him at the silvery emptiness which stretched away in every direction. But wait . . . it wasn't empty in every direction, was it? Because now he saw a shape coming toward him. Something darker in the darkness. Someone was rowing toward him in a small boat.

A very strange boat, almost as narrow as a canoe, and completely silent, manned by a single tall woman with a pole. The woman with the pole was no more than a shadow, featureless, pushing along with steady strokes, although it didn't look like she was breaking a sweat. Daneel held onto the roof with one hand

and waved with the other, opening his mouth to yell, although something stopped him at the last minute.

He realized he was scared to death.

As the woman approached, he could see a strong nose and pale skin, thin lips, and eyes like black coals, piercing. He opened his mouth again, this time to scream, when the woman said, "Little boy, I think you have a limited number of options. I'd suggest you come with me."

CHAPTER TWO

Nina Lamb was riding uptown in New Orleans six months later, sitting in a cab next to a large social worker named Alice Hopkins. The radio was on, and the cab driver was listening to Wolf News.

"WLF Newstime 10:36 . . . It's partly sunny in the Crescent City, and we got some construction out on the I-10 between the Causeway and Clearview Avenue . . ."

"So, what's the name of this place again?"

"The Daedalus School, darling. How often do I have to tell you?"

"What does it mean?"

"I don't know. That's just what it's called."

"Is it like . . . dead? Is that why they call it that?"

Loud squawks on the radio led into an ad for Pelican Air Conditioning: "Where our number one mission is keeping you . . . on ice!"

Nina tried to find the words to tell Mrs. Hopkins how uneasy this whole drive was making her. "Are you really sure I belong there?"

"Oh yes, honey, it's the absolute best place for you. Everybody agreed."

The announcer came back on, identifying himself as Wolf Radio's own Bosco Ledoux. "Folks, joining us here in the studio today is George Ingmire, who's here to tell us about his encounter last night with New Orleans' weirdest new character, the Bywater Biter. Seems George and his lady friend were just walking along last night, minding their own business, and some maniac jumps outta St. Roch Cemetery and sinks his teeth into George's friend and then runs away. No word yet on whether or not she tasted good, but the lady in question did require five stitches. So, George, you got any idea what's up with that?"

Nina turned to Mrs. Hopkins and said, "Look, um . . . I really think I'm okay, y'know? I mean, I'm guessing I'm, what? Seventeen? Eighteen? Maybe even older than that. I could get a job. Maybe even go to college. Really, I'm sure I'd be fine."

"It's out of the question. Look, you need to be taken care of, all right? You're still suffering from post-traumatic stress. All our tests said so. This school is the ideal place for you to heal up, unwind, maybe get your memory back . . ."

Nina gave up and looked out the window. The avenue un-spooling past them might have been untouched by Hurricane Katrina, if you didn't count the missing live oaks and the missing streetcars, which were still stuck somewhere in storage. The storefronts from Felicity Street to Jackson Avenue were mostly open, and the mansions looked untouched. St. Charles Avenue, all white-columned elegance and money and discreet charm.

Bosco Ledoux was talking about how the city was still messed up, and people might be acting out from all the tragedy they'd seen and the pets that had been abandoned in the days after the levees broke.

"Or it could be some kind of mutant rabies," he said. "Or some kinda mass psychosis. After all, people work through their issues the best they can. You see people drowning and being herded up and getting hysterical and dying on the sidewalk. Who knows what you do? Maybe you just gotta bite somebody. Maybe he thought he was a dog."

George explained how human bites could be especially dangerous, and Nina wondered if she could simply jump out of the moving cab and run away.

Bosco said, "Yeah, ya right. And word is it's not the first time it's happened. People are just going crazy and attacking people."

They turned onto First Street and crossed Prytania and Coliseum, then stopped in front of a very tall building and got out.

It was a big Gothic mansion, foreboding in its silence, a huge three-story fortress dominating one whole corner of the street. It had wrought-iron balconies, a high-peaked roof, long pass-through windows, and four tall chimneys poking up against the sky. All the windows were boarded up with plywood, and two very sinister stone angels wept out in front, one on either side of the door.

"Okay, here we are," Mrs. Hopkins said, and Nina could tell the social worker was nervous too.

Nina looked at the big iron gate and thought this was the very last place she wanted to be. She wondered if she could just make a break for it. Why not? What could they do to her—send her back to the hospital in Baton Rouge? Maybe she could just get lost in some bureaucratic shuffle, like half the population of Orleans Parish. She could live on the streets. That kind of sucked, but it still had to be better than this.

She'd seen people dying in the Convention Center and looting at Walgreens, but the worst part of it was she had no memory of her life before the hurricane. Which still didn't mean she needed to be here. At the Daedalus "School," a home for troubled teens, a place where she could finish an education she couldn't remember starting. She had the impression she'd be locked up here along with rich white stoners and kids who cut themselves and vomited to get their parents' attention, minor league shoplifters and major league slackers, probably with a few psychotics thrown in. Wonderful.

And there was something else, something nobody was telling her, something in the way people's eyes slid away from hers with guilty fear whenever they mentioned this place. Something unmentionable. There was a pall of secrecy over the Daedalus School that hid something furtive, like a secret shame.

"Really . . ." she tried once more, "I could go back to school up in Baton Rouge, that was okay—"

A flash of impatience crossed the social worker's face. She grabbed Nina's arm and said, "Look, let's get something straight. You need to go here. This is the only place where you'll be safe. I don't have any more dealings with these people than I have to, but every once in a while, I get a kid who belongs here, and then I just do my job and bring 'em along. I don't ask questions, and neither should you." Her face split in a conspiratorial grin, which made her look truly awful. "Hey, take my word for it, you'll like it here. It's certainly wild! You won't be bored, I can tell you that much. Now get on out of the car and ring that bell."

Nina sighed, pushed open the car door, and then pushed open the gate, feeling it give smoothly on well-oiled hinges. Well, at least it wasn't locked. And the place was strangely lovely, she realized, once she'd let the gate swing shut behind her. The silence was impressive, given the fact that busy St. Charles Avenue was just three blocks away. They might have been in another century, with errant sunlight peeking down between the trees and long strands of Spanish moss swaying from the branches. The garden was a huge green cathedral of open lawn, with gravel paths and an old carriage house over by the farthest wall. Somewhere, Nina could hear a fountain splashing. She walked up the steps and rang the bell.

"Yes, can I help you?" The tall woman who answered the door

looked harassed and tired, with flour and jam smears on her long apron.

Nina said, "Um, I think I belong here?"

She gestured to Mrs. Hopkins, who gave the woman her card and said, "Yes, we spoke over the phone. I'm Alice Hopkins, I mentioned we needed to enroll a new student here and—"

"You must have spoken to Professor Danvers. He handles all the new admissions. I'm just in charge of the physical plant."

There was a twist to the woman's lips that suggested this task was a good deal bigger than it sounded. She stepped back and added, "Why don't I give him a call."

She reached for an old-fashioned speaking tube attached to the wall, and a moment later, an impatient voice said, "Yes?"

"Visitors, Strickland. A Mrs. Hopkins and charge."

There was a momentary pause, and then the same voice said, "All right, send them up."

The woman jerked her thumb. "Professor Danvers is upstairs in the Headmaster's Office. Everyone else is in class, so you'll have time to meet with him before lunch. We serve lunch at one o'clock sharp," she added, although Nina couldn't tell if this was an invitation or a warning. "We keep to a tight schedule, as we find that helps us keep everything in line."

This sounded ominous, but the woman's straggling hair seemed to indicate keeping things in line was a lot harder than it looked. She turned at once and said, "Shit," softly under her breath, then hurried toward the back of the building, where clouds of smoke were issuing from what had to be the kitchen.

Nina and Mrs. Hopkins were left standing in a large center hall. The walls were of dark-paneled wood, so the house glowed with a shadowy beauty. There was a big chandelier hanging over an equally big rug of some dark shade. Dominating the hall was a long stained-glass window, which showed five birds in flight—a crow, a pelican, a swan, a peacock, and a fiery-orange bird with a long, plumed tail, all flying in a circle against a stormy, rain-flecked sky.

Directly in front of them rose a wide, dark-wood staircase, the banisters intricately carved, and the treads carpeted with thick red plush. The staircase ascended in a series of landings all the way to the top of the house. And when Nina and Mrs. Hopkins stood on the bottom step, they could look up and see yet another stained-glass skylight far above them. This one showed a clear glass orb containing a radiant dove.

"Are you sure?" Nina asked one last time, but Mrs. Hopkins just shook her head.

"Absolutely. All the tests said so," she replied.

All the tests. Nina shuddered, remembering the whole battery of tests she'd taken, both in Houston and later on in Baton Rouge. What was she good at? What might help her to remember? All she knew was that none of them had worked. She remembered waking up in an old, abandoned warehouse down by the river the morning after the storm, in shorts and a T-shirt and wrapped in a tattered blanket. From there, she'd wandered down to the Convention Center, to join the throngs of trapped, dehydrated, starving people who were waiting there in the brutal sun for the help that was so tragically late in coming.

Along with everyone else, she'd finally taken a bus out to the highway, where she received a ready-to-eat meal and some water. Eventually, she ended up in Houston. Where everyone had been very kind and very concerned and very baffled.

Nobody had a record of her. The Latina matron had called her la pobrecita nina, the poor girl, and the name had stuck. Later on, someone in Baton Rouge called her "lamb," and that got added. Nobody knew what to do with someone so pretty, with long, black hair and wide, hazel eyes and light-tan skin, who was also so sad. She might have fallen down out of the sky, or blown in from the ocean, a refugee from the storm itself.

Now, as they got to the second-floor landing, Nina saw a heavy oak door facing them, with the words *Headmaster's Office* on a brass plaque. Underneath it, scribbled on a white card taped to the door, were the words, Professor Strickland Danvers, Acting Headmaster. Nina stuffed her hands in her pockets, so this time Mrs. Hopkins was forced to knock.

"Come in," said a sharp voice. They glanced at each other, then opened the door and stepped inside.

The Headmaster's Office was a large room facing the street on one side and the garden on the other. The windows were all boarded up, so the light that came in was dim. The room was dominated by an enormous mahogany desk, which was covered with more papers and stacks of books than any one desk should have been able to hold. There were also obscure mechanical devices, something like a pendulum, and something else that looked like a model of the solar system. The light from an enormous gilded gaslight fell on the walls of bookcases and the thick, dark-red rug, trapping them in amber. There was also a large black box over in one corner that looked like a safe, except it had no door or hardware on it of any kind, and a man was standing facing it, a tall, dark-haired man with a beautiful, impatient face, who spun around and said, "Yes, what do you want?"

"Um . . ." Nina felt like a jerk. "I'm Nina Lamb. I'm supposed to go to school here?"

The man stared at her, although glared, she supposed, might be a better word. He was young; in fact, he looked almost boyish, although the lines on his face made him appear older. He had the darkest eyes she'd ever seen, black as coal, if coal had ever shone with such an incandescent light. His thin lips were pressed into a straight line, and his eyes looked at her warily, almost as if he expected her to attack him.

Do I know him? The intensity of his gaze made her skin prickle. She said, "I-I'm sorry—"

"Mr. Danvers." Mrs. Hopkins tried to put things back on a more professional footing. "I'm from the Louisiana Department of Child Welfare and—"

"Professor Danvers, if you don't mind." He scowled at her. "I spent a good deal of time acquiring my mostly under-utilized education, so I'd at least like to get some credit for it."

"All right, Professor Danvers," Mrs. Hopkins said with a definite sniff. They hadn't been asked to sit down, but she sat down anyway, in one of the large, overstuffed chairs that faced the desk.

Nina hesitated and then sank into the other one. She felt like she was being swallowed up in a cocoon of dark leather.

"Professor," Mrs. Hopkins continued, "Miss Lamb's file should have been sent to you—"

"Yes." He went to the desk and plucked a bundle of papers from one of the piles. "Such as it is, it's here, but I fail to see how it sheds any light on her in any way."

"Yes, well, that's rather the point," Mrs. Hopkins said. "The point is there isn't any light on her. However, we tested her attributes and—"

"Yes, yes, yes." He flipped through the sheets, coming to rest on one which caused him to narrow his eyes and read more closely. He looked over at Nina. "It says here you scored extremely high marks on existential intelligence?"

"Um, I guess so," Nina said, feeling like she didn't sound very intelligent at the moment.

He shook his head and said, "The ability to tackle deep questions about the meaning of life? Surely you're joking."

"No, why?" Nina thought, *Wait a minute. I didn't invent those tests. Or grade them. I just took them.* "Look," she said, "try and see it my way. If you don't know who you are, you have to figure everything out from scratch. Things most people never even think twice about, like do I have a fatal genetic disease, or do I have a family history of insanity? I've had to think about that stuff quite a lot. I mean, I don't think I've got a fatal disease, but who knows, right? That's at least as real a way of thinking as being able to solve logical puzzles or turn squares into diamonds by moving two matchsticks."

She licked her lips. *Did I go too far?*

Professor Danvers just looked at her for a long second and then said in a poisonously quiet voice, "Is that so?"

"Yes, sir." She swallowed. "After all, Sartre says it's up to you to give life meaning, and value is nothing else but the meaning you choose—"

But Professor Danvers had turned away from her abruptly and seemed to be wrestling with himself, or perhaps simply trying to control his temper. Then he started flipping through the papers again, but this time much more slowly.

"Ah. Yes. Yes," he said finally, sitting down and pinching the bridge of his nose. "Miss Lamb is indeed a remarkable young woman. Under normal circumstances, I'd be more than delighted to have her here. However—"

"However?" Mrs. Hopkins pounced. "Mr. Danvers, perhaps you don't understand that in today's day and age, children can't be refused an education simply because of lack of funds, so if that's your objection, there would undoubtedly be legal conse-quences—"

"Professor Danvers," he thundered, "and perhaps you don't understand not to interrupt people when they're trying to make a point!"

There was a prickly moment when nobody in the room spoke, and then the professor said with forced calmness, "We at the Daedalus School are not prejudiced. We have students here from a wide variety of backgrounds. However, at this moment, we simply have no room. We're full up."

"You're what?" Mrs. Hopkins clearly wasn't buying that. "Surely you don't mean—"

"The Daedalus School," Professor Danvers said, and his voice sounded clipped, as though he were restraining himself from shouting, "is a privately funded institution, and as such, not a receptacle for every waif and ward of the state who comes our way. We provide a secure living environment and a superior education for children who are sent to us through our regular channels, primarily the Benway Foundation. We're a Cadillac product, and as such, our expenses are high. We have a very generous endowment, but even that is limited. And since the storm—" He raised one eyebrow, as though asking them if they did remember the storm. "Our capacities have been strained to the utmost. As such, we've had to limit our enrollment—"

"Which is down 17 percent from last year!" Mrs. Hopkins said triumphantly. "Almost a quarter of your students haven't come back. You're practically empty!"

Even though 17 percent isn't anywhere near 25 percent, Nina couldn't help thinking.

And just as those words came to her mind, Professor Danvers glanced at her with raised eyebrows and what might, in another man, have almost been an involuntary smile.

"Yes, that's true," he said, after a moment. "However, the concomitant drop in tuition—"

"The state will pay Nina's tuition in full, plus a generous cost-of-living stipend, so there's no problem there," Mrs. Hopkins said, clearly having thought this all through. "She's eligible for

Family Financial Needs Assessment and state vouchers for the indigent . . ."

I sound like a derelict, Nina thought. *Then again, I guess I am a derelict.* She rubbed her forehead, wondering what Professor Danvers's smile had meant. *If I didn't know better, I would guess he'd read my mind.*

"Of course I read your mind," she heard him say in her head as clearly as a ringing bell, and she jumped.

Mrs. Hopkins patted her hand. "It's all right, honey. We have lots of children who need our assistance. It's nothing to be ashamed of."

"I'm not—" Nina didn't finish because Professor Danvers was staring at her with even greater intensity than before. His dark eyes were narrowed, as though he were drinking in every inch of her.

Why are you looking at me like that? she thought, not sure if she was talking to him telepathically or just thinking to herself.

"I'm not looking at you like anything," his voice answered in her head, a little defensively. *"Why should I?"*

You can hear my thoughts?

"As the saying goes among your verbally challenged generation . . . Duh!"

She shut her eyes, feeling her head spin. What was happening? Was she finally starting to go completely crazy? She opened her eyes again, looking around the room at the walls of books, and thought how, in a way, if she hadn't been so scared, she would have found all of this fascinating. The weird stained glass, the rich furnishings, and this tall, dark, handsome asshole. *If he wasn't so creepy,* she thought, *I'd think it was kind of cool that he can read my mind.*

But he was creepy, and this place was terrifying, and besides, he didn't even want her there, so why was he doing all this?

She looked at the professor again, and his eyes narrowed even more. She felt the touch of an exploratory hand on her cheek, and she looked down in confusion. Had he guessed that she thought he was a tall, dark, handsome asshole? She focused on the things on his desk (although she supposed it was really the headmaster's desk . . . and for that matter, where was the headmaster?) and asked, "What's that?" and pointed toward the miniature model of the solar system.

"It's called an orrery," he said. "Or sometimes a planisphere. It's for plotting the placement of the planets vis-à-vis one another and also vis-à-vis the sun." He had spoken, oddly enough, without any sarcasm, just very flatly, as though simply relaying information. But he was watching her intently.

"And that?" She pointed toward the pendulum.

"That's a Foucault pendulum. It's used for demonstrating the rotation of the earth. It works by the same principle as a gyroscope. It's also a divination device."

"Like Nostradamus had."

"Yes."

"How do I even know that?"

"You know a lot of things, Miss Lamb." His voice was soft.

And then he continued in her head, *"Unfortunately not all the things you know are either safe or to the point."*

"Mrs. Hopkins," he added, speaking aloud again and directing his attention to the social worker, "we could go on like this for hours, but it's simply impossible. We just can't take Miss Lamb."

"Let me speak to the headmaster."

"I'm afraid you can't."

"Why not?" She shot him a squinty glare. "I can wait."

"I'm sure you can, but the headmaster won't be back for several days. He's out of the country."

"Oh?"

"Yes."

He didn't volunteer any more information, and that seemed to be an end to the argument. Nina felt herself relaxing just a little. Was that it? Could they just leave now? She wasn't sure why she felt a twinge of disappointment. Surely she didn't want to stay here, did she?

She bit her lips, wondering if there was anything she could do to convince Professor Danvers of her qualifications.

"I-I'm good at languages," she said, although that sounded pretty lame, even to her own ears. "In Houston, we were all kind of thrown together, and there were some people there who spoke Spanish and Cajun French, and there were all these Vietnamese guys there, and . . . well, I could understand them all."

"How wonderful. You can apply for a job at the United Nations."

"I'm really good at solving puzzles," she said, thinking this was only getting worse and worse.

Professor Danvers raised his eyebrows and said, "Indeed?"

"Yeah, I-I just kind of got into it. Crossword puzzles, mazes, computer games . . ."

"Charming." He sounded bored. "If we offered a course in time wasting, I'm sure you'd get top marks. Anything else?"

He thinks I'm a moron. "Please, sir, I'd really like to show you what I can do. If you'll just give me a chance—"

She had no idea what she was doing. She just had an impulse to stretch out her hands to him as if she were going to beg him, but as she did so, she felt a strange tingle in her fingertips, and a moment later, everything in the room seemed to become . . . well, alive. The books on the shelves moved restlessly against one another, and some of the smaller ones fell out and inched toward her across the floor. The stacks of papers on the desk rose and blew toward her in a gentle breeze, and the plants outside on the balcony began rustling, as long tendrils of green reached in and stretched through the plywood. The orrery and the pendulum both began shifting stealthily on the desk, inching toward the edge, and even the heavy black safe in the corner gave a low groan as it tried to move in her direction.

Professor Danvers said, "Miss Lamb, stop that this minute! You're just showing off!"

"I am not!" she snapped, folding her hands in her lap.

At once, everything stopped. The papers stopped rustling and the furniture stopped moving and the long, green vines drooped dejectedly and started withdrawing back through the plywood.

Nina said, "Oh!" and then, "How on earth did you do that?"

Professor Danvers looked at her almost as if he detested her. "I didn't do anything, Miss Lamb. You did."

"But . . . but I . . . Professor? How? How could I do that? I have no idea what even happened." A pause, then she added, "I'm sorry . . ."

"No."

His voice wasn't loud, but it was peremptory.

He continued after a moment, "The power to harness what some people call 'magic' is a complicated business. It isn't understood by most people, although it's more common than most people think. It is, however, completely different from what we attempt to do here. Magic involves wishful thinking, and here at the Daedalus School, we believe firmly that this world is all there is. The material world is where we must all survive, or else perish. To distract our minds with anything else is counter-productive—"

Mrs. Hopkins cut in, "See, Professor? I told you this girl belongs here. She's part of your world. I knew it!"

"I just told you magic is not a part of our world!" Professor Danvers acted as if he was being cornered, and maybe he was. "Miss Lamb's ability at parlor tricks is a distraction, not an asset.

It certainly doesn't indicate her fitness to stay here and pursue our rather … intensive … curriculum. It could even be dangerous."

Nina opened her mouth to protest that she could control it, but Mrs. Hopkins wasn't done having her say. "Look," she snapped, "If you don't want Miss Lamb here because you're afraid of her, then say so, but may I point out some facts? There have been some bad rumors about this place. Wasn't there a scandal about some kind of a three-way going on here, between a student and two of the staff? Isn't there a tradition of private 'tutoring' that can sometimes get out of hand? I assure you, it took a good deal of convincing to get the people in my office to agree to Miss Lamb's placement here, and the decision finally came down to her being uniquely suited to your 'intensive' curriculum, and our really having no other choice. If we could have ensured her well-being elsewhere, we would have. But your school is the only place someone like Miss Lamb belongs. And—" she held up her hand, refusing to hear his argument "—can you honestly say Miss Lamb would be safer anywhere else?" She lowered her voice. "Even we know what a hornet's nest this storm has stirred up. Everything's up for grabs right now, isn't it? I'd hate to see Daedalus shut down, Professor, just when you're getting back on your feet."

For a moment, neither the professor nor the social worker said anything else, and Nina thought, What kind of a kink-fest is this school really into? And what does Mrs. Hopkins mean by "even we know"? What kind of a hornet's nest has been stirred up by the storm?

"Mrs. Hopkins," Professor Danvers said, and he sounded tired all of a sudden, "Miss Lamb is fine. She'll be perfectly fine wherever you decide to put her. You can put her in daycare if you want. The forces unleashed by this storm have far bigger fish to fry than her."

"Are you sure?" Mrs. Hopkins asked, then turned to Nina. "Look, I didn't want to tell you this, but there's something strange going on. The people who run this place, the Benway Foundation, are being very coy about the school's future, and there are some people who seem to think they're scared. Nobody knows why. Either somebody's got an axe to grind against them, or somebody wants to take them over, or somebody wants to shut them down, but they're watching their backs. And clearly, that attitude has filtered down through the ranks."

She turned back to the professor and added, "Miss Lamb is seventeen. We think. Or maybe eighteen, but she still needs to be looked after. She isn't part of whatever's going on, but she does need your help. She's still not much more than a child, and the Daedalus School is supposed to be here to help children. So, given her aptitude for your practices—"

Professor Danvers looked like he wanted to practice hitting Mrs. Hopkins, but he contented himself with flexing his long, slender hands. He said, "Your argument isn't so much ill-taken, madam, as simply beside the point. We do not have the beds!"

"Couldn't you . . . couldn't you let me sleep up in the attic?" Nina asked, too late to catch herself. *Oh shit, I'm doing it again. I'm reading his mind*, and she'd actually brought her hand to her lips as though to snatch back her words.

The assistant headmaster looked at her and said after a truly terrible pause, "Who are you, and why have you come here to torment me?"

"I-I don't know. Sir."

"How do you know about the attic?"

"Well . . . most houses have attics. I mean . . . don't they?"

"And would you really be willing to sleep up there? Alone?"

"Er, yes. I mean, I-I could, sir."

"You have no idea what you're saying." Professor Danvers's dark eyes bored into her, and she felt him reading her mind as easily as a pamphlet. Doubt. Ignorance. Innocence. Fear. And that she wasn't lying. She really had no idea who she was. Or what she was saying.

Nina had only the vaguest impression of Professor Danvers's mind as it probed hers, but what she felt more than anything else was heartbreak. There was so much sadness in him that, for a moment, she couldn't breathe. Something terrible had happened to him at some point—he'd lost something infinitely precious—up in the attic? And now he was frozen in sorrow. She was trying to figure out what that loss might have been when he got up abruptly and walked over to the window, fisting his hands behind his back.

While he stood looking at the plywood that covered the view, he almost seemed to be shuddering. She didn't know what to say. A few beats later, he turned back around, and his face was controlled again as he said, "All right. I've changed my mind, Mrs. Hopkins. Nina can stay."

Chapter Three

Mrs. Hopkins and Nina stayed for lunch with the rest of the students. Not that lunch had much to recommend it. They had lumpy gumbo, dry cornbread, sticky rice, and red Jell-O for dessert. For a lunch anywhere, it was disappointing, but for a lunch in New Orleans, it bordered on being criminal.

Nina didn't care, though, because she was much more focused on figuring out what she'd gotten herself into. And that meant figuring out her fellow students. They pretty much fell into two groups: gorgeous, and seriously lame. The gorgeous ones all sat together, toying with their food and making snarky comments while they twiddled with their perfect hair. They wore black suits and bright red ties, and long black dresses and black boots and red sashes, and while some of them looked a little strung-out—their hands twitched, and their eyes were red-rimmed and angry—they all had the undeniable air of gorgeous party monsters. Even those lovelies who had open sores on their faces looked like fashionable junkies, wiping their drooling lips on their sleeves and rubbing seductively up against their neighbors.

The loser kids sat over in a corner, and by contrast, they just looked sullen. Their clothing was strictly Walmart, mostly hoodies and sweatpants, and a few were even in their pajamas. In fact, it was like she was in two different schools at once: one a gathering place for young Goth models, one a prison. She shivered and looked down at her plate.

They ate in a large, high-ceilinged room called the Commons, where there was a bad smell, like rotten flowers. Nina sat by herself, feeling as conspicuous as a giraffe. Mrs. Hopkins was sitting up at the head table, and Nina felt the glances of both the beautiful kids and their slacker counterparts boring into her from every side. *What was I even thinking, wanting to come here?*

She reached for her glass of iced tea, and her hand brushed against the arm of the girl sitting next to her. This girl was one of the beautiful ones, with a pale, heart-shaped face and a light dusting of a mustache on her upper lip, and she seemed as cold as ice.

"Oh! Excuse me," Nina said, starting back, and the girl laughed.

"It's all right. I should say excuse *me*. We've all been checking you out, but we didn't know how to approach you." She held out her own hand. "I'm Alastaire, by the way."

"I-I'm sorry?" Nina felt like a fool, but this pretty girl (*She is a girl, isn't she?*) looked perfectly normal, yet her hand felt like she'd spent a week in a meat locker. She said, trying to be polite, "I'm Nina. Nina Lamb."

"Alastaire Roget." The girl waved her fingers. "It's all right, I didn't mean to scare you . . . I mean, with the cold. You're still amazingly warm, by the way. How do you do it?"

"Uh . . . I guess I'm just naturally warm-blooded?"

Alastaire laughed again. "That's a great line. I've got to remember that."

Nina had no idea what she meant, but she reflected that this friendly girl (or whatever she was) might be able to explain some things, so she asked, "Why were you afraid to approach me?"

"Because you have to be somebody really special. They normally never let older kids just transfer in here." Alastaire lowered her voice. "C'mon, you can tell me . . . Where are you from? New York? LA?"

Nina didn't want to admit she had no idea. "Why don't they just let people transfer in?"

"I don't know. I guess they just want to get us all while we're young, train us up in the

System, and they try to keep out as much of the riffraff as possible." Alastaire rolled her eyes at the group of loser students, who were trying to scrunch down in their seats and eat their meals as quickly as possible, to avoid the attention of the beautiful ones. "Like those lame-oids over there. They couldn't get a sponsor if they tried. *Quelles* tards."

Nina didn't like this, but she swallowed her objections and asked, "What's a sponsor?"

"Someone who pays for your education. Don't they use sponsors where you come from? See, after a certain point, people kind of adopt you and pay for everything. You become like a part of their family. If no one sponsors you, then you're really in trouble. Like those *jumbies*."

"*Jumbies*?"

"It's an old Creole word meaning low-lifes. My family's been in the French Quarter for like for*ever*. Hey, are you going to eat your dessert?"

"Here." Nina pushed her tray over. "Do you mind if I ask you a few more questions?"

"Sure. What do you want to know?"

"Well, first of all . . ." Nina didn't know how to put this. "Professor Danvers—"

"Isn't he totally beautimous?" Alastaire glanced toward the head table, where the professor was seated between Mrs. Hopkins and the woman Nina had met earlier. This woman looked remarkably like the professor—she had the same dark hair and strong, high-bridged nose, the same dark eyes, although in her case her whole appearance looked somewhat grumpy, compared to the professor's icy calm.

"So, who is he?"

"Well, first thing is, he's the acting headmaster. That's a whole other thing. The headmaster's been gone for ages . . . since way before the storm. Professor Danvers runs everything, although he's constantly having to talk to the headmaster and get everything approved."

"Does he teach anything?"

"Not regularly. He gives Divination tutorials sometimes, but they're strictly extra credit. He's basically in charge of running things. And that's his sister sitting next to him," Alastaire added. "Agatha Danvers. You do *not* want to piss her off. I think she's trying to kill us all with her cooking," she added, making a face. "That is, if anything actually could kill us."

Nina was a little surprised at the joke, but she figured she didn't know what passed for humor in this place yet. "So, all those other people up there are teachers?"

"Mm-hmm. That's Professor Hermes, he teaches Calculation Science." Alastaire pointed to a graceful man in a white suit who was so pale, he was whiter than paper—even his eyes were white. "He's also an expert in Hypnotism and Mind Control. They offer it as an elective."

Nina frowned. "Hypnotism and Mind Control? Do they really teach that stuff here?"

"Of course." Alastaire looked surprised. "What did they teach at your old school?"

"I don't know. English, Math, Chemistry . . . things like that."

"Well . . ." Alastaire said, "Calculation Science is a lot like Math, I guess, although you don't do the actual calculating, that would take forever. You use a PE."

"What's that?"

"A polynomial engine. Everybody's got one. Want to see mine?"

"Please." Nina had no idea what a polynomial engine was, but she figured she'd better learn as much about this strange new world as she could. Alastaire dug in her backpack and withdrew a beautifully carved wooden box. She pulled back the top, revealing a complex set of rods, gears, springs, and glass tubes, all interlocking as perfectly as a piece of jewelry, or the insides of an elaborate watch.

"It's simple, really. All you do is import your data, and then you place your fingers here, on these two metal plates—" Alastaire demonstrated, holding the box between her hands. "And think about whatever your problem is, like if it's math or whatever, and the polynomial engine will give you the answer. In your mind. It's simple, really."

"Why not just use a calculator?"

"A what?"

"A . . ." Nina got out the cell phone that the social services people had given her. "Check this out. I've got an app here that'll do pretty much any math problem you want. You just load in the numbers and—" But she stopped because Alastaire was staring at her as if she'd pulled out a gun.

"Put it away. Put it away! For God's sake, get rid of it before somebody sees it—hide it! Eat it! No, wait, I'll do it." Alastaire grabbed the phone, looked around wildly, and then, as if she had no other choice, plunged it into Nina's glass of iced tea and hid the glass—phone and all—under the table between her feet.

Nina would have protested, but she was too astonished to do more than stare. Finally, she said, "You *are* going to buy me another one. *Right*?"

"I'll pay you back, but you can't have anything electronic in here. It sets off all kinds of sensors. Really, seriously. You notice how everything's gas in here, and there's, like, speaking tubes instead of intercoms? Nobody at Daedalus can have anything like a cell phone or a computer or anything like that. It totally sucks, but it's a rule."

"So, what? You guys can't watch TV or listen to the radio or . . ."

Alastaire nodded. "You'll get used to it. But that's why we use PEs. Besides, they're good for lots of other things. The really good ones can do trance algorithms, but those cost a fortune. The idea is you get your raw data from observations of the world, anything from sights and sounds to smells and tastes and feelings. Then you input it, and the polynomial engine interprets it. It's based on the principle that everything in the universe can be broken down into binary data. Simple."

Nina didn't think it was simple at all, and she was still fuming over the loss of her cell, but she had to admit she was also fascinated by Alastaire's tiny, beautiful device, which would have fit perfectly in the palm of her hand. To change the subject, she asked, "So what else do you study?"

"Well, they teach us the Great Books, of course. *The Sepher Yetzirah* and *The Book of Thoth* and *The Complete Works of Simon Magus—*"

"*Excuse* me?"

"Sure, you've got to do the classics. I did my junior paper on *The Chymical Marriage of Christian Rosencreutz.* Professor Mwindo gave me an A-minus on it."

She gestured toward a reserved black man in long African robes sitting on the other side of Agatha Danvers. He was engrossed in a paperback copy of *The Complete Works of John Dee.*

Nina decided to just nod and say, "Okay, Professor Mwindo, check. Who else?"

"Well, there's Professor Aspidistrus." A portly, green-skinned man who looked like a frog. "He teaches Alchemy. And Professor

Threet." A nervous little woman like a stork. "She teaches Astronomy and Sky Geography, plotting the constellations and the planets—"

"Don't tell me—with an orrery, right?"

"Well, of course. How else would you do it?" Alastaire looked honestly curious.

"Who's that beautiful redheaded woman? The one in the long, tight dress?"

"That's Professor Ariadne." Alastaire sniffed. "She's pretty hot, I guess, but she's kind of a ditz. She teaches Hygiene."

"*Hygiene?*"

"Yeah, why?"

"I don't know. It just seems so . . . normal."

"Don't make light of washing your hands after every meal."

"Okay, if you say so. Who's that really, really old man?"

"That's Professor Seneschal. He's practically ga-ga. It's too bad—he teaches History, which could be fun, but not with him. And then there's Professor Samson." She pointed to a powerfully built man at the far end of the table, who looked like he was ready to burst out of the seams of his bush jacket. "He's in charge of Transformation and Animal Dominance, as well as Security. And he takes care of the wolf pack."

Nina just sipped her tea and thought, *I really* am *going insane.* She looked up and saw Professor Danvers looking at her with a strangely penetrating expression, and she looked down quickly. *I've got to stop looking at him so much.*

She's beautiful, Strickland Danvers thought. *I don't even know how old she is. No one does, it seems. My sister Niobe made flesh once more, and what does that mean? That I'm up the creek with-*

out a paddle. He tried to pay attention to the prattling Mrs. Hopkins on his left, but it was like nails on a blackboard. And by comparison, he knew if he turned around and spoke to Agatha, he'd be knee-deep in explanations before he even opened his mouth. Agatha was a bitch, but she knew him as well as anyone, and she knew his tastes. *Shit,* he thought, *what was I thinking, letting that girl in here?*

"He's looking at you," Alastaire whispered. "Professor Danvers is really staring at you."

"Really?" Nina tried to stifle a giggle that was threatening to burst out at the least opportune moment. The last thing she needed was to start perving on a handsome young teacher in a place like this.

"Can't you tell? C'mon, are you blushing? You are *so* blushing!" Alastaire laughed. "You're so adorable, I could just eat you up."

She was looking at Nina with the kind of frank admiration that could only mean one thing, and Nina decided she'd better nip this in the bud. "Um, Alastaire . . ."

"Yes?"

"You . . . you're a girl, right?"

"At the moment." Alastaire's lovely face was poised and calm and seemed to be waiting for her to go on.

Nina struggled with how to put this. "And, well, *I'm* a girl."

"You certainly are." Alastaire looked her up and down, and Nina felt terrible, but she had to say it.

"And, well, I'm just not into that, okay? I mean . . . going with other girls. Not that that's bad. It's just not my jam."

"Oh, that's all right," Alastaire said with a nod. "I'll be changing in the next few months, so if we wait a little while, it'll be okay."

Nina shook her head. "No, that's not what I—" She stopped and stared at Alastaire as the realization hit her. "Wait, what do you mean? Changing into what?"

"You meant that you like boys," Alastaire said. "And that's cool. So we'll wait a little while. I'll probably end up as a man. I'm definitely more male than female, and then we'll see. I'm down with that."

Nina had no idea what to say. Finally, she sputtered, "You mean . . . you're like . . . both?"

"Of course." Alastaire waved her hand (or was it *his* hand?) to indicate everyone else in the room. "We all are. Isn't it like that where you come from?" She laughed again and, without waiting for a response from Nina, pointed to the teachers' table and added, "The staff is so *completely* bi. Professor Samson wears women's underpants and a push-up bra under that jacket. Professor Aspidistrus can never decide whether he's an animal or a plant. And Agatha, well, let's just say the dyke bars in town let her run an open tab. Hey, different strokes, right?"

Nina shut her eyes. *I'm definitely losing it.* What exactly *was* Alastaire, anyway? Although a part of her mind told her she had some idea. "You're . . . you're not human, are you?"

It was Alastaire's turn to look puzzled. "What do you mean?"

"I mean . . ." Nina felt like she was drowning in a sea of double entendres. "I mean, you're not like me. A normal human being." She tried to think how else she could put it. "Warm."

"Oh." Alastaire looked down at her empty Jell-O cup. "You're kidding. Oh God, I feel like *such* a douche. I thought you knew already. You mean you really don't know?"

"Know what?"

"We're Skin Eaters."

Skin Eaters. The words were meaningless in one way, and yet they sent a chill down Nina's spine.

Alastaire looked profoundly embarrassed. "Shit," she said.

"This, like, so *totally* sucks. I can't believe they let somebody warm in here. Look, forget I ever said anything."

Nina was willing to put up with a lot of things at that point, but forgetting wasn't one of them. She snapped, "Listen, you can't just expect me to drop this. You have to explain. I have to know what's going on here."

"I can't believe I'm such a doofus. Professor Danvers is going to *kill* me. Look, what are you doing after lunch?"

"I don't know." Nina shrugged. "I guess I have to drive back with Mrs. Hopkins to Baton Rouge and get my stuff. Get checked out of the shelter there. I'm not sure."

"Look, see if you can stall her. Tell her I'm going to show you around. I've got Advanced Mist Travel after this, but I can so totally blow that off. I'll take you over to the chapel and fill you in."

"Are you sure?" Now that Alastaire had agreed to give her an explanation, Nina wasn't sure she wanted to hear it. She remembered the strange excitement she'd felt in Professor Danvers's office, but now that was again mixed with dread. She said, "I don't want to get you in any trouble."

"I'm already in trouble." Alastaire lowered her voice. "Just don't tell anybody I told you all this, all right? I mean, it stands to reason you'd learn somehow, but I don't want to be the one who gets blamed for doing it. Okay?"

"Okay." Nina felt oddly grateful to this strange boy-girl, even if she was helping her out only to cover her own butt.

Alastaire stood up and said, "I'll bus your tray. Go on and tell Mrs. Hopkins you'll meet her in an hour, and I'll catch up with you outside."

She pointed to the hallway outside the Commons, and Nina nodded, getting to her feet. "Fine. I'll see you in a minute."

Nina walked up to the front table, and her stomach did a little backflip as Professor Danvers looked up and met her eyes. She had a confused impression of anger, frustration, and anguish, and for a moment, she thought she saw a large, black bird—like a crow—attacking a woman who looked an awful lot like Mrs. Hopkins. There was blood running down the woman's face, and her mouth was open in a scream. As she watched, the bird pecked out the woman's eyes . . . and then a wall came down over whatever Nina was seeing, and Professor Danvers stood up and brushed past her.

She managed to say to Mrs. Hopkins, "One of the girls is going to give me a tour, all right?" and Mrs. Hopkins said, "Fine. Just don't get lost," and Nina ran out into the hallway.

Chapter Four

Think of something nice, she told herself. *Think of puppies. Think of kittens. Think of puppies attacking kittens and birds pecking their eyes out. No, no, no, don't think that! Don't think that at all.*

What the hell was that *all about?*

Nina had no idea what she must look like, but she figured she must look pretty bad, as she read the concern on Alastaire's face. "What's wrong?" the other girl asked. "You look like you're ready to hurl."

"Nothing," Nina said. "I . . . I'll tell you later." She changed the subject. "Mrs. Hopkins is cool with you giving me a tour, so where should we start?"

"I told you. The chapel. Come on, it's this way."

Alastaire led her down a long, dark hall away from the Commons, where the walls were lined with portraits of people in hoop skirts, Victorian top hats, powdered wigs, and even armor. The coffered wood was such a deep brown it almost looked black in the dim light. All the people in the portraits had the same dark, eerie beauty, with high cheekbones and full red lips.

As they walked, Nina noticed how every single window was boarded up.

She asked, "Did the school get a lot of damage during the storm? Is that why you still haven't taken down the plywood?"

"Um, not exactly." Alastaire led her up a flight of steps and around a bend in the corridor, where the temperature dropped.

"Does the Daedalus School go back a long time?" Nina asked, trying to keep her teeth from chattering. "These paintings look really old."

"Oh yeah. It's been here since this was the old Livaudais plantation. The whole Garden District used to belong to her. There's a legend that Madame Livaudais let her only child drown, and her husband never forgave her for it. She swore she'd do anything to bring the little boy back to life." Alastaire pushed open a heavy door. "Here we go. You'll like this. Everybody always goes 'Wow' when they first see the chapel."

And Nina decided *Wow* was indeed the right reaction, if by *Wow* you meant *Shit*! She walked into a massive octagonal chamber rising up to a vaulted ceiling at least thirty feet high, filled with soft motes of dust dancing in the colored rays from a half dozen stained-glass chandeliers.

Ruby red, golden yellow, cobalt blue, and emerald green light fell everywhere over rows of pews, all facing an altar dominated not by a traditional cross, but by a big, ugly, black cup. It looked like it was made out of cast iron. There were paintings all around them, showing an old man dismembering a child, naked men and women coupling and twisting and rutting like wild beasts, and worst of all, people eating each other, their mouths stretched open and their teeth dripping with blood.

Nina found her voice and said, "Yeah, you're right, this is certainly . . . something."

"Cool, huh? I gotta tell you, a lot of kids don't know what to say when they first come in here. It's something about the atmosphere." Alastaire gestured around the walls. "Power." She plopped down in one of the front pews and said, "Come on, have a seat, and I'll give you the basics. It just majorly sucks that they didn't tell you."

Actually, it majorly sucks that I can't just run away screaming, Nina thought, but she still sat down next to Alastaire and said, "Okay, so tell me."

"Well." Alastaire propped her feet up on the pew in front of her. She ran her hands through her dark hair before she began. "First of all, you asked me what we were."

"You're like vampires, right?"

"God, no!" Alastaire made a face. "That's so *totally* wrong. We don't kill people or sleep in coffins or anything like that. We're called Skin Eaters because, well . . . we eat the 'skins'—" she did air quotes "—off of things. The illusions that people have that cover over reality. See, everyone develops a 'skin' as they go through life, the habits and illusions that make them act the way they do without really thinking about it, and we come in contact with people and we strip those illusions away. We make people look at the world with fresh eyes. Clear eyes! We're like therapy!"

"Okay, so how do you do that?"

"Well, I'm not really sure. I'm not there yet."

"But all this stuff you're doing is to train you so someday you can do that?"

"Uh . . . yeah." Alastaire looked a little uncomfortable. "It's a complicated process."

"I'll say it is. Why don't they just call you 'strippers,' if you strip away people's illusions?"

"Because we're not strippers, okay! That's just stupid!"

"What you're talking about just sounds like self-help."

"It's a lot more spiritual than that! It's . . . it's holy!"

"Oh really?" Nina waved her hand around. "So, what's so holy about this place? Those people are fucking each other and eating each other. They're cannibals!"

Alastaire turned away, facing in the other direction, and said coldly, "If you don't want to hear about it, then I won't tell you."

"Oh, all right, come on . . . I'm sorry I freaked out. So you're not vampires."

"No."

"Are you zombies?"

"No."

"Ghouls?"

"No!"

"Werewolves?"

"What *is* it with you? For God's sake, it's a metaphor! We unwrap the human mystery, all right, we take the 'skin' off people's bullshit and reveal their true essences. We reconnect people with their souls and 'eat'—" again with the air quotes "—their complacency. What's not to like?"

"Well . . ." Nina thought about it. "I guess that's not so bad."

"It's not. It's great."

"But are you, uhh . . ." She took a deep breath and decided she'd better just go ahead and ask it. "Dead?"

"Are you kidding?" Alastaire laughed. "We're immortal! Okay, lemme explain. We all started out as human. Most of us came here when we were really little. Daedalus is, like, our only home. We're all available to be sponsored, and a lot of us get chosen right away. Usually, it's an established Skinny family that chooses us. They agree to sponsor us, and eventually they adopt us, only you can't just turn people right away. It's a whole process. That's why our parents have us stay here at Daedalus until we're finished. Once we're fully changed, we can go anywhere and do whatever we want."

"So, okay . . . I'll ask it. How do you change?"

"It's complicated." Alastaire turned back and wrapped her arms around her knees. She seemed to have completely forgiven

Nina. "It takes seven crossings to do it all, to wash the mortality out of you completely. Every time you cross with an adult Skin Eater, he or she takes a little more of your mortal life away from you, and you take a little more of his or her immortality in. It's like a process of inoculation against death."

Nina felt like pointing out that there still seemed to be a lot of death involved, but she kept that thought to herself. "Does it hurt?"

"Well, kind of. There are some gross temporary side effects. Some of the older kids take a tonic that helps. It's called Red Spur."

"Like Red Bull?"

"Actually, no. Red Spur is made of red spur valerian and brandy and some other stuff. That's the smell in the Commons, like dead flowers. That's the valerian. It's disgusting, but it's apparently great for mellowing people out."

"How do you cross with somebody?"

"Well, we each taste a little of each other's life essence and . . ."

"So, you *are* vampires!"

"No! I told you . . . it's nothing like that."

"But you still have to taste—"

"Their life *essences*. Their *souls*, all right? Okay, look. It starts when a mature Skin Eater reads somebody else's thoughts. It's like telepathy. You with me so far?"

"Yes." Nina nodded. She was certainly with her on that score.

"We call it 'tasting.' When a mature Skinny 'tastes' you, they 'taste' your thoughts. In voodoo, it's called 'mounting.' They share a spiritual connection with you, and it's really intense. You don't remember much afterward. It's like sex. Only it's actually cooler."

"Cooler than *sex*?"

"Mm-hmm." Alastaire's eyes got dreamy. "I've done it three times. I did it with Professor Threet. She was my first. She was very gentle. And I did it with Professor Mwindo, which was amazing!"

The Skinny girl giggled. "He's got this weird African way of doing it. It involves a lot of drumming."

"And I did it with Professor Samson," she added, "but that was kind of strange. He likes you to beat him with a riding crop while you're doing it. Not my thing. And a lot of kids do it with Professor Ariadne, the Hygiene teacher. There's, like, a waiting list."

Nina felt her head spinning. "Let me get this straight. Are you telling me you have to have like . . . mind sex . . . with the teachers here? Isn't that . . ." She was at a loss for words. "Isn't that *illegal*?"

Alastaire laughed. "Don't knock it if you haven't tried it. Besides, like I told you, it's a spiritual thing."

Nina shook her head. "I'm *so* not buying this."

"Why not?" Alastaire looked honestly curious. "Don't all kids get crushes on their teachers?"

Nina felt this was a dangerous topic to get into, so instead of answering the question, she posed one of her own. "And after seven crossings, that's it? You're a Skinny?"

"Yup."

"What if you cross more than that? What if you do it an eighth time?"

"You can't," Alastaire said regretfully. "If an adult Skinny crosses with another adult Skinny, you both die. It's like our lives become toxic to one another once we're both turned. Weird, huh?"

"Yeah." *Weird doesn't cover half of it.* "Is that why you're so cold?"

"That's right. I'm down to 56 degrees now. When I hit 32 degrees, I'll be able to make ice." Alastaire grinned. "That's a joke, in case you hadn't noticed."

"So you—" Nina frowned. There were so many questions she wanted to ask. "What happened to your families? I mean, your birth parents?"

"Hmm?" Alastaire was picking at a thread on her skirt. "I don't know. I don't really remember. It's all part of the process. Some of the kids aren't as cool with it as others, but eventually they settle down."

"If they get chosen."

"Right. If they don't, then they just hang around here, getting older and older and more and more pissed off. It's awful, in a way. I mean, imagine knowing there's nobody in the whole wide world who really wants you."

Tell me about it, Nina thought. "So, where did the Skinnies originally come from?"

"Well, people say we were initially created as a way to defeat death. I mean, even the Bible says something like that, right? 'Whosoever believeth in me shall never die?' Other people say there were these powerful beings who created us as their helpers. I mean . . ." She shrugged. "Who knows what actually happened?"

Nina shook her head. "I'm not following this. How did they actually do it?"

"Well, the story goes that these elder gods, the *Introim*, came down from heaven to help mankind. They taught us a lot of things, like agriculture and math and stuff. And then, when human beings first realized they were actually going to die, they begged the *Introim* to change things. To write another ending to the story. I mean, it makes sense, right?"

Nina shivered. It should have sounded ridiculous, but for some reason, it didn't. Maybe it was the setting, the strange, lush violence of the chapel, with the jewel-like lights of the chandeliers casting reflections down on the painted figures. It certainly seemed possible to believe divine beings had once come down from heaven to defeat death.

"So these *Introim* were like, what—angels?"

"Angels, archetypal forces. It all adds up to the same thing."

"Not really."

"Well, see, the thing is, they were just beings from Somewhere Else. Who knows? They weren't human, at least not in the way we understand it, but they became embodied, supposedly here." Alastaire pointed to her belly button. "In the *Dan Tien*, the navel chakra. The *Introim* became incarnate inside the navel chakras of certain human beings. And they became the Saturni."

"So who are the Saturni?"

"Oh, the Saturni are these really, really powerful people who run everything. They're like into high finance and government and the military. They saved us a while ago when there was this terrible thing that threatened us. The Skin Eaters owe their lives to the Saturni."

Nina remembered Mrs. Hopkins saying, *"There are some people who seem to think they're scared."* She asked, "What was the terrible thing?"

"Well . . ." Alastaire made a little half-and-half gesture. "We're not supposed to talk about her, but . . . Sister Aquilina."

Nina felt a chill, although she didn't know why. "Who's she?"

"She's . . ." Alastaire shook her head. "You're going to owe me big time. Okay? See, there's supposed to have been this totally wicked Super Skinny several years ago who wanted to challenge the Saturni. I shit you not. She studied all the forbidden knowledge, and she learned how to do magic. I mean really, really bad stuff. Which is supposed to be impossible, but still. Some Skinnies claimed she was the worst there ever was."

Nina looked around, not liking where this conversation was going, especially in this setting, the school, and its weird vibe. "All right," she said. "So, what did she do?"

"She claimed to have forged all kinds of alliances with the spirit world. And she did really, really bad things." Alastaire lowered her voice. "She stole children."

"You mean she was a kidnapper?"

"No, much worse. She stole little kids away and killed them. She did it all the time. People say she used to hang around playgrounds and on deserted roads. These weren't Skinny kids, you understand, just regular kids. She told them she was taking them to a better life, but that was just a scam. They were, like, never seen again." Alastaire lowered her voice until she was barely breathing. "They say she ate them."

Nina decided she didn't like hearing this at all. She shut her eyes, trying to master her breathing. *I want to go home,* she thought, *only I have no home.*

"Everyone was like totally afraid of her," Alastaire went on, much more brightly, "but the Saturni stood up to her. They were completely heroic. They banded together, and eventually, they defeated her and drove her into exile. Nobody knows where she went, but since then, there's always been these rumors that she'll come back someday. But we figure that's just talk."

Nina frowned, trying to decide how much she could tell Alastaire. She decided she had to come clean.

"Look," she said. "There are a few things you should know about me. First of all, I don't have a very good memory from before the storm. Oh, I know basic things, like how to count money and tie my shoes, but I don't know who I am. The other thing is, the social worker who brought me here. I think she knows a lot more than she's saying. And she seems to think the Benway Foundation, the guys who run this place, are scared." She looked at Alastaire. "Could that mean Sister Aquilina is, I don't know . . . back?"

Alastaire looked at her. "What? She can't be. That's impossible."

"I'm not so sure." Briefly, Nina described Mrs. Hopkins's conversation with Professor Danvers, and Alastaire didn't make a single sound.

It was only when Nina finished talking that Alastaire breathed, "That. Is. So. *Cool.*"

"No, it isn't." Nina shut her eyes. "It's terrible. Look, I don't know what it means, but Professor Danvers said you guys didn't do magic. But that's what Sister Aquilina did. Even though you people don't believe in any of that. Well, that's the other thing you should know about me . . ." She took a deep breath. "Even though it's completely impossible, it appears I can do magic."

"No way!"

"Way." She described the events in the office when she'd asked Professor Danvers to let her stay, and the strange animation that had seemed to come to all the objects in the room.

Almost as if they were alive.

Except inanimate objects couldn't come alive. Could they?

Nina sighed and said, "I don't understand it, but Mrs. Hopkins said I belonged here. I don't know what she knows, but I've got to figure, maybe it's all part of one big picture? Me and the Daedalus School and, well, Sister Aquilina? I mean, do you think that's even possible? Could that make sense?"

Alastaire looked at her for a moment longer and then appeared to come to a decision. She stood up and extended her hand, her beautiful mouth grinning underneath her mustache.

"I just want to shake your hand," she said. "I think you're right. I think this all does make sense, and it all *does* fit together, and you're incredibly brave to be here. And I want to tell you that I'm like *totally* behind you. Whatever happens. Seriously, I've got your back. To come here and . . . wow. It's like Joan of Arc. And it's so insanely cool that I know you! So shake hands and say we can be friends."

She wiggled her outstretched hand, and Nina didn't know whether to appreciate Alastaire's nice gesture or laugh. The other girl looked so serious, and also so . . . manly. Like a character in an old movie. *And that's ridiculous. Neither of us are facing death. Or anything remotely like that.*

Still, she stood up and grasped Alastaire's hand and gave her a firm shake, even as she felt the cold seeping into her warm flesh. *I hope I made the right decision*, she thought, but there was no escaping it. She had made her first friend at Daedalus.

Chapter Five

"The girl clearly has no idea," Agatha Danvers said.

"I should say that's fairly obvious," Strickland snapped. "She's an *amnesiac*. And if Miss Lamb did know anything, she'd probably be running away for dear life. So perhaps we should be grateful for small favors."

Strickland Danvers turned away from his sister and studied the wind moving the curtain of thick ivy that covered the mullioned windowpanes of the teachers' lounge. Only here, where the foliage was so thick, were the windows not covered with plywood. He could see the rain cutting long, silvery lines across the garden. He added, "What? I know you're building up to something, so you might as well say it."

"Strickland, I'm worried about you."

"Don't be." He bit the words off. *For God's sake, don't fuss over me*, he thought. *That really would be the last straw. A world in which Agatha is solicitous would be too horrible to contemplate.*

"You're aware of how dangerous this all is." Agatha's voice was crisp once more. "How angry this could make some people. Yet, you deliberately let her in."

"I did not deliberately do anything," he replied. "I *let* her in, eventually, because that atrocious pest from Social Services wasn't going to take no for an answer. Don't worry, I'll deal with her. I always do. But do you have any idea how nosy some humans are?"

"I deal with humans every day, Strickland. I go to the market.

I pay the bills. I'm aware of what they persist in calling the *real* world."

"Then you know it was either take the girl in or admit why we didn't want to do it. Admit she's exactly the straw that could break the camel's back and throw the precarious truce we've enjoyed for the past thirty years off balance. Not that it would be such a bad thing."

"Strickland, shut up!" Agatha gasped and looked around superstitiously, although they were clearly alone. "For God's sake, someone could hear you."

"Then let them. If our *friends* have taken to listening at keyholes—"

"When have they ever done anything else? It's not safe, I tell you."

"Well, it's done now in any case. Humans aren't that stupid, all evidence to the contrary. The prospect of explaining to Mrs. Hopkins that we couldn't accept the otherwise talented and personable Miss Lamb—because she might be the fulfillment of a prophecy some people detest—was one which, quite frankly, I wasn't prepared to face." He leaned against the window until his breath formed condensation on the rain-streaked glass. "I just couldn't go into it, if you want to know the truth."

"So, you deliberately endangered us."

"Stop saying I *deliberately* did this! Do you think I want her here?"

"I think the 'otherwise talented and personable Miss Lamb' is exactly what you want, and I know why! You think she's Niobe come back to you, and you're waiting to welcome her with open arms!"

"I am not—" Strickland settled his voice down into a calmer register. "You're being ridiculous. After all this time, surely I deserve a statute of limitations. Besides, there's somebody in the garden."

"That would be Bellocq Chopin. I told him he could collect mosquito larvae for his junior Animal Dominance project."

"Wonderful. Shall we double-check our supply of bug spray?"

"I don't know why you have it in for that boy. He's a very talented scientist."

"He's a little creep. Anybody who'd even think of making a polynomial engine to compute the estrous cycle of animals so he can harvest their endometria is revolting."

"It's an ingenious invention, though. The blood-rich placenta—"

"Are you really my sister?"

"I'm just saying he's *smart*, Strickland."

"I don't trust him."

"You don't trust anybody. Except, apparently, this girl."

"Oh, go to hell." Strickland threw himself down on the sofa next to the fire and reached for his glass, only to find it empty. "Damn it, pour me another one."

"You're drinking too much."

"I'd rather drink myself to death than eat. Which includes your cooking."

"Actually, I hired a new cook."

"Without my permission?"

"Oh, for God's sake, Strickland, take that pole out of your ass. You're just the assistant headmaster. Nobody died and put you in charge of everything. Besides, she's a good cook. She starts tomorrow."

"Whatever . . ." He waved his hand. "The children have few enough pleasures."

"Only you would call cheating death a small pleasure."

"Isn't it?" Her brother shut his eyes. "You don't remember what it was like before we were turned."

"I do," Agatha snapped. "I remember everything. I'm older than you are, and I remember when *you* did it. You were so eager you practically begged Father Ignatius for your seventh crossing. I remember when the Saturni first recruited you—you were ecstatic. You were going to be their right-hand man."

"Don't remind me."

"Stop evading my point. It's Crux all over again. You can't admit you made a mistake then, and for all your protests now, you're doing the same thing. Why, if you hadn't let him stay with us in the first place—"

"For the last time—" Strickland stood up and lunged for his sister, so abruptly that she took a step back, bumping into the big partners' desk in the middle of the room and sending papers flying. She hurried to pick them up, putting the desk between them, even though she could see Strickland's hands were shaking and his pallid face looking more sick than threatening.

"For the last time," he yelled, "stop throwing Crux up at me! I had no idea how that was going to turn out, and do you think if I had, I'd have let things go as far as they did?!"

"I know you were infatuated with him. You can't tell me you weren't."

"Of course I was. Who wouldn't be? You mean *you* didn't want him? He was gorgeous, that was his glamour, his utter radiant *otherness*. Why wouldn't I go mad for him? Why wouldn't Niobe, for that matter—"

"And you intentionally threw them together!"

"I did nothing of the kind." Strickland turned aside. "I wanted them both, as you say, and the easiest way to have them both was to ensure they wanted each other as well. After all, none of us were children then. What was the harm?"

"You say that about giving your sister to a *god*?"

"Oh, what the hell, it's all water under the bridge now, anyway." Strickland went to the decanter and poured himself another glass of thick, red liquid, staring at it in distaste. "This is wretched, by the way."

"It's your own damned fault." Agatha had replaced the papers on the desk and now sat down in the straight-back chair beside it, still keeping her distance. "If you weren't so stubborn, you could eat like normal people."

"Stop being a nag."

"What do you want me to say? That that stuff's better for you? That Crux was a good idea? He was an *Introim,* for God's sake. A *Lwa.* A race of beings *you* want to believe doesn't even exist. I'm not saying the existence of the magical world is either safe or pleasant, I'm just saying it's there. There are always rational explanations, but your philosophy, as was once pointed out, doesn't incorporate a lot that's in heaven *or* earth."

"A fact of which I'm aware every single second of my intolerable life, although thank you *so* much for reminding me." He sat down and drained his glass in two long swallows. "Anyway, that's all in the past. Crux played us all like a violin and got whatever he wanted. Revenge, presumably. Amusement? A second bite of the apple? The explanations to Benway and Father Ignatius alone took ages—"

"Precisely." Agatha folded her hands in front of her on top of some bills. "Don't you think they'll want to know everything now about this new girl?"

"Of course they will, but that's not the point. For one thing, she's human."

"So you say."

"So I *know*. Does she look like a *Lwa*?" Strickland frowned as if he were in pain. "And they certainly have no way of knowing this girl may be the answer to the prophecy."

"Shh! Shut *up*." Agatha lowered her voice and practically hissed at him, "I'm talking about our funding, our endowment. And our support from the Church—that is *important*."

"And I'm talking about fairness, Agatha. The girl's got talent. She may even be brilliant. And she wouldn't last two minutes if we turned her away. The Saturni would chew her up. We'd be monsters."

"So, instead, she can stay here and ruin us?"

"She may not ruin us." The assistant headmaster shut his eyes and added under his breath, "She may even save us."

"If you still believe in that, Strickland, then all I can say is, I'm sorry for you. I thought you were smarter. But not you! Oh no! You want to let someone in who's like Niobe all over again! And all I can say is you'll deserve it when she turns against you, just like Niobe did."

Strickland stood up again and walked back to the window, looking out at the driving rain, the tossing palm fronds, and the reflection of his own pale face. The rain might have been tears across his cheeks. *I had it all,* he thought, *even as I was too foolish to know how all could be lost between one heartbeat and the next. Niobe and Crux. The satisfaction of my male and female selves combined, with others equally as fluid. Sometimes we were all girls together. Sometimes all boys in the locker room. Sometimes pure mind, pure emotion, and other times pure flesh.*

The fact that Crux had been an *Introim*, a *Lwa*, of another race, arguably even of another species, hadn't mattered—it had added, God help them, a kind of spice to the mix. The unknown element in their coupling, blood and mind and soul and spirit, had always been the most intoxicating thing about it: how Crux, new to having a body, had delighted in all the things a body could do.

And he and Niobe had taught him everything. Lessons the Daedalus School could never hope to match. The purest, most forbidden knowledge, that of Love, had been their curriculum, and that, of course, had been the problem.

Because sex was one thing; in fact, sex was finally the smallest thing. Even flesh and blood were finite, but Love was large and unwieldy and made itself the biggest thing in the room. Until, finally, it was too big for three people to control, and only two could contain it.

So Niobe had sacrificed herself, and Crux had gone away, and the faculty had drawn in, denying any scandal, and Strickland's position as the youngest acting headmaster in the history of the Daedalus School had been saved. For whatever good *that* did.

"So," Strickland sighed, "what do you want me to do?"

Agatha frowned. "Well, I should think that's clear. We need to find some way to subvert the prophecy."

He made a gesture that was close to flipping her the bird, then took a small book out of his pocket and tossed it to her. She caught it one-handed, like a baseball player.

"Be my guest." He sank back down in his chair. "That book's shit. The prophecy's still impenetrable. 'After the tempest, one will appear who has no past. She will best the pelican, and the beautiful hand will be revealed. The five birds will appear all at once, and the seals that were shut will be opened. The lion rampant will do battle with the bull with twelve stars on his horns, and finally, the orphan shall rule over all, and Aquila will gush from her mouth.' If you know what it means, I'd certainly appreciate a hint."

"Well . . ." Agatha frowned. "The pelican is clearly us."

"Oh, well *done*, Aggie. Everybody knows that." He pointed toward the state flag of Louisiana hanging in the corner of the room. "The pelican feeds its young with its own blood. Yadda yadda yadda. So this person with no past who appears after a tempest is going to 'best' us."

"Which means she's going to kill us."

"Not necessarily."

"Oh, Strickland, you're splitting hairs. 'The lion rampant will do battle with the bull with twelve stars on its horns.' What else does that mean but the two factions of the Saturni? It's Jack Benway and Isolde Freeland. They've been at odds for years. But either way, it's our lives and our futures that are at stake."

"What's your point?"

"The point is, Strickland, you've been a fool."

"So?" Strickland steepled his fingers. "What do you want me to do? Throw her out now, dear sister? Would that make you happy?"

"No." Agatha frowned. "That would demand even more explanations. And besides, you said the tests showed she had aptitude—"

"More than that. She's a natural. She doesn't even know yet how good she is."

"How many crossings has she had?"

"None." He shook his head. "She's still warm."

Agatha stared at him and then jumped to her feet. "She's still warm? And yet you let her in here . . . you let her be exposed to our secrets?" Her outrage propelled her around the desk again to face her brother. "What on earth were you thinking?!"

"Actually, I'm not sure what she is." Strickland shook his head and turned once more toward the rain, his voice slow. "There are stories, you know. Of Skin Eaters who aren't doomed. Of people who can bridge both worlds. Of people who are gifted . . . and still warm."

"Bullshit." Agatha sounded a little shaken. "I don't know what metaphysics you believe in, but in my world, nothing can survive without food, and nobody can remain immortal without eating life. One way or the other. Nothing in the universe is unbalanced, Strickland. I know that much about cooking. If you want to make an omelet, you have to break some eggs. That's just the way life works."

"In a zero-sum game." He looked at her sharply. "But who says we're playing one?"

"Don't be ridiculous."

"Is it? Is it ridiculous to dream we might be kind?"

She looked away. "Of course not. To each other . . . to our children."

"We damn our children. We condemn them to hell without even giving them a choice. Besides, Nina's just a child."

"Nina's at least seventeen, Strickland, and ripe as a Georgia peach. Don't bullshit me."

"No, God forbid!" He laughed. "Never that! So, does the girl stay?"

"Oh, hell, of course. Why not?" Agatha got up and looked at her brother with fond exasperation. "When have I ever denied you anything? But look after yourself, will you this time? You're walking on a tightrope. One more slip and you really *are* going to fall."

Chapter Six

Nina spent that night back in Baton Rouge at the group home where she'd been staying since her return to Louisiana from Houston. Since there were a number of other evacuee kids there, it had been fun for a while, but now it just felt bizarre. She lay on her bed in the room she shared with a girl named Linetta and stared at the ceiling, waiting for the hours to pass until she could be driven back down to New Orleans. *So now I'm going to school to learn to be immortal,* she thought. She still couldn't get her mind around any of it.

She tried very hard to remember everything she could about Daedalus. The layout, for one thing. From the outside, the building had simply looked big and square, but inside, the corridors seemed to go on for miles. The walk to the chapel alone had seemed to take fifteen minutes. How big *was* the place? There were bedrooms upstairs, apparently, and kids earned special privileges, like having their own suite, by getting good grades and competing in contests. That way, they could stay with their friends rather than sleeping in open dormitories. *Or up in the attic,* Nina thought. *I guess I'm the only one who's currently doing that.*

She thought about the classrooms she and Alastaire had passed, hidden behind big wooden doors with stained-glass transoms and (alarmingly) heavy iron locks and keys. Were the classes so bad that people had to be locked inside once they started? She'd heard murmurings from inside—lecturing and occasional chanting. Steam had been coming out from under one of the doors, and she'd heard the flutter of wings from another room, where she also smelled gunpowder.

And everything looked so luxurious. Did the adoptive parents pay the school so much every year that their new children could live like kings? Nina shut her eyes and told herself to calm down. *Don't panic. Let it come, let memory form its images . . .* and amazingly, it did. She saw a clear expanse of water, pale amethyst under a lavender sky. Where had she seen that? A feeling of freshness and peace, and a soft purple sun shining down on her upturned face. Was it a real memory or just a dream? She felt a deep yearning inside of her for something she could barely glimpse. Her parents? Her family? Her life before the storm? She knew there was a stubborn wall inside her mind between what she could remember and something . . . someone . . . somewhere she could almost (but not quite) see.

Where are you? It made no sense, it was stupid—she didn't even know enough to be *unhappy*—but for one long moment, there was a terrible absence tolling inside of her—*Gone! Gone!*—like a lonely bell. She seemed to be floating in dark water past drowned houses, and she stayed perfectly still as a shadow crossed between her and the moon. Then she looked up to see a woman with a strong nose, pale skin, and eyes like ink. *Who are you?* Nina was frozen between fascination and fear. The woman seemed to form thoughts in her own mind, and she heard the words *I exist.* And for some reason, that thought gave her . . . not terror, but a feeling of absolute reassurance.

She closed her eyes and fell asleep, and the next morning she could barely remember her dream.

She rode back down to the Daedalus School with Mrs. Hopkins and arrived a little after nine o'clock. Agatha Danvers welcomed them in and said in her abrupt way, "Right. Here's some clothes, here's your schedule, here are your books, we'll have someone take your, uh, *things—*" she arched an eyebrow at Nina's worldly possessions, all stuffed in a Sav-A-Center bag "—up to the attic, and you can go on ahead to your first class, which is Alchemy, Professor Aspidistrus, Room 201. It's just down that hallway, then take a left and go all the way to the end. I've included a map. Right. Off you go."

Nina stared at her. She wondered why she couldn't wear her own clothes, although she had to admit these new things were really nice: one of the long black dresses and red sashes, and a pair of neat black boots in place of her sneakers. She said, "Um . . . where should I change?"

Agatha rolled her eyes, but jerked her thumb and said, "Use the cloakroom. It's just under the stairs. Be quick about it, though, I haven't got all morning."

Nina changed in the small room underneath the stairs, shoving her old clothes into the bag (presumably she could wear them during off hours?) Then she returned to Mrs. Hopkins and said, "Um, thanks. I mean, thanks for everything."

"That's fine, honey, no problem. I'll be in touch." Mrs. Hopkins gave her a perfunctory peck on the cheek. "Miss Danvers, call me if you need anything. You have my number. Bye."

And she was gone out the front door, the sunlight winking and then disappearing again, as she shut the door behind her.

Nina looked at Agatha and said, "Well, she's busy," and Agatha raised her eyebrows and said, "Scared's more like it," and for the first time, Nina thought she saw a glint of cruel amusement in her eyes.

Nina trudged down the hallway carrying her load of heavy books and didn't stop until she was out of Agatha's line of sight, at which point she sat down in a handy window seat and looked at what they'd given her.

There was *Elementary Materialism, Sky Watching for*

Beginners, Transformation Theory, and a small pamphlet called *Daedalus, A Tradition of Service,* which appeared to be a brochure for the school itself. It included photographs of distinguished trustees, among them a man in a Roman collar with a pale, fine face identified as "Father Ignatius Ragoczy, head of the Vatican's *Curis Dei,*" and another man with dark, wavy hair who was, "John Benway, noted philanthropist and head of the Benway Corporation." One thing was clear, this place was majorly connected. She looked at Agatha's map, but it looked like a road map for the Pentagon. There were hallways going every which way, staircases, classrooms, and something called the "Riding Ring" at the back of the school, and another room called the "Observatory" out in the carriage house. She was supposed to go Alchemy, Room 201, so she straightened her shoulders, stuffed her books into her bag, and trudged down the length of the dark hallway, past closed doors and the unnerving sound of something skittering inside the walls.

She turned left and headed down another darkened hall, but halfway to the end she found her way blocked by a collapsed ceiling and a barricade of hazard tape. There was a sawhorse with a sign taped to it: *Further Access Forbidden Due to Storm Damage.*

She looked around. What was she supposed to do now? Was there another way? She studied the map again. Nope, this was it. Why hadn't Agatha told her this part of the school had been damaged? She glanced into a deserted classroom where the desks were piled up against the wall and mildew spangling the ceiling, and thought, *Ugh. This place smells like a sewer.*

"Can I help you?" came a polite voice, and an old man entered the room carrying an armload of books.

A very impressive-looking old man, unusually tall, with long, flowing white hair and a close-cropped white beard. His face was lined and craggy, and he had ice-blue eyes like a stern grandfather. Nina felt immediately shy in front of him.

"I, uh . . ." She gestured. "I'm new here. I-I think I'm supposed to go to Room 201 for a class, but I can't seem to find it. Sir." And then she added, trying not to sound like she was about six years old, "They told me to go down this hallway to the room at the end, but I can't seem to get there. It's blocked."

"Really? Room 201?" The old man frowned. "That's ridiculous. I wonder why they sent you this way if it's blocked. Do you have any idea?"

Nina didn't want to say, *"No, sir, that's why I asked you,"* because she was afraid that might sound rude. She said instead, "Um, it's Professor Aspidistrus's class. Alchemy. Do you happen to know where I could find it?"

"Ah, Alchemy . . ." The bearded man smiled. "With Professor Aspidistrus. My, my. Old Aspy's been teaching that since Paracelsus was a pup. You'll like it. The transmutation of matter, the search for eternal truths in the guise of physical properties . . . the cosmic egg—"

"Yes, sir." Nina didn't like interrupting him, but she was afraid she was going to be late.

He stopped reminiscing and his brow crumpled as he looked at her. "Don't you already know all of that?"

"No, sir, I told you. I'm new here. Um, I'm sorry, but . . . I don't mean to be impolite, but have we ever met before?"

His gaze was very sharp for a moment, not necessarily threatening, but just very keen. She felt like a butterfly pinned to a board. He looked her over from top to toe, and then said, "Ah, well, we can't expect miracles all the time. Excuse me, I'm forgetting the niceties. I'm the headmaster of the Daedalus School. Among other things. You can call me Mr. O'Brien."

Nina wondered if she ought to curtsey. *Isn't the headmaster gone, though? But Alastaire said Professor Danvers was in constant contact with him. Maybe he comes back for visits?* She said, "I-I'm pleased to meet you, sir. I-I thought you weren't here, sir."

He smiled thinly. "News of my absence has been much exaggerated." He turned and tapped his finger against his lips thoughtfully. "You know, I wouldn't be much surprised if there isn't some perfectly natural explanation for your inability to reach Room 201. That often is, you know. Young people . . ." He frowned. "You like things simple. You've become impatient with mysteries. You don't like to wait to find out the ending of the story. Don't you agree, Miss Lamb?"

Nina jumped at being addressed so directly by this sharp-eyed, somewhat intimidating old man. "I don't know, sir," she said. She wanted to say, *"I don't know the answer to any mysteries,"* but she said instead, "How do you know my name?"

"Oh, word travels fast. 'The walls have ears,' as they say." He shrugged. "It's a cliché, but then many a true thing is ultimately banal."

Nina had no idea how to answer this. "Um, sir, do you mind . . . well, now that I've got you, would you mind looking at the rest of my schedule and this map and telling me where everything is? I mean, if it's not too much trouble . . . I just feel so stupid, not knowing my way around."

"Pure impatience, as I said. No one really knows their way around in a place like this. I myself feel like an idiot at least half the time. I think it adds some much-needed spice to my life. Feeling like an idiot's an overlooked pleasure."

"Um, okay."

"The rooms *are* clearly numbered. You just have to read the signs, and they'll take you wherever you need to go."

"Okay. Uh . . . thanks." This was the least helpful advice anyone had ever given her. She waited for him to say something else, and when he didn't, she asked, "Is there anything more?"

"Only that I'm very glad you're here, Miss Lamb. May I take the liberty of saying you are in many respects an extraordinary young woman? Professor Danvers did very well to admit you. I think you'll be surprised at how well this all turns out. And now, may I suggest you run along? Professor Aspidistrus is probably well on the way to separating out the sulfuric from the mercuric elements, and you don't want to miss that."

"But I . . . sir, I can't. I still don't know where to find Room 201. The way's blocked, and I can't get past it." She pointed out to the corridor, and when she turned around again, the headmaster was gone.

Great. Where was he? How was she supposed to—

When she looked again, the way was completely clear. There was no debris, no sawhorse, and no sign saying access was forbidden. There was just a row of doors clear down to the far end, the last one marked as Room 201. It had been there all along.

She went in and stood near the door, waiting for someone to notice her. Everything was clean and bright and as antiseptic as an operating room. If she'd been expecting a Gothic potions lab, this certainly wasn't it. It appeared the students at Daedalus all studied together, working at whatever level suited their individual skills. There were little girls and boys sitting at desks, copying out what appeared to be a list of rules on the blackboard, among them:

No Calling Up Elemental Forces for Trivial Purposes.
*Hands of Glory Are To Be Used **Only for** Immobilizing an
    Enemy.*
Keep Your Grimoire with You at All Times.

Other students, slightly older, were studying a kind of periodic table, although she noticed as she peeked over their shoulders that the names of the elements were somewhat unusual, with earth, air, fire, and water listed right alongside with hydrogen and helium. The last element was the Philosopher's Stone.

Meanwhile, at longer worktables in the back, students were paired up brewing things over Bunsen burners and drawing runes in chalk, ash, and cornmeal. She saw Alastaire wearing a rubber apron, boiling a black liquid in one retort and distilling it through a long, glass tube into a second, where it became first white and then bright red.

Professor Aspidistrus glanced her way, then waddled over, his green skin gleaming and a smile stretching his almost lipless mouth.

"Ah, Miss Lamb," he said, as bright green leaves appeared all over his face and twisted like ivy into his hair. "I'm so glad to make your acquaintance. Welcome to my class."

She tried to answer him, but she was too fascinated by the greenery that seemed to be sprouting from him everywhere, small ferns bracketing his eyes and grass growing out of his ears, delicate vines climbing up his cheeks and then settling back into his skin. This whole facial garden seemed to come and go with each breath he took, all of it living and faintly whispering.

She shook his hand, grateful to feel that although ice cold, it wasn't particularly vegetal.

She said, "Sir, I'll be happy to do whatever I can, but I'm afraid I'm pretty much of a beginner."

"Don't be afraid. We all move at our own speed, and some of us move with surprising swiftness. *Qui capit ille sapit.*" He turned to Alastaire. "Perhaps you can help Miss Lamb get started. And will you also assist, Miss Chopin . . . or is it *Mister* Chopin? If so, please forgive me."

"Yes," snapped a slim Vietnamese boy standing next to Alastaire, who looked bored and defiant at the same time. "I should think it would be perfectly apparent that it's *Mister* Chopin."

He wasn't particularly manly, but he *was* wearing trousers, along with a gold stickpin in his tie and what Nina recognized as Gucci loafers.

"My apologies . . ." said their strange plant-like professor with a graceful flick of his leafy fingers. "You young people change back and forth so swiftly now."

Nina turned to the boy and said, "How do you do—I'm Nina Lamb. And you are . . . ?"

"Bellocq Chopin," he murmured, shaking her hand and glancing at Alastaire. "So this is the girl you were gushing about? Your newest paramour?"

"She's my newest *friend*," Alastaire said smoothly. "Suck it up, Bella. You know you like boys no matter what sex you are. Come on, Nina, we're brewing Balm of Sulfur into a decoction of First Matter, so you can help me with the alembic."

Chapter Seven

Nina felt the rest of the day pass in a blur. She went from brewing Balm of Sulfur with Alastaire and Bella to Literature with Professor Mwindo, who taught them about the dangers of symbolism.

"The idea that something stands for something else is a common misapprehension, but one against which we must all be on our guard. For example, 'The mountains rise' is just a description, but to see them as some sort of acme of achievement, from the Greek *akme,* is to completely misinterpret them. It's the same way with the Pathetic Fallacy. The idea that inanimate objects have feelings is preposterous. For example, in Tennyson's *Maud . . .*" And he proceeded to recite an excerpt from the poem:

> *There has fallen a splendid tear*
> *From the passion-flower at the gate.*
> *She is coming, my dove, my dear;*
> *She is coming, my life, my fate;*
> *The red rose cries, "She is near, she is near;"*
> *And the white rose weeps, "She is late;"*
> *The larkspur listens, "I hear, I hear;"*
> *And the lily whispers, "I wait."*

"In that excerpt," the professor went on, "Tennyson is committing the first cardinal sin of art, implying that flowers have emotions. I want you to pay special attention to this failing as we study Goethe."

"But I *liked* that poem," Nina whispered to Alastaire as they left the room. "I thought it was beautiful."

Alastaire rolled her eyes. "Oh, Mwindo's a real classicist. He thinks if it wasn't invented by the Saturni, it's completely worthless. And of course, the Saturni are all materialists. No souls, no magic."

"Alastaire, exactly how powerful are the Saturni?"

"Look." Alastaire stopped on her way down the stairs, and Nina stopped too. The Skinny girl was looking unusually serious. "You should understand that the Saturni pretty much run everything that goes on in our society, and they've made everything a lot more efficient and practical. Everything was, like, a real mess before they cleaned things up."

"By warning against talking roses?"

"Oh, it's so much more than that. The Saturni taught us if you look at anything closely enough, there's a pattern that can be predicted. Sense impressions, abstract concepts . . . Objectively, they're all really value neutral. Everything from a beautiful sunset to a fatal disease, it's just a *fact*." Alastaire shook her head in frustration and added, "Just wait till you study Calculation Science, okay? It's cool."

Nina looked at her schedule and saw she had Calculation Science in the afternoon. She wasn't sure she liked the sound of everything in the world being value neutral.

Bella brushed past them and said over his shoulder, "Don't be late for the Petting Zoo, girls," and Alastaire glared at him.

"What's the Petting Zoo?" Nina whispered.

"It's Transformation and Animal Dominance. Bella just wants to pretend like those wolves don't scare the living shit out of him too." And then Alastaire seemed to realize she probably shouldn't have said that, adding quickly, "Not like it's really scary, just . . . exciting. C'mon, stick close to me and you'll be all right."

Transformation and Animal Dominance was held in the Riding Ring, a big, covered barnlike room attached to the back of the school. Nina noticed there were no little children in this class, only people her age or older. Professor Samson was standing with his hands on his hips when they came in—an enormous whistle stuck in his mouth.

He removed the whistle from between his lips and shouted, "Right!" then looked at the whistle as though trying to think of a good excuse to blow it. "Okay, you squirts, time to see how you do with the school pack. Hey, Roticus!" he added, addressing a round-shouldered *jumbie* who was dressed in an oversized T-shirt and hiding in the corner. "Release Thor and Vladimir!"

Roticus swallowed, and going over to a wooden door, he pulled up a latch and let out two enormous gray wolves. They raced straight for the class, teeth bared and froth flying from their jaws, and everyone scattered, students jumping up onto hay bales and grabbing one another to pull each other to safety. Alastaire grabbed Nina's hand, and they both climbed up on top of a big wooden crate, where they sat with their legs pulled up while the wolves snapped and jumped frantically below them. Looking disgusted, Professor Samson blew his whistle.

"All right, all right, *all right!*" he said, clapping his hands, which made the wolves immediately lie down and look at him with their big, dark eyes. "What did I tell you last time? *Don't run!* It only excites 'em, makes 'em think it's all just a big game. You want to show a wolf who's boss, what do you do? Show of hands, please!"

Bella put up his hand and said reluctantly, "You look them straight in the eye and say, 'I am your master.'" It came off a little awkwardly because he was climbing down one of the hay bales as he spoke.

"Right! 'I am your master!' How hard is that to remember?

Not 'Come out and play!' Not 'Eek, eek, a nasty old wolf!' It's *'I am your master!'* Come on, troop, it's not rocket science! Let's try it again."

They all returned to the center of the barn and stood looking nervously at the wolves, who were glancing at the professor expectantly. Professor Samson waited and then blew his whistle. This time, the wolves took off in two different directions, one toward a fat boy who turned and ran right out of the room, and one toward a lovely girl with chocolate-brown skin, her hair a cascade of rich, dark waves and her eyes so tawny they looked like topazes. The girl stood her ground, clenching her fists against her black skirt but otherwise appearing calm, and when the wolf was no more than ten feet away from her, she held up her hand and said in a ringing voice, "I am your master! I command you to stop!"

The wolf skidded to a stop and looked at her as if confused, shaking its head, and then it snarled and let out a blood-curdling howl of what sounded like frustration. But it didn't attack her. The girl slowly lowered her hand, and as she did so, the wolf lowered himself as well, until he lay down flat on the ground. She turned around to the rest of the class and smiled, and the students—even Professor Samson—broke into spontaneous applause.

"Okay, well done, Simone. That's the ticket! You gotta be tough! You gotta read 'em the riot act! Okay, now everyone else line up over there. We'll take this one at a time. I'll work the wolves in tandem. Thor, Vlad, c'mere. Sit. Okay, now, who wants to go next?"

Everyone tried to huddle behind everyone else, which resulted in Nina being pushed into the front by sheer accident. She braced herself, and thought, *I can't do this. They'll know I'm a fraud. They'll know I can't control an animal; I can barely control my own bladder right now.*

Well, at least I can die without making a complete fool of myself. She gulped and said, "Okay, I-I'm ready."

Professor Samson looked like he clearly doubted it, but he stepped back and left the two wolves sitting with their mouths watering. When he said, "Thor!" and blew his whistle, she thought, *I am so dead.*

The wolf raced toward her, and as it leaped for her throat, she put out her hands instinctively to shield her face and grabbed hold of its thick, soft fur. There was a confused blur of movement as the wolf pushed her down, and they both rolled over onto the ground. She felt hot raw meat in her mouth and bones cracking between her teeth, and it tasted *good.* She felt a rich, ripe pleasure in all of her sinews, as though she could run forever without tiring. She also saw a pale-gray vista of snow and pine trees and frozen ground, mountains in the distance, and somewhere, the sound of water running over ice.

She was in the wolf's mind! She realized what was happening as she was already thinking, *Don't hurt me, oh please don't hurt me,* and as she tried to take a deep breath, she felt the hot breath of the wolf on her face.

And then it started licking her.

She lay on the ground and let the wolf lick her, laughing with relief, and gradually she became aware of a confused murmur of voices all around her. Professor Samson was blowing his whistle helplessly, and finally, he simply hauled the wolf off, saying, "Okay, Thor, that's enough!" as though the animal had done something embarrassing, like piddle on the rug.

Alastaire and Bella were there to help her up, and she saw Alastaire beaming at her like she was a hero, and even Bella had a reluctant smile on his face.

"I wouldn't have believed it if I hadn't seen it with my own eyes," the Vietnamese boy whispered. "You can read their minds, can't you? Communicate with them telepathically? That's *incredibly* rare."

"Really?" she asked, standing up and brushing the dirt off her dress. She wanted more than anything now to take a bath. She looked at Professor Samson and asked, "Is that true? That most people can't read animals' minds?"

"Well, not as a general rule, no," he admitted. "It's a whole cross-species thing. That's why you've got to dominate animals, bend 'em to your will. You can't ever let an animal get the better of you."

Why not? Nina thought.

Simone, the beautiful black girl, was staring at her with narrowed eyes, and she said, "So it's true, then?"

"What?"

"That the Daedalus School has started going to the dogs."

Everybody fell silent, some of them, Nina guessed, curious what she'd say in return, and others, she supposed, frankly hoping for a fight. Which made her want to play nice. She said, "I'm sorry, I don't know what you mean."

"I *mean*, bitch, that you and that wolf looked awfully friendly." She glanced around at her equally beautiful white girlfriends and smirked. "You like doing it on the down-low in the kennel?"

"Well—" Nina thought of a lot of ways to answer that, but politeness still seemed the better part of valor. "I'm really more of a cat person."

"I'll have to remember that." The other girl grinned. "You like pussy."

Nina looked at this lovely girl, who really was fairly perfect, with a face like Nefertiti's, and tried to guess what her problem was. Clearly, it wasn't a racial thing. She looked like a pampered princess, someone even the teachers deferred to. Professor Samson was dragging Thor and Vlad back to their cages and allowing the whole scene to unfold without interfering.

Everyone else was hanging back, and Nina felt her recent

triumph morphing into shame. Did Simone think she was a freak because she could do something the others couldn't do?

She tried one last attempt at conciliation. "Hey, look, I just did whatever I could think of. I was scared to death."

"Clearly."

"You were much more prepared."

"Of course. I *was* prepared. You could have been chewed up like a Happy Meal. Not that that would have been much of a loss."

"Simone . . ." someone said, and the black goddess snapped, "Shut up, Bella. I'm talking to the new school mascot."

She advanced on Nina and gave an audible sniff. "Just what I thought. You need a bath. I wouldn't want to get mange."

Nina had had about enough of this, but before she could say anything, Bella grabbed Simone's arm with a surprisingly strong grip. He said quietly, "She's new. Give her a break."

"Butt out, rice boy, or I'll tell your daddy you're getting into bestiality."

"No. You. Won't." He didn't tighten his hold on her arm or do anything else, but still, his power over her was obvious, if only in that it made her hesitate. "Your parents need *mine* every bit as much as mine need *yours*," Bella said, so softly only the nearest students could hear him. "So let's just call it a truce, okay? You go back to being Queen Bitch, and I'll go back to just being richer than you are, and we'll call it a draw. Otherwise, well . . . the next time we all have dinner down at the Fortuna Club, things could get, say, a little *tense*?"

He let go of her and stepped back, making an almost invisible gesture of dismissal, and Simone stepped back as well, massaging her wrist and giving him a look that was nearly cobralike in its venom.

Professor Samson returned at that point from kenneling the wolves and said, "All right, gang. I guess we're done with the pack for today. Let's try something else. What say you give me a quick transformation and then hit the showers? Not you," he added, pointing at Nina. "I think you've already done enough."

Which was probably just as well, since she had no idea how to transform. She was a little taken aback by the fact that everyone else in the class started stripping stark naked. No one seemed embarrassed, and they piled their clothes up on the side of the ring before changing into various creatures.

Alastaire transformed into a borzoi and went sniffing off into the corners, while Bella became a tiny fruit bat that immediately zigzagged around the barn, catching flies.

One of the other kids, a big boy with some of those sick gray sores on his face, became a gigantic rat, while Simone became a cloud of dark smoke.

Everyone changed into something, until Nina and Professor Samson were left standing in a sea of manifestations all creeping, bounding, flying, and drifting around in every direction. The professor blew his whistle, and they all changed back and picked up their clothes again, looking pretty pleased with themselves.

Professor Samson said, "Right! Okay, class dismissed!" and the students headed to the showers.

"What was that all about?" Nina whispered to Alastaire, as they stood soaping their armpits, keeping as far away from Simone as possible. The black girl was standing under the water with her white posse, gossiping and preening while they washed each other's hair.

"Transformation? Well, it's about changing on the molecular level and rearranging your cellular makeup and—"

"No, I meant Bella and the Queen of Sheba over there. And . . . well, me."

Alastaire grimaced. "Well, it's like Bella said. Simone's a real Queen Bitch. Her family's ultra-famous and influential. Her father's Archer Freeland, a big cheese in the Saturni, and her mother's this big-deal doctor. *Very* important people."

"Why was she so mad at me?"

"You mean, aside from her being a huge King Kamehameha *bitch*? That's easy. You did something she couldn't do. Skinnies aren't into racial prejudice, because we can all change so much, but that doesn't mean there aren't cliques. Simone's your typical alpha female. Besides, she's really smart—I'll give her that. She's always top of the class, and she wins the school Hadiade every year without even trying."

"The school what?"

"Hadiade. It's like the Olympics, but . . . well, it's named after Hades instead of Mount Olympus." Alastaire shrugged to indicate *she* wasn't responsible for calling it that. "Each year at the end of the spring term, there's, like, a test of all the top students at the school, and they compete in different things, and the best student wins a trophy. Simone's probably got a whole set by now. I'll bet her parents display them right next to their Mardi Gras favors."

Nina reflected that she probably couldn't have chosen a worse Skin Eater to be her enemy, but the damage was done now. While they were walking back to the school, she asked Alastaire, "So, what's up with Bella? Why was he allowed to tell Simone off?"

"Because, like he said, his sponsors are *really* rich. They're from Saigon but, like, ages ago, and that's why they have a French last name. They're really into the whole ancestor thing, which is why Bella is such a disappointment to them." Alastaire sighed. "Poor Bella. His parents never even want to see him. Plus, they're like super homophobes, which is a whole other drag. Hey, c'mon, it's almost lunchtime. Not that it's any great shakes, but we still gotta eat, right?"

Chapter Eight

Nina wished she had time to ask Alastaire about a thousand more questions, but her grumbling stomach made her agree to head for the Commons. After another disastrous meal (gray hamburgers and undercooked french fries), Alastaire went to a special seminar on Advanced Symbology, and Nina went to Calculation Science with Professor Hermes, History with Professor Seneschal (who slept through most of the class), Hygiene (where Professor Ariadne explained how to use red spur valerian to relieve something called "late sixth stage convulsions") and finally Sky Geography.

She looked at her schedule and saw her last class was being held out in the carriage house, which would give her a chance to walk across the garden. She caught up with Bella as they were going out the door and said, "Um, thanks for sticking up for me before, in Animal Dominance. That really meant a lot."

"I was just trying to put Simone Freeland in her place," he said, hunching his shoulders. "Don't get excited. I'm not a fan of warm wannabes like you either."

"Bella—" she began, but he interrupted her.

"Look, Alastaire told me a little bit about you. Yes, it's interesting, I grant, that you're here going to school with us when you haven't been sponsored. I suppose Professor Danvers had his reasons. And the fact that you don't remember your past—that certainly is strange. At least you haven't been relegated to *jumbie* status yet."

"And that would be a bad thing . . . why?"

"Well, let's just say I wouldn't want it to happen to my worst enemy, whoever they are."

He continued walking quickly, hugging himself and keeping to the shadows, and she guessed the sunlight must hurt him. For people who kept protesting they weren't vampires, the Skin Eaters certainly acted like them.

"So, what are the *jumbies*?" she pressed, unable to let it go. "Why aren't they in the same classes as . . . well, the rest of us? Are they all stupid?"

Bella sighed. "Pretty much. They're losers. The saddest of the sad, really. You could break your heart worrying about every stray, but it's like the SPCA, the cute puppies are the ones who get adopted. The rest of them go to the gas chamber."

"Yes, but I mean . . . I mean, eventually the *jumbies* do grow up, right? And go out on their own? They don't . . . they don't really go to the gas chamber."

"Oh, sure. Look," he said, stopping at the corner of the building, where an overhanging balcony left a tiny wedge of shade. "I'm going to make a run for it, okay?" He took off his jacket and held it over his head. "Do you think you can handle it on your own, or do you want me to get you an umbrella?"

Nina smiled. "It's all right. I can handle it. So, you guys really don't like sunlight?"

"It speeds up our metabolism, so our tissues break down." Bella's voice was tight. "Our bodies aren't really that stable while we're still changing. We don't melt or burn up or anything like that, but we do become a little . . . fluid." He allowed himself a quick, tight smile. "Think of it as getting really, *really* sweaty. I guess you don't have that problem?"

"Not so you'd notice." She smiled a little warily back at him. "You go on ahead, and I'll catch up."

She didn't want to tell him that the opportunity to spend even a minute or two out in the late afternoon sunlight seemed like heaven, after the gloomy chill of the school. Bella made a dash for the carriage house, and Nina followed more slowly, savoring the warmth.

The carriage house looked derelict and spooky when she got up close to it, with chunks of mortar falling away and weeds sprouting from the cracks between the bricks. But when she went inside, she was pleased to see it was swept clean, and the steps going upstairs looked more or less sound.

She walked up to the second floor, hearing a babble of voices above her, and came out into a high chamber where there was a big window facing back toward the school and two huge skylights. The room was dominated by a big telescope-like contraption, sporting wheels and cogs and brass dials and even something that looked like a gyroscope. There were large maps of the night sky tacked to the walls, showing the different constellations. The windows were all shrouded with thick, black drapes, which could presumably be pulled aside at night.

Professor Threet was standing there waiting for the class to assemble, and when they were all gathered around her, the nervous little astronomer explained how they'd be using the school's noctoscope during the next full moon.

She actually waxed poetic as she talked about the procedure. "The moon is our mother," she said, stroking the big brass cylinder of the scope as it gleamed next to her. "The noctoscope can intensify, focus, dissipate, or project her rays. It enables us to safely study the quality of light she emits, the light that kindles all our thoughts and prompts our deepest aspirations. For she is the radiance that calls us back to ourselves, and when we look at her, we can see the primordial light from which we sprang."

Nina thought how odd it was that she'd dreamed about the

moon the night before. The Skin Eaters were clearly a lot more in love with magic than they let on—pretending their shape-shifting and sex-changing were just some weird kind of science. And Professor Threet looked even more nervous than usual when she told them how powerful the moon was.

When the time came for questions, Nina raised her hand. "Um, Professor Threet?"

"Yes, ah . . . our newest student. Miss . . . Lamb," she added, consulting the class list. "What is it, dear?"

"I-I understood people here at the Daedalus School don't really believe in magic, but . . . well, aren't you talking about the moon in kind of magical terms?"

"Er, no." Professor Threet's pale, long-nosed face got, if anything, a shade paler. "No, not at all. That's completely wrong. I can't see how you would think that!"

"But you just said the moon was our 'mother.' And you said 'she kindles all our thoughts' and calls us back to ourselves. That sounds like she's . . . well, a spirit."

Professor Threet looked so scared she practically dropped her glasses, and she glanced around furtively before she said, "Well, dear, a lot of people used to believe that in olden times, but we've grown beyond that now. We only believe in processes we can count and calibrate and *control*. Change we can predict and measure. The ability to summon spirits . . . the actual existence of such things . . . well, that's something we've left far behind, and good riddance, too, if you ask me! Er . . . any more questions?"

Alastaire, who was lounging two rows behind Nina, piped up and asked, "Professor, is it true the moon is made of green cheese?"

"Er—no," Professor Threet said. "Nobody believes that now. As I said, now we're all very modern and practical—"

"And can it drive people crazy?"

The class was openly giggling now, and Nina thought Alastaire was being a little mean, but she supposed it was Professor Threet's own fault if she didn't realize she was being made the butt of a joke.

"Er, yes, sometimes," the professor said, flipping through her notes. "I believe . . . um . . . there are numerous cases of moon madness recorded in the book *My Life with The Lunatics* by Dr. John Seward—"

"And the moon can tell you who you're going to marry?"

She winked, but Professor Threet still didn't get it, saying, "Well, yes, Miss Roget. Certain young British ladies once believed you could simply address the new moon and say, 'New moon, new moon, I hail thee. Grant this night that I may see he who my one true love will be' and your future husband would appear to you in a dream."

"Professor," Bella interrupted, clearly impatient with what he surely viewed as a childish waste of time, "is it true the moon's light can actually bring someone back to life?"

Professor Threet raised her eyebrows. "Why, yes, Mr. Chopin, it certainly can. That's a fairly obscure fact, so I commend you on your knowledge. In times past, it's been recorded that certain of our kind, perishing for want of our immortal food, could be brought back to health almost miraculously by the moon's rays. You see, during the full moon, all rules go backward: the dead can live and conversely, the living and even the ever-living can die. Nothing can change our essential nature, but the moon has been known to have vast powers—"

A bell rang, distantly audible from the main building, and all the students made a mad dash for the stairs, clearly eager to be finished with Professor Threet. Nina, who wished she could stay longer and ask her some more questions, dawdled out after everyone else. There was a girl on the stairs being sick—Nina heard violent whoops and gurgles and caught a quick glimpse of her bulging eyes before looking away—and she came down the last few steps feeling a little queasy herself. Fortunately, Alastaire and Bella were waiting for her.

"C'mon," Alastaire said, acting like it was no big deal, although they'd all passed the girl on the stairs, "Let's go to dinner. Safety in numbers, right? The sun's almost setting, but Bella here might still collapse, and then we'll have to carry him."

She ducked as the slender boy tried to hit her, adding, "Besides, if we sit together, if one of us gets food poisoning, the other two can perform the Heinie-Lick Maneuver."

Nina smiled, more grateful than she could admit that they'd waited for her. After everything else that had happened that day, she was glad *somebody* at the school liked her. As they walked back across the beautiful garden in the darkening twilight, she asked, "Is that really true, all that stuff about the moon?"

"I don't know." Alastaire laughed. "I was just trying to get a rise out of old Threety-bird."

"Yes," Bella sighed. "It *is* true, if you'd ever pay attention. The moon is a powerful healer and destroyer. Why the ancient Sumerians in the time of Gilgamesh—"

Alastaire made a *yakkety-yak* gesture with her hand behind Bella's back, and Nina tried to control a smile. She was thinking of all the strange things she'd learned that day—not the least of which was the Skin Eaters' absolute refusal to believe in anything spiritual—when she saw a sight up ahead of them that made the blood freeze in her still-warm veins. Simone was standing by the side entrance to the school, and she had her posse with her. One of the girls was a redhead and the other two were blonds, so Simone shone between them like a luminous black pearl.

"Oh," she drawled, affecting surprise, "look who's here. Mowgli and the other cubs."

Nina made a snap decision right then and there that she didn't want Alastaire or Bella fighting any more battles for her.

She walked over to Simone and said in a tone of polite curiosity, "How's the air up there?"

"Up where, dog-breath?"

"Up your butt. I thought it must be a little hard to breath with your head so far up your ass, but I guess you guys have special powers. Forgive me, I'm new."

Simone didn't say anything, and then, very slowly, she smiled. It was a *very* nasty smile. She paused as if choosing her words, and said, "Well, what do you know, the dog's trying to be funny. You think you can take me on?"

"We'll see, next time I transform."

"Don't be ridiculous. You have no idea how to transform."

"Yes, I do." Nina remembered what Alastaire had told her the first day they'd met. "It's done by controlling the forces of metabolism and cellular regeneration. Your bodies are unstable, which is why you avoid sunlight. Simple, really."

"Not for a *mortal.*"

Simone made the word sound like the worst kind of insult. Nina pretended not to notice. "I don't know," she said, frowning. "Didn't you all start off as mortal? Maybe *you* have something to hide."

"Maybe you'll just start off and end up as meat."

"Simone . . ." Bella shot her a warning glance, but the black girl just tossed her head. "What? Afraid I'll hurt your little girlfriend's feelings?"

"She's not my—"

"Oh, no, that's right, you like guys, don't you? Well, you'd better change sexes soon, sissy pants. Don't want any nasty incidents in the boys' room."

Nina saw Bella flinch, and her anger at having him insulted made her act without thinking. She drew back her hand to slap Simone, but before she could bring it across her cheek, the force of an unseen blow made a crack in the air—nearly knocking the other girl against the wall. She staggered and was caught by her acolytes. A cut appeared at the corner of her full mouth, and her hand flew up and unintended tears filled her eyes—although they were tears of rage.

"You whore," she snapped, stepping back and letting her minions close in around her. "I'll tell. I'll tell you used magic. You should *never* have done that."

"I thought magic didn't exist."

Simone glared at her. "You're such a smart-ass, you tell *me*. You think you can just waltz in here and become whatever you want? You think because you're the latest Daedalus charity case, you're one of *us*? You're nothing. You're nothing but a dirty little *magician*."

Nina balled up her hand into a fist and held it behind her back, because she was still so mad she was afraid she'd do more magic and give Simone a black eye. Simone settled herself and put her usual sneer back on her face, although it looked a little crooked because of her split lip. "You can kiss your special status goodbye, once I tell Professor Danvers about this."

Oh great, Nina thought.

"He'll be fascinated to learn our newest welfare student broke our most basic rule. No magic. No fairy tales. No little green men and dancing pixies. You just screwed up big-time, girlfriend. You'll be out of here so fast you'll get whiplash."

She looked like she almost wanted to add something else, then thought better of it and turned on her heel and allowed her gang to help her back into the school.

Right, like I broke her ankle, Nina thought. Nina turned back to her friends and realized Bella and Alastaire were staring at her as if they were half afraid of her as well. "What?" she snapped.

Alastaire said, "Wow. So it's really true, then. You *can* do magic."

Bella was looking at her with an expression somewhere between nervousness and something else, maybe sorrow, and suddenly, it was all too much. Nina felt naked, stupid, defenseless, and hopelessly confused, and having the two people she liked best look at her like she'd just sprouted horns was the last straw. Tears stung her eyes, but she was damned if she was going to let Bella and Alastaire see her cry. She said shortly, "Yeah, well, now you know. I guess you'll want to stay away from me," and then she hurried away from them, not caring where she went, only knowing she wanted to put as much distance as possible between herself and everyone else in the whole world.

She ran down one corridor and then another and finally pushed open a door and realized she'd run straight into the kitchen. Which was the last place she wanted to be, between Agatha and Agatha's cooking. Except in this case, everything was different.

For one thing, the room was full of the most delicious smells. There was the aroma of chicken frying in big, deep pans, biscuits baking in one of the huge ovens, and apple pies in the other. Dinner actually smelled wonderful.

The kitchen was also as neat as a pin, with big bowls holding shredded cabbage and red onions ready to make coleslaw, and others filled with fruit. There was a nondescript young woman in a chef's jacket and a baseball cap standing in front of the stove singing, "Sleep, little one, sleep, if you don't sleep, the crab will eat you, *dodo titit*, crab in okra gumbo."

Nina asked, "Who are you, and what have you done with Agatha?"

Chapter Nine

The woman at the stove turned around and looked at her for a long moment, and then said, "Whoever you are, girl, you look like you're having one seriously bad day. Get your ass on in here and have some biscuits. You'll find it very hard to be completely miserable when you're stuffing your face with biscuits and jam."

Nina didn't know what to say. Finally, she repeated, "Who are you?"

The woman looked surprised and said, "That's right, we haven't been formally introduced. I'm Sally Bowman, the new cook."

Nina knew it was stupid, but she said the first thing that came into her head. "You're the first person I've met here who has anything like a normal name."

"That's probably because I'm pretty normal." Sally took a tray of freshly baked biscuits out of the oven and slid them onto a plate. She brought them over to the big center island of the kitchen and motioned for Nina to sit on one of the stools there. Then she got a jar of raspberry jam out of the fridge and a crock of sweet butter and handed Nina a knife. "Dig in. I'll just keep flipping the chicken. Cooking's a pretty normal thing, when you get right down to it. You can't get too far out there when you're dealing with things like starch and hot oil."

Nina buttered one flaky biscuit and took an experimental bite. It was beyond good. She spread some of the jam and took another bite, and it was even better. This woman seriously knew her biscuits.

"How did you . . ." She paused to swallow, and Sally finished for her, "Get here? The usual way. I took the streetcar. Ha-ha. Seriously, I found the listing online." She closed her eyes and pretended to quote from memory. "'Want a challenge at a private institution with a hundred hungry mouths to feed? Then Daedalus is the place for you!'" She looked around and added,

"And it's true. I love cooking for a lot of people. I used to run a kitchen that fed hundreds, but that was way back before the storm. Lots of places closed since then. You ask me to make myself a ham sandwich, I won't bother, but a banquet for a thousand? Child, that's fun."

She turned the chicken expertly in the hot oil, and Nina reached for another biscuit and grinned. This felt so . . . normal. She had no memory of whether or not she'd ever had a mother, but this felt really nice. Too nice, in fact. She said, "I probably shouldn't be bothering you . . ." as she stood up.

"Nonsense, sit back down and eat. The only thing about cooking by yourself is it's too damn quiet. You need company." Sally looked over at Nina, and there was a weird moment when Nina wondered if the cook was another mind reader. She certainly felt like an open book. "You want to tell me why you were so upset, or you just want me to guess?"

"I . . . It's nothing." Nina laughed. *Right. I've been enrolled in a school for immortals, and I've found out I can do magic, and I can talk to the animals like Doctor Doolittle, and there's this African bitch-goddess who hates my guts, and even my kinda-sorta friends think I'm creepy. So, no, nothing much is going on. Just your average teen drama. Don't give it another thought.* "I'm having trouble fitting in," she finally mumbled.

"Tell me about it." Sally walked over to the table and pushed up her sleeve. "Look at that."

She had an enormous scar on her forearm that reached all the way around. It looked like a big piece of her skin had been torn away. It was beyond strange, because it should have looked hideous, and in a way it *did* look hideous, but at the same time, it also looked ferocious—like she was wearing a bracelet of scar tissue all around her wrist.

"I was mauled by a dog a while back," she said matter-of-factly. "Nothing life- threatening, but it definitely put an end to my career as a hand model. Ha ha, that's a joke. But everybody was like, are you gonna start frothing at the mouth? Making lame jokes. It's because they were embarrassed, but it still made me feel lower than low. Like I'd become some kind of a leper."

"So, what did you do?"

"What do you think? I became a total jerk about it. I completely overreacted. Started keeping to myself and acting like everybody was out to get me. *Not* a good idea."

"I don't know." Nina decided to eat *one more* biscuit (she'd already eaten three) and reached for the butter. "Maybe if you stick to yourself, you don't get hurt."

"Right. And then maybe you don't feel anything." Sally went back to the pans and started tossing more chicken pieces around, careless of the sputtering oil. Nina guessed that once you'd dealt with practically having your arm bitten off, a little thing like hot cooking oil didn't bother you.

"And no, it didn't make me particularly brave," Sally added, as though she'd just read Nina's mind again. "I was just scared of dogs for a long time after that. Silly, really. You give something power over you if you fear it. The easiest way to deal with a fear is to just put it out of your mind and only look at it when you have to. That way, you're not constantly obsessing over it. Puts it in perspective."

She lowered the heat on the chicken and added, almost as an afterthought, "That works pretty well with people who scare you too. Or people who piss you off."

"You just ignore them?"

"Mm-hmm. Drives 'em crazy. *They* start obsessing about *you* and trying to get a rise out of you, and pretty soon you've totally blown their minds. As we used to say back in my youth, 'Smile, it'll make people wonder what you've been up to.'"

Nina looked at the new cook and tried to figure out how old she was. She looked maybe thirty, thirty-five at the most, but Nina wasn't sure if she was a Skinny, so she might be older.

Nina didn't know how to ask her outright if she was human, so she tried to sneak up on it. "You're a terrific cook," she said, gesturing at the crumbs from the five biscuits—*five?*—she'd eaten and wiped her hands on a towel. "I guess when everybody found out what good food you made, you had a lot of new friends. The way to every normal person's heart is through their stomach, right?"

"Not necessarily." Sally sounded highly amused. "Depends on their tastes. And no, since you ask, I don't necessarily share the tastes of most of the other students and faculty here at Daedalus. Nor, apparently, do you. Not that I mind, of course. Live and let live—that's my motto. Now, you ask me to cook all that macrobiotic stuff, ground-up nuts and tofu—" She shuddered. "I'm outta here. But otherwise, I'm pretty broad-minded, taking it all in all."

She wiped up a spatter of grease with a paper towel and added, "I guess if you've known real hunger, you don't worry too much about what people eat, just that the inner emptiness is filled up somehow. That inner . . . craving. People are so unhappy; they long for real food, but all they get is fast-food ideas and empty calories. We stuff ourselves with mental Chee-Wees and call it progress."

She stopped, and Nina saw a rueful smile, thin as a crescent, shape her lips. "God, I'm such an aged hippy. 'All you need is love.' I'm surprised I'm not still wearing bell bottoms. All right, so now you know all my secrets. Now go on out and get yourself a place in the chow line, I'm almost done here, and I've still got to plate all this shit."

When Nina found a seat in the Commons—next to Alastaire and Bella, who fortunately looked like they were still happy to see her—big platters of food were just being brought out, and everyone started *ooh*ing and *ahh*ing. When they finally pushed back their chairs from the tables an hour later, they felt like they'd eaten enough to feed an army—or at least enough to feed a school full of hungry teenagers who hadn't enjoyed a decent meal in months. Fried chicken, mashed potatoes, coleslaw, and apple pie kept on coming until everybody was ready to burst, and even Agatha and Professor Danvers seemed happy. Nina had watched the professor out of the corner of her eye all through dinner, and he didn't look like Simone had blabbed to him yet about being hit with a disembodied bitch-slap . . . so she could only hope.

After dinner, Nina excused herself and went upstairs to the attic. When she got there, she discovered it was a big, spooky room under the eaves, but at least somebody had swept it clean. Rough-hewn beams crossed high above her head, and there were cobwebs and decades of dust obscuring the small-paned windows—which were all, of course, boarded up and nailed shut. They'd furnished the otherwise empty room with an old iron bedstead, a desk, a chair, and an old-fashioned wardrobe, where she could at least hang up her clothes. *Well,* she told herself, taking a deep breath, *it could be worse. At least I'm not sleeping on the floor.*

The school had sent up someone to help her "unpack," the round-shouldered boy named Roticus. As she took her clothes out of the Sav-A-Center bag—no way was she letting him get his hands on her bras and panties—he stood in the corner and mumbled, "Are you actually going to sleep up here?"

"Yeah, sure." Nina tried to make it sound like it was no big deal. "Why not?"

"There are ghosts, you know."

"Really?" Nina didn't particularly want to hear that, but she shrugged it off. "Roticus, um . . ." She decided to pump him for some information. "Do you *jumbies* ever get hassled because you don't have sponsors yet? I mean, because . . . well, you should know, *I* don't have a sponsor yet, and the way things are going, I don't think too many people are going to be lining up for the job."

Roticus didn't look at her while she hung up her red vinyl jacket with the faux biker tattoo patch on the back. The school, she saw, had provided her with several more dark dresses and skirts and blouses in shades of black and gray, already hung up neatly in the wardrobe, and she guessed that was a not-so-subtle hint.

"No," he said finally. "They know we're all just killing time here. Nobody expects us to be anything special."

This sounded so sad that Nina decided she couldn't possibly leave it at that. "Well, I-I think you're cool," she told him, even though anyone less cool than this depressed little kid was hard to imagine. He seemed to think so, too, because he made a *big whoop* gesture and stuffed his hands in his pockets.

"At least you guys can go off campus on weekends," he added. "You can probably go over to Magazine Street anytime you like."

"Roticus, what do you mean?" She sat down on the bed. "Why can't you go over to Magazine Street? Aren't all the kids allowed the same privileges?"

"Oh." He looked aside. "Forget it. You want me to put your bag someplace?"

Nina told him to just throw it out. While he stood there, she finished arranging her books and then checked out the rest of the attic (there was a bathroom with an old claw-foot bathtub, a pull-chain toilet, and a cracked mirror that reflected back a watery version of her face, and that was it). She came back and said, "Um, thanks. Oh, one other thing . . . do you suppose we could open a couple of windows?"

His eyes got as big as saucers. "You want to open a *window*?"

"Um, yeah. It's kind of stuffy in here."

"But . . . but the moon's almost full! There'll be light!"

"Yes, I know. I-I know about that. Professor Threet said that during the full moon all rules went backward, so maybe it's okay. Besides, it doesn't affect me." She looked at Roticus. "What? What's wrong?"

He was edging farther away from her, and his slacker sullenness was gone now, replaced by an out-and-out fear that would have made more sense in a much younger boy. He swallowed and said, "Don't hurt me!"

"I'm not going to hurt you." Nina tried to keep her voice from sounding indignant. She wasn't used to being accused of wanting to hurt someone. Roticus almost looked like he was going to cry. "C'mon," she added more softly, "It's okay."

He turned and ran away down the stairs, and she sighed and closed the door behind him, hearing his footsteps fade away as she threw the bolt. *Well,* she thought, *now I can scare small children.* She sat down on the bed and bounced up and down a couple of times. It actually felt pretty comfortable, so she changed out of her black clothes into a bright pink T-shirt and got under the covers. Then she thought, *This is ridiculous,* and went over to one of the small-paned windows and tried to see if she could open it. Two big nails were holding it closed, and she easily pried them loose. She opened the window and pushed against the plywood until it fell down into the bushes in the garden far below.

The soft night air and the rich fragrance of jasmine and gardenia were a full reward for her efforts. She looked out over the rooftops and chimneys of the Garden District, a lovely vista that had scarcely changed in more than a century. The moonlight gave a cool, silvery wash to everything, more delicate than day. She went back to her bed and snuggled down, only realizing then how bone tired she was. She tried to concentrate on the Alchemy book she had to read for Professor Aspidistrus's class tomorrow—and what on earth were the Consonances of the Mundane Monochord?—but it was no good. Within five minutes she was asleep.

Which was when she had a very strange dream. In it, an angel appeared to her and asked if she wanted a bite of an apple, and guessing where this might be leading, she said no. But the angel looked so disappointed, and he was so handsome. Tall, dark, forbidding . . . Did he look like anyone she knew? She finally took a bite, and abruptly she could see a rainbow of colors: red, blue, green, a kind of shimmery yellow halfway between gold dust and silvery sunlight, and a white so bright it looked like an atomic flash. She could smell flowers, fresh grass, the iodine tang of the sea, and she could feel ripples running all over her skin like trickling water. Every part of her body felt alive, impatient . . . yearning. She ran her hands over her own skin, wishing she could feel someone else's hands, someone strong, masterful . . . dangerous . . .

What on earth was she *thinking*? And with that thought, as fear lanced through her, a black darkness filled her vision so absolute it blocked out anything else, and she could smell mud, gasoline, wet smoke, and burning rubber.

She was standing in a vacant lot within sight of the New Orleans Convention Center, and there was a man standing next to her, a tall, pale man with a waxy complexion and wavy hair, dressed in a dark business suit. She recognized him from the *Daedalus, A Tradition of Service* brochure as "John Benway, noted philanthropist and head of the Benway Corporation."

She said, "What are you doing here?"

"I could ask you the same thing." He sounded annoyed. "You don't do things by half, do you?"

"I don't know what you mean."

"Showing up now. Your timing couldn't be worse."

"I'm sorry I—"

"You don't know what I'm talking about, do you? Of course not. That would be too easy."

"Really, I—"

He was sweating, though he ignored it. The streams of moisture running down his face were like tracks of water over smooth white porcelain.

"The Mundane Monochord represents the major gradations of energy and substance, between elemental earth and absolute unconditioned force. In other words, between that which is *seen* and that which is *willed*. Your being here is just the visible manifestation of a will the size of the Spiral Nebula. *Whose* will, of course, remains the question."

"Say *what*?"

"You can't know everything. But we who know much know there are limits to our knowledge, and 'all' is a concept reserved for the most mercurial of forces. Don't count your chickens before they're hatched. It never rains, but it pours. We who are about to die salute you. And keep your powder dry. We'll meet again very soon."

Then the dream changed, becoming sensuous again. Cool breezes tweaked her exposed flesh—and when had she taken off all her clothes?—sending sharp signals of mingled pain and pleasure. She felt a wind that was almost icy chill her nipples, and a moment later, the wind changed and became warm as her belly was bathed with a hot huff of breath. Had she ever been touched like this before? She didn't know. She knew she was lying down, and someone—or something—was moving over her, exploring, changing directions. She felt the flutter of lips and fingers, teeth, a tongue, a cool sigh as *something* trailed moisture down the center of her body from her throat to her navel and then further . . . further down . . . *ah, yes.* She arched her hips, and her pulse trembled. And then she realized she was lying naked on her bed, and Professor Danvers was staring down at her.

He stood looking at her without speaking, his eyes burning.

"You remind me of someone I knew once," he thought, and she could hear his thoughts. And then, *"Someone I once loved."*

I do?

"Yes. That's not necessarily a good thing."

No?

"I don't even know how old you are."

She didn't know, either, and had no idea where this conversation was headed, but she realized, even in a dream, that she was spread wide open, shamelessly displayed to him. He could see her body in excruciating detail, and she could tell how aroused he was.

"Love isn't simple," he thought. His lips didn't move, and he seemed angry with her.

It isn't? Then to herself, *I'm not even very clever in my own erotic dream.*

Could she be any more lame? She felt afraid to move, and she barely breathed.

"Nor is it easy," he thought. He moved to the side of the bed and continued to look down at her. He stretched out one long-fingered hand and brushed her hair back from her face, his own face coming so close she could feel the coldness of his skin. His pale mouth parted, and she felt his breath brush her throat. And then, just when he seemed about to kiss her, the dream faded, and she awoke to the alarming sensation that there really *was* somebody else in the room with her.

She pushed herself up on her elbows. "Who's there?"

No answer, but she was more convinced than ever that she wasn't alone. She tried to see by the faint moonlight shining in through the open window. There, a black dress, short like a smock, and a child's bare legs.

"Who are you?" she whispered, pulling her T-shirt and panties back on. She heard a low whimper, like a sob, and then the words, "Help me."

"Who are you?" she repeated, trying to keep as quiet as possible. She could see a dark face now, dark hair in braids, dark eyes hollowed and sunken, and a bloodless mouth—presumably a girl. The voice that answered her was soft and very young.

"Zoolie."

"Zoolie what?"

"I don't remember."

"Where are you from?"

"I don't know."

"Do you know where you are now?"

"No."

"Are you, um . . ." Nina wanted to ask the child whether she was alive or dead, but she didn't know how to bring it up. She said instead, "What's the last thing you remember?"

"Nothing."

Right, Nina thought. *No surprises there.* She sat up in bed. "Don't be scared. I'm just going to turn the light on . . ."

"No!" The child darted behind the wardrobe and crouched down.

Nina said, "Okay, okay, I won't do it! All right? Why don't you . . . um, why don't you come over and sit on the bed?" She shifted her position to make room. "Come on, I won't bite you."

The child let out a low wail of such hideous, muffled horror that Nina only realized at that point what she'd just said. "Oh my God! I'm sorry! I'm sorry! I just meant I-I won't hurt you. I'm not going to . . . I'm not going to do *anything*!"

The child didn't move but continued to stare at her with big, frightened eyes, and after a moment, Nina took a chance and got out of bed herself, her feet cold on the bare floor. She crouched down in front of the little girl and said, "There, see? It's okay. Here, give me your hands. I'll warm them up for you."

And the minute she touched the child's hands, she knew she wasn't alive. Her hands weren't merely cold; they had a terrible elastic *give*, like pressing her fingers into foam rubber. She could feel no bones, just rubbery flesh all the way through. "Jesus!" she said, starting back and dropping the child's hands as if she'd been stung.

She got up and went to the kerosene lamp by her bedside without even stopping to consider what she was doing, only knowing she needed to see more clearly what was going on. But as she touched the lamp and fumbled for a match to light it, the glass globe shattered in a bright explosion, and when she turned around again, she couldn't see anything at all.

"W-where are you?" Nina whispered. "Are you still here?"

"I'm here." A voice like a sigh, like nothing.

"Did you do that?"

Silence.

"Who are you?"

"I told you, I'm Zoolie."

"And . . . and what happened to you?" Nina asked it very quietly, trying to keep her voice as level as possible.

"I told you. I don't know."

And then Nina heard the words in her head, *"Help me."*

Then all of a sudden there was a knock on the door, and Alastaire's low voice said, "Nina? Are you in there? Let me in! I've got to talk to you for a second!"

"Hold on!" Nina said, and bent down to the little girl again. "How'd you get in here?"

"Through the wall." The girl gestured. The wall looked like regular plaster, but when the little girl put her hand on it, it gave like marshmallow, and she said, "We can go through. It's sticky, but we figured out how."

It seemed the dead (or whatever they were) had more than a few tricks up their sleeves.

Nina asked quickly, "How many of you are there?"

"I don't know."

This was getting silly.

Then the girl said, "There are lots, but they're different. Some of them are just . . ." She shivered. "Bones. Some of them are like me. We're all . . . trapped here. Trapped in the walls."

This was so absolutely horrible that Nina couldn't think of a single thing to say for a moment, and *stat*, the little girl sank back into the wall like she was disappearing into vertical quicksand. After a deep breath, Nina went to the door and opened it, rubbing her eyes with unsteady hands as she did so.

"I'm sorry," she told Alastaire. "I was just, um, sleeping."

"That's okay." The Skinny girl came in without apologizing and sat down on the bed. "I just wanted to check on you. It's, like, the weirdest thing. I was just coming up the stairs and there was like this big explosion and I heard you yell and—Jesus, you look like shit," she added, finally registering the strange expression on Nina's face. "What happened? Are you sick?"

Nina forced a laugh and said, "I guess I've been having bad dreams, that's all. What made you come up here?"

"Uh . . ." Alastaire fiddled with a loose button on her bathrobe. Her mustache was a little more pronounced than before, and her voice was a little deeper, but she was still wearing pink, fluffy, bunny slippers, so she looked pretty harmless. "It's not what you think. I'm not hitting on you, okay. I was just worried about you. There are rumors of all kinds of strange stuff going on up here at night, ghosts and everything."

Nina made a quick decision. "Well, nothing strange happened tonight. I just knocked my lamp over, that's all, when I heard you coming up the stairs, so you can go back to your room now with a clear conscience and—"

Another knock on the door frame, and Bella stuck his head in. Since they hadn't closed the door, he wasn't *exactly* trespassing, but Nina still sighed and said, "What? Does the whole school want to see me in my underwear?"

"Probably." Bella allowed himself a little smirk as he closed the door behind him, and then he frowned when he saw Alastaire. "So what are you doing here, Groucho?"

"Same as you, Bird-legs. I was just checking up on Nina."

Bella really did have super skinny legs, which were currently on display in silk boxers and a Sulka robe. He contented himself with sitting down at Nina's desk and sticking his tongue out at Alastaire. Nina decided things were rapidly getting ridiculous—again.

"Well, there's no need for either of you to check on me. I'm *fine*. It's not like I need somebody to watch me sleep." *I've already got plenty of people doing that*, she thought.

Bella frowned. "You sound like sleeping up here is nothing unusual."

"It *isn't* unusual!" Nina almost screamed. "It's normal. There's a bed. There are sheets." *I'm tired. What else does it* take?"

"You don't know." He said it flatly.

Oh no, that can't be good, Nina thought. "What?"

"Nothing."

"*What?*" She said it more firmly this time.

Bella glanced at Alastaire, who was suddenly fascinated by her fingernails. He hesitated and then said, "This is where it happened."

"Where *what* happened?"

Bella sighed and settled himself down as if to tell a long story. "Okay, so you know there are two people named Danvers who pretty much run this place, right?"

"Bella, she already knows that." Alastaire sighed. "She's not *dumb*."

"Whatever. Well, once upon a time there were three of them. The Danverses. They had a sister. Niobe."

You look like someone I once knew, Nina remembered his words in her head. *Someone I once loved. And that's not necessarily a good thing.*

"What happened to her?" she forced herself to ask.

"Well, she and Professor Danvers were very close. I believe they were in love." He blushed and added, "It's not like that. Skin Eaters aren't biologically related to one another, so so-called siblings fall in love all the time. In fact, we fall in love with all kinds of people." He shot Alastaire a glance. "With some of us, it happens practically every day."

"Blow it out your butt, Sissy-drawers."

"Anyway, years later, there was a war, and Niobe fought alongside her brother Strickland."

"Against Sister Aquilina?"

"Right. Sister Aquilina made a pact with the *Lwas*. They are the darkest of dark spirits. The word *Lwa* is the voodoo word for god or supernatural force. The only problem was, Niobe Danvers at that time happened to be in love with a *Lwa*."

"She was in love with a supernatural force?"

"In human form."

Nina considered this. So Professor Danvers's sister had been in love with an evil god? "So what happened? Did Niobe get in trouble?"

"Worse than that. The Saturni called her a traitor. Finally, she saw the only way to prove she hadn't gone over to the dark side was to go up against Sister Aquilina herself. She fought Sister Aquilina in this very room and . . ." He lowered his voice. "Sister Aquilina crossed with her."

"She—What? Wait a minute—" Nina looked from Alastaire to Bella and back again. "I thought you said your lives became toxic to one another once you both turned?"

Alastaire nodded, and Nina belatedly got it. She said slowly, "So Sister Aquilina and Niobe were both adult Skin Eaters, and Sister Aquilina shared her life essence with Niobe, and that . . . that killed her? Is that what you're saying happened?" She swallowed, and her voice came out a lot higher than she intended it to. "Up *here*?"

"Uh-huh." Bella looked around at the bare room. "Of course, nobody would come up here for ages. Professor Danvers wanted to burn the whole school down. He was insane with grief."

Nina remembered the waves of anguish she'd felt coming from the professor the first time they'd met, and she remembered his drawn, unsmiling face as he'd gazed down on her in her dream. She whispered, "I'm so sorry."

"Why? *You* didn't know her!" Alastaire rounded on Bella. "Why are you frightening her like that? I just figured she might be uncomfortable sleeping in a strange room. I wasn't going to tell her somebody *died* up here!"

But Nina was thinking about something else. "Why didn't Sister Aquilina die too? Wouldn't it kill her to share Niobe's life the same way it killed Niobe?"

"No one knows," Bella said after a moment. "It may have been the powerful darkness Sister Aquilina commanded, or she may have known some way of giving Niobe Danvers her poisoned life and taking nothing in return. All we know is, Niobe died. And I did *not* want to scare her," he added to Alastaire. "I just wanted to . . . to warn her."

Nina had another thought. "What happened to the *Lwa*? The one Niobe was in love with?"

"I don't know," Bella admitted. "For that matter, no one knows exactly what happened to Sister Aquilina. She just disappeared. The Saturni claim to have bound her somehow, but that's just bullshit if you ask me. If you ask me what *really* happened—"

Another set of footsteps sounded on the stairs, and then Agatha Danvers's stern voice came very clearly through the closed door. "Miss Roget, Mr. Chopin, I know you're in there, so you might as well come out now and let Miss Lamb get a decent night's sleep."

Busted, Alastaire mouthed to Bella, who rolled his eyes, picked up a pen from Nina's desk, and scribbled something on the wooden surface. He then immediately put the pen down and strolled over to the door, opening it. "I'm *so* sorry, Miss Danvers. You caught me as I was just leaving. I was saying goodnight to Nina."

"At three o'clock in the morning?" Agatha raised one eyebrow. "Surely you can do better than that."

"Um . . . I couldn't sleep?"

Agatha came into the room and saw Nina sitting on the bed in nothing but her T-shirt, with Alastaire sitting next to her, and a nasty smile curled her lips.

"Well, well, well," Agatha said. "Miss Lamb. *And* Miss Roget. In a state of . . . undress. Tell me, Miss Lamb, are you already making conquests?"

Nina said, "No," and raised her chin. "Alastaire, Bella, and I were just talking about our classes. They were explaining some of the rules to me."

"Alastaire . . ." Agatha held the name in her mouth like a bitter pill, "could explain the rules of contract bridge and make them sound obscene. And Mr. Chopin is, I believe, only allowed out after curfew for certain specially approved research projects. What exactly were you researching up here?"

"Termites," he said, glancing up. "You have them in the roof, in case you're interested."

Agatha was staring at Nina now, as if she truly hated her. Or as if she were truly afraid of her. "Miss Lamb," she sneered, "Please don't think of challenging my authority. I've been running things at Daedalus since your great-grandma wore diapers."

"I thought Professor Danvers was in charge here."

Agatha scowled even more than she already was. "Professor Danvers can barely govern his own thoughts, much less a school full of unruly children. And if you think you're going to get special treatment by making up to the assistant headmaster—"

This was so profoundly unfair that Nina had to open her mouth to answer, but before she could say anything, Bella and Alastaire had both crossed the room to link arms with Agatha Danvers, one on either side.

Alastaire crooned, "C'mon, Danny. You know you're just jealous because I didn't choose you for my third crossing. But you can be my fourth, I promise!"

"And I'll let you do me if you'll give me some extra time out in the garden," Bella whispered in her ear. "The larvae are just getting good."

"Come on . . ." Alastaire tickled the older woman's ear.

Agatha looked like she was getting ready to murder both of them and was just trying to decide on the most drawn-out, painful method of doing it.

"Please do me the favor of getting your hands off me," she hissed through her teeth, and then snapped, "Out. *Now.*"

"C'mon, Danny, don't be mean . . ."

"Now!"

"Okay, okay . . ."

Bella and Alastaire both winked at Nina before they left, strolling off down the stairs.

Agatha turned to Nina and said, "Watch yourself. Not everyone wants you here. And close that window," she added, slamming the door behind her as she stormed out.

Chapter Ten

There was a garden filling up with night. Rain pattered overhead on the leaves, although up here on the porch Daneel and the rest of them were dry, sitting in big old leather chairs. The rich smells of the flowers and the earth made him feel like he was drunk or high, like smoking weed, if weed ever smelled this sweet. It made him think of the perfume his mother had worn once, before she disappeared into the streets. Better not to think about her now. Better not to think about his Nani either, or any of the kids he'd once known at school. Better just to drift and lie down and wait for his tummy to be rubbed like a big old dog. Big old dogs didn't have to worry—they got fed and a warm place to sleep. If they were tough enough, nobody messed with a dog.

If I were a dog, Daneel thought, *everything would be all right.*

There was a warm, fresh wind blowing from someplace, but that surely couldn't be right, could it? This close to the river, it should have been muggy and sticky by now. It should have smelled like rot, like oil, like all the rest of the Ninth Ward still swimming in all that shit and mold and old clothes and pulled-out plasterboard, all that soggy shit, all the way from Jackson Barracks to St. Claude Avenue. Most of that area had just gotten the electricity back, if there were still people in their houses to use it. Most of those houses, in fact, stood empty, just piles of boards and sticks and bricks and the sodden mess of lives washed out onto the sidewalk.

But here it smelled like fruit, like that sweet incense they used to light down at Ti-Bon's, like freshly cut grass, and like something that smelled like chocolate. But there couldn't be chocolate in a garden, could there? Couldn't be a lot of things, but Daneel didn't know.

He tried to make his thoughts make sense, but there was nothing around him to latch on to.

He'd given up trying to understand it all, just let it wash over him. He was content at the moment, sitting on the porch. Staying in this big old house was cool, but he knew he'd have to get his ass in gear soon. This couldn't last forever. Nobody just let you stay in their house and left food around for you. Lots of food, good food . . . He'd eaten better here than anywhere else he could remember. Nobody did that without wanting something in return. He wondered what the strange dark woman who'd rescued him really wanted.

Catch and release—wasn't that what they did with fish? Catch and release. He wondered if he'd wake up one morning (or one evening, because the days all ran together here) with a hook in his mouth, reeled in on the end of a pole. The dark woman called them "mounts." She smiled like it was all a big game, but he knew he couldn't trust her, didn't dare. She was some kind of scary, and when he thought about it, he was afraid she'd grab him one night with those beautiful, long, slim hands and he'd be stuck, gigged like a frog, and gutted with one quick move.

And yet she didn't do it. She never touched him. She never did anything.

And she could be nice, but you never knew. Like that girl Billie, that runaway with the big tits who had pissed the woman off just by asking if she could go home. The dark woman had finally whirled on her and said, "All right, you want to see what you've done, then see," and the girl had fallen to her knees. Later, the girl had told them what she'd seen in a flash, like a movie: her stepfather slumped in the front seat of his Lexus in the garage, with the door closed and the engine running. Daneel guessed Billie must have felt bad after that, because she'd never mentioned going home again, although she'd told them enough about her stepfather's own little games of catch and release that you didn't need to fill in too many blanks. That's what the dark woman was like, kind, but tough. The little ones, the ones who still cried and wet the bed, could expect to be comforted, but the older ones had learned to shut up after that.

Even when the *horroi* were howling, they didn't complain too much.

The *horroi*. It had taken Daneel a while to get used to *them*, and he supposed "used" still wasn't the right word. Huge dogs the size of lions, with gaunt black empty faces and eyes scoured clean like the eyes in skulls. He kept away from them as much as he could. The dark woman could call them to her hand with a snap, and they'd come fawning, but they could send anyone away who came too close, running after them, their silence worse than a snarl. They patrolled the outer edges of the "camp," as they'd come to call this place, for want of a better name: as if this was someplace where you'd earn merit badges. Daneel sometimes thought maybe he was dead, but he couldn't figure out if this was heaven or hell. One thing about the place, though—it was beautiful. Crazy-ass batshit weird, but beautiful.

The rain was getting stronger, and Daneel heard a noise to his left and looked over to see Tish and Flyboy coming out to sit on the steps. They'd get wet, but Tish never seemed to care what happened to her, and Flyboy went wherever Tish went, like he was stuck to her with Gorilla Glue. Tish looked up at the sky and let the water cascade down over her face, plastering her red hair to her cheeks like seaweed. In her short lifetime, she'd clearly seen a lot, pale and skinny with cigarette burns all over her arms and legs, but Daneel never asked her what had happened. That was one of the unspoken rules of the camp, that nobody there talked too much about the past.

"You see the new kid?" Daneel asked, keeping his voice low.

Tish nodded, and Flyboy just made that strange buzzing sound he always made, like he was humming but could never remember the tune.

"He says the dark woman's wanted by the police." Daneel didn't say her name out loud.

"He doesn't know shit." Tish sounded certain. "He's just scared."

The new kid had arrived the day before—or was it the day before that?—a skinny white punk with bars in both eyebrows and tattoos all over his body, and a stud in his dick (so he said, but they thought he was just bluffing). *Be pissing in his pants with that stud dick*, Daneel thought, sniggering.

"He says she's a child molester."

"He's full of shit. You think the police ever even *heard* of her?"

"What *you* think she wants?"

Tish shrugged. "Don't know. Know I sleep safe, that's for sure."

"You think she's bad?"

"Shut up."

Daneel tried to keep his voice low, but it was hard. "I think she wants us all scared,

'cause it makes us foul up, makes us stupid. That's how it works."

"You don't need to be scared to do that. You can do stupid all by yourself."

"I've been here longer than you," he said defensively. "Longer than most. I was here right after the storm."

"Bully for you. That's not being smart; that's just lazy."

Over beyond the tall palms and the battered magnolia trees where the leaves moved and clashed together in the wind, there were moving shapes, solid shadows like spilled blood. The dogs the size of lions. The *horroi* always knew when the children fought, and it made them restless.

"I had that dream again." Tish's voice was soft now. "That girl. She's sleeping up in some attic."

"You mean, like, here?" This house had storage space up under the eaves, but it wasn't anywhere you wanted to stay for long. Some of the kids had checked it out when they first got there, in case it flooded again, but they'd come back down in time for lunch.

"No, in my dreams, that attic where she's staying is bigger. Spooky. There's windows, but they're mostly boarded up." Tish shivered, and Daneel knew he definitely didn't want to hear about any of this.

Didn't want to hear about anything spooky right now. They had *spooky* down cold.

"You think this place is haunted?" He hated himself for even saying it, but he had to ask.

"I don't know." Tish looked up at the ceiling of the porch, where the paint was peeling away in long strips. "It's crummy enough."

And yet it wasn't crummy. It was rundown, but beauty dripped from the vines twined around the windows, burst with flowers from the wild bushes in the garden, and sprouted in the overgrown grass.

Daneel sighed and said, "You think she means it? She gonna let us go sometime?" He was back to the dark woman again.

Tish shrugged. "Say her name, why don't you? *Sister Aquilina.* She's not Candyman. And yeah, I think she means it. Though I doubt we can just split. Besides . . ." She looked around. "Where you gonna go? Back to your Nani's? You gonna scrub everything down with Clorox and it'll be fine? Shee-it . . ." She looked up at the sky and opened her mouth, letting raindrops fall on her tongue. "Ain't nothing gonna be *fine* again."

There was a sound inside, of music playing softly, and with it came the enticing aroma of dinner. Daneel tried not to let his stomach growl. He had the idea that all this food was a bad idea (was she fattening them up for something?) but every time a meal appeared, it seemed impossible not to eat like a horse. Red beans and rice and sausage so juicy the grease ran down your chin, and mustard greens and fresh cornbread, and corn pudding too, and crowder peas.

Pork chops fried crisp and turkey wings so big they hung off your plate. French bread and butter. Thick cakes with icing and whiskey sauce on the side. Even though Sister Aquilina wasn't there all the time, she made sure they always ate well—and to everyone's liking. But when she was there, they had music with dinner, and it was playing now, some kind of New Age-y thing but with a beat, harps, and funky drumming at the same time, lovely.

Tish and Flyboy stood up, and Daneel did too, and Sibelle, who was an albino and so was kinda creepy in her own right, and Bacalou, the scary-looking Arab guy who was blind in one eye and had been wounded somewhere (Iraq? Lebanon?), and they all trooped into the kitchen, where they started gathering up their plates. They ate family style, and nothing better to call the family to the table than the feast that was currently being laid out. It might be three o'clock in the morning (Daneel suspected it was; time was strange here) but here was the new tattooed kid, his name was Sharazz; and Santangelo, who was gay and funny and wore bright silk shirts and played the harmonica; and Stephen, who was weird and Goth with platinum hair and always wore black leather; and Joe Trunza, who was built like a bull; and Emma and Ella, who were twins and always hung together and rarely spoke. And here was Billie, the rich white runaway, looking good in a pair of short-shorts (*guess that's why her stepfather kept hitting on her,* Daneel thought) and the dreadlocked guy from the neighborhood who often ate with them, whom everyone called Legs.

And here was Sister Aquilina in her long, black dress and her black robes, and her long, black hair hanging down her back like some weird kind of Wicked Witch nun or something. A beautiful nun.

And there was Mr. O'Brien, and Daneel thought Mr. O'Brien was probably the strangest guy in the bunch. He was tall and strong, but old, really old, with an old white man's skin and an old white man's beard and ice-blue eyes and the kind of stern, no-nonsense face that made you think he'd chew you out just as soon as look at you. And even though he was generally nice and brought them all candy and magazines—and had even bought Santangelo his harmonica—Daneel didn't trust him an inch.

He'd seen him with Sister A. and heard them talking, and Mr. O'Brien telling her, "They really do suit their roles perfectly, you know. Where did you find them?"

And Sister A saying, "Oh, here and there. I learned a lot from you, you know."

"How flattering."

"Don't flatter yourself. I learn from whoever will satisfy me and give me what I want."

"That, my dear, is precisely why I'm flattered."

Mr. O'Brien called them all to the table now and stood up, folding his hands together. "Children, shall we pray?" Daneel caught a fleeting glimpse of Sister Aquilina's face and realized she thought this was as much bullshit as Daneel did. Mr. O'Brien had some kind of arthritis that made his knuckles all big and blue, and sometimes Daneel thought he was just waiting to pick them all up and break them between those big, strong, awful blue hands. Daneel didn't even know why he thought that, but he did. He put his own hands together now and said, "Thank you, God," as fervently as anyone, hoping it would keep him on Mr. O'Brien's good side.

Then Sister Aquilina said, "Welcome," and quirked an eyebrow at Sharazz, adding, "I hope you're hungry." And then she turned to Daneel, and he felt his bowels turn to jelly with a combination of fear and love.

She said softly, "Ah, Daneel, my first conquest. I made you a special dessert tonight. I don't know why, but I just thought you might like chocolate. It's a devil's food cake. Now make sure you eat up every bite."

Chapter Eleven

I t wasn't until the morning, after Nina's first night at the Daedalus School, that she discovered Bella had scribbled on her desk: *CC's, tomorrow, 10 a.m.*

Wondering who CC was, she went downstairs, determined to find out. But there was a delay. Just as she was sitting down to breakfast, Professor Hermes rose to make an announcement.

"Students," he said, turning his blind white gaze toward them all, "Pending the return of Professor Danvers, who has been called away unexpectedly, I'd like you all to know that I shall be taking over his duties as *assistant* assistant headmaster. Please feel free to see me with any administrative concerns you may have. Now I . . . um, where was I? Oh yes, I have one other announcement to make . . . ah, where is it? Ah, yes, thank you—"

Professor Samson had handed him a piece of paper, and he stared at it, as if unsure what it said.

Then he took out a pair of very thick glasses, put them on, and looked at it again. Then he leaned down to Professor Samson and pointed at a word, but the other professor made a quick *get on with it* gesture and turned back to finish his coffee.

Professor Hermes said, "Er, yes. The pliers have asked to speak to any stud walls who have knuckles regarding the disappointment of Mrs. Cockle Hodgepodge. If any of you know of her moonmen yesterday, after her visor here, please comb and set me at once in my offramp."

This was met with universal exclamations of "What?" "Repeat

that!" and "What did he say?" and Professor Hermes blinked and held the paper up a little more to the light.

"Ah, yes, now I can see it. The polecats have asked to spooge to any sandwich who have kow-tows regarding the dishrag of Mrs. Crinkly Hoopleskirt. If any offers know of her mudman yestiddy after hair vision here, please can and shine me at oon in my orifice."

This didn't make any more sense than the first announcement, and finally Professor Samson tore the paper out of Professor Hermes's hands and read, "The police have asked to speak to any students who have knowledge regarding the disappearance of Mrs. Cecilia Hopkins. If any of you know of her movements yesterday, after her visit here, please come and see Professor Hermes at once in his office. Or not. Frankly, I for one, don't even care anymore!"

The room exploded with laughter, but Nina felt uneasy. Mrs. Hopkins had disappeared? How could that be? She glanced around, but neither Bella nor Alastaire was there. Since it was Saturday, a number of students were absent. A tall, blonde person plunked down next to her and started scarfing up a plate of scrambled eggs, and Nina handed the blond some bacon and whispered, "Do you know anything about this?"

"What, that Blindo Hermes is a trainwreck? Please. The guy can't see as far as his nose."

"No, I meant about Mrs. Hopkins."

"Isn't she the old lady who brought you here?" The blond laughed. "What'd you do, push her in some swamp?"

Nina decided to let the matter drop. She asked instead, "Do you know who or what CC's is?"

"It's a coffee shop. Down on Magazine Street." The blonde yawned. Nina truly had no idea of the person's sex, since they were tall and strong and possessed of some impressive biceps, but equally impressive tits. They also appeared to be hungover.

"God, and speaking of coffee, I need about eight more cups!" The blond rolled their eyes and poured themselves another cup. "I was up all night with Professor Danvers doing my fifth crossing. Wheeee ... what a rush!"

Nina winced, although she tried hard not to let the blond see it. Was that why Professor Danvers was also missing this morning? Was he sleeping off a particularly strenuous encounter? Of course, as Alastaire had admitted, such encounters were beyond pleasant. Why wouldn't Professor Danvers want to share life with this person? Nina told herself she was being ridiculous, although she couldn't resist asking, "Really? What was he ... I mean, what was it like?"

"Are you *kidding*? *Haaawwt!*" The blonde giggled.

Definitely female, Nina thought. Despite the biceps. Damn. "Did he ... What did he do, exactly?"

"God, what *didn't* he do?" The blond rubbed her head and fingered what might or might not have been a hickey on her neck. Or a bite mark. Shit. "I feel like I've been rid hard and put away wet." For all her alleged satisfaction, she also looked like she was in some considerable pain. "He said he doesn't do it with everybody, you know ... he's *very* particular."

Right, Nina thought, *'roided-out sluts are probably his favorite type.* She stood up abruptly. "Look, I gotta run, thanks for telling me about CC's. I-I'll see you around ..."

"Whatever," the blond said, reaching for the orange juice. "Right now, I gotta build up my strength. That was a l-o-o-ong night."

Great, Nina thought as she brought her tray into the kitchen. *Now I'm jealous of anybody who comes near a man who says I bedevil him. I need to get a grip.*

She could remember the cold seeming to radiate from Professor Danvers's skin, and his breath against her throat.

She remembered the languorous, trailing touch of an invisible force caressing her, sending shivers up her spine and down to her toes. She remembered the expression of power, command, and authority in his eyes as he'd stared at her. And she could remember the tight, almost anguished look on his face as she read his thoughts: *Love isn't simple.* Damn, it had all felt so *real.*

But, in fact, it meant nothing. She reminded herself it was all just a dream. She set her tray down as Sally was wiping down the stove, and Roticus and two other *jumbies* were glumly loading the dishwasher, and as she approached the cook she asked, "Sally, did you ever hear of Sister Aquilina?"

The cook turned away to toss her sponge in the sink, and when she turned back she said, "Nope. Who's she?"

"She's . . . well, she's supposed to be this really nasty magician who was once the enemy of the Skin Eaters." She gestured. "The . . . um, the people here. You know."

"Sister Aquilina." Sally quirked an eyebrow as she thought about it. "Was she a nun? I've known some pretty scary nuns in my time."

"No, I . . . actually, I don't know why she was called that." Nina realized for the first time how odd it was. "She supposedly learned all this magic, which the Skin Eaters don't believe in but kind of do, and it scares them. So then the Skin Eaters had to band together and defeat her."

"Like Hitler, huh? I mean, without the magic." Sally shrugged. "Unless you count *Raiders of the Lost Ark.*"

"Yeah, something like that."

"You know . . ." Sally sat down on one of the stools next to the kitchen island and gestured for Nina to join her. She poured them each a cup of coffee. "I always think it's kind of curious what people are afraid of. Like magic. By the way, what do you think of

Calculation Science? Do you really believe all life can be turned into raw data, just numbers, and stored in a polynomial engine?"

Nina's eyes widened. For someone who'd just arrived, Sally seemed to know a lot.

The cook made a dismissive gesture. "I had a crash course in the curriculum from Agatha Danvers. Calculation Science seems like basic Materialism 101. Matter is all there is, right?"

"Yes." Nina remembered her conversation with Alastaire. "Someone told me the Skin Eaters believe everything is value neutral. Nothing but facts."

"Yeah? Well, don't *you* believe it." Sally got up and went to the counter and reached under the sink. She brought out a tiny kitten, jet black with bright yellow eyes. She reached down with her free hand and turned on the garbage disposal and was just about to drop the animal into its grinding gears when Nina yelled, "Stop it!" and ran over and grabbed the little kitten away from her. She backed away from the cook as though she'd gone crazy, and Sally just looked at her with raised eyebrows.

"Why? What's wrong?"

"What's *wrong*? Because . . . because it's terrible, that's why! This poor little thing . . ." Nina cuddled the tiny animal to her throat, where it began to purr against her skin. She felt like she was about to cry. "He didn't do anything to you! He's just a baby, and you're going to grind him up like hamburger? What kind of a monster are you?"

"A value neutral one." Sally smiled, taking the cat back from her and stroking its chin. It curled up in Sally's two hands like a tiny soft black ball, obviously feeling safe. "See? So much for calculation. You're not a monster, and neither am I, but there are those who would grind whole populations down to dust and never break a sweat. Remember that the next time people tell you logic is everything, and everything can be boiled down to just 'facts'."

Nina took a deep breath, still upset about the kitten, and noticed Sally wasn't holding anything anymore. "Wh-where did it go?"

"That? Oh, that was just a Schrödinger cat, just a thought experiment." Sally smiled, as if surprised. "I just made it appear to show you. Why? Do you really want it back? Okay." The cook cupped her two palms together again and then deposited a soft, warm, still purring creature into Nina's hands.

As she held the little cat, Nina felt a strange warmth running all through her. She nuzzled the kitten and asked, "What's his name?"

"I should say his name is Mercy, since you showed him Mercy."

Nina smiled suddenly, liking Sally a lot, and liking what Sally had told her almost as much as she liked the kitten itself. "You're right! You can't just boil down everything into data! There's how we feel and who we love and what we think. It's what we do and what we decide to do that matters. Thoughts aren't just *things*."

"Well, idealism's a little more complicated than that, but that's the basic idea. Someone once said, 'materialism is the philosophy of the subject who forgets to take account of himself,' which is pretty damn neat, when you come to think of it." Sally stood up. "Now, don't you have somewhere to be and someone to meet?"

Nina glanced at the clock and realized it was already ten. Mercy was squirming to get down and investigate a pitcher of milk on the counter, so she handed the kitten back to Sally, then ran for the front door.

It felt odd being outside without a chaperone, as she opened the big iron gate and let herself out into the street. Would anybody stop her? Everything looked so ordinary. The beautiful live oaks stretched their limbs across the sidewalk, and the columned houses drowsed in the sun. A man walked by yelling into a cell phone—"You told me we could get the sheetrock by Tuesday, now you're telling me a month?"—but despite his angry words, he just smiled at her and waved as he went past. She'd been worried she'd stick out like a sore thumb in her dark clothes, but apparently Goths were common here, and nobody gave her a second glance.

As she started to walk down First Street in the direction of what she hoped was Magazine, she thought, I could go anywhere right now. I could just disappear. The odd thing was, she wasn't sure she wanted to. The Daedalus School might be scary—make that terrifying, sexy, and possibly life-threatening—but after twenty-four hours, it was also starting to feel like home. *In spite of everything, maybe I do belong here.*

She thought that until she saw the words "Community Coffee" written on the glass-front wall of a welcoming café, and looking inside, she saw Alastaire sprawled in a plushy chair, wearing dark sunglasses and hiding from the sun. She had a full five o'clock shadow now, and she was rubbing her chin like it itched. However, Nina told herself, friends didn't bail on friends just because they needed a shave. She went inside and sat down and said, "Hi, I was afraid I'd missed you guys."

"What? No, we're here. Bella's just getting us lattes." Alastaire indicated a big chunk of carrot cake on the low table in front of her. "And I'm busy stuffing my face. God, I hate the sun," she added. "My head hurts."

"I-I'm sorry."

Alastaire gestured to indicate it didn't matter. Nina thought about the other kids she'd seen, who looked like they were sick and hurting and wondered if she should express more concern, but just then, Bella came over carrying three lattes and a folded-up newspaper, and his face told her something worse was going on.

"Hi, Nina. Have you seen the *Times Picayune*?"

"No, I just got here."

"Okay. Prepare yourself. Oh, yeah, here's your coffee." He handed her a frothy cup. By contrast with Alastaire, Bella was looking pretty good this morning: his Armani shades complemented his thin, honey-colored face, although he was looking more feminine than ever. Nina could even see curves underneath his jacket.

But his frown spoke volumes, and after she'd taken a sip, Nina opened the paper and read the headline: "Social Worker Found Dead, Eaten By Birds."

"Oh, shit," she whispered. "Yes. Wasn't she the woman who enrolled you a couple of days ago? It says here she left a note saying she was onto some vast, terrible conspiracy, and she was found out in Audubon Park with her eyes pecked out and half her face gone—"

Nina wasn't listening. She remembered the horrifying image she'd seen for a split second two days before, when she'd looked into Professor Danvers's eyes and seen . . . what, exactly? A vision? A glimpse of the future? Mrs. Hopkins with blood running down her face . . . She'd been attacked by a monstrous crow, while her mouth stretched wide in a scream nobody could hear. Nina remembered the bird pecking out her eyes, and then an iron wall coming down.

As though she'd seen something by accident.

She came back to herself and looked down at her cup and said, "I don't want to be here. I just want to go away. Anyplace. I don't care. Just go."

"Nina—" Alastaire touched her hand.

Nina flinched. "You don't understand."

"I know it's a shock—" Alastaire began.

Bella had been looking at her cooly, and he interrupted Alastaire with, "You aren't surprised, are you?"

"No, I just . . ."

"You knew about this."

"Well, Professor Hermes said something at school, but it's not that." She pressed the heels of her hands against her eyes, very hard—hard enough to see stars. Was that the last thing Mrs. Hopkins had seen? Stars or a beak? "I-I knew this was going to happen." There. She'd said it.

"So now you're, what? Clairvoyant?" Alastaire snorted. "Come on, Neen, I know you're special, but stop trying to freak us out. What are you going to do next, bend spoons?"

Nina shook her head and said, "Never mind, forget it. Why did you ask me here?"

Bella drank half of his latte in a gulp and pushed his cup to one side. "Because we didn't finish our conversation last night. About Sister Aquilina. And other stuff."

"What else is there?"

"Just this." Bella lowered his voice even further. "There's a prophecy. And I think it's about you."

Nina shut her eyes again. No, she thought, none of this could be happening. She remembered the strange events in Professor Danvers's office, and Mrs. Hopkins's mysterious words.

She remembered Alastaire saying, "I think this all does fit together, and I'm behind you, whatever happens," and she thought, *It's all real, isn't it? And it all has to do with this strange evil magician who's come back?* She asked, "What does the prophecy say?"

"It's incredibly complicated." Bella shrugged. "I only got a look at it once for about half a second, when Professor Danvers left a book open in the library. Fortunately, I have a photographic memory. Let me see." He steepled his fingers. "'After the tempest, one will appear who has no past. She will best the pelican, and the beautiful hand will be revealed.' That's all I got to see. Professor Danvers came back and grabbed the book and gave me the dirtiest look, like I'd read his private stash of porn. But that doesn't matter. I've been working on it ever since, trying to put it together with other things. Here, look at this."

He pulled out a marble composition notebook and opened it. The pages were covered with notes, arrows pointing to other notes, scribbled drawings, and even shorthand. It looked like a treasure map drawn by Albert Einstein.

"Okay, so here's what I think. The Skin Eaters are obsessed with riddles and prophecies. I've been studying them for years. And the one with no past is clearly you." He pointed at Nina. "It's just too much of a coincidence, you showing up like this so soon after the storm. And the pelican is a symbol for the Skin Eaters. In the Middle Ages, it was believed that pelicans kill their young and then pour out their own life's blood to revive them. It's an old symbol of love and sacrifice, something like Jesus. The idea is that you have to die and be reborn into a new life."

"Sometimes literally," Alastaire said, scraping the last of the cream cheese icing off her plate and getting up out of her armchair. "I'm gonna go get another piece. Anyone else want something?"

Bella rolled his eyes. "You're disgusting."

"I'm *hungry*."

"Never mind," he said. "Moving on. As far as this part, where you're going to 'best' the pelican, all I can think of is that you're going to beat us at something. Like a contest."

"Well, forget about that," Nina said, leaning back in her chair. "I couldn't beat you guys at tic-tac-toe. I'm a moron."

"Not necessarily." He got out a pen and made a few quick notes. "I'm also wondering if it means you're going to do something good for us. Like make us the 'best' at something."

"That's a weird way of putting it."

"That's how riddles work. Maybe you're going to do something that turns out for the 'best.'"

"Maybe." Nina still wasn't convinced. "So, what's up with the beautiful hand?"

"Well, there are hand symbols in every culture, so that's kind of vague. Maybe it's like a hand behind the scenes, or a hand you can't see what it's doing, that's going to be revealed. It's complicated."

"Or it could mean Nina's going to get a job as a palm reader," Alastaire said, sitting back down again. "Or give somebody a hand job. A bee-yoo-tee-ful hand job!"

Nina spoke up quickly before Bella exploded. "I thought you were going to tell me what happened to Sister Aquilina."

Bella looked around and said, "No. Not here. It's too dangerous."

"Then where?" Nina practically stamped her foot. "Come *on*." She looked around. "There's nobody in here but that really scruffy guy—"

She pointed to a very filthy young man with blond dreadlocks who was sitting at a table in the far corner, tapping on a laptop. Bella and Alastaire glanced over at him, and she saw a look pass between them.

"What?" Nina asked. "Do you know him?"

"No, but we know what he is." Alastaire bit her lip. "A gutter-blood."

"A *gutterblood*?"

"A Skin Eater outlaw. Bella thinks they're uber cool."

"I do not!" Bella snapped, then remembered to lower his voice. "Alastaire's the one who's always talking about how wouldn't it be great to just go off to the Bywater and hang out with them?"

"I said it would be 'interesting,' Mister Know-It-All. So would shoving this packet of Splenda up your nose!"

"Don't be so immature."

"*I'm* immature? *You're* immature!"

Nina sighed, feeling like she needed Professor Samson's whistle. "All right . . . well, he's not paying any attention to us right now, and there's only him and . . ." Her voice faltered. "And the two guys who just came in."

But Bella had already spun around to look, and Nina felt her stomach lurch as she realized the full implication of those two men being in the café. Not that they looked that out of place on a street in New Orleans: a businessman and a priest. But the priest was "Father Ignatius Ragoczy, head of the Vatican's *Curis Dei*" from the school brochure, while the businessman was—

"Oh God, I've seen him before too," Nina said, scrunching down in her seat before she remembered that when she'd seen Mr. Benway before, it had just been in a dream. He wouldn't recognize her.

But Bella was whispering, "Damn it, what are *they* doing here?"

"How do you know—" Nina began.

"Shh," Bella said, hunching over his coffee, and Alastaire moved to block him from being seen by the priest, who had gone to the counter to order.

Alastaire added, "They're not alone, either. Look who's with them. Miss Gulch."

Of course, it wasn't really the Wicked Witch of the West, but a close approximation: Agatha Danvers.

Alastaire and Bella and Nina all huddled down in their big squashy armchairs and tried to make themselves as inconspicuous as possible, which fortunately wasn't that hard, since the café was starting to fill up with people. A tourist couple came in wearing matching his-and-her Jazz Fest shirts and ordered Grande Iced Mochasippis with extra whipped cream. A woman in scrubs entered and got a coffee, black. A toothless old homeless woman shuffled in wearing Mardi Gras beads and what looked like a floral bathrobe, and the barista smiled and got her a small café au lait on the house. The priest brought his tray of coffees back to the table and sat down opposite Agatha and Mr. Benway, and they started to talk quietly together.

"I'm going over to see what I can find out," Alastaire whispered, standing up and smoothing down her skirt.

"Be careful," Bella whispered back, but she just turned and stuck her tongue out at him. Then, as casually as she could, she walked toward the counter, stretching her arms up over her head as if she didn't have a care in the world. Nina and Bella peeked over the backs of their chairs as she placed her order and then turned and pretended to notice Agatha and the two men sitting there. She smiled and dropped them a curtsy, and Father Ragoczy smiled a thin smile back at her.

While she waited for her second latte, Alastaire twiddled her fingers in her hair and made small talk, which Father Ragoczy seemed to enjoy, while Agatha and Mr. Benway frowned.

Nina leaned toward Bella and whispered, "Why did you say 'damn it' when you first saw them?"

"Because that's what anyone in his right mind would say. They're both bastards.

Especially Father Ignatius. Traces his lineage back to Prince Ragoczy of Moldavia, and he's a complete prick."

"Yes, but—"

"Shh." Bella watched as Alastaire, waving bye-bye like a five-year-old, got her order, and went to put sugar in it. "He's also my godfather."

"Your *god*—" Nina felt out of her depth. "But he's a—"

"Yes, he's a priest. And a Saturni. And oh yes, he's Caucasian. Our society breaks a lot more boundaries than you humans do."

"But doesn't the Church hate . . . well, you people?" Nina blushed. "I don't mean Vietnamese people, I mean . . . well, you know . . . crosses and all that, and holy water? Isn't all that stuff dangerous to you?"

Bella smiled grimly as Alastaire started walking back toward them again. He said, "Tell that to the Muslims whom the Wallachians impaled for Rome, and the Lutherans and the Calvinists they burned. Tell that to the men in the *Curis Dei*. They know we have different tastes, but we're all monsters in the end. Whether we eat skins or we eat the bread of Christ, we're all destroyers."

He broke off as Alastaire sat back down again. "Dammit," she said. "Acting like a retard's a colossal pain in the ass."

"Really? I would think it would come naturally."

Alastaire just glared at Bella, and Nina asked, "What did you find out?"

The other girl shook her head. "Not much. They're in town because Agatha Danvers sent for them. Something big's going down, but they're playing it close to the vest. Or cassock, as it were."

Nina thought about the idea of these powerful men being summoned just on Agatha's say-so. A shiver ran through her. "Does this have anything to do with *me*?"

"I don't think so." Bella finished the rest of his coffee. "They're probably just in town for some fundraiser. They're big cheeses down at the Fortuna Club with my father. That's a club down on Canal Street where all the wealthiest Skin Eaters hang out and play cards. It's very exclusive. You have to be a member of the Krewe of Lycidas just to join. Six-figure poker games, and they put on *skits. Merde.*"

Nina thought of something. "So, why is Sister Aquilina called 'sister'? Is she a nun?"

"No. The Church certainly has no control over her. I think it might be a way of saying she's sexless, like someone who's inhuman. Although some people say she made it up herself as a kind of inside joke."

"What about the *Curis Dei*? I've never heard of it."

"That's because it's a secret." Bella made a face. "*Curis Dei*, the Spear of God. It's an organization founded in 1591 by Pope Innocent IX, a singularly ironically named clergyman. It was the first time an open bond was established between the Skin Eaters and the Church. The Spear of God is a group that does dirty tricks for the Vatican—you know, assassinations, wet ops. Things like that."

Nina looked shocked, and he laughed and said, "Don't kid yourself. A lot of Skin Eaters are up to their armpits in spying. That's what the Saturni are all about, really, secret alliances between the Church, the Army, politicians, and private industry. There aren't that many Saturni, they're immortal, and they can shape-shift, so they can appear and disappear at will, but they use the Skin Eaters as their secret agents. We're their foot soldiers. Come on." He stood up. "Let's get out of here while they're not looking."

They walked back to the school without saying much, Bella scuffing his Guccis through last year's magnolia leaves. He said, "I'll probably be asked to join my godfather for dinner tonight. I'll see what I can find out. My parents love to trot me out, even though when we're alone, they treat me like something the dog threw up."

"What are they like?" Nina asked, then added, "If you don't mind telling me."

"Mind?" Bella laughed. "Nhi Trung's beautiful, in a Dragon Lady kind of a way. Very into tight red dresses. And Ly Than looks like Ming the Merciless. I kid you not—he's bald, and he's got this little droopy mustache and everything. They're *such* cartoons."

"And they're rich?"

"Oh, yeah. Whoop-de-doo."

Nina suddenly stopped and looked up ahead of them, where she saw a group of Daedalus girls walking toward them. She recognized the long, lustrous black hair of the tall girl in the middle. Simone. She was flanked as usual by her three beautiful cohorts, all of them walking under decorated Mardi Gras umbrellas, so they looked like gorgeous birds of paradise with multicolored feathers. And they had a fat white kid between them whom they were pushing back and forth, in and out of the sunlight. One of the *jumbies*.

"You want to give me a kiss, piggy?" one of the lovely girls asked, puckering up her lips and blowing against his ear. He cringed away from her and shut his eyes, crying, although he didn't dare to pull away completely. They held onto his arms, their fingers cruelly tight.

"Here, pig-pig-pig ... sooo-eee, pig-pig-pig ..." Simone giggled, and then she pinched his cheek. Nina could see how it must have hurt him—tears ran down his face—but he also seemed strangely quiet, like he was drugged. She felt like she was seeing a replay of Sally's prior behavior with the cat, only Sally had been faking it, just to teach her a lesson. Alastaire and Bella had stopped as well, and she could feel them tense beside her, although they didn't say anything.

Nina said, "What—" but Bella said, "Shh, don't interfere," and Alastaire whispered, "Assholes," under her breath.

"Hey piggy-piggy-piggy . . . you want to give us a bite . . ." One of the girls actually lifted his fat little hand and bit him, lightly, not breaking the skin, but licking and sucking against the flesh. The little boy seemed to become, if anything, *more* passive, just standing there, his head lolling to one side and his eyes half shut like he was catatonic.

"Aw, he's sleepy." Simone kicked his shin. "C'mon, piggy, wake up and play."

"That's enough." Nina didn't know she had spoken aloud until she heard the words, but when she did, she didn't regret them. If she'd been closer, she would have pulled the little kid away by force—and maybe would have used more force than was necessary.

"Oh, look, it's the dynamic trio." Simone strolled ahead of her friends until she was close enough to Nina to look her up and down, and then she smirked, as if she were observing a gutterblood. She said sweetly, "Oh, Nina darlin', I'm *so* glad I ran into you. You see, I spoke to Professor Danvers . . . yes, he just got back. I met him just as he was putting his things away in his office."

Nina flinched but knew better than to rise to this bait. Whatever Simone had said to the professor, that was a bridge she'd cross when she came to it. She jerked her chin at the little boy and said, "Let him go."

"Or what? You'll *fight* for him? A *jumbie*?" Simone curled her beautiful lips in exaggerated disgust. "How incredibly brave. You actually feel sorry for one of the cattle? Or . . ." She glanced at her friends. "Do you want him for yourself? Feeling hungry? He won't mind. He's pretty well worn out. We can barely get a rise out of him."

Nina punched Simone. She didn't waste time with a slap; she hit right in the solar plexus, and the girl went down, clutching her stomach. Her friends surged forward, but they were pushed back by what could only be described as a gust of wind. It sent their parasols flying up into the trees and the magnolia leaves swirling around and snarling their hair, and it kept them away from Nina and her friends as effectively as a shield. Simone struggled to catch her breath and then got slowly to her feet, still bending over and her arms wrapped around her. Her face was drawn, and her eyes were full of hatred.

"You'll be sorry . . ." she spat out. "Professor Danvers wants to see you. *Now*. In the carriage house. He said he wanted to see you the minute you got back. I'll bet he's going to expel you, bitch. You'll be out of Daedalus by dinnertime."

Chapter Twelve

The first thing Nina felt was disappointment.

She had to admit, Simone was probably right—Professor Danvers probably *did* want to expel her. And despite her fear, her first reaction was, *Damn. I really wanted to stay.*

She sucked in her breath and said, "Hey, it's all good," and waved to Bella and Alastaire as she started back toward the school. *If you're about to go eat shit,* she thought, *you might as well do it with your head held high.*

The sun was hot now, and she concentrated on enjoying the beautiful day and the beautiful garden. There were winding paths everywhere and overarching trees, towering hedges, and a fountain where a bronze woman stood pouring water down from her open wrists into two other bronze figures' waiting mouths—a little extreme, but there it was. The garden was exotic, lush and opulent, and she wondered why the Skin Eaters were so afraid of chaos. They wanted to simplify everything, but nature wasn't like that at all.

It was . . . natural.

Wild.

They feared what they couldn't measure, catalog, control, and cut up into little pieces. But the world wasn't like that.

It was . . . magic.

And if I go on thinking like that, she told herself, *I'm going to be totally screwed by the time I see Professor Danvers. He hates magic.*

But it was hard not to feel poetic and scared and romantic and desperately confused as she smoothed her hair and tried to keep from hyperventilating. Why did he want to see her? What was he going to do? Kill her? Cross with her? What did Skin Eaters do to the people they were mad at? And was he really mad at her? She desperately hoped he might think Simone Freeland was as big a lying ho as she did, but perhaps that was too much to ask.

She called out "Hello!" as she came up the stairs of the carriage house, and as she did so, she noticed that the whole interior was lit by a strange red light. When she got to the top, it was almost like the inner room was on fire, light spilling under the door. She touched the wood to see if it was hot, but the heavy cypress was cool under her hand. She hesitated, then knocked.

"Come in," said a quiet voice.

Stepping inside, she saw at once where the red light was coming from. There was a fire kindled inside a black cup like the one she'd seen displayed in the chapel. Professor Danvers was standing next to a table on which the cup stood, along with a mirror and a sword and a long piece of wood. The huge shadow of the noctoscope loomed above him, its gears and wheels illuminated with flickering flames, but Professor Danvers looked the same as always: tall, graceful, and forbidding.

"Thank you for coming," he said.

"Um . . . sure. Is this a punishment?"

"Not necessarily. Do you *want* me to punish you?"

No! she thought, then, *Well . . .*

"It's just that Simone said—"

"Ah, Miss Freeland. She can be a little melodramatic sometimes, don't you agree?"

A quick, almost fugitive smile crossed his lips and then was gone.

But if she *wasn't* in trouble . . . "Is this a class, Professor?"

"In a way."

"Is there going to be anyone else here besides me?"

"Why?" His voice was like velvet. "Are you afraid to be alone with me?"

Yes, she thought. *Obviously.* Hoping he couldn't read her mind. "Um . . . no, sir."

"Miss Lamb, I'll be frank with you. You present a puzzle to us here at Daedalus. Your unknown provenance, your indeterminate level of expertise . . . Yes, your professors told me you did very well on your first day of classes, the unfortunate episode with Thor notwithstanding. To be honest, we don't quite know what to do with you. Therefore, in consultation with our board of directors, I've decided I should try some basic divination exercises with you, in the hope that we may learn more. So—" He turned to the table. "Please come here."

She stepped forward and had the sensation she was passing through something thick, almost resistant, like a sheet of invisible plastic. Professor Danvers sighed and flicked his fingers.

"Oh yes, I forgot to tell you. I've created a Circle of Force around this table. Neither of us can leave it until I lift it. I hope you don't mind?"

She bit her lips sharply. The last thing she was going to do was tell him or show him how scared she was. She forced herself to shake her head no.

"Good." He picked up the mirror. "Please gaze into this and tell me what you see."

"Uh . . . my face?" She looked into the polished surface of the mirror, which wasn't glass, but some sort of gleaming silver metal, so it reflected back her features through a cloudy sheen.

"Obviously, Miss Lamb. The trick is to look beyond the obvious. That, incidentally, is the wellspring of the popular superstition that Skin Eaters cast no reflection, because we've learned to ignore it." He quirked an eyebrow. "I presume someone *did* fill you in on the basics?"

"Actually . . . yes, sir. Bella and Alastaire both told me something about your . . . kind."

She hoped that didn't sound prejudiced, but Professor Danvers took it in stride. "Very well. Then . . . *concentrate*." He stood behind her and touched, with the very tips of his fingers, her temples. She tried to repress a shiver. "Look deep into the mirror and tell me what you see."

She looked again and saw a pair of young people walking together through a garden. It was, in fact, the garden of the Daedalus School itself, although the trees and the bushes all looked smaller. In the vision, it was nighttime, and the boy was holding his arm around the girl as they walked, the girl leaning against him.

In her mind's ear, Nina could hear his words, *It's all right, you'll feel better once you get used to it. You had to do it. It was the only way*, and then she couldn't hear or see anything more.

"Professor?" she asked, turning around to look at him.

"Yes?" He was standing close, not quite touching her, his body a shadow curving toward her, a shadow with slightly unsteady breath.

"Sir, am I supposed to be seeing the future? Or the past?"

"Well." He moved a little away from her. "That's a good question. Technically, mirror scrying is an open-ended process, not unlike crystal gazing. Some people liken it to lucid dreaming. The point isn't to ask specific questions, but to just let the images flow."

"Okay." She nodded, thinking, *I can do that*. "What I mean is, sir, if I see something, should it make sense? Should it be part of a bigger picture? A story?"

"Everything's part of a story, Miss Lamb."

"Yes, I-I guess I'm not making sense. Should it tie in with anything else I know?"

"If possible, yes."

"Okay, then." She took a deep breath. "I saw these two kids. Walking in the garden outside. They were walking close together, and one of them was holding the other one up. Kind of. The girl looked like she might be sick. And the boy said, 'It's all right, you'll feel better once you get used to it.'"

"Indeed." Professor Danvers didn't appear to be questioning her vision, but he clearly didn't want to give her any hints either. "What else?"

"Well, the thing is . . . I think I know one of them."

"Can you describe that person?" For some reason, his voice sounded tense or perhaps a little hoarse, as though he were having trouble breathing.

"Tall. With long black hair and very dark eyes. She . . ." She looked up into Professor Danvers's suddenly startled face. "She looks kind of like you, Professor."

"Oh really?"

"And the thing is . . . well, I think I've seen her before."

"You have? Where?" He grabbed her shoulders. "Where have you seen her? Where is she?"

"In my dreams. The night before I came down here." She shook her head. "I mean, the night after you interviewed me. I spent that night up in Baton Rouge, and I saw her then. I mean, I *dreamed* I saw her then and . . . well, you know what I mean. In my dream, it was the same girl. Or woman—she looked older then."

Strickland spun away, thinking, *Damn it, I should have foreseen this. She read my mind. She saw Niobe in my mind the day we first met, and she's seeing her now. Niobe and I walking in the garden after her first crossing. Damn Jack Benway for treating her so roughly. He's a loutish pig who ought to have been hung up by his heels ages ago. I remember I told her I'd cross with her the next time,* all *the next times, just to let her see how wonderful it could be . . .*

He pulled himself together and said, "Miss Lamb, I assure you the woman you saw means nothing. *Nothing.* Please try again."

"But I—I'm not sure.

And by the way, what were you thinking? Why is Jack Benway a pig?"

"Miss Lamb." He made his voice sound ominous by lowering it, so now it was almost inaudible. "Can you follow a simple direction, or do I have to write it out for you in *crayon*?"

"A-all right." Sighing in frustration, Nina looked back into the mirror. "There's a little black boy sitting on a roof."

"All right." Strickland waited, and then asked, "What's he doing?"

"He's just sitting there. He opened a window to get out of the attic. There's water all around him; it's completely flooded. He's just kicking his feet. And there's that woman again!"

"Oh, come on!" Professor Danvers snapped. "You're not trying! I told you, forget about that woman!"

"But she's there, Professor! She's . . . okay, she's in a boat, and she stopped the boat and she's speaking to him. She's saying, 'I think you have a limited number of options right now. I'd suggest you come with me.'"

"And the boy?"

"He's going with her. He's getting into the boat. Although he doesn't want to."

Professor Danvers hesitated, his voice softening infinitesimally. "How can you tell?"

"Because he's frightened. Wait a minute, I see a house in . . . somewhere that's really, really overgrown. It's by the river. There's been flooding. Mud. But the house is beautiful. There's water nearby, but you can't see it. It's dark. Really dark. And there are

. . . these creatures in the bushes. Like dogs. But they're not." She hesitated. "They're horrible."

"*Are* they?"

Something about his emphasis made her turn around to look at him, and he said almost absently, "*Horroi*, the hounds of the dead. Like mastiffs with big dead eyes?"

"Yes. And . . . there are all these children there."

Professor Danvers pressed the pads of his fingers against her temples again, turning her head back to look in the mirror once more. "What? Tell me."

"I'm frightened." She shook her head. "There's something terrifying there. Something I can't see."

"Try."

He stood behind her, touching her shoulders, encouraging her, and she saw children, young (two little girls), older (a boy almost of a man's height, and one with a wounded eye), a girl with red hair and one in shorts, and a boy with tattoos and a boy who made a strange buzzing sound, and a wraith, and a boy in black leather, and a tattooed guy, and one who played the harmonica, and . . .

"Oh! It's him! I've seen him before!" She felt a burst of relief. "That old white guy. I met him my first day here, I mean my first real day. Mr. O'Brien. He said he was—"

And then she stopped and caught her breath, because Professor Danvers had leaned in suddenly much closer, pressing his cheek hard against hers. She could feel his cold, smooth skin, his *very cold* skin. *"When I hit 32 degrees,"* she recalled the words, *"I'll be able to make ice."* He was looking at the same scene she was seeing, and she felt him suddenly go completely still.

And then he started back from the mirror and said, "No! That's simply not possible!" very sharply.

"Professor, what—"

"I'm not in the least prepared to accept that!"

"I'm sorry?"

"Miss Lamb, are you playing tricks with me?"

"No!" she yelled, much louder than she needed to. "I don't even have any idea what I'm

doing! How could I be playing tricks?"

"I'm sorry." He walked away, smoothing his hair, and she reflected how its dark color, shiny as a crow's feathers, set off his pale, beautiful face to perfection. He looked like a fallen angel.

"Miss Lamb, this is trying for you, I know. Let's just say that it's trying for me too. Let's try something else, shall we? Can you pick up this sword, please?"

She shrugged and then did as he asked, although it was much heavier than she'd expected, dragging her arm down and making her fingers go all pins and needles. She thought, *It's not just that it's heavy. It's powerful in some way.* She felt her arm go numb and said, "I-I think I've got it, sir."

"Good." Professor Danvers stepped back. "Now, please draw a circle with the point of it, all around you on the floor. Go ahead."

He stepped back, his eyes narrowed, and he put up one hand in an unconscious gesture of protection. Puzzled, Nina lifted the heavy sword and tried to do as she'd been told.

It was like pulling a lead weight. *Ow!* she thought, as the weight of the sword made the pommel bite into her palm. She managed to drag its point a little forward, scraping it against the wood. It cast up sparks as it went, red as fire, like metal scraping against metal, and left a slick wet stain behind it.

It was almost as if she were making the floor *bleed*. She pulled harder, and it was definitely as though she were cutting through something, slicing through some invisible matter on the floor. She dragged the heavy, sharp blade around her, even though there was the smell of blood in her nose now, and her arm was shuddering as though a hundred needles were being stuck into it. Desperately, she grasped the handle with her other hand and fought to drag it around her, feeling her shoulders ache and the blood pooling around her feet in a hot, wet puddle that seeped into her shoes.

She finally finished, having made a complete circle around her, and the smell was still horrible, but she realized there were other smells there too. Food, for one thing. She could smell spices and chocolate and rich gravy and something sweet, like incense. She could smell rain, and the wind rising through clattering palm leaves. And she could hear voices: "What do you think she wants? If I was a big old dog, everything would be all right."

She looked at Professor Danvers as if across a huge divide, space, time, and the separation of molecules from one dimension to the next, and heard him say inside her head, *"What is it?"*

"They're living there." She wasn't sure what that meant at all, but she knew that's exactly what she had to tell him. "They're real," she tried to explain. "It's like this dream I had where that woman—I know, I know, you told me not to mention her again, but I saw her, and she said, 'I exist.' It's like that. They *exist*. They're not just some . . ." She bit her lip. "Some kind of propaganda, or an urban myth, or a way for the Saturni to recruit people and raise money." She stopped. "Sir, I don't even know why I said that."

"It's all right." His voice sounded distracted. His thin lips were taut with what could, she supposed, be either anger or amusement. "They certainly do use propaganda and scare tactics to recruit people. That's arguably how they recruited me. But it's not something I would have expected you to know about."

"I don't, sir. Not really. I just . . ." She stopped again. It probably wouldn't do to say, "I've been gossiping about you and the Saturni and Sister Aquilina with Bella and Alastaire and everyone else I can think of, because I don't know anything and I'm grasping at straws here." She said instead, "It's like I can sense things all around me. Or, I don't know . . . *smell* them . . ."

"It's a different kind of scrying." He assumed a detached voice. "The human mind can only absorb information by certain neural pathways. The sense of smell trumps sight and sound in its importance to primitive mammals. If the blood is a little melodramatic, I apologize, this type of work is usually done by members of our kind, and scent follows appetite. It's like tuning in to a radio frequency. Go on."

She shut her eyes, willing the tears away, although she thought, in a way, this was torture. She didn't want to be where she was, smelling what she was. And where was she, anyway? "I-I . . . The old man is there. They're all having dinner. Cake. She's saying . . ." She shook her head. "'I don't know why, but I just thought you might like chocolate.' Now someone else is saying . . ." She frowned. "'Don't flatter yourself. I learn from whoever will satisfy me and give me what I want.'"

"Really? Selfish." Professor Danvers's voice sounded distant. "What else?"

"Someone's saying, 'They really do suit their roles perfectly, you know. Where did you find them?'"

"Who's talking now?"

"The old man. I think. It's confusing." She shook her head. "They're all there, for some reason—because of who they *are*, I think. What they're like, their central essences. It's not random, although they think it is." She breathed deeply, letting the terrible blood-incense-chocolate-gravy smell flood her nose. "They think she's just creepy, that she's abducted them there to hurt them or eat them, but I don't know. They're right, the whole thing *is* creepy . . ."

"'Creepy' is a ridiculous teenage euphemism," Professor Danvers said, making a gesture, and the smells and blood immediately vanished. He came to her and grabbed the sword out of her hands and flung it away, sending it clanging into the farthest corner of the room. "The word you're looking for is 'uncanny.' The sense that what is familiar is somehow wrong or strange." He took her palms in his. "That's all right," he added, laying cool, soothing fingers against her burning skin. "It'll fade. See?—there, it's getting better already."

And it was true, the burning in her palms was fading away under his cold, hypnotic touch.

"You did that very well, by the way."

"Was that a test?"

"Yes," he said. "A test of will, among other things. Sometimes, the key to doing something unpleasant is simply knowing you can stand it." He stroked her hands some more. "Now," he said abruptly, stepping away from her. "Let's see what you can do with the cup."

He made a little picking-up gesture, and privately thinking, *Screw you,* she grasped the cup and lifted it up in front of her. It was heavy and cold, despite the fire burning in it, and she felt her fingers growing slippery with sweat or condensation, she wasn't sure which.

The flames in the cup sent flickering reflections all around the room and shone against Professor Danvers's stark white face.

"Throughout history," he said, speaking very softly now, "our kind, by which I mean the Skin Eaters, have walked a fine line between courting death and defying it, between embracing oblivion and asserting our wills against it. We were not created lightly, nor do we take our creation for granted. You will find, Miss Lamb, if you continue in our company, that some of this ambivalence will no doubt rub off on you. Drink."

She looked down and saw that the cup was now filled with a thick, red liquid. She looked up at him and asked, "What is it?"

"Can't you imagine?" His voice was barely a murmur.

"I—" She thought, *This is crazy, I can't drink that,* and at the same time, *He thinks I'm afraid*, and without giving herself time to consider, she lifted the cup to her mouth and swallowed a big mouthful of the red liquid.

Which wasn't exactly blood, she realized. There was blood there, coppery and metallic, but there was also something with a rotten undertaste, like dead flowers, and something else like grit. She felt it slide down her throat, and it was worse than swallowing a mouthful of very cold ice cream. Brain freeze was nothing compared to this. She felt the frigid cold making her esophagus spasm, and then it was making her gag, making her cough, and then her guts were twisting in knots and she felt her head spin, and it was as if she'd swallowed an enormous icy stone that plunged down into her belly and rolled around in there like a bowling ball.

She felt petrified with cold. That was it—she felt frozen. It was freezing everything inside of her . . . stopping her . . . killing her . . . and she thought, *What* was *that?* She thought of the smell of rotting flowers: *red spur?* She felt her heart slowing in her chest, beating in frozen, frantic beats . . . *bang, bang, bang* against her ribs and faintly she heard . . .

"Miss Lamb? Miss Lamb!"

"Yes," she whispered through rubbery lips and saw Professor Danvers's face float into focus in front of her.

"Miss Lamb, look at me! What are you experiencing?"

"I'm dying," she wanted to say, but she couldn't summon the words. Whatever she'd drunk felt like it was worse than poison, felt like it was the ultimate enemy of her body itself, a substance that couldn't coexist with her cells without destroying them. She gestured helplessly at her throat, and the professor got the hint and moved quickly. He cupped his hands around her neck and pulled up sharply, as though he wanted to lift her up by her chin, then moved his hands down to her chest and pulled up again, his thumbs pressing in, and finally held on to her belly and pulled up on her a third time, forcing the contents of her stomach up into her esophagus and then out of her mouth.

Everything came up, the blood mixture and also her coffee and her breakfast. She collapsed to the floor in a state of embarrassment bordering on rigor mortis, but that didn't matter—she could breathe again. It was all right, and she could feel her heart beating at a normal, steady pace, not that cold, dead thudding of frozen flesh.

Professor Danvers made a gesture, and the mess disappeared from the floor, and she sat there staring at the bare wide boards for a long minute without seeing them, until he said mildly, "I'm up here, Miss Lamb. Please stand up."

Unsteadily, she got back to her feet. What did he want *now*? Looking into his face, she was surprised to see the sorrow there, etched around his eyes as sharply as tattoos. She heard him say in her mind, *"Forgive me."*

"That's okay, Professor." She averted her gaze, looking down at the floor. "I-I understand. I guess. You were trying to find out if I could do that."

I was trying to find out if you were human, he wanted to say, at least in her head. *And you're not. At least not entirely. What are you?* . . . but no, he couldn't think that. Couldn't let her see any further into his mind than her natural abilities, which were already beyond his, would let her. *Dammit*, he thought only to himself, *why am I always given fragile things only so I can break them?*

She still didn't think she could stand up by herself, so she rested one hand on his shoulder, and he said, "Miss Lamb, I realize all this is new to you. Would you like to continue this tomorrow?"

She looked up at him, wondering if he actually meant it. And then she thought, did she really want to come back and do all this again? She was sore, exhausted, shaken. She said, "Actually, I think I'd like to get this all over with. What exactly happened to me?"

"I don't know." He frowned. "You drank a potion which quells our hunger, at least temporarily. A normal human being should have merely found it mildly disgusting. It's a blend of blood, in this case, a sheep's blood, valerian root, and human ashes." She made a choking sound. "Yes, as I said, it's not particularly nice, but it shouldn't have affected you so drastically. Again, I apologize."

He turned aside as if that settled the matter. "Now, if you're ready, let's move on to the wand."

That wasn't a word she'd expected to hear outside of a movie, although a quick glance confirmed it didn't look much like a magic wand. The piece of wood on the table was about two feet long and covered with bark and knobby twigs. One end still held a small leaf. Professor Danvers said, "Pick it up."

Which she did and was immediately surprised by how warm it felt. It felt like the stick had been lying out in the sun. She asked, "What should I do with it, sir?"

"Just hold it. See what happens."

A small flame ignited at the end of the wand and gradually grew stronger until she was holding a lighted torch. The fire didn't burn red but cycled quickly through several colors: green, blue, yellow, purple, until it settled on a pure white light. She felt the radiance spill out all around her, warm and comforting, and the flame from the wand danced and grew taller still, a clear illumination as happy and bright as the sun.

She turned to Professor Danvers and saw his harsh, beautiful features warmed by the light, and she couldn't help but offer a smile, which was answered by a tight, almost painful smile of his own.

"It's lovely," she murmured.

"Yes." He wasn't looking at the flame, but at her.

"What is it?"

"It's *lignam leukos*. Literally 'wood light.' It's a kind of litmus test. It tells what kind of power people have in them. Power over matter, power to heal, power to transform, or power to kill. Roughly comparable to earth, air, fire, and water, although those are ridiculously simplistic metaphors."

"And what am I?"

"You're something else. An amalgam. A mixture. Like all the colors of the spectrum coming together to make pure light."

It didn't sound like a stupid compliment, but instead like the reluctant admission of a man who abhorred stupidity and who wasn't used to giving compliments in any case. She blinked and asked, "But what does that *mean* exactly?"

He didn't answer. Instead, he walked away from her, and when he spoke again, she could tell he was trying to keep things light.

"Several things. It could mean you're just a stew of unformed possibilities. Like mixing all the colors in a paintbox. You get mud. Or on the other hand . . ." He hesitated.

"On the other hand?"

"On the other hand, Miss Lamb, you could be exactly what we've all been waiting for. You could be the key to exploding every filthy, stale, deadly, predictable thing in our world. Blowing a hole in the whole thing and letting in madness. Lunacy. Something new. In which case . . ."

He turned and looked at her. "In which case, there would be a decision to be made, wouldn't there?" His voice was very low again.

She swallowed. "Whether or not you're going to let me do that."

"Bravo, Miss Lamb. Full points for stating the obvious. Oh, you can put the wand down now. I've learned all I need to know."

Well, good for you, she thought. *I don't know anything.* "Sir?"

"Yes?"

"Why did I see a crow attacking Mrs. Hopkins the other day? When I looked in your eyes?"

He spun around to face her, so quickly she took a step back. "*What* did you say?" he breathed.

"I-I saw it in your mind. When I looked at you at lunch the other day, Professor." She forced herself to continue. "I saw a crow pecking her eyes out, and then I read in the newspaper that she actually *was* pecked to death by birds. I was just . . . curious."

"Really?" he murmured. "You were just curious."

"Um . . . okay. Yeah. Scared. That too. I just wanted to know . . ."

"Whether I knew anything about that? Whether I was—" he took a step toward her and flexed his hands "—responsible?"

He stood very still, and for a moment, she could hear him say very clearly in her mind, *"Go away. Go away now. Get out of my sight before I hurt you."*

"Um . . ." she said, "maybe I should go back to the school now?"

He turned away and ground out, "Maybe you should."

"Sir . . ." She gathered her courage, because when was she going to get another chance like this? "Sir, who's Zoolie?"

"*What?*" he exclaimed, his face still turned away from her.

She thought from his outburst that he was going to say more, but that was all. He just stood turned away from her, clenching his hands. She tried again.

"Sir, are there ghosts in the walls of Daedalus? Do they live up in the attic?"

"I can only assume you're trying to drive me mad, Miss Lamb. In which case, you're succeeding. Now please get out."

"The *jumbies*, sir. Why are they so unhappy?"

"Might as well ask why all teenagers are unhappy. It's the nature of the beasts. Now *go*."

"Sir, what did you see in the mirror? That made you think I was playing a trick on you?"

He finally turned to look at her again, his eyes not guarded at all but bruised, dark, furious, and he said very softly, "Take care, little girl. Don't push me too far. I'm not really a nice man, and I'm certainly far from patient."

Nina swallowed and stood her ground. "You saw something. I know you did. You said you refused to accept it, and I know you glimpsed something, and I want to know what it was." She took a shallow breath and added, "I don't know anything, sir. I don't know what any of this means, or whether any of it can hurt me. Please, at least give me the tools to protect myself."

"Ah," he said finally, looking off into the distance, as though all the fight had gone out of him and he was just tired and bemused. "You really want to know what I saw?"

"Yes, sir."

"Well," he said, looking to the side now, as if a mote of dust had caught his attention. "I suppose you can know that. I saw a man, Miss Lamb. A man who was once our headmaster. A man, I might add, who was once the most important person in the world to me. But not anymore." He narrowed his eyes. "Because, Miss Lamb, Mr. O'Brien has been destroyed. The Saturni got a hold of him, and now he's gone for good."

Chapter Thirteen

Nina walked back to the main building feeling like she'd been hit by a truck. What was *that* all about? Who was the old man she had met, and why had he told her his name was Mr. O'Brien? Why had Professor Danvers hurt her, threatened her, fed her poison, and allowed her to feel all the grief and rage and longing and loneliness inside of him, and then simply pushed her away?

Why had he made her *see* those things at all?

I'm too stupid, she thought. *I can't figure any of this stuff out,* and she sat down on one of the long, uncomfortable wooden benches that lined the corridor leading down to the chapel. She felt the grim portraits all looking down at her in disapproval, gazing at her with their cold red eyes, and then she heard a low chuckle.

"You're right. This *is* a strange place. Daedalus would scare anybody silly, if you ask me.

Anybody normal, that is."

Nina looked over to see Sally sitting there, having a smoke under the portrait of a beautiful, hawk-faced woman in a severe black dress. She looked up at the portrait as well and shrugged.

"Madame Livaudais herself would have been creeped out. 'Course, they say she started it all. This phase of things, anyway."

"So I've been told."

"You have?" Sally chuckled. "You get around, don't you?"

"Yeah, well . . ." Nina pulled her legs up and hugged her knees.

"Right now, I wish I didn't know as much as I do. It seems like the more I learn, the more complicated things get."

"That's usually the case." Sally shook her head. "Remember, ignorance is bliss."

"Sally, do you think I was wrong to come here?" Nina shrugged and bit her lips. "I mean, not to fight it more, not to demand that they send me someplace else?"

"Where would you go?"

The question was so simple it cut like a knife, and its wake brought emptiness too painful to face. Nina changed the subject. "Can somebody really know another person? I mean *really* know them?"

"You got a certain tall, dark, handsome assistant headmaster in mind?"

Nina had the feeling yet again that Sally was reading her mind, and given the current circumstances, she wasn't sure whether or not she liked it.

"Oh . . ." She made a little gesture. "I'm probably making a big deal out of nothing. After all, he's just a teacher."

"From what I see, Strickland Danvers is scarcely 'just' anything. And the circumstances here . . . well, let's just say it puts a whole new spin on the idea of 'teacher's pet.'"

Nina giggled, thinking once more about the 'roided-out blonde. "You certainly know a lot about the Skinnies for somebody who just got this job online."

Sally laughed. "God help me, a smart student. *Mirabile dictu.* No, you got me. I like to know what I'm getting into. I've been trying to find out as much as I can."

"So what have you found out so far?"

"About Professor Danvers?"

"About any of this." Nina gestured around at the dark, shadowy hallway, where the portraits of the school's founders seemed not so much to hang on the black walls as to emerge from the age-stained wood.

It was Sally's turn to gesture. She flicked the ash from her cigarette and said, "I've seen worse."

"You have?"

"Sure. You ever spend a summer in Biloxi? Now *that's* scary."

She smiled, and Nina appreciated the joke, even though she said almost angrily, "I don't even understand why they want me here! I'm not like everybody else. I don't look like everyone else, and I'm not from the same background—" And there, she stopped, because she wasn't sure about that. After all, she didn't know.

"Look," Sally said. "Let me give you some free advice, which you can take for whatever it's worth. You're a smart, nice person. That's worth a lot more than you think. There's more stupid people in this world, and more unkind people, than you can shake a stick at, and that may be a little uncharitable, but hey, prove me wrong. I'd be the happiest person on earth to admit it. You throw a stone in a crowd and you'll hit somebody who's resentful and greedy and an asshole more often than you'll hit somebody who's principled and noble and kind, or even just decent and sweet and dumb. I'm just saying. So, maybe you're more valuable than you think."

Nina blushed, then she thought of Alastaire and Bella, and said, "Not everybody's an asshole."

"No, of course not. And you're inclined to find them, because like calls to like. It also calls to the best in people, which is a mixed blessing, because expecting people to live up to their better natures is never the best way to be popular. However, it's also a good idea to keep a low profile, fly beneath the radar." Sally drew on her cigarette and frowned. "You stand out in a crowd, and they'll strike you down every time."

She spoke lightly, but something in her tone made Nina

wonder if she'd once stood out in a crowd. Nina said, "You sound like you've had some experience."

"Who, me? Nope. I'm just an ordinary wage slave." The cook's eyes lit up. "'Silence, exile, and cunning' . . . you know who said that? James Joyce. Shortest sentence he ever wrote. Now." She dropped her cigarette on the stone floor and ground it out with her shoe. "I've got to get busy. These two big cheeses came by to visit the school, and they demanded a whole fancy dinner party tonight."

Nina had a brainstorm. "Is one of them Jack Benway, of the Benway Corporation?"

"You know him?" Sally's eyes widened momentarily. "Yeah, that's him, along with this priest. They're apparently big Saturni mucky-mucks, whatever that means. They were doing the whole tour-the-grounds thing, trustees seeing where their money was going. Blah blah blah." Sally stood up. "They asked for this big feast to be prepared . . . sautéed sweetbreads, kidney stew, rare tenderloin with marrow forcemeat, mince pie . . ." She stuck out her tongue. "I'm getting nauseous already. I've ordered in pizza for the students, but I've still got to get to work. All the Waterford and china hasn't been unpacked since the storm, and I've got to go polish the silver."

Nina took the plunge and asked, "Can I help you?"

"Sure. But are you really that bored that you can't think of anything better to do for the next several hours than polish soup tureens?"

Nina shook her head and grinned. "Not a thing. But what I really want to do is help you serve tonight. Can a friend and I do it?"

Sally looked at her. "I've got a feeling I don't even want to hear why you're asking me this."

"Nothing special." Nina stood up. "I just want to see what

they're like, that's all. You said *you* like to know what you're getting into. Well, so do I."

She looked at the cook, who was looking back at her with an expression that plainly said she knew the difference between shit and chocolate pudding, but she wasn't about to press the point. Then Sally laughed and said, "Sure, why not? Okay, girlfriend, you got yourself a deal. But don't think you're going to get off easy. We've got to clean the kidneys and blanch the sweetbreads and crack the marrow bones, and that's just for starters. You're going to be a vegetarian by the time you're done with all those organ meats. C'mon, let's get started."

Six hours later, they were ready to start the final preparations. Nina and Alastaire had eaten lunch in the kitchen while they helped Sally simmer the stock, chop the vegetables, make the pie dough, and prepare the truly amazing amount of food they were serving. Alastaire had a burn on her thumb and three Band-Aids on three separate cuts and an abiding hatred for cooking that rivaled even Agatha's in its ferocity. Nina, on the other hand, had quite enjoyed herself, even though her hands were still tired from mincing all the garlic, lemon zest, and parsley.

Nina pushed her hair back from her face and asked the cook, "Do you do this every day?"

"More or less." Sally wielded a heavy cleaver to crack several long bones that lay on the counter and remove the marrow from inside them. Her face was contorted. "Not quite as—" *whack* "—complicated, and not quite as—" *whack* "—time-consuming, but these guys wanted the deluxe menu. No, don't touch that," she added quickly, as Alastaire reached to taste the mixture of finely chopped meats simmering on the stove. "It's not ready yet."

"Okay, okay." Alastaire stepped back from the pot.

Sally turned the heat down and said, "Okay, what's next?" consulting her scribbled list. "You got the suet ready, Nina?"

"Check." Nina handed Sally a bowl of freshly ground white kidney fat. She thought the idea of actually putting meat and fat into a dessert pie was kind of gross, but it was what their guests had ordered, and she figured Sally would make it taste great. Sally mixed in the cooked meat, added cinnamon and nutmeg and a good splash of brandy, and spooned the mixture into the pie shells. She made two quick latticework crusts, opened the oven door, set the pies in, and kicked the door shut all in one fluid motion. It was like she was dancing around the kitchen.

"O-*kay*. Nina, slice me some more truffles for the Sauce Perigueux while I get the sweetbreads ready." She opened the fridge and took out a dish that had been chilling in there for several hours.

As she started to slice the large lumpy pieces of meat, Alastaire asked, "What are these things again?"

"Actually, they're glands. Thymus glands." Sally put one of the lumps down and touched the base of her throat. Her eyes twinkled. "They're lymph nodes that are in most young animals, right here, on either side of the neck. They control the immune system." She gave it a beat and then added with a perfectly straight face, "and they're considered a delicacy."

Alastaire looked like she was going to barf, and Sally made several small cuts in the sweetbreads and studded them with smaller pieces of red meat ("tongue," she told them succinctly). The Skin Eater girl turned green and excused herself to go to the bathroom.

"All right." Sally chuckled. "So, the kidneys are ready, and the tenderloins just need to be seared at the last minute. I've got the forcemeat *avec des cervelles . . .*"

"Should you tell Alastaire that means brains?" Nina asked,

having seen Sally poach the soft lobes of brains earlier in a reduced Sauce Allemande.

"No, let's not push her completely over the edge." The cook grinned, dredging the sweetbread slices in flour. "These'll be ready in no time." She tossed them lightly in a pan with melted butter. "Here, just sauce around the plates . . ." She handed Nina the Sauce Perigueux and showed her how to drizzle it in artful swirls. "Here we go . . ." She slipped the sweetbreads out onto the sauced plates as Alastaire came back in, looking a little better. "And we're all ready with the first course. Which means you guys are on. You all set?"

"Just a sec." Nina whipped off her dirty apron, and Sally tied a clean one around her.

Sally starting loading their serving trays with plates and then added, "Wait a minute, I just thought of something."

"What is it?" Nina asked, juggling her tray of hot food.

"You don't want them to recognize you, do you?" Sally shook her head, as though wondering to herself, *Why didn't I think of that before?*

"Here," she said, giving them each white kerchiefs to tie up their hair. "This should do it.

Makes it easier to see what you're doing without being, um, messy. Okay, knock 'em dead, kids. Poor choice of words, but . . . you know. *Bon appetit.*"

Alastaire nodded, although she looked more baffled than ever, as she and Nina headed down the corridor toward the teachers' private dining room. She whispered, "So tell me again why we're doing this?"

"To find out what's going on." Nina rolled her eyes. "God, it's so obvious. We're going to try and hear what they're talking about."

"And we're going to do that while we're serving them these weird glandy things?" Alastaire grimaced. "That'll take about five minutes. They're not going to ask us to sit down and join them. Besides, people don't talk while they're being served food, they just clam up and say *thank you* if they're feeling polite."

Nina had to admit she had a point. "I don't know. We'll try and see if we can figure out some excuse to stick around once we're inside. Maybe pour some ice water or something."

"And why do we have to wear these do-rags?"

"I don't know," Nina hissed as they got to the door. "Sally just seemed to think it was a good idea. Now come on."

She pushed open the door to the teachers' dining room—and then stopped short. Inside, the room was lined with coffered wood like all the other rooms in the school, but here the paneling was painted a rich, deep red, and there was a thick, dark red carpet on the floor. The mahogany furniture looked almost black by comparison. There were ten chairs arranged around a big, intricately carved table, with snakes and dragons writhing up the legs and obscene bats spreading their jointed wings across the tall carved chair backs. The service was heavy silver, polished to a gleaming sheen, and the room looked rich, plush, suffocating, and dangerous. There were no windows.

There were ten people sitting around the table, and Nina scanned them while trying not to be too obvious about it. There were several people she knew: Professor Danvers, Agatha, Bella, and (her heart sank) Simone Freeland. Bella was sitting between two severe-looking people who had to be his parents—Ly Than Chopin did indeed look like a much better-looking Ming the Merciless, with a narrow, bald head, and his wife was gorgeous in a red satin *cheongsam* poured over her slender body like lacquer. Next to her was the priest, Father Ragoczy, so white he looked like he'd been blanched like the sweetbreads, and next to him was another handsome man, this one blond with bright-blue eyes, who looked like a movie star or a male model—he had the same vacuous smile and perfectly capped teeth. Simone was for some reason sitting between him and another dazzling blond, and Nina realized these had to be her adoptive parents: for some reason, these two ice gods had decided to adopt a black girl. The woman had a sharp cameo profile and an imperious gaze and was dressed almost mannishly in a tailored black suit and white shirt with a simple red scarf around her throat.

That left the last person at the table to draw Nina's attention: John Benway.

Who didn't look any happier to be there than he'd looked at CC's. Actually, he didn't look like he'd really be that happy anywhere. He was staring around the table with a suspicious frown on his face, slouching down, as though he expected the evening to be a big disappointment. For a well-dressed man—with his expensive suit and his Rolex and his nice gold cufflinks—he somehow looked rumpled and bulky. His waxy cheeks were almost bluish, as though being immortal hadn't stopped him from having to shave. He was rolling a pen back and forth on the table, and she didn't want to go anywhere near him.

It was Professor Danvers who broke the silence as they entered, and his voice was controlled, if sarcastic. "Well, I see we have two of the school's children waiting on us tonight. What's the matter—the chef couldn't serve us in person?"

"No, I . . . we . . ." Nina ducked her head. "Sally just asked us to help, that's all." She quickly handed around the plates, trying not to look too closely at anyone, although when she handed Bella his plate, he looked up at her curiously. It was almost as if he didn't recognize her—or as if he *did* recognize her, but didn't know why.

When she gave Simone her plate, the black girl pointedly moved her arm to avoid letting Nina touch her—*right,* Nina thought, *remind me to spit in your food next course*—but it didn't seem like Simone recognized her either. It was more like she was deliberately being rude to someone who was simply beneath her.

Nina thought excitedly, *Whatever Sally did, she made it so nobody knows who we are!*

She handed a plate to Simone's mother and then moved on to the assistant headmaster, who glared at her as she heard quite clearly in her head, *"What do you think you're doing, Miss Lamb?"*

Well, okay, *he* recognized her, but that was probably because of the special bond they had. *I'm serving you your sweetbreads*, she thought stubbornly back, refusing to rise to the bait of carrying on a psychic conversation with him, as much as part of her wanted to.

"That's not what I meant. You shouldn't be here at all. Certainly not after today."

Why not?

"You have no idea what you're meddling in, Miss Lamb. No idea."

All right, then, tell me. What am I meddling in?

Professor Danvers sighed and said aloud cooly, "I don't eat sweetbreads. Please take those away."

"Strickland, you can't mean it! You *love* sweetbreads!" Nhi Trung Chopin had clearly had a few drinks already, and she leaned toward him, trailing her fingers on his arm. "Don't tell me you've developed an allergy, you poor man! You should let Isolde prescribe something for you."

"Actually, that's not possible," Dr. Freeland said, picking up her fork. "Skin Eaters don't get allergies."

"Oh, you know what I mean, Isolde. Something *like* an allergy. I don't know, like getting a rash. *Some*thing. Don't get all medicinal on us."

"I'll have to remember that the next time you need my services, Nhi." Dr. Freeland speared a crisp sweetbread slice and popped it into her mouth. "Skin rejuvenation only works for so long. If you swap life with any more infants, we'll have to get you a crib."

She seemed not to be aware of Nhi Trung's gasp and Ly Than Chopin's angry sputter, but her own husband said quickly, "Oh, Izzy's just in a bad mood today because the Benway Corporation turned down the funding for her latest research project. Didn't they darling? Something about polynomial DNA restructuring... I'm afraid I can't make head nor tail of it..."

"Then you shouldn't try, darling." Dr. Freeland patted his hand. "Just sit there and look pretty. Here, Strickland, have the girl give me your sweetbreads. I adore eating at the top of the food chain," and she stretched out her hand as Nina picked up the plate and handed it to her. Nina felt a jolt of electricity jump across the dish as both her hand and Dr. Freeland's hand touched it for a moment, and one of the sweetbreads gave a little jump and fell off the plate onto the floor.

Dr. Freeland laughed. "Well, they're certainly fresh, at any rate," she said, although Nina thought there was something unconvincing about her voice. Nina bent down to clean up the mess, trying to avoid everyone's eyes, although she felt she only half succeeded.

She glanced across the table at Alastaire as she stood up, and of one accord, they stepped back and folded their hands, and Professor Danvers's voice rang in Nina's head like a bell, saying, *"Please leave now!"* and she couldn't think of any reason not to. They both curtseyed and got out of there fast.

When they were back in the hallway again, Nina made a quick *zip your mouth* gesture and nodded toward the kitchen.

"What. Did. You. Think. You. Were. Doing?" Alastaire panted the minute they got back behind the swinging doors. "Why on earth did you do magic in there? In front of them? *All* of them? Are you insane?”

“First,” Nina whispered furiously, “I didn’t deliberately do magic, and second, it’s because they were there that it happened! Or at least that woman, Dr. Freeland.” Nina shook her head. “It was strange. It was like an electric shock happened when we both touched the plate at the same time. I don’t know—for all I know, maybe *she* did magic!”

“Not a chance.” Alastaire kept her voice low, although Sally was absorbed at the other end of the room with spooning out the kidney stew onto warmed plates, and she didn’t appear to have heard them.

“She’d be an idiot to try anything like that in front of Benway. He can fund her new research project with his spare change. And from what I hear, Dr. Freeland’s the last person anybody would call an idiot. No, Nina, you did it, even if it was an accident, and they noticed. At least I’m sure Professor Danvers did.”

Yes, Nina thought, *I’m sure he did.* She shook herself. “Well, anyway, we just have to hear as much as we can the next time we go in there and not let anything distract us.”

Alastaire raised her eyebrows as much as to say *she* didn’t plan on doing any more magic, and Nina figured she’d earned that. They both went over to Sally, who was garnishing the stew plates with croutons.

“Did everybody like the first course?”

“Professor Danvers doesn’t eat sweetbreads, but Dr. Freeland ate his,” Alastaire said.

“Really? I’ll have to remember Professor Danvers’s preferences in the future.” Sally sounded a little distracted. “Did anything else happen?”

“Well . . .” The two girls looked at each other, and then one said, “No,” and the other said, “Nuh-uh,” almost simultaneously.

Sally glanced back and forth between them, and Nina said, "Well, when Dr. Freeland took the plate from me, I felt an electric spark. That's all. I guess the carpet's all static-y."

"Yeah. Right." Sally frowned, but there wasn't time to get into this any further. "Well, you'd better go serve them their kidneys. Oh, and bring them some wine. Grab a couple bottles of the Romanee-Conti. That'll go well with the stew."

Nina grabbed two dusty bottles of wine and balanced them on her tray as they headed back to the dining room. "This is great," she whispered to Alastaire. "Now I can make a big deal out of opening the bottles and letting them taste it and letting it breathe, and everything will take ages. We can really listen to what they're saying now."

Alastaire just sniffed and said, "Terrific. Now if you can manage not to piss anybody else off, we might actually get out of this in one piece."

Nina made a *shh*-ing gesture as they opened the door again to the dining room, and Mr. Freeland said, "Oh, good, here's the wine! Come in, ladies . . ." and waved his cocktail glass around, which was a good indication that everyone was already pretty well lubricated. Nina took the bottles of wine to the sideboard and started to peel away the foil wrapping, being as slow and meticulous about it as possible. Alastaire was going around the table putting out the wineglasses, and from the sound of things, their presence wasn't putting much of a dent in the conversation.

"So the point is, Strickland, Agatha, you're *here*. I mean, I know . . . shaping the youth of tomorrow is all very well, but you're also pretty isolated here from the day to day hurly-burly. I tell you, things are a mess out there, and they're not getting any better. This storm has fouled everything up, and I don't just mean down in the Ninth Ward."

Strickland touched the stem of his wineglass, turning it a

quarter turn. Nina had the feeling he was holding onto his temper with difficulty.

"Archer, I think we all know there have been changes in the last six months," he said finally. "Even holed up here in kindergarten, we *do* read the newspapers."

"That's not what I—"

"I know what you meant. She's back. Yes, I know, let's all draw a deep breath. Now. Shall we talk about what we're all thinking about, or do you still want to discuss the weather?"

There was silence for an instant, and then Ly Than Chopin said, "Strickland, given the fact that we have children present, don't you think a little . . . discretion might be in order?"

"No, he's right," Dr. Freeland said, interrupting him. "Why waste time? They'll have to face facts soon enough, and I don't believe in coddling anyone, patients *or* children. Simone already knows what's happening, don't you, dear?"

"There's a risk that Sister Aquilina could disrupt everything," Simone said, as though she were parroting back something she'd heard. "Bring back the bad old days. Isn't that right, Mom?"

"Exactly, dear. I scarcely need to remind you what things were like back then."

She glanced around the table, and Nina guessed the "bad old days" were when they fought Sister Aquilina the last time. But they don't look that brave now, do they? In fact, Nhi Trung Chopin and Archer Freeland were looking distinctly scared.

"That's why you're so upset, isn't it, Mom?" Simone went on, confirming Nina's point. "Because you think Sister Aquilina might be back and trying to start the war again?"

"I told you—" Ly Than repeated, glancing meaningfully at Nina and Alastaire. "Not in front of the *children*!"

Waving her hand, Agatha then spoke up. "Oh, I wouldn't worry about them, Ly. All the students here are woefully naïve. They believe, as all infants do, that the whole world revolves around them." She sighed. "I sometimes think we should consider all young people *jumbies* and leave it at that."

Mr. Chopin seemed relieved, although Nina thought angrily, *I'm not a* jumbie*!* She heard Professor Danvers's voice in her head again saying, *"Shh. Aggie's a bitch, but her prejudices are useful to you at this particular moment."*

He continued out loud, "For God's sake, girl, bring that wine over here and start pouring it!" and she nodded and came toward him to fill his glass.

She tried to keep her hand steady as she did so, but she heard Simone say to the table at large, "It's the fact that the school's been taking in refugees that particularly upsets Mom and Dad. Losers, kids with no memory . . . frankly, all kinds of rubbish."

Nina felt her hand shake, and she spilled wine onto the table.

"God, girl, you're hopeless," Strickland sighed, picking up a napkin and mopping up the spill. Nina resisted the impulse to pour the wine onto his head and continued carefully around the table.

"Iggy, what do you think?" Nhi Trung asked the priest, and Father Ragoczy took his time answering, while Alastaire filled his glass.

"I think," he said finally, "that no one knows entirely what Sister Aquilina is doing, which is, of course, the problem. Science can only take us so far, and even those of us skilled at divination—" he inclined his head toward Professor Danvers "—have their limits. Fire cannot know earth, or else it will smother. Air cannot know water, or it will drown. I sometimes think the forces that made us still have much to answer for, in the field of natural selection. It takes a rare visionary to see into every mind at once."

Nina's eyes flew to Professor Danvers, who caught hers for a split second before he looked down. *That's why he'd asked me to the carriage house,* she thought. He was a fixed element—earth, air, fire, or water—and he couldn't do divination in all directions at once the way she could. *You goddamn son of a bitch.* She didn't know whether to feel flattered or pissed off. *I* should *have poured wine on his head. He used me, and he didn't even tell me why.*

"So, you don't think she's a menace?" Mr. Freeland pressed him.

"I didn't say that," the priest went on. "The greatest menaces are those we don't fully understand. The late headmaster—" he held up his hand in a gesture halfway between a benediction and a dismissive wave "—understood such things far better than I, and look where it got him. I think if Sister Aquilina is back, she's scarcely here for a vacation. Then again, we have far greater resources than we had the last time. She can't simply walk in here anytime she wants."

Most of the guests looked relieved to hear that, but Simone said, "But that's why you're so upset, Mom, isn't it? Because you think she *can* do that."

"That's right, dear. You're very perceptive. I think I speak for us all when I say the risk of having to completely rearrange our whole system, if nothing else, is far too tedious to contemplate." Dr. Freeland made a lovely gesture with her hand like shooing away butterflies. "The calculations alone would take weeks. Now I know, we're talking fairly advanced stuff here, but we don't know what our *friend* has been up to for the last thirty years—"

"We know she was crippled," Agatha said quickly. "She had to hide herself away. She can't be much of a threat now."

"Not necessarily. We don't know if anyone else helped her." Dr. Freeland let that hang in the air, and nobody at the table seemed to enjoy the silence. "The possibility of a spy, or I suppose in this case I should say a *mole,* is something that can't be discounted."

Nina and Alastaire continued around the table pouring wine, and Nina tried desperately to make sense of what she was hearing. Sister Aquilina was back, and the guests in the room seemed to take that fact for granted. Professor Danvers was still speaking to her telepathically, but was he mad at her or not? And was she mad at him or not? She wasn't sure about that either. Not to mention the fact that Agatha had just called her a *jumbie,* but she didn't care about that. Did she? Well, maybe just a little.

She stopped in front of Mr. Benway and said, "Sir? Would you like some wine?"

Benway regarded her, his heavy gaze holding hers in a way that was somewhere between reptilian and . . . caressing. His eyes were blue, as flat as storm clouds, and Nina found herself thinking about shipwrecks, whirlpools, and slime-covered rocks. He let his attention travel down from her face to her boobs, then to her waist, and then down the long length of her skirt to her black boots, where it rested for a moment. He said, "Oh, yes, dear. I'd like all sorts of things from you."

She saw Professor Danvers move his hand instinctively, not quite closing it into a fist but wanting to, and the fact that he was there gave her courage. "I'm only offering you wine, sir," she said levelly.

"And that's fine for now." Benway held out his glass. "We share all the appetites of our underlings, even if we don't have the same needs as they do. Their addictions are our . . . delicacies." He glanced at Professor Danvers, and then at Agatha and the Chopins, and none of them could hold his gaze. They all looked down at their plates. "Yes, dear, I'd love some wine. And I can't wait to see what the rest of the meal brings," and Nina and Alastaire didn't need to be told twice. They plunked down the kidney stew in front of everyone and got out of there fast.

"Majorly yucky," Alastaire said when they were behind the swinging doors again. "That's it, I quit. You serve the rest of dinner."

"No, wait a minute—" Nina was quickly scribbling things down on the back of the list of courses Sally had discarded, trying to remember them before they slipped her mind. She wrote:

They know Sister A. is back. Bad old days.
We don't share the same needs? War?

And then she realized that she had no time to think about any of that right now. She stuffed the list in her pocket and hurried over to where Sally was slicing the tenderloins. The cook said, "Got to be quick with these. Could you hand me that marrow sauce? Don't burn yourself," and Nina handed Sally the hot pot. Sally spooned the sauce over the meat, saying, "There, that should do it. Bring it all out and let 'em make pigs of themselves for all I care."

Nina was a little surprised at Sally's disgust, but she figured it was because she was tired and wasn't sure they appreciated all her hard work. She gestured to Alastaire, and the two girls loaded up their trays and headed back in.

". . . The need for the appropriate means to continue our control is self-evident," Ly Than was saying, but he clammed up as soon as he saw them, and everyone else followed suit.

Nina went to the sideboard and got the second bottle of wine and said weakly, "Would anyone like anything more to drink?"

"Bring it here," Professor Danvers said between gritted teeth. It looked like he hadn't eaten anything at all, although his plate of kidneys was stirred up and cut into little pieces. She remembered him playing with his food on her first day at Daedalus, but she didn't have time to ask him what was wrong. She poured him some more wine, then moved around the table again. Alastaire started handing out the plates of meat.

"Excellent, excellent," Mr. Benway said, tasting the tenderloin and chewing with enthusiasm. "Even without necessity, it's always so nice to *enjoy* oneself!"

He grinned at everyone else around the table, and once again, everybody there, with the exception of the Freelands and Father Ignatius, looked extremely uncomfortable. Nina noticed that while everybody except Professor Danvers was eating, there was a strange furtiveness about their movements. The Chopins and Agatha were shoveling the food into their mouths like they hadn't eaten in weeks, as though they were starving, but also as though they wanted to get it down as quickly as possible. Bella and Simone were just doggedly working their way through their plates. Benway and his friends, on the other hand, were savoring each bite and practically smacking their lips.

"Really, Aggie, you've outdone yourself! This new cook is a perfect gem," Benway said.

"She's all right," Agatha said. "I have to keep a close eye on her, though."

Nina poured a little wine for Bella, who looked at her again and whispered, "Who *are* you?" She shook her head and didn't answer. She moved on to the Freelands, making sure she didn't touch Dr. Freeland or come any nearer to her than she had to.

"I think," Father Ignatius said, "the real thing we need to worry about is the prophecy."

There was a moment of silence when everyone stopped eating, and then Professor Danvers said, "The real thing we need to worry about, Iggy, is whether we believe any of the headmaster's bullshit or not. I, for one, frankly do not."

Father Ignatius smiled but didn't say anything, and Nhi Trung giggled, and Archer Freeland blinked, and Ly Than said, "Come on, man, you shouldn't joke about that."

"I'm not joking." Professor Danvers leaned back and swallowed a big mouthful of wine. *At this rate,* Nina thought, *we're going to need another bottle.* "The crackpot maunderings of a silly old fool may be of interest to those who like Plato's cave, but I for one prefer to look things in the face. No one knows what the prophecy means. What we *do* know is that Sister Aquilina's back, and she'll be trying to get hold of what she couldn't get the last time."

He nodded toward Father Ignatius and Mr. Benway, and added, "That's why you're here tonight, isn't it? I mean, besides rubbing our noses in your superior tastes. The Four Gifts may reside at Daedalus as a matter of tradition, but I can't imagine the Vatican or the Saturni or the Army *or* the Benway Corporation much appreciating their theft. Am I right or am I right?"

He looked across the table, and Nina wondered, *What are the Four Gifts? What's he talking about?* Dr. Freeland was sitting with her fork poised in front of her mouth, but for the moment, she'd forgotten to eat. And then she laughed and said, "Point taken. My father would be furious."

"How is General Azazel these days?"

"Fine. Getting on in years."

"No lingering ill effects from facing a *Lwa*?"

"I told you, Strickland, he's fine." She waved her hand again, although the gesture wasn't quite as perfect as before. "Are you threatening me?"

"No, Isolde." His sarcasm was heavy. "I would never do that. I'm merely pointing out what should be apparent to anyone with half a brain—that the Four Gifts are valuable, and you might want to *protect* them. Unless that's too much trouble."

Nina and Alastaire, having served all the plates and all the wine, couldn't think of any other reason to stay there, but since no one in the room was telling them to leave yet, they didn't leave. And then Nina heard the words she'd been dreading someone would say, "What about this new girl, Strickland? Is she involved?" Dr. Freeland frowned. "Surely there's some connection."

Nina thought, *That's it. I'm so screwed.* Fortunately, only Professor Danvers seemed to know who she was at the moment. He yawned and said, "Oh, right, Miss . . . what's her name anyway? Some kind of animal? Miss Cow? Miss Pig? She's all right, I guess." He turned to his sister. "What do you think, Aggie? Not the brightest match in the box, but then, we can't have everything."

"Who is she?" Dr. Freeland wasn't giving up that easily.

"Just some girl they found after the storm." He shrugged.

"Is she one of *us*?"

"I really couldn't say." And then Professor Danvers speared a piece of meat from his plate and brought it to his lips. "You're right, Jack, this really is good," he said, changing the topic completely. "Aggie's new discovery is certainly working out," although Nina watched his jaw muscles clench as he swallowed, and he looked like he wanted to vomit.

The only thing left to serve were the mince pies, which they brought out a few minutes later, each wreathed with pungent steam. Everyone got a thick slice and some coffee, and then Nina and Alastaire waited to see if there was anything else.

"Now, I can only think of one thing missing from a perfect evening," Mr. Benway said, pushing back his chair. "A willing young girl to join me in a nightcap. Either of you young ladies want to oblige?"

Nina froze, and Alastaire went very still next to her. She looked across the table at Professor Danvers and sent him a quick, *Help!* and he shut his eyes.

Then he said quietly, "No."

"No?"

"That's not going to happen. Sorry, Jack, you can find someone else to share life with tonight. Not one of my students."

"Oh, come *on*." Benway narrowed his eyes and his quasi-jovial expression slid across his face like it was slipping off. "Since when have you become so dainty? Haven't *you* had them?"

"No more than I have to," Professor Danvers said. "And I'm not letting you anywhere near them."

There was a moment then that was more strained than anything that had gone before.

Ly Than Chopin said, "Oh, come on, Jack, let's go down to the Fortuna Club. You don't need *schoolgirls*. We'll find you something a little more ripe out of the gutter of Bourbon Street," and he appealed to Archer Freeland, who knew enough to say, "Oh sure, Jack. C'mon, man, it'll be fun." Their wives either didn't seem to mind or maybe didn't think now was the time to object, and everyone scraped back their chairs. The Chopins kissed Bella on both cheeks and told him to be good. And then everyone was leaving, and Nina noticed Dr. Freeland and Simone holding back, and as they left, Dr. Freeland grabbed her daughter's hand and twisted it behind her back and whispered, "Don't screw things up," and Simone answered grimacing, "Don't worry, Mom, I won't."

Nina and Alastaire went back into the kitchen and sat down on two of the stools there, completely exhausted and more confused than ever. Sally had already cleaned up and left.

Alastaire finally said, "I'm hungry, I wonder if there's any more tenderloin?" and went over to the stove to check. Nina let her, because she was staring at the list she'd made, and what Sally had written on the other side. And suddenly something, at least, about the dinner made perfect sense.

Five jumbies = ten servings, the cook had written. *One kidney per person, half a brain, one thigh bone each, one tenderloin. 10 hams = approx. 20 cups of human meat.*

Chapter Fourteen

"Stop," Nina said before Alastaire put the meat in her mouth. And then she threw up. Her first thought, even as she gazed at the mess on the floor, was, *I have to get out of here.*

Everything she'd known about the Skin Eaters, everything she'd ever known about anything, was wrong. Everything was different, horribly different. The *jumbies* weren't just losers, were they?

They were *food.*

And if they were, then that meant . . .

Nina felt her head spin as she fully processed what that did mean. All the strange inconsistencies. The things that had never added up. "Tasting" life, and Agatha's disdain for cooking. The scared, helpless children who were just "killing time." What had Simone said? "You actually feel sorry for one of the cattle? Or do you want him for yourself? Feeling hungry?" And Roticus had said, "Don't hurt me."

What if the process Alastaire had described as a kind of spiritual thing, "We're called Skin Eaters because we eat people's illusions," was something much more literal?

What if the Skin Eaters were called that because they ate . . . skin. Flesh. Human flesh.

She tried to get her mind around what that would mean. They didn't eat human meat all the time, obviously. Sally cooked regular meals for the students. Fried chicken. Pancakes. She even made salads. So, was this just for special occasions?

Was that what "crossing" meant?

And Professor Danvers had eaten a bite of that awful meat, although, to be fair, he'd looked sick while he was doing it.

She tried to get that image out of her mind, but all she could think about were his jaw muscles working and the pale, tense look on his face as he swallowed his bite of tenderloin and his words, "No more than I have to." She didn't even want to think about the others. Did Bella know? Could he really have eaten all that stuff if he *had* known? Or did he believe what Alastaire said—that the Skin Eaters just fed on people's bad habits?

Nina realized she was leaning against the kitchen counter, and her hands were shaking.

Alastaire was saying as if from a great distance, "What's wrong, Neens? Talk to me . . ."

"I have to go outside," she said, pushing past Alastaire and heading for the door to the garden. Once out there, the soft perfume of the spring night couldn't push away the smell of blood that was still in her nose, and she turned away and threw up again in the rose bushes.

"Nina, c'mon, you're freaking me out." Alastaire followed her outside and shut the door quietly behind her. "Let's go find a bench somewhere where you can sit down. Okay? C'mon, deep breaths. Just relax. I mean, that was tense in there, but not . . . Hey, maybe you're just hungry? Do you want me to get you something to eat?"

Nina knew her laughter wasn't kind, but she couldn't help it. Hysteria bubbled up inside of her, tight and panicky, until she felt like hands were clenched around her throat. When she could finally breathe again, she looked at Alastaire and saw the moonlight molding her pretty, heart-shaped face, her dark hair hanging loose down her back, her worried frown and her little mustache, and she looked so innocent and sweet and kind that Nina's breath caught in her throat again.

How innocent they all are. All the students here. They simply don't know.

Or do they?

She held out Sally's list without a word, not knowing how to say it. There was certainly enough moonlight for Alastaire to read it. She waited. Alastaire read the list of ingredients and didn't say anything for a long moment. Then, "Well, it's a joke, obviously."

"Is it?"

"Of course. I mean, we all know people pick on the *jumbies*. I mean, I've laughed at them too, but we wouldn't . . . no. That's not what anybody would . . . do. It's not like anybody would actually do that . . . unless they were . . . unless they were . . ."

"Unless they were what?"

"Monsters," Alastaire whispered. And then she dropped the list and backed away and said, "No, that's just stupid."

"Is it?"

"Yeah. You're sick, Neens. You wrote that list yourself."

"You know I didn't. That's what this is really all about, isn't it? When the adult Skinnies cross with you? You said it felt really sexy and physical and you don't remember much afterward and there were some gross side effects? They feed off you, don't they? And they feed off the *jumbies*. They're cannibals."

"No. No." Alastaire was whipping her head back and forth. "It's not like that. It's *nice*."

"Then how do you get to be immortal? How do you 'wash the mortal' out of you and become like them? You get colder and colder and sicker and sicker and more and more *dead*! That's what's really going on, isn't it? You're not evolving, you're dying! And then when you're completely dead, you're like them, and you have to eat the living to stay alive!"

Alastaire took off running, running as fast as she could, away from Nina into the dense darkness of the garden. And Nina went after her, even though a part of her mind said she shouldn't. Even though a part of her mind said Alastaire was dangerous and might hurt her if she were cornered. She ran without a thought, because Alastaire was her friend, and because that's what friends did when they were in trouble. They believed in each other, and they trusted each other, even when there was some doubt, even when they were still reeling with shock. When she caught up with the Skin Eater girl by the carriage house, Alastaire was crying and screaming and banging her open hands flat against the old brick wall, over and over again.

"No, no, no!" she shouted. "It's not true. I'm not going to turn into something like that. I'm not! I'm not! Goddamn it!" She punched the wall. "It's not fair! I didn't even know!"

"Shh," Nina said, grabbing Alastaire around the shoulders and hugging her, trying to get her to calm down but also trying to get her to shut up and stop throwing punches before they were discovered. She felt like they were making enough noise already to bring the whole school out after them.

She wrestled Alastaire down onto the grass, and all the while the other girl was screaming, "They're inside of me! Shit! Their lives are inside of me, and I crossed with them! And I didn't even know!"

"*Shh*," Nina said, hugging her and rubbing small circles against her back. "*Shh*. Be quiet.

What did you tell me? Just breathe. It's going to be all right." Even though she had no idea at the moment how any of this was going to be all right.

Alastaire finally calmed down enough to say, "I feel terrible," and Nina said, "Me too."

Nina sat looking at the dark writhing shapes of the trees and the black bulk of the school looming above them and the bronze fountain nearby with the woman bleeding from her wrists. *Oh, I do not want to see that right now*, she thought, but she couldn't think of a single thing to say.

"I don't remember it," Alastaire whispered.

"What?"

"What they did. Professor Threet and Professor Mwindo and Professor Samson. When they crossed with me. It's all a blur. I felt really good, but yes, I guess there was a little pain." She scrunched her eyes shut. "I remember I had a scrape on my inner thigh after the first time, and, like, a really bad paper cut after the second, and my ass hurt after Professor Samson, but it went away. I, like, I don't have any scars or anything." She held her hands up and looked at them. "I guess that's how all the Skinnies can regenerate. Our flesh grows back really fast."

"Handy."

"Yeah. I guess so." Alastaire sighed. "I want to take a shower."

"Do you think Bella knows the truth?"

Alastaire shook her head but then made a little *maybe* gesture. "He's pretty smart. He might know." She stared out into the darkness, and then, "Neens?"

"Yes?"

"Do I make you disgusted?"

Nina felt dizzy. She dug her fingers into the grass on either side of her, as though she could hold on to the earth to keep from falling off into space.

"No, of course not," she said finally. "I don't think any of you are to blame. Even the teachers here. I mean, presumably *they* were turned too, and probably without their knowledge."

And where did it start? What had Benway said? "We share all the appetites of our underlings, even if we don't exactly have the same needs." The Saturni must have given the Skin Eaters this unholy appetite as a way of controlling them, but while Benway and the others had relished their meal, she remembered the furtive, famished gestures of the adult Skin Eaters, stuffing the forbidden, desired meat into their mouths, and she thought, *They weren't just hungry, were they? They were ravenous. And they were also* ashamed.

Nina added, "I don't know . . . maybe you don't have to do it. Maybe that's what red spur is for. Professor Danvers said it quells their hunger, at least temporarily."

She fell silent and listened to Alastaire crying next to her, which broke her heart.

Finally, the other girl asked, "Neens? Do you think there's any way . . ." She sounded much younger all of a sudden. "Any way to just stop it? Just stay the way I am now?"

"Maybe." Nina pulled at the blades of grass. "I feel like I don't know anything anymore."

She wanted to say something else, but she didn't know what to add. A few beats later, she said, "It was a weird night, even without all that. I mean, who'd have thought they'd be so cool with the idea of Sister Aquilina being back."

"They weren't cool." Alastaire sounded like she knew Nina was trying to cheer her up, and she wasn't buying it. "They were scared to death. Besides, I told you." She lay back on the grass. "The Saturni never defeated Sister Aquilina. They just drove her away." She bit her lip and added, "Simone's parents are real assholes, aren't they?"

"Tell me about it." Nina lay down next to her. "Did you know they were white?"

"I heard rumors. Her father looks like he bleaches his teeth with Clorox."

"And her mom's the original Ice Queen. Did you catch that bit when she twisted Simone's arm?"

"Yeah. I mean, not like I wouldn't like to twist Simone's neck sometimes, but still." Alastaire put her hands behind her head. "And Bella's parents are such suck-ups. If I was that rich, I wouldn't be such a kiss-ass."

They fell silent, and it was almost all right for a moment. Then Nina asked, "Do you think the real headmaster is really dead?"

"No idea." Alastaire sat up and hugged her knees. "I told you he's been gone for, like, ages. I barely remember him."

Nina sat up as well. "You met him?"

"Yeah. When I first came here, he was around a lot. He used to have this weird little habit of eating pistachios. Everywhere he went, you'd find, like, this trail of shells. When I first came here, I was really scared, and he helped me out. He said I'd make friends, because like always calls to like."

"Somebody else told me that recently." Nina frowned. "I've seen him too, you know."

"Who?"

"The headmaster. I saw him the first full day I was here."

"No way." Alastaire shook her head. "I told you, he disappeared years ago."

"Still, he was here." Nina described the meeting. "I told Professor Danvers about it, and he said it couldn't be, because Mr. O'Brien is definitely dead. But I know I saw him. Even though he disappeared. And there's something else . . ."

She hesitated. She didn't want to freak out Alastaire any more than she was freaked out already, but she had to say it. "I felt like I knew him, somehow," she whispered. "Besides, how can any of you guys really be dead?"

"I have no idea." Alastaire frowned. "I feel like I'm about three years old, and I don't know how to tie my own shoes."

"Well," Nina said, getting to her feet, "one thing I do know is we ought to be getting back inside. If Agatha catches us out here, she'll be majorly pissed off. Besides, I think we need to talk to Bella. He . . . he needs to know about the . . . you know. I mean, it's disgusting and awful, but it's still better than letting him think he was eating filet mignon."

Chapter Fifteen

But when they found Bella, he was in the empty Alchemy classroom rummaging around in the cupboards.

"I think there's some Tincture of Apomorphia in here somewhere," he said, as he pulled away from them and knelt down to search on the bottom shelves. "If I throw up quickly enough, I won't keep much of it in me."

Alastaire shot Nina a look. "He knows." Then with a sigh, she turned to Bella. "We were hoping maybe you didn't."

"I've known for years," he snapped, grabbing a bottle from the back of the cupboard and chugging the contents. "Why do you think there's always so much drama between me and my parents?" He wiped his lips. "I *saw* them. They were eating a rib roast, and it didn't come from a cow, lemme tell you." He vomited copiously into the sink. "It had *shoulders*."

Alastaire said, "Jeez, give us some warning next time—"

Bella shot back, "The next time you engage in a primal taboo, remind me to be so critical of *your* table manners." He turned to Nina. "By the way, I guessed it was you two in there when Professor Danvers started lying about knowing what your real name was. I had a feeling, but that clinched it. And then when Alastaire had seven kinds of fits when Benway propositioned you, I was sure of it."

"I did not have seven kinds of fits!" Alastaire protested. "I was *fine*!"

"Oh really? You were ready to have a stroke."

"Well, you try having some perv put the moves on you and see how you feel!"

"Stop it," Nina said, sitting down at a desk and rubbing her forehead. She still felt sick, and she suddenly felt horribly tired. The long day and the night's terrible revelations all felt like they were pressing around her head like a helmet of lead, and she just wanted to crawl into her bed and sleep. Instead, she spread out Sally's list in front of her and tried to concentrate. She turned it over and wrote at the bottom of her other notes:

Four Gifts.

General Azazel.

And the last and biggest question: *What does Sister Aquilina really want?*

She looked at the list and thought that Alastaire was right. They were all like little kids trying to solve problems way beyond their abilities. Something was nagging at her mind, but she didn't know what it was.

"Well—" she sighed "—look. We can start with the Four Gifts. Professor Danvers said Sister Aquilina wanted to steal them. So, what are they?"

Bella shoved a handful of Tic Tacs into his mouth to freshen his breath, then shook his head. "I have no idea."

Nina gave him a flat look.

He raised his eyebrows. "What? Don't look at me like that, I'm not your own personal search engine! I don't know every-thing!"

"Well, listen," she went on. "I think I may have an idea. Professor Danvers said they were kept at Daedalus as a matter of tradition, so they've got to be valuable. So where would they keep something like that, something that's really priceless?"

"In the chapel," Bella said at once. "That's where they keep the headmaster's cup, and the sword of Valentinus and the mirror of Simon Magus, and the wand of Asphodel and . . . *hmm* . . . I wonder . . ."

"Are those the things they use for divination?" Nina asked. She blushed a little, because she really didn't want to describe her private meeting with Professor Danvers, but when Bella nodded, she said, "I think I've seen them."

"Really?"

She nodded, recapping the main points of her private lesson and trying to keep it short. "I drank from the cup, looked in the mirror, and dragged the sword around me in a circle."

She left out any reference to the sword bleeding and the cup being full of blood, but Bella still stared at her with newfound respect, as though she'd described working with plutonium. "And I held the wand, and it gave off a white light."

"Wait a minute, *white*? Really?" He whistled. "That's amazing. What else?"

"Um . . . that's about it." She didn't want to tell them anything else. "So, do you think those four things . . ."

"Are the Four Gifts? Sure, why not?" Bella looked better than he had all evening. "It stands to reason. They're incredibly old, and they're steeped in history and tradition, so they're immensely powerful. Why wouldn't they be looked on as gifts from the gods?"

"I don't know." Nina shook her head, frowning. "They just seem so obvious. Besides, they're human artifacts, like tools. I still think there's more going on."

"Well, I still think it's a good possibility. Although . . ." And now it was Bella's turn to frown. "It *is* scary to think of them being hidden in plain sight like that."

Nina abruptly decided she needed to take action. "Well, there's one way to find out. We need to sneak into the chapel tonight and see what those four things are."

The others looked at her as if she'd proposed breaking into the White House. "Oh, for God's sake!" she snapped. "What are they going to do to us? We go to school here. We have as much right to be walking around the place as anybody else. And besides, right now we're in a really good position to find out what Mr. Benway and all those other people are up to. Professor Danvers said the Four Gifts were at Daedalus, and everybody would be really upset if they were stolen. So obviously, we need to find out why!"

"You need to watch your back," Bella pointed out. "Jack Benway's already far too interested in you. If Professor Danvers hadn't lied tonight, they'd all know that the new girl is named Nina Lamb, then they might put two and two together and guess you're the one the prophecy is all about. You can't just go wandering around at night asking for trouble."

Nina privately wondered why not? Wasn't it a better idea than just hiding?

"Look, I know Benway's a creep," she agreed, "but the point is, for whatever reason, Professor Danvers *did* lie tonight. Which means right now, they *don't* know who I am, which means we've got some information they don't. Which is always a good thing."

She stopped and looked at each of them in turn. In their own ways, they looked scared and sick, and she thought, *How can I ask them to go through anything more tonight?*

How could she, who knew nothing of what their lives were really like, threaten the core of their beliefs . . . and for what? Her own curiosity?

Her compassion warred with her frayed nerves, and she said, "Look, if you don't want to go with me, then fine. I'll just go by myself."

She stood up, and of course, they both said, "No, wait!" and "I didn't mean—" and she thought, *Oh well, I guess we're a team, aren't we?*

"Okay," she said, "here's what I think we should do. We'll wait until everybody else is asleep and then meet at midnight down in the corridor that leads to the chapel. Do they lock it at night?"

Bella gave a little grunt, not quite a laugh, but like he was trying to. "Even if they do, I have a key." He dug in his pocket and pulled out a big brass one. "Agatha Danvers gave it to me, so I can go out into the garden at night. This key unlocks every door at Daedalus."

"Wow." Alastaire looked at the key with mingled awe and desire. "You must be the biggest suck-up in the world if she trusts you that much."

Bella bowed modestly, although he added, "I think she just trusts that my parents would tear me apart if I ever got into trouble. Which by the way, now seems likely."

"No, it doesn't," Nina said quickly. "We'll play it real safe. Just go into the chapel and look around. If we get caught, we can say we were, um . . . praying."

"Right," Alastaire snorted. "Like they're going to believe *that* of a bunch of kids."

But the idea of adventure had plainly cheered her up, and when they parted, she looked more like her old self. She even told Bella to go brush his teeth, that his Tic Tacs weren't making it. Nina thought, *I hope I'm not ruining their lives,* and then, *I hope I'm not ruining mine, either.*

They went off to their separate rooms to wait for midnight.

Nina felt the minutes drag by, and at eleven thirty she couldn't stand it anymore and opened her door. Anyone around? *Of course not,* she thought. *No one wants to come up here. It's haunted.* She crept down the stairs, testing each tread to make sure it didn't squeak before letting it take her full weight. She finally got down to the big main hall. Because of all the plywood over all of the windows, it was very dark.

"Nina?" came a whisper, and she jumped.

"Shit!" she said, recognizing Alastaire. "I said we'd meet by the *chapel*. At *midnight*. Not here where you could scare the crap out of me!"

"I just wanted to tell you Agatha's still up. She's patrolling. Should we rethink this?" "We can't." Nina shook her head. "Bella's going to meet us. If we crap out on him, he'll be all alone to take the heat. C'mon, I think we can fool her if we do what she doesn't expect."

"Which is what?"

But Nina didn't stop to explain. Instead, she stomped over to the front door as loudly as she could, noisily threw the bolt, and walked out into the night.

"Great!" Alastaire said, running after her. "Great! That made about as much noise as ringing the doorbell. Nina, are you totally nuts?"

"I want her to hear us. I want her to follow us outside. That way, we can lose her in the garden while we go back inside."

"And how do we lose her?"

"Duck back in through the kitchen. If we're fast enough, she won't see us."

They walked down the long path bordered with boxwood hedges, brushing their hands against them, but that didn't make much noise. When they got to the big magnolia tree at the corner of the garden, they had better luck, finding lots of dry, leathery leaves to step on. A beam of light shot out through the front door, and they heard Agatha call out sharply, "Who's out there?"

"Good. Let's put some distance between us." Nina sprinted

across the big lawn, which was far too open for comfort but would clearly show Agatha someone in a long, black dress running, and being followed—a little reluctantly—by a second nearly identical figure. They heard Agatha yell, "Stop!" and the beam of the flashlight swung their way, but by then, they were already in the shadows of the banana trees, hiding behind their thick stalks.

"Eewww."

"What?" Nina whispered.

"I think I stepped on a banana. It felt all squishy."

"So wipe it off."

"I *hope* it was a banana."

"Alastaire, focus. Now's not the time to go grossing ourselves out!"

They could see Agatha walking across the lawn toward them, sweeping the beam of her flashlight from side to side. Just then, a small creature flew out of a live oak far over to their left, and Agatha turned her light toward it. They could see her scanning the branches of the trees.

"Come on," Nina said. "She's as distracted as she's going to get. Let's get going."

"It's a lucky thing that bird showed up," Alastaire muttered as they crept back toward the school, now moving as quietly as they could. "She'd have caught us for sure!"

"Don't you know who that was?" Nina asked when they were back inside the kitchen, with the door safely closed.

"Who?"

"Bella. He must have heard her or figured it out. You saw him turn into a bat the other day in Animal Dominance. He's very good at it."

"Oh. Oh, yeah. I knew that," Alastaire said, picking at a fingernail. "I was just wondering if you did."

They walked as quietly as they could down the long hallway to the chapel, and when they got there, Nina wasn't entirely surprised to see Bella putting his pants back on.

"Glad you made it," he said, grinning. "I do like the chance to get a little exercise. Well, ladies, shall we break and enter?"

He held out his key, and he fit it in the lock and opened the door. They slipped into the chapel, locking the door again securely behind them.

The room was, if anything, even more intimidating and beautiful at night than it was during the day. A low fire burned in the cup on the altar, not the red blaze Nina had seen in the carriage house but banked and flickering. It lit the strange, larger-than-life-size paintings on the walls into a far-too-realistic impression of animation, so the lovely, muscular creatures seemed to coil and throb and pulse with their own strange energy. The chandeliers, thirty feet up, looked dark and threatening, like dangerous torture implements, and the pews could have held anything in their Gothic shadows. Nina stopped and could hear her own heart beating in her ears, and she wondered if the others could hear it too.

"Okay, so where do we start?" Bella whispered.

"The cup." Nina took a deep breath. "Maybe it's got a clue, something we can decipher." Stepping up onto the altar, she reached out her hand for the cup and then hesitated.

"Do you think it's got an alarm attached?"

Bella and Alastaire both shrugged. Nina could imagine a siren going off, or a steel cage dropping down around her, or even the cup exploding. Hoping very much that none of those things would happen, she counted to three, took an even deeper breath, and snatched up the cup.

Nothing happened. Absolutely nothing. Not even a flicker in the glowing fire inside, which shone up at her as placidly as a candle flame. She felt a little embarrassed and, frankly, more than a little surprised.

"Okay, um . . . well, that was easy. Let's take a look at it."

It was just then that the cup started to vibrate in her hands, and a moment later, the fire inside drew together and changed again to a dark red liquid. *Definitely blood this time*, she thought. She could smell it, unmixed with anything else. She could also feel it, as the cup started filling and then overflowing with what seemed like an ocean of blood, a geyser, that started running down over her hands and spilling onto the floor. The blood was hot and oily and sticky and totally disgusting, and it was all she could do not to drop the whole filthy mess.

The cup was *beating* like a living heart—there was no other word for it—and it pumped what felt like gallons of blood out to splash all around her, soaking her. She looked wildly at Bella and Alastaire, but they were backing away with equal expressions of horror. She thought, *Quick, what would Professor Danvers do?* and the answer came to her: *Of course, he'd drink it. He'd drink every drop.*

She looked at the cup that was still pumping up huge gouts of blood like a sliced artery. She realized she had very little choice. She had to do *something* before the blood started running out under the door. Telling her stomach not to betray her, she lifted the cup to her lips and drank.

The blood disappeared the moment her lips touched the edge of the cup, as did the light.

They were plunged into total darkness, thick and stinking as a slaughterhouse.

"Great," Bella whispered. "You certainly know how to put on a rock show."

"Shh," Nina said, trying to see around her. The cup hung

heavily from her hand, and the blood had definitely disappeared. The iron cup felt cold and dry to the touch.

Just then, a soft whisper of light became apparent against the farthest wall, like a hand pressing against a soft, stretchy surface. Nina watched in fascination as the wall stretched and stretched and grew thinner and thinner, and then the little girl Zoolie was standing there again, cold and shivering in her short, black dress.

"Zoolie!" Nina said. "I didn't know you could do that, go other places than in the attic!"

"Yes," the little girl whispered. "We can go through the walls. I heard you."

"You, um . . ." Nina swallowed, not knowing how to ask this. "Did you just see that?"

"Yes." The little girl didn't come any closer, so after a moment, Nina put the cup back on the altar and walked slowly down between the pews and ap-proached her. She could feel Bella and Alastaire huddling behind her, but they'd just have to wait for explanations.

"Zoolie, if you could see that, I should tell you why we're here. We're trying to find out more about the Four Gifts. Do you know anything about them?"

Zoolie smiled. "Yes, I know."

"Do you know what they are?"

Zoolie's pressed her lips together, then, "There's a riddle. I'll tell you . . ."

> *I am that thing that beggars gold and makes jewels hide in*
> *   shame,*
> *But vaults and banks can't hold me, and misers shun my name.*
> *For blessed is he who owns me, though a pauper he may be,*
> *For he shall see things clearly, when he learns to see through*
> *   me.*

I am the thing men long for most, and struggle to procure, But only when I'm cast away will my gifts become yours. My ways are subtle, secretive, and faith must be your goal, If you would own my fire, and let me warm your soul.

In forests dark I'm hidden, and oft passed by unseen, For I'm that deepest part of you that's only known in dreams. Your past, your gains and losses, are all contained in me,

So if you would see clearly, touch my leaves and climb my tree. I am the wind and weather that can blast the world away. And blood is mine, and life is mine, and death is in my sway. All life must bow before me, for in time you all shall see, That run the wide world over, you all belong to me.

"Great," Alastaire muttered, "like the prophecy wasn't enough . . ." but Zoolie was already fading back into the wall, pushing back through the soft goo of matter.

And then she was gone.

The chapel was pitch dark for a moment, and then the light flickered on again in the cup and everything was the same as before. Completely normal.

"What the holy hell was that?" Alastaire exploded, but Nina had to admit she didn't know. She felt a terrible pounding in her head, and her mouth tasted foul and metallic from even the little sip of blood she'd swallowed. She thought she might be going to puke again.

"I-I met her before," she whispered. "Up in the attic," and she sat down in the nearest pew to keep from falling. "Her name's Zoolie. She . . . I don't know . . . I think she's a ghost or something. The thing is, I think I know what the answer is now."

"A mirror, a cup full of fire, a wooden wand, and a sword that bleeds," Bella said. "That's the answer to the riddle. The Four Gifts."

"I guess so," Nina said, and then she fainted.

Chapter Sixteen

Nina didn't know how she got back to her own room. She imagined Bella and Alastaire must have helped her upstairs—Alastaire was pretty strong. She woke up in her own bed the next morning, fully dressed, stiff from head to toe, and with the terrible wish she could just believe the whole previous day had been a dream. Or make that the last couple of weeks.

She smelled scrambled eggs and fresh coffee as she walked downstairs, but she was still trying to convince herself this was all an illusion. Bella and Alastaire were already in the Commons, and she sat down next to them and said, "Did anyone ever hallucinate breakfast when they were going out of their minds?"

"I don't think so," Bella said.

"Then I guess this is all real, huh?"

"As real as it gets." Alastaire handed her a cup of coffee. "Drink this. You look like ass."

"Thanks." Nina sipped. "So, what do we do next?"

"Well . . ." Bella pushed away his eggs. "I need to do some research. I wrote down Zoolie's riddle. Here's a copy. I've got to go to the library and start reading up on the Four Gifts—what powers they have and what someone could do with them. And I think we'd better check out General Azazel and see what he's been up to."

"Oh, I know all about him," Alastaire said unexpectedly, pouring half a pitcher of cream into her coffee. "What? Haven't you two ever read *My Life and Lives*?"

Clearly, Bella hadn't read it, and even more clearly, he didn't seem to want to. "That self-serving piece of crap? I wouldn't use it to wipe my dog's butt, if I had a dog, which I don't."

"Well, smarty-pants, then you don't know he's a big deal pundit now. His memoir sold like a gazillion copies, and he writes for the *Midnight Times*. He's in practically every issue. He's like a total right-wing nut-job, of course, saying we should kill everybody who's not a Skin Eater and start a holy war to take over the world." Alastaire stuffed a big forkful of eggs into her mouth and added, "Ma p'rnts think hs grt."

"What?" both Nina and Bella asked at once.

"My parents think he's great," Alastaire said, swallowing. "They're both pretty much right-wing nut-jobs themselves. They're very anti-Sister Aquilina."

Nina was starting to think maybe Sister Aquilina had her good points, if the people who were against her were that much worse. But she didn't say anything. *After all, what do I know? They're probably right to be scared.*

"Anyway," Alastaire continued in between chews, "I guess it makes sense his daughter's married to one of the Saturni hotshots. And of course it makes sense that his adoptive granddaughter's a skanky ho."

"Actually, Alastaire, there's no evidence whatsoever that Simone Freeland is a skanky—"

"God, Bella, you're so literal! What*ever*. At any rate, I'll bet he knows everything about the Four Gifts. It's a pity we can't ask him."

"Maybe we can," Nina said after a moment. "You said he writes a column?"

"Yeah, it's called "My Views" or "Why We Should Arm Bears" or something like that." "Does he answer letters?"

"Sometimes." Alastaire looked at her. "You can't be thinking what I think you're thinking."

"Why not?"

"Because he'd know where a letter came from, for one thing. He'd know it came from here at Daedalus. And we can't email him, because you need a computer for that."

"So we don't send it from here, and we don't use our own computer." Nina lowered her voice. "Lots of people at CC's have laptops, right? We'll just ask to borrow one. That one gutterblood we saw looked like he'd do anything for twenty bucks."

Bella bit his lip. "You know, Nina's plan actually might work. Not that General Azazel would necessarily answer us, but at least we could see what he'd do."

"And then we'd know more about what Professor Danvers was talking about when he mentioned him to Dr. Freeland." Nina frowned. "It seemed like he was almost threatening her when he brought her father up. There's got to be more going on there than meets the eye."

They agreed to meet next Saturday at CC's, which still left them with six days to pretend nothing was the matter. Glancing up at the teacher's table, Nina wondered how many of the faculty were having the same problem. Professor Danvers had on dark glasses, and he looked like he was nursing the Hangover from Hell. And Agatha looked even worse. She had a big Band-Aid on her forehead, and Nina wondered if she'd hit her head chasing them around in the dark the night before.

She went off to her first class wondering how she'd meet anyone's eyes, now that she knew what she knew. She wanted to scream at all the *jumbies,* "Run!" but she knew she couldn't do that. For one thing, they probably wouldn't believe her. She watched them in the hallways, slumping off to whatever remedial classes they were allowed to take. *Why teach them at all? Why don't they just let them smoke dope and eat ice cream? Was it to keep them from knowing, keep them from abandoning hope? What had*

Alastaire said? "Imagine knowing there's nobody in the whole wide world who really wants you?"

History with Professor Seneschal was in some ways the hardest class, because she wanted to scream at him to "Wake up!" and tell her something she could *use,* when all he did was sleep.

The first glimmer came when he roused himself with a snort and said, "Naturally, Bernard de Marigny never forgave Francois Livaudais for abandoning his wife."

Nina raised her hand and asked, "Was this the same Madame Livaudais who used to own the whole Garden District?"

"The very same, yes."

"But why did Bernard de Marigny care what happened to her?"

"Because she was his sister, of course. De Marigny was her maiden name. Ah, names . . . names are such perplexing things, aren't they? After all, we have alliterations, synonyms . . . The Arabs saw puns as a kind of cosmic code . . ." He seemed to be drifting off again.

"Professor, is there anything—" she tried to think how to put this "—special about the number four?"

He blinked at her. He seemed to be really trying, fighting against the cobwebs in his own brain. "Four is, of course, a very important number. Four compass points . . . four cardinal virtues for our kind—Wisdom, Love, Memory, and Destruction—and of course, the Saturni are based on the number four."

"They are? How do you figure that?"

"Well, the Saturni were originally called the Party of Four. Didn't you know that? Mmm, let's see . . . General Azazel, he represented the military." He held up one trembling, arthritic finger. "And John Benway brought his great wealth to bear." He carefully held up a second one. "And Father Ignatius Ragoczy represented the Church," and he slowly raised a third finger. "And of course, our own beloved headmaster represented both spiritual and temporal power."

"But—" Nina shook her head. "But I thought the headmaster just ran things here at the school? Was he something more than that? Was he a teacher?"

"He was. The greatest teacher the world has ever known. He wrote a book, *The Science of the Mysteries.* But you know . . ." Professor Seneschal's eyes blurred as he gazed into the middle distance, and he seemed to be trembling. "There's a great power in teaching. You hold a person's mind in the palm of your hand. You can bend them, break them, tear down everything they know, and burn the ideas out of their heads like wildfire. The greatest teachers in the world have always in some ways been the most merciless . . . Mercy me. Now, what was I . . . Oh yes, names. Bernard de Marigny . . . well, of course he was crazy about his sister . . ."

And he nodded off, his head falling forward onto the desk with a surprisingly loud thump, although as far as she could tell, that still didn't wake him up. Nina tried to ignore the laughter all around her and scribbled down what he'd just said, but by the end of the class, she still had no clear idea what he'd been talking about.

The rest of the day was pretty much the same, and by that evening, she was still no closer to solving any of the riddles facing her. After dinner, she strolled into the library, where some students were reading and others were playing Hearts. She had a morbid desire to ask them if they were using real hearts to keep score, and if so, whose. She looked for a copy of *The Science of the Mysteries,* but she wasn't entirely surprised to find it wasn't there. If the Saturni had decided to erase Mr. O'Brien, they'd certainly have made sure to ban his book. She walked back upstairs to her attic and sat down at her desk, thinking about the number four. Four gifts. Four divination objects. The four cardinal virtues.

Four parts of the Saturni: the Army, Big Business, Education, and the Church. The Four Horsemen of the Apocalypse. Professor Seneschal was right; the number four certainly did mean a lot of things.

She took out a piece of paper and wrote down Bella's answers to Zoolie's riddle. Bella had said there were the four divination objects: the mirror that you could see through, a cup full of fire, a wooden wand that was obviously part of a tree, and a sword that bled death. Why were those answers so unsatisfactory to her?

She frowned. Because the riddle seemed to mean so much more than that. Bella's literalism seemed to have missed the point. She looked at her copy of Zoolie's riddle.

I am that thing that beggars gold and makes jewels hide in shame, But vaults and banks can't hold me, and misers shun my name.

For blessed is he who owns me, though a pauper he may be, For he shall see things clearly, when he learns to see through me.

She tried to puzzle it out. What beggared gold and made jewels hide in shame? What made a pauper rich if he had it, because then he could see clearly?

And the answer came to her as if she'd glimpsed it in her own interior mirror: Wisdom.

Which made it a piece of cake to figure out the rest of the riddle. What did men long for most and struggled to procure?

Love.

What hid in forests dark, in dreams, and showed you your past? Memory.

What wind would blast the world away and, ultimately, claim all men? Destruction, death.

Nina gaped at the piece of paper in front of her. It wasn't necessarily *the* answer to the riddle, but it was certainly *an* answer, and one which was a lot more satisfying than just figuring out how the Four Gifts were four material objects.

The Four Gifts were four *ideas.*

Except that couldn't be right either, because then how could somebody steal them? What had Sally said? "Thoughts aren't things." So how could Sister Aquilina steal the Four Gifts if they weren't four literal things?

She rubbed her eyes, her head spinning. She was tired. She was sick. She still felt her skin crawling with the knowledge of what she'd learned about all these people. Changing into a T-shirt, she got into bed and, leaving the lamp lit, tried to will her mind into unconsciousness. The air in the attic was warm, and there were soft breezes blowing once again through her open window, but she shuddered as a feeling of dread suddenly overwhelmed her, and then she felt a cold, soft touch against her throat.

It wasn't tight, like a strangling fist. More like a single icy finger moving up to her lips.

She tried to move, but the finger commanded obedience, *hush,* and she lay still. She felt someone tracing, with infinite care, the soft lines of her mouth.

Ohhh . . . She shut her eyes. Oh, this was lovely, but what was going on? She tried to scream. She tried to concentrate. *There are so many mysteries here* . . . as the pad of a cold thumb parted her lips, and she was helpless to restrain her tongue from darting out to taste . . . nothing.

No taste, no scent, but the thumb entered her mouth, and she gave in to the urge to suckle on it. She felt the rest of a hand come up to cup her cheek, and as she sucked greedily, she thought, *I can't believe I'm doing this. What's come over me?* She felt another hand come up and tangle itself in her hair, and she sighed, and then she felt a strong sense of longing. She was surrounded by such a silent, lonely ache that she shut her eyes, and felt tears starting at the corners of her eyelids.

What did he want? Who did he even imagine she was? She thought about all the lost children there, the lost parents, the lost families of the Skin Eaters. How did anyone find out anything when facts were like needles in a haystack and memories were as slippery as lies? The cold hand finally moved and slid down to her throat again, caressing and molding her neck, and she heard Professor Danvers's voice in her head, whispering, *"Mine, always mine ... Oh, Niobe ..."*

She got up then and went and stood by the open window, trying to breathe in the fresh night air and still her racing heart. Something *majorly* strange was going on here, and she needed to put some distance between it and herself. Gradually, her pulse slowed. Here, looking out at the Garden District, her vantage point gave her trees, rooftops, and a vista of scudding clouds.

The moon was shrouded. Birds—or were they bats?—flew like individual scraps of burned paper here and there, and the softly breathing night, rich with new life, settled her. There had always been storms here. There had always been surface glitter and balls and, beneath that, danger and, beneath that, stubborn life. Maybe she shouldn't be so frightened by anything she'd learned about the Skinnies. Maybe even the horrible facts of what they did could be made to fit into a universe that still made sense. Maybe she just needed to get used to it, like learning the facts of life. Maybe all that was happening was that she was scaring herself, playing at doing magic and learning terrible secrets in this strange, dark house.

Yeah, right, she thought. *Maybe.*

She narrowed her eyes. She could see directly across to the

carriage house, and suddenly she realized that the curtains on the top floor there had been drawn back. The whole top floor wasn't so much illuminated as lit by a stealthy glow, like a single candle flame. She thought, *Are they scanning the night sky? But surely it was too cloudy.* Whatever it was, someone was moving around in there who didn't want to be observed, and who didn't think they *were* being observed, either.

She held her breath. Shit, I wish I could see better. What I really need is a good pair of binoculars. Was that a faint beam of moonlight striking the noctoscope? Someone seemed to be moving it slowly from side to side, as if searching the night sky for something. She saw the moonlight glint off it again as it was pushed roughly to one side, and then the light brightened and she could see clearly for a moment. Two figures seemed to be grappling there together, or embracing, she couldn't tell which—and one of them looked an awful lot like Agatha Danvers.

And the other one? The other figure was a tall woman dressed all in black, whom she'd never seen before except in her dreams, and in Professor Danvers's mirror. She had a strong nose and raven dark hair and dark eyes and a pale, coldly beautiful face. Sister Aquilina.

Sister Aquilina turned around just then and seemed to be looking right at her, and Nina fought the impulse to yell, even though no one could have heard her. And a moment later, another cloud covered the moon, and she couldn't see anything anymore. *Shit.*

Shit shit shit shit shit! She flung herself away from the window and sat back down on her bed, hugging her knees. Had she seen me? It was entirely possible. *I'm such a jerk. Why didn't I at least put the lamp out?* But the damage was done. The question now was what should she do next?

Should she tell someone? Who? Run downstairs and say, "Oh,

I just happened to be looking out my window, which is supposed to be closed, when I saw your worst enemy wrestling with Agatha Danvers . . ." Right, like that would win her any more friends.

Okay, so what *could* she do? She closed her eyes and breathed in a measured cadence a few times to steady herself. She could tell Professor Danvers, that's what, if she could find him. So . . . could she do that? Could she locate him now simply by thinking about him, calling out from her mind to his? It was certainly worth a shot. She sat up and pressed her fingers against her temples and thought, *Professor Danvers, I really,* really *need to speak to you.*

Nothing happened.

Perhaps she just needed to try harder. She concentrated on his beautiful face, his compelling voice. *Professor, it's me. It's Nina Lamb. Something important has happened, and I really need to tell you about it.*

This time, she felt a faint, a *very* faint vibration in the pit of her stomach—was it ESP or just gas? She tried again. *Please, Professor, if you can hear me, let me know. Send me a sign. I've got to know if I'm crazy to even be trying this.*

She heard what sounded like an impatient sigh, and it certainly sounded like him. She decided to try out in the hallway, or maybe even on the stairs? She could always run back inside if she heard someone coming. Stealthily she opened her door, thinking, *Professor, please, let me know where you are. Tell me how to find you . . .* and there was a very slight but definite vibration in the air in front of her. She thought she could see a pair of dark eyes for an instant. Taking a deep breath, she started down the stairs. What was the worst they could do to her, anyway? She couldn't just stay in her room doing nothing. If they literally bit her head off, that would at least be the end of all her troubles.

She reminded herself to watch the treads on the stairs that

creaked. She gave herself time to let her eyes get used to the dark. The school was asleep all around her, no whisper of movement stirring, no intruder's footfall or the sweep of a long black dress giving anything away. She thought, not for the first time, surely drapes would be a little less oppressive around here than plywood, but now was not the time to think about redecorating. When she reached the second floor, she felt her way along the wall, making her way stealthily toward the Headmaster's Office.

Which was empty. *Well, of course,* she told herself, *you didn't really think he* slept *there, did you?*

She crept over to the window and peeked through a crack in the boards. She could see past the wrought-iron balcony to the street, deserted and strangely unreal-looking at night. Could she light a lamp? It might be seen. But one of the boards was just leaning up against the long pass-through window, she noticed, as though . . . as though perhaps Professor Danvers had taken it away himself and let in a shaft of ambient light. She lifted the heavy board away as quietly as she could, and the moon's faint glow illuminated the room. Then she turned and looked around.

Well, the office was certainly impressive, even faintly lit. Here were the strange machines, the orrery and the pendulum gleaming faintly. Here was the safe, looking squat and ugly and dark, and . . . oh. Did it really have Acme Security Company written on it in raised letters? It sure did. She giggled. It was like an old Road Runner cartoon.

Here, too, was the big, heavy desk, piled high with papers and notes and what even looked like scrolls. Here was a litter of pens, a pair of reading glasses, chewing gum wrappers—he chewed *gum?*—and more obscure things, like a strand of cowrie shells, a black crow's feather, and . . . What was this? She held it up.

A small book. Inscribed with faded gilt letters, *The Science of the Mysteries.*

All *right*. The headmaster's book. She didn't waste a second but brought it over into the light.

On the flyleaf was written: "To Strickland, With All My Love, C. B," and she turned the page and read "Epigraph: All Things Will Die."

Clearly the blue river chimes in its flowing Under my eye;
Warmly and broadly the south winds are blowing Over the sky.
One after another the white clouds are fleeting; Every heart this
*   May morning in joyance is beating.*
Full merrily; Yet all things must die.
The stream will cease to flow; The wind will cease to blow;
The clouds will cease to fleet; The heart will cease to beat;
For all things must die. All things must die.

Well, *that* was kind of depressing. Who wrote that? She looked down at the bottom. Alfred Lord Tennyson. Him again. She turned to the Table of Contents.

1: The Truth About Crossing.

2: The Semiotics of Lies

3: Eat or Be Eaten

4: All Changed, Changed Utterly

5: Orphans

She hesitated. Maybe she shouldn't be reading this? What she really wanted to do was just stick the book in her pocket and read it later, but that inscription—"To Strickland, With All My Love"— made her uncomfortable about actually stealing it. She turned over the page to the first Chapter and read the first passage:

It is a truth universally acknowledged that when the Saturni created the Skin Eaters, they had no thought but for their own ease in crafting a source of willing labor, bound by their own damnation. They made them to be their shock troops, fed on flesh. No one should glamorize the Saturni's cold-blooded decision in thus condemning the unhappy beings they engendered, or minimize the self-replicating nature of the curse they placed on them, to endlessly infect others over the years. However, for those undergoing the transformative process, it may be helpful to understand the various stages.

Well, that pretty much said it, didn't it? She wasn't entirely surprised to discover the Saturni had created the Skin Eaters, but she was impressed the headmaster had been able to say so that plainly in a book.

And the next words appalled her:

Skin Eating is a virus secreted through the saliva, by means of transdermal inoculation (i.e., a bite) or by direct contact with infectious material, e.g., saliva, cerebrospinal fluid, nerve tissue, etc. In most cases, the infectious host bites, chews, or in some cases, tears a hole in the subject's skin with his or her fingernails, so the viral material is introduced. This may be done anywhere on the subject's body, although ganglia-rich sites such as those near the spinal column, the brachial plexus (the neck), the sacral plexus (the lower back), and the femoral and pudendal nerves (the sex) are often used. In rarer cases, material from an infectious Skin Eater may be directly ingested by the subject. Thus, you can "cross" with a Skin Eater either by being bitten by them, or by eating them.

Oh my God, she thought. *No, no, no, I don't want to be reading this! I don't want to know any of this!*

But something made her go on.

Luckily, most subjects experience a feeling of dreamy euphoria, which leads to the perception of crossing as a spiritual process. This is indeed fortunate, since subsequent crossings entail more and more physical discomfort. In the later stages, subjects experience pain, severe headache, stumbling, difficulty seeing, vomiting, delirium, convulsions, and terror, all leading eventually to complete bodily paralysis and a seeming death-in-life of suspended animation. It is from this last cataleptic trance that the subject will finally emerge, as if reborn, fully transformed into a functional and autonomous Skin Eater.

She sat down in Professor Danvers's chair and stared at the book in horror. This was the truth; finally, an explanation for why some of the students looked sick and dizzy, why some of them vomited and staggered and twitched and drooled. They were becoming Skin Eaters. They were becoming more fully infected with a *virus.* She read further:

Unlike rabies, in this case changes occur to the actual structural anatomy of the subject's cells. Once introduced, the virus works to transform the body, suppressing the human and stimulating the primal animal instinct, while at the same time intelligence, strength, and recuperative powers are also heightened.

They can do extraordinary things, she thought. *They can transform. They can heal really quickly. And it's true, it's not magic, it's not magic at all. Everything they can do, everything they become, is the result of a* disease.

"Aggression rises," she read aloud this time. "Inhibitions melt away. The infected subject now is set on its inexorable path to becoming a Skin Eater, and will likely spend the last period of its transformation on the attack, chasing and lunging and biting, as if in the throes of madness . . ."

She felt sick. Someone had written in the margin, "We become beasts," this handwriting far different from the inscription, an angry black slash. She flipped through other pages, reading at random:

It has become an unfortunate dogma of modern Skin Eaters that students should be kept ignorant of the changes they will be undergoing, under the assumption that this will lessen their feelings of dread. But on the contrary, deliberate lying will only result in a general breakdown of confidence in authority . . .

No shit, she thought. *They don't know what's going to hit them.* She also read:

Changes brought about on the mitochondrial level make it necessary for all mature Skin Eaters to ingest a certain amount of human meat weekly, usually at least six or eight ounces, or else run the risk of eventual starvation . . .

A potion which quells our hunger, at least temporarily, she remembered. *It's a blend of blood, in this case a sheep's blood, valerian root, and human ashes.*

And finally, she read:

I find myself imagining the nightmare existence of those whom our hungers have left behind, and I confess myself full of sorrow and regret.

And at the very end of the book, there was a handwritten poem:

The spirits that did once us make Now make us theirs, as they
Did once live solely for the sake Of Him whose realm is day.

Now night in fastness closes all And makes all gray, until
One shall arrive to lift the pall And open the jars of ill.

And just then the doorknob turned and Professor Danvers came in and turned the light on and saw her reading the book and yelled, "Put that down this instant!"

She jumped up and put the book back down on the desk. The professor looked sleepy and rumpled in a long, dark robe, his hair disordered and falling into his eyes. They stared at each other for a moment longer, and then he exploded, "Good God, girl, what the hell is wrong with you? Are you stalking me? Isn't there *anything* of mine that you don't have the overwhelming need to *paw* over?"

She felt angry as well, and snapped, "I just picked up the book because it was lying right there in plain sight. I didn't . . . I didn't do anything wrong. And besides, I have something really important to tell you. That's why I called you here—"

"*You* called *me* here?" he asked, his voice venomous. "To my own office?"

"It's not your office, it's the headmaster's. And besides . . . it . . . it wasn't locked."

"Do I have to lock my own *toilet* to keep you out of there too?"

"I—" Nina decided this was getting her nowhere. She started again. "Look, I needed to see you. That's why I called out to you. I was trying to call out to you from my bedroom, but I couldn't reach you, so I had to come down here."

Damn it, that didn't sound right either. Why was everything she was saying sounding like some kind of weird, sexy *come-on?* Maybe because she was standing there in a T-shirt, and he was standing there in his bathrobe and clearly nothing else.

She tore her eyes away from the sight of his bare feet and said, "Professor, there's something terribly wrong."

"Tell me about it." He ran his hand over his face. "I'm going to have a drink, Miss Lamb. And no, you may not join me." He walked over to his desk, got a bottle and a glass out of the bottom drawer, and poured himself a tumbler of thick, red liquid. "Besides—" he smirked as he took a sip "—we've already determined this isn't your beverage of choice."

"Sir, how can you do it?" That wasn't what she'd wanted to ask him, but she'd just blurted it out. Seeing him grimace as he took another swallow, she thought, *He hates it. He hated eating that one bite of dinner the other night. The whole bloody business makes him sick.*

"Miss Lamb," Professor Strickland said, clearly enunciating each syllable, "there are many, many terms for what you are at this moment, but the most descriptive one is Pain in the Ass. A *Colossal* Pain in the Ass, to be exact. If you can manage to keep your utterly misplaced pity to yourself, you can stay. Otherwise, please go back to bed while you're still in one piece."

He sank back in his chair and pressed the glass against his forehead, and she moved quickly around the desk away from him, taking a seat in one of the two big armchairs. She wanted to ask him so many things, but she realized now wasn't the time. She kept a tight hold, instead, on her reason for coming there.

"Did you hear what I was saying?" she said. "I need to talk to you about something."

"What?" He looked at her finally, clearly challenging her to spit out whatever foolish, childish, ridiculous thing she had to say.

She almost told him, "Your sister's fighting with Sister Aquilina up in the carriage house," but she knew if she did that, he'd just laugh at her. Instead, she put her chin up and said, "Look for yourself, sir. You can read my mind. Check it out."

He raised his eyebrows. "Much as I appreciate the offer, I'm afraid I'll have to decline. Adolescent daydreams don't interest me."

"Oh, for God's sake!" She slapped the arm of her chair. She had no idea how she had the nerve to be this rude to him, but it *was* two o'clock in the morning, and he *was* just sitting there getting sloshed on blood in his bathrobe, and she *had* just seen a majorly dangerous Skin Eater on the grounds. "I'm not flirting, Professor. I'm serious! Look inside my goddamn mind and you'll see what I saw! She might even still be here somewhere if you'd just stop farting around!"

He was out of his chair in a flash, and his hand grasped her chin in an iron grip, and she thought, *Uh-oh, bad move,* before she felt him plunge into her mind. It was like being swept away by a tidal wave. She struggled against the assault as she felt him hunting here and there in her thoughts, trying to see what she'd seen, and then he flung himself away from her and said bitterly, "That's ridiculous. She can't be here; it's just not possible."

"Why not?" Nina rubbed her jaw. "Have you got some kind of security system that keeps out powerful magicians I haven't heard about? Otherwise, what's so impossible?"

"She can't be here, because she's *dead*, that's why. My sister is dead, Miss Lamb."

And all of a sudden it hit her. It was like someone had turned a light on in her head.

Sister Aquilina. Why was she called that? "Is she a nun?" Sally had asked. "I've known some pretty scary nuns in my day."

Niobe Danvers had known the only way to prove her innocence was to cross with Sister Aquilina. But Sister Aquilina hadn't died, because she'd been the only person up there in the attic in the first place.

What had Bella said? "Some people say she made it up herself as a kind of inside joke."

Niobe Danvers and Sister Aquilina were the same person. Sister Aquilina was Professor

Danvers's sister.

Nina felt lightheaded, as a flood of other things made sense as well. Bernard de Marigny never forgave Francois Livaudais for abandoning his wife. He was crazy about his sister. And Sister Aquilina had disappeared right after that conflict in the attic. Nobody knew where she'd gone. But if Sister Aquilina and Niobe were the same person, and she had known she had to get out of sight, then she might just have made a brilliant escape by faking her own death.

Nina said very quietly, "Actually, Professor, I don't think she's dead."

And Professor Danvers just looked at her and sighed. "No, I guess she isn't."

She looked up at him sharply. "You *knew*? You *knew* she was alive all along?"

"I . . . hoped. I . . . suspected. I . . ." He got up, walked over to the window, and leaned his full weight against the plywood. He looked like he wanted to break through it and throw himself down into the street. "All right. *Yes.* I knew she was alive. Happy?"

He swallowed, then proceeded in a calmer tone. "I've known Niobe was alive for the past thirty years, but she made herself into something I can't go near now, something I can't touch. I have the exquisite pleasure of knowing that the only person I care about in the whole world is alive *some*where, and I can never even say her name without pretending she's a myth or a goddamn metaphor! I hope the irony isn't lost on you, Miss Lamb, because it certainly pisses the hell out of me."

Nina felt his anger washing over her, but most of all, what she felt was sorry. She was so, so sorry for him. And she was so, so sorry for *herself*, because what did that make her? A kid. A nuisance. Someone with a stupid crush on a teacher who wasn't remotely interested in her. After all, he was ages older than she was. In fact, if her hunch was right, he was at least two hundred years old.

She asked, "Sir, when were you born?"

His lips quirked. There was something almost comical in his look of complete and utter surprise. Whatever he'd been expecting, it wasn't that.

"A while ago," he said.

"How old are you?"

"I'm . . . older than I look."

"I know, sir. I mean, I know all Skin Eaters are, like, effectively immortal, so you could be like two or three hundred years old, and she . . . she could be . . ."

She stopped. He continued to look at her, and she could hear his thoughts again, except they were all mixed up. *"She's smart,"* he was thinking, *"She's so smart and so young, and goddamn Crux and Jack Benway and the Saturni and me, me, me for being a horse's ass and letting this go on this far. I should never have let myself be alone with her. I should never have dreamed of her, and . . . Wait a minute, have I got this right? Did she dream that dream too? And what does that mean, that she dreamed of me the way I dreamed of her, and she doesn't just think I'm a dirty old man? Does that mean that she . . ."*

"In 1749," he said, shutting his eyes. "Yes. All right? I'm *that* old. Although I haven't used the name Bernard de Marigny for a long, long time."

She sat still and let her mind try to take it all in, but Professor Danvers wasn't giving her enough time for it. "Miss Lamb, let me make this perfectly clear to you. In order for my sister to survive, she had to become what she is now. A pariah. An outcast. A . . . I don't even know what she is anymore! She's probably more spirit now than anything else. But yes, she's alive. Although quite frankly the idea of her being *here* at Daedalus is beyond ludicrous."

"But I-I saw her."

"Whatever you 'saw,' Miss Lamb, it was clearly a trick of the moonlight and nothing more. I'm telling you *it could never happen*. Niobe and I shared a bond that makes *our* bond look like wet Kleenex. I'd know if she was in the same state, much less right out there in the carriage house."

He turned away from her again, but not before she could see his lips were pressed so tightly together that he looked like he was trying not to scream. She felt her own heart clench with a despair so profound she could literally feel it breaking in her chest, and she finally said, "You could go out and check."

"What do you mean?" His words were like ice.

She swallowed. "You could go out there now and see if she's there. I-I don't mind. I'll stay here, or I'll go back to bed and forget I saw anything. Um, what I mean is, I won't give you away."

He turned around slowly then, running his palms over his face to wipe away what she realized suddenly were tears. How could someone cry without moving a muscle? When he finally spoke again, his voice was low. "You really would do that, wouldn't you?"

She started to answer him, but he went on with, "You really would keep my secret, wouldn't you? God, you have no idea what you're even talking about! You truly have no idea what you're wading into, what muck you're already into up to your armpits, and goddamn it, I still don't know how old you are! You may still be a child, and yet you're willing to be so insanely . . . stupidly . . . *gallant*. God, it's enough to make someone puke."

He shook his head and seemed visibly trying to control himself. He went and sat back down in his chair and said, "I'm sorry, Miss Lamb. You're a very nice young lady. You should be going to Sacred Heart Academy or Huey Long High School in East Bumfuck, Louisiana. Not here. You should be worrying about who's going to take you to the senior prom, or who's going to ask you to dance at the next Carnival ball. Why on earth you're here instead, meddling in . . . I'm sorry . . . 'involved' in things you don't understand and can't possibly understand and, by any yardstick of common morality, shouldn't *have* to understand, I have no idea. That's not for me to say. What you should know is, right now, your girlish romantic notions of sex and love and tragedy are not only inappropriate, they're almost obscenely wrong. My sister and I knew no tragedy. What we knew, what we *know*, is heartbreak. Nothing more. I'll never be able to see her again because I simply don't *believe* I'll ever be able to see her again. That's all. Niobe might have believed. But I don't."

He fell silent, and his long, pale fingers strayed to the book on his desk. He touched the binding with an exploratory gesture, almost as though he expected it to bite him. Nina held her breath as he said softly, "'The heart will cease to beat; for all things must die. All things must die.'"

"Is she the person who gave it to you?"

"No. That was somebody else."

"But you still love her."

"Yes."

"So, why don't you give her a chance? Why don't you at least try and see her again?" The question was almost torn out of her against her will, because she didn't *want* him to see her again. She wanted him to forget all about Sister Aquilina. "You believed in her once, sir. Why don't you believe in her now?"

She saw his rage then. She saw the familiar flash of fire in those dark, oh-so-sexy eyes, and the familiar curl of disdain to his lips, which made him look like a dangerous soul in torment. He drew in his breath, no doubt to say something cruel and unbelievably cutting, and then let it out again, as though incapable of putting his fury and frustration into speech. There was even a hint of melancholy laughter in his voice as he said, "You never quit, do you?"

"I guess not."

"Why do you care?"

"Because you…" She licked her lips. "Because in that book, you wrote a note in the margin, 'We become beasts.' You don't like any of this any more than I do. I can tell. And Sister Aquilina is… well, she's trying to fight it, isn't she? I mean, I don't know, maybe she's even worse than those people who asked for that awful dinner party. But if you love someone, you give them a chance, right? You root for them. You don't just despair. I mean, I-I don't know." She turned aside. "You're not like me. Maybe you do."

"I wrote that," he said finally, giving each word weight, "a long time ago, when I felt differently. A little less tired, perhaps. And when I'd thought my sister was our savior. Now, surrounded as she no doubt is by gutterbloods and foundlings, her appreciation for heresy may have dwindled, and mine is worn out. God, you really are funny. I could quite enjoy your being here, if it wasn't… well, if it all wasn't so serious. And now, Miss Lamb, I'd like you to get out. I can't bear to be civil to you a moment longer, and I-I don't want you to see me like this. Just leave and forget you were ever here. No—" he added, as her hand crept toward the desk, "Leave the book. This has been a thoroughly awful evening. Now please go away."

Chapter Seventeen

"I wonder what he meant, 'surrounded as she is now by gutterbloods and foundlings'?" Bella frowned as he sipped his latte, and Nina rolled her eyes. After everything she'd told them, everything she'd described to her friends about her meeting with Professor Danvers (and she hadn't even mentioned her second erotic dream) *this* was what he decided to worry about?

"Who cares?" she snapped. "I just told you he's, like, two hundred years old, and Sister Aquilina is his sister, and I saw her upstairs in the carriage house and all you're worried about is who she's hanging out with? According to *him*? What difference does it make?"

They were sitting in CC's and had just composed the letter to General Azazel.

Dear General,

My friends and I have a bet. Are the Four Gifts real, and if so, what are they? I've heard about them, but no one seems to know exactly what they are. And if they're real, where can I find them?

Signed,
Curious

"I agree, though," Alastaire said, wiping her fingers with a napkin, after having returned the borrowed laptop to the scruffy, blond gutterblood they'd seen the other day. He'd barely looked up enough to grunt a *yup*. "This whole thing is weird. You got these crusties suddenly hanging around here, and Professor Danvers mentions them, and yet he hasn't seen his sister in ages, and so Bella's right—what's up with that? And yuck, I feel like I got fleas now." She scrubbed at her hands again. "How can people let themselves go like that? It's just gross."

"I guess you don't want to go down to the Bywater and chill with them now?" Nina teased.

"I never said—Oh, forget it. What I'm saying is, Nina's right too. How could Professor Danvers know what Sister Aquilina's been doing? He admits he hasn't seen her in thirty years."

"And *I'm* saying, ladies, that you're missing the obvious." Bella put his cup down. "Hello? Who was Sister Aquilina wrestling with when Nina saw her? Who might be in closer contact with Sister Aquilina than her brother? And who could be hiding her presence from said brother?"

Nina and Alastaire both stared at him and then said at the same time, "No way!" and Nina said, "Are you kidding? They were fighting, not talking!"

"That's just what you think you saw." He grabbed Alastaire and appeared to be choking her and then turned it into a hug and gave her a big kiss. He let her go a split second later, blushing as red as a tomato, then got up and almost ran away to the boys' room. Alastaire stared after him and didn't say a word.

"Your mouth's open," Nina said finally.

"Oh. Yeah." Alastaire closed her mouth.

"You're staring."

"Yeah." Alastaire shrugged. "Now I feel like I've got *cooties*."

"He's got a point, though." Nina decided the best way to deal with this extremely un- Bella-like behavior was just to ignore it. "They could have been hugging, for all I know. Agatha could be on Sister Aquilina's side, I guess. Or not. Or it could have been something else entirely. God, now I'm more confused than ever."

"Tell me about it." Alastaire, true to form, took an enormous bite of the chocolate éclair in front of her and followed it up with a big gulp of coffee. "And if Agatha and Sister Aquilina *are* on the same side, then what? Are they *both* bad guys?"

Nina shrugged. She was wishing she'd asked Professor Danvers what he meant about gutterbloods. Should she and Alastaire interrogate the guy sitting across from them? And if they did, would he even talk to them? And what about the word *foundlings*? That sounded like orphans, and weren't orphans a part of the prophecy?

She was distracted by the arrival of the homeless old woman, dressed in her dirty bathrobe and Mardi Gras beads. The woman went up to the counter and got her usual free cup of coffee and then sat in the corner, mumbling. Nina chuckled. "I guess she's a regular."

"Oh, you can say that again." Alastaire smiled. "That's Slippery Annie. They also call her the Old Maid. She's been around for years. Supposedly she was some kind of beauty back in the day, but that must have been back when Jean Lafitte was hanging out in the bayou. Anyway, she's harmless. I'm glad she survived the storm."

Bella came back and sat down, trying, with limited success, to pretend like nothing had happened. "Okay," he said, "so at least we know this much—Sister Aquilina is Niobe Danvers, who's also Madame Livaudais."

"Whose child died," Nina said. "Yes, Alastaire told me about all that."

"Well, but what she probably didn't tell you, since it's *Alastaire*, is that people say she learned the black arts to bring the boy back. Now, we know what that means. Madame Livaudais was a Skinny, so she probably just turned her kid into a Skinny too. Of course, the stories about Madame Livaudais being an evil magician may also be true. People say she learned to command certain voodoo spirits and sealed them into clay jars. They say that's how she got the spirits to do her bidding."

Nina and Bella stared at each other, and then they both got it in the same instant.

"She sealed them," Bella said. "Sealed them in *jars*."

"*The jars of ill*."

"And everything will be gray until the jars are opened."

"At which point, the pall will be lifted and night's fastness will be broken." Nina laughed. "The Four Gifts! They aren't just concepts! Wisdom, Love, Memory, and Destruction. They're spirits! They're four voodoo spirits! And they're trapped somewhere in jars!"

Bella slumped down in his seat and covered his face with his hands. "Shoot me. Shoot me now. Draw and quarter me. How could I *ever* have missed that?"

"Easy," Alastaire said, still not getting it. "You're a dork. By the way, what the hell are you two talking about?"

They both turned to face her at once. Nina said, "The last poem I read in the book. It basically said darkness was going to last forever until someone arrived to 'open the jars of ill.' And what's in those jars—"

"Are personified ideas." Bella nodded. "Like you figured out last night. Wisdom, Love, Memory, and—"

"And Destruction. Right." Nina stopped and thought about it. "Zoolie said she knew about the Four Gifts. Of course she does. But what she didn't tell us is that the Four Gifts aren't just ideas, and they aren't just *things* either. They're forces. Spirits. What do you call them . . . *Lwas*. Four . . . four beings."

And then she stopped, because the word she wanted to use wasn't one she felt quite comfortable with yet.

Four gods.

"Holy shit . . ." Alastaire said slowly, then shoveled the rest of her éclair into her mouth and wiped the cream filling off her chin. "That's fucking weird, but you know, it makes sense! I mean, if she is . . . well, who you say she is . . . well, then I guess it makes sense."

"Brilliant," Bella said. "Your powers of analysis are beyond belief."

"All right, brainiac, so tell me this. If the Four Gifts are four trapped *Lwas*, then why does Sister Aquilina want them?"

"Well, I'm guessing she wants them *back*," Nina said. "Since she's the one who trapped them in the first place. Unless . . ."

"Yes?" Bella prompted her when she'd been silent for some time.

"Well, I was just thinking . . . Madame Livaudais, or Niobe Danvers, or whatever you want to call her, has to have been mortal at one point."

"So?"

"So . . . somebody made her a Skin Eater. But before that she was human. She had a baby.

You guys can't have children the normal way, right? That's why Skinnies adopt. She had a baby, and she was so upset when it died she supposedly did all this black magic hoodoo to bring him back to life. So—" She spread her hands "—she wasn't some big bad witch. She was somebody's mommy. I mean, how do we really know Sister Aquilina is really that bad?"

"Well, we—" Bella stopped. Nina wanted to interrupt him, but watching Bella think, really think, was an impressive sight, so she kept quiet. He looked down at the table and seemed to be running over in his mind all the times he'd ever heard a reference made to Sister Aquilina, reviewing every time he'd read her name in print, and trying to remember who'd called her a legendary villain, and Nina could almost see him checking things off: no, not reliable . . . not firsthand knowledge . . . hearsay . . . gossip . . . people who had their own axes to grind . . .

He looked up finally and said, almost against his will, "You're right. We *don't* know she's evil. It could all just be one big gigantic *lie*."

Alastaire looked back and forth between them, and then, when Nina didn't say anything, she exploded. "What do you mean we don't know? She's *Sister Aquilina*, for god's sake! She's, like, the Devil! Like Satan! Like Voldemort! She's . . . she's . . ." She sputtered and then finally said in a very small, dubious voice, "Isn't she?"

And when they didn't say anything, she slumped back and said, "Boy, have we all been fed a load of horse shit."

"You can say that again." Bella almost looked like he wanted to pat her hand, but he pulled back at the last minute and sat cracking his knuckles. Nina turned away and glanced around at the rest of the coffee shop, which was unusually empty that morning. It was just the three of them and the old lady and that one lone gutterblood, who was putting his laptop away in a filthy knapsack and pulling a tattered raincoat around him as he prepared to stand up. His face, she noticed, was fine, almost handsome beneath its coating of dirt and piercings and several days' growth of beard. His eyes were hidden behind blue-tinted glasses, and he wore his blond hair in long, elaborate dreadlocks.

What a pain in the ass, she thought, *to have to get all dressed up like that every morning. Why not just shower and comb your hair?*

He turned around and looked at her, and she felt a momentary shyness, although his gaze was more curious than aggressive. A moment later, when she'd looked down and then back up again, he was gone. But he'd left something behind him on the floor, as if it had fallen out of his pocket, and she went over and picked it up.

A matchbook printed with a crude drawing of a ringed planet and the words *Saturn Bar, 3067 St. Claude Ave., New Orleans, LA.*

She took it back to the table and set it down and said, "Okay, so tell me about this place."

Bella looked at the matchbook and then slid Alastaire a glance, and she just shrugged and made a *whatever* face.

"It's a hangout," he said finally, a little defensively. "A dive bar, okay? It's just a . . . a joint. Okay, look, it's the kind of place our kind have in every city, where, if you want to meet Skinnies, you go there, and if you're a Skinny and you're hungry, you can find some humans there and hook up." He held up his hands. "Not like crossing. It's not like that. Just a . . . oh Lord, I'm actually going to say it . . . a snack. A quick *bite*. God, this is so embarrassing. See, some humans get off on having Skin Eaters bite them, it's kind of a kink, and if you don't want to go the whole crossing route, and you haven't got a fresh supply of *jumbies*, you can go to places like that and well . . . find them." He appealed to Alastaire. "Come on, you knew about the Saturn Bar, and you didn't even know we were *cannibals* until a week ago."

"Yeah, well, I just thought it was some weird kind of fucked-up subculture," Alastaire said. "Like S&M."

Nina turned the matchbook over in her hands, and surprisingly, she felt very little fear. *There's got to be a connection,* she thought. *Gutterbloods. Surrounded by foundlings. It's all too much of a coincidence.*

"Okay," she said, making a decision. "Bella, Alastaire? Which one of you has a car?"

They both blinked like she'd asked for a space shuttle.

"You're kidding, right?" Alastaire asked. "Why?"

"Uh, to *drive* somewhere? Hello, Earth to Alastaire . . ."

"But we don't drive." Alastaire shook her head. "Skinnies don't, I mean, as a rule. We have various ways of traveling through mirrors. Or else we take mass trans if we don't want to be too obvious. We're, um . . ." She looked down and mumbled something.

"What?"

"We're claustrophobic, okay? We don't like small spaces. Like, for instance, *coffins*? *Duh*? Besides, with a car, there's always the chance that something will break down and then we'd have to get out and walk, and we don't do walking so great either. I mean, like, long distances. Like in the sun and . . . well, you know."

Nina reflected that for immortals, Skin Eaters were the biggest pussies on earth. She said, "Okay, we'll have to take a cab, then. You two can sit in a cab for, like, fifteen minutes, right?"

"Take a cab where?"

She sighed. "To. The. Saturn. Bar. God, did everybody drink stupid juice this morning? I want to go to the Saturn Bar and see if I can find out anything more about Sister Aquilina and the gutterbloods."

She gestured toward the table where the filthy guy had been sitting. A couple who'd just walked in had overheard her last words, and they blinked and then chose to sit on the other side of the room. Nina realized she'd spoken a little more loudly than she'd intended to and lowered her voice. "Look, you told me they hang out down in the Bywater. Which is where you told me this bar is. Which is probably where *she* is, if she's here in the city somewhere and I didn't just hallucinate her. So, what's the big deal?"

"The big deal is we could be expelled," Bella said. "We're not supposed to leave the school grounds at night. They might send the wolves after us—that's one of the things they're there for. Besides—" his eyes shifted "—that bar's not for kids. They probably wouldn't even let us in."

"What are they going to do, card us?"

"Well, yeah. Maybe." He looked down.

"You're afraid for me, aren't you?"

"Um . . . yeah." He glanced at Alastaire, who'd gone uncharacteristically quiet.

She made a little gesture and said, "Yeah," as well.

"You could get killed," Bella said finally, his voice flat. "We're already partially dead, but you're not. And we'd really like to keep you that way. We love you, Nina." His ears got red, and he swallowed. "If something happened to you, I don't know what we'd do."

"Well, look . . ." Nina felt herself blushing as well, and she figured the best way to deal with this was by being as honest as she could in return. "You said I was the person this prophecy might be about, right? And I don't know, maybe I am. Maybe I knew all this stuff once, but I don't know it *now*. I don't even really know my own name, so what kind of a life is that? I'm just wandering around in the dark. Yeah, you're all orphans, but I'm more of an orphan than anybody. I might as well have been left on the front steps of the Daedalus School in a basket.

I've *got* to find out what this all means, because otherwise what's the goddamn *point*? Just to exist? To keep breathing?"

She turned away but continued. "I might as well be dead, then, or immortal like you. If that's all it comes down to, just about eating and drinking and hurting people and boiling everything down to raw data, then count me out. That just *sucks*."

They were all silent for a moment, then Alastaire said, "Whoa . . ." and Bella said, "See? You are the prophesied one. Nobody else could be so kick-ass. Miss Lamb, I'm proud to know you," and he followed that up by grabbing Nina's hand and kissing it, proving to all three of them that Bella Chopin had definitely been replaced by a pod person.

They agreed to go a week later, in the late afternoon. By then, the full moon would have passed, and, since it was a Sunday, no one would object to their going off campus for a while. No one, hopefully, would notice when they didn't come back before dark.

Chapter Eighteen

As per the plan, they all tried to dress as much like twenty-somethings as possible, although with varying success. Bella had decided to embrace his female side, wearing a black leather mini-dress and thigh-high boots. Nina gaped when she first saw him. Bella might be a wimpy guy, but he was a flat-out gorgeous woman.

She said, "You should always—" and then stopped, but Bella was already smiling a little.

"Yeah, I know." He shrugged. "My father would probably rather see me dead, as in *really dead and buried in the ground* dead, than as a woman. And my mom's always like, 'Oh, honey, it's so much harder for women in the world.' Like she would know. The hardest thing she's ever done is have, like, a million youth treatments from Dr. Freeland."

Nina had hit a local thrift store and bought ripped jeans that gave a nice booty view, a clingy top, and high-heeled Mary Janes. Her hair was worn loose down her back. Alastaire, by contrast, showed up wearing Doc Martens and khakis, an untucked Oxford shirt, and a yellow pork-pie hat with Disneyland printed on the side. She looked like a Yalie going slumming.

"Nice hat," Bella couldn't resist saying, and Alastaire checked out both girls' cleavages and said, "Nice, um . . . hair." Nina hurried them outside before anyone could notice them, and they walked together in silence down First Street to St. Charles Avenue.

"There's a cab," Nina said after a minute, and Alastaire put two fingers in her mouth and whistled. The driver pulled over, and they all piled in.

"Saturn Bar," Alastaire said, putting her arms around her two "dates" and squeezing their shoulders. "And make it snappy."

The cab driver just grunted and floored it, clearly familiar with student passengers. *He probably expects us to stiff him for a tip,* Nina thought. She felt a little ripple of excitement as they peeled away from the curb and headed down St. Charles Avenue through the gathering dusk. The streetlights—those that were working—illuminated the trees overhead. She was actually going away from the school! She was actually going to see a part of the city she'd never seen before!

The trips to and from Baton Rouge had been mostly spent on highways, and the short trip from the I-10 to the Daedalus School had merely shown her more of the Garden District. Now she was looping around Lee Circle and heading up in the direction of the Superdome. Businesspeople began the long commute home to their temporary houses on the Northshore, and truckloads of Mexicans returned from their day jobs to the temporary refuge of the closed gas station on Howard Avenue.

Lights were going on in some of the high rises, despite the many windows that were still blown out, and the city looked beautiful, an indigo mirage, gearing up for the night with a rakish swagger. Once they crossed Canal Street, the architecture got older and funkier, and by the time they reached St. Claude Avenue, there were shuttered storefronts and slapdash galleries, auto repair shops, laundromats, and bars. There was trash still piled up on the sides of the road, and the occasional rot-filled refrigerators still reeking on the curb. The houses were once-bright gingerbread painted every color of the rainbow, most of them peeling now and banded with a brown stain showing how high the water had risen.

As they drove further downtown, many of the houses were

also marked with Day-Glo X's inside circles, the spray-painted signs used by rescuers to indicate what they'd found during the flood: how many people inside, how many dead. But if this area of the city had suffered and was still half in ruins, it was also full of life. Bohemians in feathers rode bicycles and walked mongrel dogs. Gangstas in limos drove by kids squatting on the curb eating boiled crawfish. There were shaved-headed young men who might have been Iraqi war vets or Neo-Nazis or loose mental patients— or perhaps all three—laughing and drinking beer in barely lighted doorways, and butchy women and barely dressed young men sharing joints and groping in the dark.

And there were a surprising number of gutterbloods all walking around openly, chatting with one another and checking out the meat. As the cab pulled over, Nina thought for a split second, *This is insane*, even as she grabbed money from Bella and paid their fare (tipping lavishly) and stood on the sidewalk in front of the Saturn Bar with her two friends . . .

Where they created a mild sensation.

First of all, they were sober. Most of the other patrons lounging outside were already halfway to unconsciousness, and the rest were blowing their FEMA relief money to get there. Then, too, Nina and her friends were younger, but that was apparently no problem—the grizzled regulars practically had thought bubbles forming over their heads spelling out *Jailbait*.

And finally, she and her friends looked rich.

Shit, Nina thought, *we're going to get robbed before we even get inside.* She whispered to her friends, "Let's go in while they're still staring."

But inside it wasn't much better. The scribbled neon decorations on the facade of the building continued along the walls, as did the buzz at the arrival of fresh faces. Nina and her friends walked into a reception that might have made sense if they'd been rock stars. Shouts of "Whoo-hoo!" and "Bring that sweet thang over *here*!" echoed around the smoke-filled room, which seemed crammed with every kind of visual stimuli imaginable: paintings, posters, signs, old records, photographs, old calendars, Christmas wreaths, and a five-foot-tall can of Dixie beer, inside of which someone was currently sleeping.

The air was so thick it seemed ready to spontaneously combust, and a band was rocking away in the corner with a song that featured the refrain, "Trouble always catches up to everyone."

Alastaire looked uncertainly around and said, "Um, you guys want a beer?"

"I want some aspirin," Bella said, pinching the bridge of his nose. "But sure, let's have a beer. Pabst Blue Ribbon, the *Vin de Pays* of the Upper Ninth Ward."

Alastaire didn't even bother to ask him what that meant but just shouldered her way to the bar and returned with three overflowing plastic cups. She also brought back a very drunk woman named Gypsy.

"Here," Alastaire said, handing around the cups to Bella and Nina, and then turning to her new best friend. "Look, lady, I already told you. I'm not Rick from Datona! I don't even *know* any Rick from Datona! Gimme a break!"

"I *know* I've met you someplace," the woman insisted, wafting a cloud of bourbon at them from a mouth missing two front teeth. "I just *know* I know you, baby . . ." She was dressed in a very short, white-lace dress and clearly nothing else. "C'mon and let's get reacquainted . . ."

She started rubbing herself insinuatingly against Alastaire, who turned to the other two and mouthed, *"Help."* Bella looked entertained, and Nina took the opportunity to raise her cup to her lips and glance around the room. The place was packed, with Skin

Eaters and mortals both. Some were easy to spot, the Skinnies aggressive, while the mortals were giggling and acting skittish.

Other couples, it was harder to figure out who was who: whose hunger was for what satisfaction, food or drink or sex or distraction or death. A bald man in a heavy leather vest was kneeling in front of a very young girl and licking and sucking at the ring in her navel; the girl, who looked scarcely any older than they were, took out a tiny Swiss Army Knife and cut his head and dabbled her fingers in the blood that flowed, sticking them into her mouth. A pair of women in long ballgowns were lying on the pool table, head to toe, each nibbling on each other's ankles. An old man in a wheelchair was begging a young man to let him bite him on the arm, just this once, while the young man laughed and let a boy lick beer off his outstretched hand. It was a hot, crowded, messy, chaotic dance of pain and pleasure, life in the midst of devastation, and Nina found it both disgusting and, oddly, shamefully exciting to think of Professor Danvers being there and taking part in this whole shameless, desperate feast of flesh.

She shut her eyes and shook her head, thinking, *Eyes on the prize, girl. You don't need to picture him with someone like Gypsy.* Just then, Gypsy started showing off, kicking her booted foot up over her head and grabbing her ankle, thus revealing the fact that indeed she *wasn't* wearing any underwear. Bella choked, and Nina had to moisten her throat with a sip of beer. Just as she thought Alastaire would die of embarrassment, a face she recognized appeared in the crowd.

The young man approached them, saying, "Good, I'm glad you made it."

It was the blond gutterblood from CC's.

She recognized his chiseled features and his vivid blue eyes, even though he wasn't wearing his blue glasses tonight. He also looked a little cleaner, although not much. He glanced at Gypsy, and she slowly lowered her foot until she was standing normally again, slurring, "Hiya, Legs," in greeting. She tried to hold the blond gutterblood's eyes, but she couldn't do it and still maintain her balance, so she shrugged and stumbled toward the bar.

The young man turned to Nina and her friends and said, "You're popular."

"Yeah, well, I could kind of stand being a little less popular right now, if you want to know the truth," Alastaire mumbled.

The gutterblood laughed. "I know what you mean." He looked at Nina again and said, "I guess you know why I asked you here."

"Um . . . to see me again?" she asked, frowning, although she didn't remotely want to flirt with him. "To buy me a drink? To see Bella in black leather?"

It was his turn to frown, and he said, "Are you telling me you really don't know?"

This is getting really old. "No," she snapped. "I don't know. I don't know you, and I don't know this place, I don't know fucking lingerie-challenged Gypsy over there, and I'm about to scream if one more person looks at me with that *oh I'm so sorry* expression on their face and tells me I don't know something!"

This little outburst used up her remaining breath, and she chugged her beer while she recovered. *Careful*, she thought. She didn't want to get drunk.

The blond man, Legs, was shaking his head now, almost smiling at his own mistake. "I keep forgetting how different things are for you now," he said. "Even after all this time. Well, of course, when you get right down to it, time *is* the major difference. I'm sorry. All right, I'll explain it to you. I asked you here tonight, all of you, because I couldn't help overhearing your conversation earlier today, and I thought—"

Bella said sharply, "Whatever you heard, that's none of your business!" and Legs just raised his eyebrows.

"Really? Don't you think Sister Aquilina is everybody's business?"

They all stared at him, and in that bar, in that drowned city, surrounded as they were with sweating and dancing and groping and gnawing couples in that atmosphere of blood and booze, it was almost like a bubble had formed around them, keeping their conversation separate. Nina wondered if something like that had actually taken place. She looked more closely at the scruffy young man facing them and had a feeling like vertigo, as if she were standing on the edge of a cliff looking down into a bottomless well. Gravity and depth and endless space both drew and repelled her, and she thought, *Who is he? What is he? Do I know him?*

She felt eons of age flowing off him, stars, space, distance, and the overwhelming difference of being with another species altogether, even though she had no idea what kind of species it was. And she didn't know what to say, although he was clearly waiting for a response.

Finally she said, "Um . . . sure," feeling like she was maybe ten. "I guess so. I mean . . . uh, I guess she is."

"Good," he said, and then pulled his filthy raincoat tighter around his slender shoulders and started buttoning the buttons. His fingers were graceful and, she realized, completely clean. "Then come with me. I'll take you where she is."

Chapter Nineteen

The crowd out on the sidewalk wasn't any less drunk and rowdy when they walked back outside, but the revelers seemed to part before them. *It's like we're ghosts*, Nina thought, or like we emit some kind of a force field. They walked down the street following Legs, and by the time they'd gotten half a block away from the Saturn's neon glow, the area began to feel very empty and very desolate and very ruined indeed, and more than a little scary. Most of the streetlights were out, and the oil-deep shadows between and behind the buildings could have held anything: monsters, killers, or water to drown them all again.

They turned right on Pauline Street, at an old, shuttered building that might have once been a school, and walked down the block past a chain-link fence on one side and a row of dilapidated houses on the other. Columns and steps white as bleached bones shone in the moonlight, and the grass here was high and unkempt. There was the rich perfume of ripe and over-ripe vegetation. Nina could smell bananas fallen and gone black on the ground, and there were magnolia blossoms scattered underfoot.

The light here was deceptive: strange, large shadows seemed to be moving all around them, their forms like huge dogs, silver saliva running from their mouths. Nina swallowed and reached for Bella's hand on one side and Alastaire's on the other.

"Um . . . Legs, are we . . . is this something we could come back and, like, do maybe tomorrow?"

"No, unfortunately, it's only available in the darkness. I'm sorry, milady," he added. "I wish I could bend the rules for you, but there's really no other way."

O-kay, she thought. *I can do this. I wanted information, and now I'm getting it.* She continued to follow their guide, whose movements were almost unearthly. His feet seemed to barely touch the ground, even as his filthy raincoat fluttered behind him. She wondered if there'd been something in her beer that was making her sense things differently. Truly, the farther she walked, the darker the night seemed to become—and yet, the softer everything seemed to be around her. She wasn't walking on hard concrete anymore, but soft grass. Her low heels sank into the earth. The scent of a warm breeze and the soft chirp of insects made it seem like they were walking across an open field . . . *But that's impossible. There were houses all around here a second ag—*

And just then, she almost stumbled when her foot hit a wooden step, and then another and another one, and she followed Legs up onto a porch.

"Tish?" came a quiet voice, and then a darker shadow detached itself from the doorway. A black boy of about eleven or twelve years old came toward them.

A boy she knew.

She'd seen him in the scrying mirror with Professor Danvers. She'd seen him sitting on a rooftop and getting into a boat with Sister Aquilina. She said softly, not knowing how she knew his name, "Daneel?"

"Uh-huh." He stopped. "You're new here."

"I'm Nina." She stepped forward. "Daneel, where are we?"

"The camp." He shrugged. "That's what we call it anyway. What are you doing here?"

She shook her head. She could feel Bella and Alastaire standing behind her, and Legs somewhere nearby, but she seemed to have a special connection with this little boy.

Or with something behind him.

She squinted. Standing just to the right of the little boy's shoulder, with one hand poised on it as if protecting him or supporting him, was a large black man. A large man whose hand wasn't quite solid, nor his face quite visible. A man with a crown of feathers on his head. A warrior king.

"Shango," she said softly, inclining her head. And the image dissolved a second later, but not before the black man had nodded his head as well, in recognition.

She turned to Legs and said, "I—" but he held up his hand.

"Shh. Come inside first. You should meet the others. Then I'll answer your questions."

She glanced back at Alastaire and Bella, but they both shrugged and indicated they'd follow her lead. Pushing open the screen door, she walked past Daneel into a big, old-fashioned parlor where there were a few sofas and chairs and standing lamps, and about a dozen other kids.

There were too many for her to keep track of them all, but she noticed a skinny redheaded girl and, next to her, a pale boy humming or buzzing and occasionally rubbing his forehead against her arm. There was a girl with white hair and pink rabbit eyes sitting on a sofa, and huddled next to her were two other little girls, barely toddlers. A dark young man hulked by the unlit fireplace, his face marked with a weeping slash that had taken out one eye, and a Goth boy in black leather stood next to him, and there was a girl in denim short-shorts, and a boy with multiple piercings, and a big young man who looked like a bull.

And there was food piled in serving bowls on a sideboard, and on plates sitting on everybody's laps. Massive amounts of food. They'd just walked in on a feast.

"I—" Nina started to say again, but the redheaded girl said, "That's her. That's the one I dreamed about."

And there was a rustle as everyone else around the room stirred, and the strange boy

standing next to the redhead raised his eyes to her, and Nina saw they were the color of purple bruises. He hummed loudly, "*Bzzzzzz, bzzzzzz, bzzzzz . . .*"

Nina shivered. She looked around, and it seemed, for one dizzy moment, as if everyone in the room had someone else standing right beside them. The two little girls on the sofa had two soft, transparent figures laced around them, twins, so identical it was impossible to tell which one was which. The albino girl was sitting on a woman's lap, and the woman had frayed palm fronds covering her face like a veil. The redheaded girl had a terrible woman standing behind her, her face slashed with knife cuts. The woman tried to speak and could only go "*Kak-kak-kak,*" around the bloody stump of her tongue. There was a boy in a bright shirt holding hands with a man in a straw hat, while the Goth kid had a man in a full formal suit beside him, in a top hat and sunglasses. And the girl in short-shorts was flanked by a mermaid, her skin blue and silvery cool.

Nina looked around and saw that the boy who'd been blinded in one eye had a man standing next to him supported on a crutch, his skin covered in sores. And the big boy who looked like a bull was flanked by an actual bull, while the pierced boy had a man with a hammer and tongs beside him, his eyes red as the coals of a forge.

Everyone seemed to have a spectral figure standing right next to them, a figure who was almost real, almost visible, and yet whose transparency made them look like ghosts glimpsed through a haze of smoke. She turned to look at Legs and saw that he was changing almost too quickly for her to glimpse each shape. Here was a young man with dreadlocks, and here a man whose skin was so bright it outshone the sun, a man with wings, a man with a beard, an old man, a youth, and every change was anchored by his bright-blue eyes which glittered with amusement, whirled with stars, and shook her with the absolute sense that she was looking at someone who, far from being human, was both less and infinitely more.

"I can't," she whispered, and he said, "Of course not. Not yet. Come on, sit down and eat something first. That'll help you."

He led her gently to a chair, and Alastaire and Bella came and stood right next to her, like they were her own two shadows. Legs heaped up a plate with black beans, fried pork, rice, a hard-boiled egg, white grapes, red Jell-O, and for some reason, gummi snakes, then handed it to her.

"Um . . . thanks." She glanced at Bella. "You think any of this is, you know . . . ?"

"Human? I don't think so," Bella whispered back. "But to be on the safe side, stick with the gummi snakes. They might not be very healthy, but the worst they'll do is give you diabetes."

She nodded and reluctantly put one of the candy snakes into her mouth and chewed it. She felt a flood of clarity come to her, and a little calm along with it.

"I think these are all offerings," she said, looking at Legs. "Aren't they? I mean, I don't know, but . . . all of these things represent something, right?"

"Mm-hmm." He grinned at her. "Snakes are the symbol of Damballa, the wisdom- serpent, as are eggs. Red Jell-O is my personal favorite. The white grapes are a particular treat of the mermaids. And of course, Mr. O'Brien likes plain old white rice."

"Mr. O'Brien! Is *he* here?"

Legs shook his head. "All in good time. First, eat. You know, food is such a misunderstood thing," he added thoughtfully, almost to himself. "We all have to receive nourishment of one kind or another. Even immortal beings, to whom many of the rules don't apply, aren't allowed to get off scot-free. We all have to fill our bellies.

"And I suppose that's horrible, in a way," he added, frowning. "Even freely given, food always involves a sacrifice. But what are you going to do? Take babies away from their mothers' breasts? Love would lie stillborn if we couldn't ignore the fact that it hurt so much. The mysteries of the world are myriad. How are you feeling now? Better?"

"Yes," Nina said, shoveling the last bite of hard-boiled egg into her mouth, although she wasn't sure the combination of Jell-O and black beans was one she'd be ordering again anytime soon. She looked around and said, "This all has to do with voodoo, right?"

"You got it." Legs sat down on the floor next to her, Indian style. "All these things are offerings to call forth various spirits. 'Gods' is another word for them. People think the old gods are gone, but that's just their short-sightedness. When you eat the gods' offerings, you can sometimes . . . almost . . . see them."

He gestured around, and Nina thought, *It's true, I* can *see them more clearly now.* There was sorrow in the mermaid's silvery scales, wild rage coming off of the woman with no tongue, grim patience coming from the man in the straw hat, while the man in the dress suit and top hat lifted his sunglasses and showed her his eyes, which were sewn together—blind.

Everyone here, all the spirits, were sorrowful, hurting, angry, helpless, and frustrated, in ways ranging from the bull's baffled strength to the immobility of the figure with her face covered with palm leaves. They were all half visible and half not, half present and half absent, as if they couldn't go one way or the other. They were all trapped.

"Who did this?" she asked Legs quietly.

He sighed. "It's a long, long story. Far too long for right now. Suffice it to say, we're all here, but diminished—some of us more than others. We came to this plane of existence to help mankind, and we became incarnate, here—" He gestured at his abdomen.

Nina remembered Alastaire telling her, "They became embodied, the legend says, here, in the navel chakra."

The *Lwas*. So were these the Saturni?

"The Saturni were our brothers and sisters," he said, seeming to have read her mind and answering her question. "They were once pure spirits like us, but they coveted. They hungered for mortal appetites, and they overpowered us. We had no idea of the inherent contradictions between being and non-being. If you mix fire and gasoline, you don't get a steady blaze. You get an explosion. Yes, milady, I, too, am a *Lwa*. My name is Legba, or Legs for short. My other name is Crux."

Nina felt a shudder run down her spine, and in her heightened state, it felt like a discreet, almost visible flash of lightning starting at the top of her head and ending at her tailbone. She said, to keep herself from asking all the more important questions she was afraid to ask, "Why did you call me 'milady'?"

"It's a form of respect. You *are* kind of special."

She looked at Alastaire and Bella, who both shrugged. *Okay,* she thought, *I guess having a prophecy written about you should entitle you to something.*

"All the children here," Legs went on, waving his hand again, "have been chosen in some way. They're 'horses,' mounts waiting for the gods. In due time, they will serve their purpose, but right now, all you need to know is that they're being kept safe." He quirked his eyebrows and added, "Haven't you found out by now how difficult it is to separate the good guys from the bad guys?"

No shit, Nina thought, but right now, she was less concerned with questions of good or evil than she was with simple honesty. "Look, I'm really flattered that you think I'm special, and I'm sure you're all very nice, but what am I even doing here? I mean, aren't *you* the powerful ones? Aren't the *Lwas*, like, angels or something? If it's a question of good and evil, surely that's your department! What can I do? I don't even know who I am!"

And Legs looked right into her eyes and said, "Are you sure?"

It was like falling through a trap door. She felt her brain opening up like a flower in fast motion, and vistas appeared in front of her. She saw a savanna full of tall grass and standing stones, a mountaintop, and an island with a sheer cliff falling into the sea. She saw a building made out of glass, and a horse with a fish's tail, and a world beneath the waters that was full of shapes and movement and with terrifying things at its center . . . and then a moment later, she was back in the shabby parlor of the house on Pauline Street.

Shit, was I actually there? *Did I actually see all that, or is Legs just messing with my head again?*

She narrowed her eyes and said, "Okay, so WTF?"

"What did you see?"

"An amethyst ocean," she said, reluctant to tell him. "And a city. And great big stones."

"The stone circles," he said, nodding. "There were three great ones once, in what's now the Sudan—of course, it wasn't a desert then; it was all grassland—in Malta, and on the Isle of Man. They predate Stonehenge by more than a thousand years. Mankind worshipped them as places where the membranes between the worlds were exceptionally thin, and people could cross back and forth." He smiled. "New Orleans is another place like that."

Nina wondered how many frat boys on Bourbon Street knew they were near a portal to another dimension, but she decided to keep her speculations to herself.

"And what happened there? Is that where you guys . . . came through? Where you entered this world?"

"Mm-hmm."

"I still don't . . . ?"

Legs looked at her encouragingly. "Ask."

"Okay, so . . . the *Lwas* were originally, like, pure energy, right?"

"In a rough way. Initially, we were pure potential. Pure thought."

"And you became incarnate . . ." She touched her belly button uncertainly, and Legs nodded. "Yes, that's right."

"And then the Saturni did what? They got greedy?"

"That's a very good way of putting it." He smiled. "They wanted the whole world to themselves. So, they weakened the others of our kind who wanted to help your world, and they drove us into exile. We were barely able to manifest ourselves as perceptions to the most lowly people on earth . . . slaves. And they imprisoned the four most powerful *Lwas,* the ones they couldn't conquer, in four earthen jars. You may have heard of them? The Four Gifts?"

He looked at her with the ghost of a smile, as though daring her to contradict him. And at the same time, there was distant sadness in his absolutely unblinking bright-blue eyes. The children in the room had fallen completely quiet, all staring at the floor, while the half-visible beings behind them looked at her in stony silence. But outside, she could hear the movement of big animals and the inconsolable howling of dogs.

"The *horroi* feel it," Legs said. "They know what torments their masters feel. They know what dangers they pose if held too long in bondage. I don't mean to sound alarmist, but reality is scarcely a steady state. Things change. The center cannot hold. Dwell in possibility too long and you could wind up in hell."

"You mean we need to free the Four Gifts?" Bella spoke up for the first time. His voice was a strange mixture of male and female, bravery and fear, but it still held a Little Professor squeak that Nina found immensely endearing. Especially since her own lips were suddenly as dry as chalk.

"Yes," Legs said, raising his eyebrows. "Very good. The Four Gifts must be released if we're to stand a ghost of a chance at maintaining a balance, at least in the foreseeable future.

The forces arrayed against us . . ." He shrugged. "Let's just say they're powerful and leave it at that. But, of course, you'd know that." He brushed Nina's forehead with the briefest of touches. "If you were in your full mind."

Nina felt the same frustration well up inside her as before, and this time, she said, "Okay, now just stop it! I am *sick* of being told I can't remember things. I *know* I can't remember things. That's just a goddamn tease, so quit it!"

"Fair enough." Legs, she realized after a moment, was laughing, almost silently.

She snapped, "So, where's our hostess? What about her?"

"She's . . . elsewhere."

The care in Legs's voice made her realize at once that this had been set up in advance. She'd been brought to the house while Sister Aquilina (or whomever she was) was away, so she could learn some things, but not the full truth. *They're toying with me again*, Nina thought.

"Okay, then let's try something else. How are we supposed to free the Four Gifts?"

"Oh, you'll figure it out." Legs got gracefully to his feet. "You're pretty resourceful."

Nina jumped up to face him. "No! Dammit, you all ask for too much. You and everyone else. I'm not your puppet, and I'm not going to just sit here and eat black beans and candy and wait for you to tell me what's going on! What's happening? What do you really *want*?"

Thunder rumbled outside, and the *horroi* howled, their unearthly baying sounding like hurricane winds. Legs looked uncertain for a moment, and then said, "All right. I want to do my job, what I was created for, but I'm not sure whether my job was ever a good idea to begin with, and even if it was, I'm not sure I have the faith anymore to see myself through to the end of it.

You're frustrated? Fine—we're all frustrated, so join the club. The experience of being dumped into a world without rules or signposts isn't unique to orphans, or Skin Eaters, or even little gods. We all open our eyes on the inexplicable every morning."

"Your choice—" he nodded to Alastaire and Bella "—the *Skin Eaters'* choice is reason. Earth. Pure matter. Ours—" he glanced behind him at the children "—is Magic. Who's crazy? I haven't the faintest idea at this point. If the headmaster—" He stopped again and shut his eyes. "No. I won't go that far. I'm sorry, milady, but the Four Gifts haven't been seen in decades. I really don't dare say too much. Remember the moon, and the circle, and the highest point; that's all I can tell you. Maybe the world, your world, would have been better off without our intervention, but that's water under the bridge now. Even I can't unknit the past."

CHAPTER TWENTY

Finally, they had to accept the fact that Legs wasn't going to tell them anything else. He took them back to the Saturn Bar, and when they got to the corner of St. Claude Avenue, Nina said, "I'm sorry. I didn't mean to get hysterical back there. It's just, you know . . . this is pretty hard stuff."

"That's true," Legs said dryly. "I wish I could do more. By the way, how's Strickland?"

She gaped at him. How's *Strickland*? That sounded awfully personal. She swallowed and said, "Uh . . . he's fine, I guess."

"Really? I can't imagine him coping with any of this too patiently. Or too carefully, for that matter. Sitting idly by was never his style."

"Yeah, well, he—"

"In fact, he's the most passionate, reckless man I know."

I know, she thought miserably. *He's just not passionate and reckless about me.*

Legs shook his head. "Is he still drinking red spur?"

Nina hesitated, feeling like it might be in bad taste to admit this particular habit of the professor's in front of a relative stranger. "How do you . . . ?"

"Oh, he's been doing that for years." Legs smiled. "He does that rather than eat."

Nina took a moment to realize her intuition had been right. Professor Danvers drank that filthy stuff in order to avoid doing something even worse. Legs was looking amused. "Strickland's like a Russian doll, always secrets within secrets. Although I suppose that's rather his strong suit."

And she finally caught onto where Legs might be going with this.

"You're asking me which side he's on, right? What he's going to do if there's an all-out war between the . . . um—" she gestured helplessly "—between the *Lwa* and the Skin Eaters?"

"I already know which side he's on." Legs continued to look at her thoughtfully, his completely alien, detached gaze as unsettling as ever. "I probably know more about his allegiances than he does himself, but that's neither here nor there. What I meant was—" he stretched out one long, slender finger and touched her face "—how is he managing to keep his hands off you? I can't imagine it's been easy. He is, as I say, reckless and tends to leap before he looks. You must be very special to him, since he's restrained himself from crossing with you so far."

That was probably the very last thing I needed to hear, Nina thought, although she felt a guilty, warm sensation in the pit of her stomach. She also felt her cheeks flaming and knew Alastaire and Bella were staring at her.

She said, "Yeah, well, that's great, but we've got to get back to the school now," and she gestured at her clothes and her companions. "We're already going to be in *such* deep shit if they figure out we've been out without permission."

"I think I can help with that." Legs reached into his pocket. What he pulled out was a small atomizer, like a perfume bottle. "Give yourselves a quick spritz each, and you'll be unrecognizable for thirty minutes, give or take. It's a cheap trick, but it'll give you a chance to get back inside before anyone spots you. You can also put it on a piece of clothing. A friend of mine cooked it up."

"What is it?" Nina asked, looking at the bottle, which held a clear amethyst liquid. "Bilberry, eyebright, damiana, and a small amount of atropine, to dilate the pupils. Plus water from the ocean beneath the world. Don't worry, you'll understand what I'm talking about later on. All you need to know now is it's completely harmless."

And then, "Here's a cab. Come on, you're right—you'd better head back. Don't worry; we'll meet again soon. All of us." And he sketched a bow to Bella and Alastaire. "Sir, ma'am, it's been delightful." Then he grinned and stepped back, shutting the cab door on them and seemed to melt into the crowd.

Once they were a few blocks away, Alastaire let out her breath and said, "Holy fucking shit, Nina, lemme know the next time we're going to the Twilight Zone, okay? And can we like *never* ever *ever* do something that weird again in our lifetimes?"

And Bella simply settled back into the farthest corner of the seat and hugged his leather-clad shoulders with his slim, bare arms and said, "Well, one thing I'll say for you, Miss Thing. You're never boring."

Nina decided it was better not to respond to either of these comments, and they were silent for the rest of the ride uptown. When the cab driver let them off in front of the Daedalus School, the street was deserted.

"You sure you kids know where you're going?" the driver asked, looking at the darkened houses all around them and the boarded windows of the big building in front of them. Nina wanted to ask him why he hadn't been worried when he picked them up at a gutterblood bar, but all she said was, "Yes, yes, we're fine, they're expecting us," and hurried inside the gate.

They stopped then and gave each other a quick spray of invisibility juice, which smelled beautiful, like a kind of expensive body wash. And as they were hurrying up the steps, Alastaire said, "Jeez, I hope they aren't really expecting us—" and Bella whispered, "God, you are such an idiot," and Nina hoped that meant things were more or less back to normal.

It was a hope she was able to hold on to only until the next morning. Just as she was coming into the Commons, she felt her foot catch in something sticky. Looking down, she realized she'd stepped in a large puddle of black tar that had been poured onto the floor. Her boots were covered with it, and as she walked forward, she realized she was tracking it across the wood floor. She heard giggling all around her, and Simone said, "Uh-oh. Looks like she stepped in something."

Nina thought it was the lamest excuse for a practical joke she'd ever seen. Rolling her eyes, she said, "Sweet Jesus," and bent to untie her bootlaces.

Someone sniffed, "Won't come off that easy, baby," and someone else started crooning, "Uh-oh, you in some shit now . . ."

"Remind me to give you all a call next April Fools'," she snapped. "Looks like you're all ready."

And the snide remarks kept coming . . .

"Better wipe that thang . . ."

"How ridiculous."

"Watch out, tar baby."

She was still working to get her second damn boot off when Simone walked over, bent down, and smeared some tar on one of her long, perfectly manicured fingertips. She wiped it across Nina's cheek, leaving a pungent smear.

"That's for my grandfather," the ebony girl said, her voice still sounding snotty and bored, although she didn't look bored. Her eyes glittered like two golden slits. "I hope you and your little friends enjoyed humiliating an old man. You may be high yella, baby, but you ain't nothing but a field slut."

"What the—" Nina started to say, but just then Bella and Alastaire came in, and Simone stepped back, holding up her hands in mock innocence.

"Why, hush ma mouf, ef it ain't Br'er Rabbit and Br'er Bear. Better get the tar baby outta

here." She turned and sauntered away, and Alastaire let Nina lean on her shoulder while she finally pulled off her second boot and carried them both over to shove them under the tablecloth next to her place.

"Nail polish remover," Bella said after a moment.

Nina said, "What?"

"Take that right off." He shrugged, pointing. "The tar."

"So will spit," Alastaire said, then moistened a napkin and wiped Nina's face. She said after a decent pause, "So, to what do we owe *that* pleasure?"

"I don't know." Nina looked around to where several late-arriving kids and some of the teachers were stepping in the tar now, or else carefully going around it. She said, "She's pissed off, but all she said was it involved her grandfather."

Alastaire was still wiping her face with more than necessary care, and she pushed her away, saying, "It's all right, for God's sake, I'm not *that* dirty!" Bella, on the other hand, had immediately left the table and gone out to the hall, from which he returned a few minutes later carrying a newspaper.

"Hot off the presses," he said, spreading it out. It was a copy of the *Midnight Times*.

"He must have answered our email," Nina exclaimed, forgetting Simone entirely as she searched for the article. Her friends craned over her shoulder to look, and she turned the pages until she found a column entitled:

TODAY'S YOUTH IN TROUBLE

It happens every day. Our children start to question the old stories, and pretty soon, everything's up for grabs. When Sister Aquilina was vanquished thirty years ago, it didn't take long for the Far Left to come up with a new way to advance its agenda: Secular Mysticism. Nowadays, under the guise of being "modern," young people are taught to believe that anything is possible. They're encouraged to see witchcraft and sorcery as just "alternative technologies." Well, I'm here to tell you that's just not so.

The Far Left's real purpose in promoting a belief in magic is to soften up our resolve in the face of our real enemies, devious and powerful as they still are. I recently received a letter from "Curious," asking me if I still believed in the Four Gifts. Well, I was shocked, and the fact I was shocked probably says as much about my own innocence as it does about the questioner's honest inquiry. When I was a boy, we took it for granted that the Four Gifts weren't literally real. We knew, like Santa Claus and the Easter Bunny, that this was a way for our elders to teach us important lessons: watchfulness, and sticking with our own kind. We knew we were being taught to be good citizens, and we saw the Four Gifts as examples of that teaching. Now, however, it seems those days are long gone by.

Yes, Curious, there are indeed Four Gifts, but not in the literal sense you mean. They exist in the place of the highest honor in all our hearts, as goals to which we can all aspire. They exist as certainly as courage and loyalty and love and danger still exist. You may tear apart a watch to see what's inside it, but certain symbols are far more important than the sum of their individual parts. And the Four Gifts are indeed such symbols.

No Four Gifts? No, a thousand times no! Saying there are no Four Gifts would be as bad as saying there is no young letter-writer named "Curious"! A thousand years from now, we will still believe in the Four Gifts as our forefathers did: not as magical talismans, but as self-evident truths. We will value and love them, not as occult totems, but as ideals! Yes, in that sense, Curious, there are indeed Four Gifts. And I for one say God bless them, every one!

"Now *there's* a guy who's full of crap," Alastaire said, reaching for a basket of cinnamon rolls. "I'm sorry I even suggested him. He's so full of it he probably burps turds."

"I'm not so sure." Nina was studying the small photograph of General Azazel next to the byline. The general, who was white like his daughter Isabel, had a lean, hard face, and she guessed he might still be a tough customer. "Simone must have been really angry to go to this much effort. This could actually get her in trouble."

She gestured as Professor Hermes slipped in the tar, which, of course, he couldn't see, and went down hard saying, "Whoooaaa!" There was a burst of laughter, and Professor Samson swore he'd "fix" whoever had made this goddamn mess.

"She said she hoped we'd enjoyed 'humiliating' an old man," Nina added. "But I don't think he sounds humiliated. He just sounds like your average reactionary bigot."

Bella was studying the article, frowning. "There's something funny here, but I can't quite put my finger on it."

By now, a large enough crowd was standing around the tar slick—commenting on it, laughing and high-fiving Simone and cutting glances at Nina and her friends—that Nina felt like a goldfish in a bowl. She looked up at the teachers' table, but as luck would have it, or maybe luck wasn't responsible at all, most of the teachers had already finished their breakfasts and left the room. Only Professor Seneschal still sat there, fast asleep, and Professor Ariadne was fixing her lipstick. It appeared none of them wanted to get involved, and Nina guessed they didn't want to piss off Isolde Freeland's kid any more than the students did.

But this was ridiculous. What was really bothering Simone? General Azazel had answered them with nothing but platitudes. Why was she so bent out of shape?

And then Nina thought, *Something did come through in his answer, didn't it?* At least, he'd admitted the Four Gifts were real. Was that what Simone meant about his "humiliation"? Had he been humiliated, not in the eyes of the wider world, but in the eyes of the other Skin Eaters?

She stood up and walked over to the beautiful black girl, who was standing there smirking. "We scared him, didn't we?" Nina said. "That's what this is really all about. He's superstitious enough that he can't quite bring himself to say those things we talked about don't exist. But he wasn't supposed to say that. He messed up, didn't he? He didn't say he had no idea what we meant."

"I don't have any idea what *you* mean," Simone said softly.

"He said they were real . . . that letter."

"Clueless, you'd need help just to be *wrong*."

"He knows, doesn't he?" Nina pressed her advantage, despite all the other kids standing there listening, despite everything, because she felt if she could just put her finger on what General Azazel had actually *said*, she might understand this whole thing. "He knows, right? What did he say . . . 'They exist in the place of the highest honor'—"

"You should go out for the school Hadiade," came a mocking voice, and Nina spun around to face Agatha Danvers, who seemed to have appeared out of nowhere. She was watching them both now with a faint smile on her face. "You girls have such vivid imaginations, you really ought to go up against one another." Agatha's eyes narrowed. "What does our reigning champion say? After all, shoe-ins are so tedious."

"I-I have no idea—" Nina began.

But Simone cut her off. "You wouldn't survive the first round of the Hadiade, bitch."

"Oh, really?" Nina knew she shouldn't rise to this particular bait, but Simone was really getting on her last nerve. "How hard could it be? I mean, if *you* can do it?" It felt like some force outside of herself had taken her over now and was pushing her straight toward disaster. She kept her eyes fixed on Simone and said, "You knew this was coming, didn't you?"

"I had a feeling." Simone wasn't pretending she didn't care anymore.

"You knew we'd have to fight eventually."

"The first rule of fighting is to never admit you want to fight. This is just going to be fun. Like taking candy from a baby."

"Babies can be ruthless. They don't know they're not supposed to win."

"Oooh, I'm shaking."

"I'm stronger than you think."

"Bully for you. I'm stronger than you can *imagine*."

Nina opened her mouth to answer this, but the door slammed open from the corridor, and there was Professor Danvers.

Looking like a thundercloud. A particularly handsome thundercloud, with his black hair ruffled and his tie loose, but a thundercloud nonetheless. His face was ashen.

"Where the hell have you been?" he roared at Nina, raking his dark eyes over her. "I've been looking everywhere—" And then, realizing he had an audience, he caught his breath and added,

"Miss Lamb was absent without leave last night. I don't suppose any of you have any information about that? And what's all this . . . this *tar* doing here?"

Nina had a perverse desire to laugh. It was just too bizarre. She had no idea how he guessed they'd been out, but she didn't even have any time to bluff it through.

Agatha just looked at her brother and smiled, a very wide, very nasty smile, as she said, "Oh, Strickland, I've got the most wonderful news! Miss Lamb has agreed to compete in the school Hadiade against Miss Freeland. Isn't that great? Given your opinion of her talents, I'm sure you'll agree that for once we're going to have a real knock-down drag-out contest."

Chapter Twenty-One

"Shit, you're really in for it now," Alastaire said, as they hurried away to class shortly afterward. "Nina, what were you *thinking* challenging Simone like that?"

"*I* didn't challenge her! It was that bitch Agatha—"

"Well, you didn't exactly back down," Bella pointed out. "Simone's a class-A pain in the ass, but you're still going to get creamed."

"Maybe not," Nina shook her head. "Maybe I can learn enough to beat her."

"In less than a *month*? The Hadiade's three weeks away."

"Well, you two could teach me!"

"I could try," Bella admitted, "but I could teach you for a whole year, and you still wouldn't be prepared. And as far as Miss Middlebrow here . . . forget it. What Alastaire knows could be written on the front of an envelope and you'd still have room for the stamp."

"Eat crap, sissy-boy," Alastaire said, but her heart didn't really seem to be in it. They'd reached the door to Professor Aspidistrus's classroom, and Nina could hear the professor inside saying, "Please pair up and select a sample salamander from the box on my desk. Today, let's try and see if we can't keep the salamanders *alive* in the fires, shall we?"

"Damn it, stop telling me what I can and cannot do!" Nina exploded. Immediately there was a loud clap of thunder, and torrential rain started pouring down in the hallway. The lights flickered, and an icy wind blew down the corridor.

Bella and Alastaire both backed away from her and said at the same moment, "Okay, we'll try it!" and then fled into the classroom, as Nina sagged against the wall. She shut her eyes, and the rain stopped. What on earth was wrong with her? She hurried inside after her friends and grabbed a wriggling salamander from the box on Professor Aspidistrus's desk, and thought, *I've got to stop doing that. Whatever it is.*

She tried to concentrate for the rest of the day, but even the excitement of burning salamanders alive—they writhed and danced in the flames, but didn't die—and making the wolves howl on cue couldn't distract her. By evening, her thoughts were still chasing each other around her head like mice. Why was she still doing magic? How had Professor Danvers known she'd been gone? And what about all the things Legs had told them? She could accept the idea that freeing the Four Gifts was a good thing, but she was no closer to knowing how on earth to do that.

And now she had to worry about this Hadiade business, whatever it was.

She sighed as she walked back upstairs to her bedroom after dinner. She and her friends had agreed that the attic was the safest place for her to train, but she felt tired and empty now that all the excitement of the past twenty-four hours had worn off. *I almost wish we'd stayed in the house on Pauline Street, at least until Sister Aquilina returned. I'd at least know what she really looks like. As it is, all I've got to go on are bad dreams and worse publicity.*

"Hey," she said as she pushed open the door with her shoulder. Her hands were full of plates. "Sally hooked us up with a whole bunch of stuff to snack on while we're working. I've got cookies, éclairs, petit fours, sponge cake . . ."

"Sally's the best," Alastaire said, bouncing off the bed and coming to relieve Nina of several cookies, which she immediately stuffed in her mouth. "What would we do without her?"

"I don't know," Bella said, without turning around. "You might have to go more than one or two hours without *eating*."

"What are you doing?" Nina asked, once she'd put the rest of the plates down. He was sitting at her desk, working on a series of calculations and biting the end of a pencil. Mercy the black cat, who'd followed her up from the kitchen, came over and wound around her legs, and she reached down and picked him up.

"Trying to figure out how you can shape-shift without being at least a partial Skinny. But it's impossible. Your cells just don't work the way ours do. It's like one of us going to the doctor and trying to show a normal body temperature. We'd probably just freeze the thermometer."

She felt a stab of panic. "Is shape-shifting going to be part of the Hadiade?"

"It might be. It's hard to say. The games change every year, but they're supposed to test 'the skills and knowledge most valuable to the average Skin Eater.' Or something like that."

"Great," Nina said, sitting down and taking an éclair. "What other kinds of things do they test?"

"Everything we've been studying, plus *Introim* lore, Skin Eater customs, Polynomial Calculations, Flying . . ."

"You're right." Nina shook her head. "I'm going to get totally creamed."

"Actually, I was wondering . . ." Bella frowned again. "Nina, stand up and try something for me."

"Okay." She wiped her hands and stood up.

Bella motioned for her to stand in front of him and then said, "All right. Now, what I want you to do is to make me believe you can shape-shift. Make me *see* it. It doesn't matter if you can really do it, just make me *think* you can do it. See if you can get inside my mind and do magic."

That sounded fine in one sense, but—

"Wait a minute," she snapped. "Won't they know if I do something that's completely outside the laws of consensual reality, especially in *front* of everybody? Then I'll be breaking two rules at once!"

"Not if you do it well enough." Bella looked excited. "We already know you can change the weather and move objects and see spirits and talk to gods. It ought to be a cinch to fool a bunch of Skinny judges. See, I think we've been thinking about this whole thing the wrong way." His eyes gleamed. "You're powerful enough that you can make people believe all sorts of things. So, let's *cheat!*"

Nina hesitated. Cheating sounded fine, but could she just do it blindly? *I can get inside Bella's and Alastaire's heads because I know them. Who knows who'll be judging me?* Still, it was worth a shot. She looked back and forth from Bella to Alastaire, trying to sense the humming of their minds, and she could almost feel it, although their thoughts weren't in any way clear to her.

She thought, *See me,* and she felt their attention sharpening, focusing on the surface of her skin. It felt almost like tickling or a little dancing force field all around her.

She thought, *See me as fluid,* and she could almost *feel* them seeing her skin sliding, moving easily over her bones. In her mind's eye, she saw them seeing her becoming as soft and fluid as warm candy, even though her own sense of herself remained the same. She didn't try for anything elaborate like changing into a bat or a dog. She just lightened her eyes, lengthened her hair, and changed it from dark to bottle blond. She gave herself a snub nose, pale lips, and chubby cheeks. She dressed herself in a pink tube top, short-shorts, a navel piercing, and stacked heels, and laid the imaginary mascara on thick. She knew none of this was really happening, but she concentrated on making them *see* the changes she was imagining. And she heard Alastaire gasp.

"Nina, you look like . . . God, it's true! You look exactly like Britney Spears!"

"You definitely look different," Bella said, shaking his head. "Now, please change back. I can't stand to see you doing this to yourself."

Nina laughed—and the illusion vanished. She didn't so much shift back to her normal self as just release her hold on their minds, and they both blinked and looked at each other in near amazement and then said, "Wow!" at the same moment.

"Okay, well, we know you can do *that*," Bella said, pleased that his idea had worked. "Quick! Let's try some other stuff."

They practiced her making them think she was brewing a complex alchemical potion, making them think she was making salamanders do high dives, and making them think she could fly. After they'd applauded her zooming around the room only to have her break the illusion and reveal she'd been sitting on the bed the whole time, Alastaire said, "That's it, she's going to blow them all away! I wish we had some money to bet on her—" and Nina laughed and said, "I'll lend you some!" and then she looked at Bella, who was frowning again.

"What's wrong?" she asked, her heart sinking.

He bit his lips and admitted the flaw in his own plan. "You can only do this with things you already know the answer to. You know what someone would *look* like if they flew, and you know what Britney Spears looks like, and you know what the salamanders looked like in class today. You can't get inside my head and make me think you know the answer to something when you don't know it."

She stopped, realizing he was exactly right. She could only make him think *two plus two equals four* if she knew that two plus two actually *did* make four.

"Well . . ." She took a little breath. "Couldn't I read your mind first and find out what the answer is and *then* answer the question?"

"Not without having me sense it. Try it. What's the polynomial equation for plotting the hypotenuse of Venus?"

Nina looked at him and tried her best to sneak into his mind, but the minute she touched the answer—it had something to do with the square root of negative pi—Bella said, "Nope, I felt that. I'm sorry. And I'm not even trying to stop you. If anybody suspicious realized you were rooting around inside their consciousness, this whole plan would go down the toilet. We've just got to cram you on all the correct answers to anything they could possibly ask you."

Nina thought she'd have a better chance of actually trying to get herself to transform on the cellular level. She looked wistfully at the plates of food Sally had sent up and said, "We'd better get some more snacks. This could take a while."

"Actually, it's okay, we've got three weeks left." He tapped his fingers together. "I think we could pace ourselves and do three or four hours a night and—" He broke off suddenly and looked at the cookies and cakes and other goodies. He looked at them very strangely, as though he'd never seen anything like them before. Finally, he said in a flat, detached voice, "She sent up gummi snakes."

"*What?*" Nina flung herself at the nearest plate and pushed the remaining éclairs and cookies to one side. There on the bottom, sure enough, was a little plastic package of the same candy snakes as she'd eaten the night before.

"Go on and try one," Alastaire suggested after a couple of seconds. "You know it made you wicked smart the last time."

Nina was already tearing open the plastic wrapping, although she thought, *One pill makes you smaller and one pill makes you tall, go ask Alice if eating gummi snakes makes you a genius.* She crammed two snakes into her mouth and chewed them up quickly and swallowed them. "Okay," she told Bella. "Ask me something."

"What famous event took place in 1791 that directly impacted the Skin Eaters?"

"I haven't the faintest idea. Maybe it takes a while to work. What's the answer?"

"The Voodoo Ceremony at Bois Caiman that launched the Haitian revolution. Let's try something else. Who said, 'The greatest truths comprise the shortest numbers'?"

"Einstein?"

"Oliver Occam in 1601. It's a calculation engine theory that's come to be called 'Occam's Knife.'" He sighed. "Let's try an easy one. What are the fourteen leaves of Hermes's sacred tree?"

"I don't effing know!" Nina shouted, picking up the rest of the gummi snakes and throwing them at him. "This is all shit! I'm going down in flames. I'd better quit now before I make an even bigger fool of myself than I already have!"

She sat back down on the bed and tried to laugh it all off, although angry tears still stung her eyes. In one way, she told herself, it didn't really matter. With everything else that was going on, who cared about some stupid game? But she hated feeling ignorant. If she had more than a couple of months to study all this, she'd know as much as Bella, although she had a feeling Bella was always going to be able to beat her when it came to sheer geek retention.

I want to win, she thought miserably. *I want to impress him,*

Professor Danvers. And I want to show creepy-drawers Agatha that I'm not just some dumb jumbie. *I—*

And as she thought those thoughts, she suddenly knew, she just *knew*, that something important was going to happen to the *jumbies* at the Hadiade. She didn't know how she knew it, but it was as clear as if she'd read it in a newspaper or seen it on TV. It was as clear as her own name—if she knew what her real name was.

"Listen—" she began, but Bella put up his hand, and Alastaire said, "Wait a sec; there's somebody at the door."

She strolled over to the doorway, yanked it open, and said, "Okay, Aggie, you got me. Me and Nina are making out up here!" but nobody was there. "Shit. I really thought I had her this time."

Bella came to Alastaire's side, and they both looked out into the hallway, but nobody could be seen. There was, however, a clue. A pile of pale beige crescents lying on the floor. A pile of—

"Pistachio shells," Bella said, picking up one. "What on earth does that mean?"

Nina felt as if her stomach had suddenly fallen through the floor. She said shakily,

"Um . . . I guess somebody likes pistachio nuts?"

Bella just looked at her like that wasn't even worth a response.

Alastaire said, "Funny, you know, the headmaster used to like . . ." And then she looked at Nina's white face and said, "Uh-oh."

Chapter Twenty-Two

There were few things that could stop a conversation better than "Uh-oh."

Nina said, "Okay, so, here's the deal," and explained to Bella how, on her first day at Daedalus, she met a man who'd said his name was Mr. O'Brien.

"He said he was the headmaster. Then later on, I saw him again in the scrying mirror, when I saw all the kids we met the other night on Pauline Street. And then Professor Danvers freaked out and told me that none of that could be true, because the headmaster wasn't just away on business, he'd been terminated by the Saturni."

"That's true," Bella said, biting his lips and clearly thinking hard. "I mean, everybody I know certainly thinks the headmaster is dead. My parents even joke about it. It's kind of gross."

"But I still know what I saw. And remember, Legs said, 'Mr. O'Brien likes plain white rice.' I'm guessing another thing he still likes is pistachio nuts. So . . ." Nina spread her hands, "that must mean he's still alive, and still around here someplace."

"Maybe." Bella looked troubled, and went and sat down at Nina's desk again and doodled some marks on the papers in front of him.

"What? You think I've just got very hungry *mice* up here? You think someone else is lurking around in the attic eating pistachios?"

"I don't know, I don't know." He turned to look at her. "I do know Mr. O'Brien was a really scary guy, back in the day. He was like—" he lowered his voice "—crazy."

"No way," Alastaire said, grabbing another handful of cookies and sitting back down on the bed. "Not to me. He was really nice. He reassured me and told me I'd fit in, I'd be okay."

"That wasn't my experience." Bella shut his eyes. "Mr. O'Brien terrified me. He took me into a closet my first week here and showed me . . . things."

He stopped, and Alastaire said after a minute, "Okay, major gag-making, but it's not like he's the first or the last guy who ever showed a little kid his wiener. I mean, I'm sorry, but—"

"No, you don't understand. He didn't show me anything sexual, or anything really . . . anything. What he showed me was *nothing*. Utter emptiness. *Lack*."

Nina and Alastaire looked at each other, and then they both said at the same time, "What's it look like?"

Bella was still shaking his head. "It's hard to explain. He showed me his age. He's incredibly old. He put his hands on either side of my head and squeezed, and I felt like my head was going to crack open like an egg. He showed me what it was like before the standing stones, before anything, and it was all just . . . dust. Just ashes. I saw him killing things, just because he could do it. Whole worlds. Just to see the life suddenly blink out of them, or drain slowly out of them like a faucet. I saw him hurting things, just because he had that power. He showed me the whole world, and it was just that. Devastation. Waste."

"But . . . but . . ." Alastaire sputtered. "But that's ridiculous! He wasn't like that at all. He was nice. He was really *nice*!"

"Don't you believe it. He said he'd shown Professor Seneschal these things once, and it had driven him mad. That's why the professor falls asleep all the time—he prefers unconsciousness to having seen what he's seen. The headmaster said it took an unusual strength of mind to hold meaninglessness in your head for any length of time, and I was probably one of the few ones who could do that." Bella looked down and added quietly under his breath, "I was six."

Nina felt revolted, but she also felt as if something major didn't add up. "Look, if the headmaster's really that old, and that powerful, and that scary, why does everybody think he's dead? Could you . . . I mean, could you actually even *kill* somebody like that?" She shrugged. "After all, you guys are pretty indestructible, and you're nowhere near that strong. Why is everybody so sure he's gone?"

"Because they want him to be." Bella rubbed his forehead. "Mr. O'Brien, the headmaster, whatever you want to call him—and he has lots of other names—isn't anybody's idea of 'cuddly.' For all Alastaire's memories, I don't think anybody really liked having him around that much, not the teachers, not the students. Not anybody. Nobody likes having someone around who's that unsettling. It's like living next to a fault line. You don't know if you're going to fall in. I think when he disappeared, everyone's reaction was, *Great, at least now we don't have to worry about* him *anymore*." He hesitated. "That is, if he *is* gone. I suppose we have to, at least, consider that."

Nina felt exhausted and strangely shaken by this latest mystery. One more puzzle was one too many at this point. *Stick a fork in this camel's back*, she thought, *I'm done*. She said, "Look, guys, it's late, and I'm personally beat. Can't we do some more cramming tomorrow? The Hadiade's still almost a month away, and you two can probably help me memorize everything before that." She looked at them both. "Please?"

And whether it was the weariness in her voice, or the fact that they were all tired and shaken—they'd been through as much shit as she had recently—they didn't put up much of a fight. Alastaire just shrugged and said, "Sure," and Bella said, "Sleep tight, Nina. We'll see you tomorrow," and then they both left her alone in the attic.

Nina threw herself down on the bed and wondered whether she'd be able to sleep a wink. What did it all *mean*? Was Mr. O'Brien alive or dead, bad or good, outside her door eating pistachio nuts or dragging innocent kids away into closets to show them the void? And what did it mean that she kept getting these teasing little *hints* of something else, something more, some other reality beyond what she knew and what she could remember, which was practically nothing. Why couldn't she put it all together? She longed to know, to understand, but also to sleep, to be unconscious and not to have to worry about any of this anymore. She stared up at her high, cobwebbed ceiling. *Now's the one time I could really use a vision or two, and I got nothing.* And later on, she cursed herself for having had that thought.

It started with the distant sound of sobbing, not Zoolie's disembodied distress, but someone distinctly human, repeating those perennial human words over and over again, *No* and *Please*. She sat up and looked toward the window. Was anybody out there? The night breeze was soft, rustling the leaves of the big oak trees and swaying the trailing moss, and she told herself she might just have been hearing things. Or else someone was in the garden crying. It happened, after all. People in a school cried for all sorts of reasons, from the tragic to the merely hormonal. Still, she got up and went to the window and looked out—even though later on, she wished that she hadn't.

The garden was lit by a waxing moon, not big enough yet to cause trouble for the Skin Eaters, but light enough that the smooth, flat lawn below her looked like a dark green stage. It seemed all the members of the faculty were out there: Mwindo and Samson, Hermes and Aspidistrus, Seneschal and Threet, and Strickland

and Agatha Danvers, all standing in a rough circle. The moon shone down on their bowed heads. They were all formally dressed, in frock coats and long gowns, and she might have thought it was some kind of a religious ceremony, were it not for the Skin Eaters' strong opposition to anything remotely spiritual.

And were it not for the unconscious child bound hand and foot, lying in the grass in the center of the circle.

It wasn't anyone she recognized. Later on, she wondered if that would have made any difference. Would she have cried out if it had been Roticus, or the fat little boy she'd seen with Simone and her friends? Probably not. She was paralyzed with fear, and the last thing she wanted was to call attention to herself. She watched as the warm night wind stirred the long dark dresses and the long dark coats the faculty were wearing, and she watched as all their heads turned, their faces etched with a single grief, as someone had approached them and entered their circle.

Nina recognized the girl she'd seen outside of Sky Geography class, the girl who'd been sick, vomiting, her face feral and distorted with pain. Now she looked calm, almost numb, although it was her voice that kept murmuring in a soft, dull, constant, defeated whisper, "No. Please. Please, no . . ."

"It has to be." Professor Danvers's voice wasn't loud either, but it carried on the hushed quiet of the night air, thick with pain. He left his place and went to stand by the Skin Eater girl and supported her, his arm around her shoulders.

"I know how you feel." His voice was a hoarse whisper. Nina strained to hear him. "We all know. It gets easier as it goes along. *Trust me.*"

"Please."

"You must eat. Otherwise, the hunger will destroy you."

"It makes me sick."

"I know."

"It sticks in my throat."

"Yes."

"It's terrible."

"Yes. But it's who you are now."

"I want to die."

"No, you can't. Not anymore."

The girl nodded and seemed to bow to the inevitable, bending in on herself, but Nina realized, after a moment, that it wasn't in weakness. Rather, it was to drop into a crouch, making herself small and compact, bunching herself up and then crawling forward on her hands and knees toward the unconscious child, moving like a dark spider, a hunched-up insect across the grass. A beetle. A tick. A bug, scuttling across the grass now at terrific speed and scooping up the child almost too quickly to be seen, carrying it away in a blur, while Professor Samson and Professor Mwindo broke ranks and grabbed Professor Danvers to keep him from going after her. Nina heard his strangled cry of "No!" and she pressed her own knuckles against her mouth so hard that she tasted blood. *No,* she thought, *no, that's not what they are, that's not what they really are. It's not, it's not,* but she couldn't bear to look anymore.

She fell down, hugging herself on the floor, and eventually, she crawled back into her bed. That image of a hungry insect, a parasite, a louse, stayed with her, and she couldn't get it out of her head.

Even though, by the following morning, she'd convinced herself it had all been a dream.

Chapter Twenty-Three

Nina continued to practice with Bella and Alastaire, and she managed not to dream that much over the next three weeks. What sleep she had was haunted by polynomial formulas, alchemical theories, historic dates, and sky geography charts. She practiced making Mercy tap dance and swing by his paws from a miniature trapeze, and she practiced making Bella and Alastaire think she could transfigure herself into everything from a rat to a Shetland pony, while she studied Skin Eater literature until she could quote huge chunks of John Dee and Edgar Allen Poe by heart. She practiced exercising, working out with dumbbells and doing ab crunches because Bella said some of the tests might be physically demanding, especially for someone with normal DNA.

And she tried to eat as many gummi snakes as she could, although the only effect she noticed was that they ended up making her skirt tight.

And the morning of the Hadiade, she woke up thinking, *I am so dead. Really. I might as well cross with somebody right now, because before midnight, I'll be lucky if I'm not a body in the Mississippi River.*

Only the thought that she had the whole day ahead to goof off gave her a little comfort. The Hadiade didn't start until that evening—twelve hours grace until her execution. She dragged herself downstairs and ate breakfast. Not gummi snakes, but bacon and eggs and toast and grits, and she drank several cups of black coffee. When she brought her empty plate into the kitchen, she asked Sally, "You got any Alka-Seltzer?"

"Thanks. I'll take that as meaning you ate far too much of my delicious food," the cook said, rummaging in a drawer and handing her a packet. "You want to puke, though, do it outside."

"That's okay," Nina said, dropping the tablets into a glass of tap water. She pretended to be engrossed with the *plop-plop-fizz-fizz* until Sally asked, "Nervous?"

"Duh."

"Don't be. You've done things far worse and far harder than this dumb-ass Hadiade. And that's just since *I've* known you. God knows what you did to get through the storm."

"That's just it," Nina said, swallowing her Alka-Seltzer and trying not to burp too loudly.

"I wish I knew what I'd done, so I could tell myself how smart I am or how strong I am or how whatever I am, but for all I know, I'm just a flop." She sighed. "A loser. Which is what I'm going to be tonight, in any case."

"No, you're not," Sally said. She seemed to be at a loss for a moment. She stood there with her hands on her hips, as though furious that she couldn't think of a quick way to cheer Nina up. Finally, she asked, "Do you know the story of Sir Gareth in the kitchen?"

"No." Nina put her glass down and sat on one of the stools. "Tell me."

"Well, Sir Gareth was one of King Arthur's knights, and when he came to Camelot, he was disguised and got a job in the kitchen, and all the other knights were like, 'In your face, pretty boy,' because they said he was such a big sissy since he was only good for kitchen work—and that his hands were too smooth and white for him to be any good at that, either. They said he must be a bastard, because otherwise he wouldn't have had to hide his identity. And they talked all other kinds of trash about him, you know, and *yadda yadda yadda*. Of course, he was really a nobleman, and his brothers were already there, being all knightly, but he didn't want to ride on their coattails, so he'd come disguised. Anyway, he finally got fed up with everyone calling him 'Softy' and 'Pretty Hands,' so he went away on a quest and defeated a bunch of ogres and rescued a princess and things like that, and he went back to Camelot and everyone was like, 'Oh, so it's you!' when he finally revealed himself.

"But the point is, he was the *same person* all the time. Even his own brothers didn't recognize him at first, because they weren't looking at him the right way. They were expecting him to be All That, and strutting around looking for a fight, and instead he was very mild. Some people even say the name Gareth is based on an old Anglo-Saxon word for *gentle*."

Nina said, "So he should have been a little less gentle, and then people would have realized he was as tough a knight as they were?"

"In a way." Sally shook her head. "Not really. People see you as threatening when they, themselves, feel threatened. He didn't kill any of the bad guys he defeated. He just made them swear fealty to the Round Table and the idea that Good triumphs over Might. He tried to do the right thing. And in the end, he was killed by a mistake. Guinevere was sentenced to die because of her affair with Lancelot, and when Lancelot rescued her, he killed Gareth by accident. Sir Gawaine and the rest of Gareth's brothers insisted King Arthur go to war against Lancelot, and the Round Table was broken up and destroyed. Gareth would never have wanted that."

"Sally . . ." Nina looked at the cook out of the corner of her eye.

Sally pretended to be engrossed in wiping down the counter, as usual, as she said, "Hmm? What's on your mind?"

"Have you ever heard of a prophecy about somebody destroying the Skin Eaters?"

"Nope. Sounds like a great idea, but no, I haven't."

"It's incredibly complicated. Bella knows it all by heart, but there's this one line that made me think of your story. It says, 'the beautiful hand will be revealed.' I was just thinking about how Sir Gareth was called 'Pretty Hands,' and they all made fun of him for having such smooth hands. Do you think that's . . . well, that's something like what you were talking about? That someone's going to find out who someone else really is and reveal it? Maybe . . . um . . . someone like me?"

She said that last word very softly, almost under her breath, because she didn't want to admit even to Sally how much she wanted someone to do just that. Tell her who she was. The visions she'd seen in the house on Pauline Street had only whetted her curiosity, to know what she knew of standing stones and mountains, a glass city, and a purple sea. She remembered Legs saying, "The forces arrayed against us are powerful, but, of course, you'd know that if you were in your full mind." And she wanted to beg someone, anyone, *Give me my full mind!* But there was no one there she could ask.

I want to go back there, she thought. *I want to go back home.* But where was home? For all she knew, home was a strange stone circle where cavemen met to worship. Home wasn't anywhere near New Orleans, that was for damn sure. Even though Legs had said New Orleans was one of those places where it was easiest to cross between the worlds.

Nina got up and put her glass in the dishwasher, to avoid meeting Sally's eyes. "It's dumb," she mumbled, "I know . . . I'm sorry I mentioned it."

"Not dumb." Sally chuckled. "Although not unexpected. Sometimes I astonish even myself with how obvious I can be. However, no one ever said subtlety was my strong point."

She continued to look at Nina with raised eyebrows, clearly

encouraging her to figure it out for herself, and Nina said, "So it . . . it *does* have something to do with all that, doesn't it?

And that's why you told me that story! Because you want me to know there's somebody out there who *knows* who I am and who can tell me! Oh, thank you, Sally! Thank you! I love you!"

She couldn't stop herself. She flung her arms around the startled cook and gave her a big hug—and only noticed a fraction of a second too late how Sally had tensed up. For a split second, the older woman stood perfectly still and then reluctantly raised her own arms, patting Nina on the back. And Nina felt the cold go through and through her. It was like she was hugging a frozen body.

Or a dead one.

She flinched. And then she said, "Oh, Sally, I-I didn't know . . ." She was struggling to find the right words. "I'm sorry, it's just . . . I didn't realize you were a Skinny."

"It's all right." The cook stepped away, dusting her hands on her apron. "I told you, I'm obvious. Not entirely *honest* always, but obvious. I misdirected your attention: it's an old magician's trick. I told you I didn't share the tastes of most of the students and staff here, and I don't. That doesn't mean I'm not—how does the old song go?—'in that number.'"

Nina felt like she had profoundly hurt the other woman's feelings, even though Sally was pretending it was no big deal. She wanted to explain to her that it didn't matter, that she loved Bella and Alastaire, and *they* were Skinnies (well, nearly), and Professor Danvers was a Skinny, and she certainly didn't hate *him*. So, she could never hate Sally, either.

She said awkwardly, "Sally, you said it would be a good idea if somebody destroyed the Skin Eaters, but is that really how you feel? Doesn't that mean . . . well, you too? Is that what you really meant?"

"Don't *you* think it would be a good idea?" There was a slight edge to Sally's voice. She turned away and looked down at the stove, gleaming clean as always. "Wouldn't you expect that, knowing what I know and having done what I've done, that I'd feel that way? Most people don't want to acknowledge their appetites. Pork chops are always more palatable when they come wrapped in plastic. No one wants to be the one who actually slaughters the pig. So, perhaps the person who should have the final say for our kind should be someone like me, who actually knows where our food comes from. A happy butcher. Okay, that's it. I don't want to talk about it anymore."

Chapter Twenty-Four

Nina got through the rest of the day somehow, but she was never sure afterward exactly how. By sundown, she was shaking so badly Alastaire said, "Hey, you want me to score you some weed or a drink or something? I-I mean, um, ahem . . . assuming any of the kids here have anything like that."

"No, thanks," Nina said, smiling with what she knew must be a very sick-looking smile. "The last thing I need is to try and get through this thing drunk or stoned. I'm barely going to be coherent as it is." She looked at Bella, who was approaching them carrying a huge stack of books.

"What are you doing?" she asked him. "I can't ask you a question during the contest.

Why the library?"

"I know, but I figured maybe I could nod to you, or shake my head, or . . . or I don't know! It was the only thing I could think of!" Bella looked even more nervous than she did, and she had a sudden thought.

"Bella, I could read *your* mind during the contest! Why didn't we think of that before?

Here I've been busting my butt studying, when all I have to do is channel *you* and . . . and . . ." She lost steam as she saw him shaking his head. "No, you can't. They set the judges' polynomial engines to pick up any direct telepathic messages going to any of the contestants. You can send stuff out, because they've never had anyone as skilled at manipulating other people's thoughts as you are. But I can't send thoughts back to you. They'd know."

"Oh." She thought of something else. "Bella, why haven't *you* ever competed in the Hadiade? You could mop the floor with Simone. You're the smartest kid here. Unless..."

She knew he'd guessed where she was going with that train of thought—he was nodding glumly. He dumped the books onto one of the empty folding chairs that had been set up on the lawn and shrugged. "You're right. I'm a coward. I get terrible stage fright. Even during exams, I always ace everything, but I have to drink like a bottle of Kaopectate beforehand just to get through it." He mumbled, "It's called irritable bowel syndrome."

"Irritable— What? You're kidding! You can't do it because you ... you ..." Alastaire could barely finish her thought, because she was laughing too hard. "You can't do it because you get the shits?"

Bella scowled at her and said, "Oh, put a cork in it, Miss Claustrophobia. Remind me to put you on a bus sometime and send you to Chicago."

Nina left them to squabble together and walked over to the small stage that had been set up at the far end of the garden. Professors Mwindo, Hermes, Seneschal, Ariadne, and Samson were already milling around there. Professors Aspidistrus and Threet could be seen hurrying over from the side door together, an unlikely couple, tall and thin accompanied by short, fat, and green. The students who were going to compete in the Hadiade were all grouped together on the far side of the stage, not really touching one another, and not really talking to one another either, but giving each other quick, covert glances. There were five of them in all: Nina, Simone, a girl named Kathy Hareton whom Nina recognized from Sky Geography, Armand Louis from Calculation Science, and the boy from Animal Dominance who could turn himself into a barn owl at will.

Everyone settled down as Professor Danvers came striding toward them across the grass, just as the last rays of the setting sun were filtering through the skeins of moss in the trees. The shadows cut across his pale, expressionless face. He paused to briefly nod to the other teachers before walking up onto the stage and sitting down. The rest of the staff followed suit in the row behind him. The competitors shuffled onto the stage and sat in a row as well, Simone contriving to be first while Nina was pushed to the farthest end.

All the students found seats in the rows below them on the lawn, some of them carrying signs that read *Simone's #1!* and *Team Armand!* Some were carrying bags of popcorn and other snacks. Professor Danvers stood up and an uneasy silence fell.

"Ladies and gentlemen—" Professor Danvers's lips twisted to indicate he thought this honorific was scarcely justified in their cases, "—we've come to the end of another school year, and as such, it is my pleasure to welcome you to another Hadiade. The Daedalus School prides itself on not merely sheltering its charges, but educating them to take their rightful places in the world, and as such, this contest represents one of our oldest and most revered traditions.

"These five contestants—" He turned and his eyes swept over them, lingering for a moment on Nina, although she couldn't read his expression, "—have agreed to subject themselves to the rigors and the potential triumphs of testing their mettle against the hardest and most difficult lessons our kind has to learn and bear. Only one of them will emerge victorious. Although all of them are to be commended for their . . . nerve, if nothing else."

He hesitated and looked out over the audience, his eyes narrowing. "Now. Points will be awarded on the basis of accuracy, skill, strength, flair, and subtlety. At the end of the contest, the winner will be determined among those who haven't been previously disqualified, based on their overall accumulation of points. There will be no calling out, no signaling, no 'accidental' interruptions, and above all, *no stopping* once this contest has begun. Is that understood?"

All the students found reasons to look at their hands or their laps or their shoes.

"Very well," he said. "Then let the Hadiade begin, and may the most worthy win."

He sat back down, and Professor Hermes came forward and stood at a lectern in the center of the stage. Nina noticed Bella and Alastaire sitting tensely in the second row, Bella almost hidden behind his stack of books, while Alastaire sat forward, her hands clasped between her knees, her knuckles white.

Nina looked around and saw Roticus standing over by the carriage house, holding two of the wild gray wolves on a leash, although she suddenly realized none of the other *jumbies* were present. She swallowed, thinking, *Breathe, breathe,* and pictured a clear expanse of water, flat and silvery under a night sky. She imagined a woman coming toward her in a boat, and the words being spoken, *I exist.* And she felt as ready as she'd ever be.

Glancing over toward the kitchen door, she wondered if Sally was watching, but she couldn't tell.

Professor Hermes turned his moon-white eyes toward them and said, "Children, I'd like to start our first round off with some Calculation Science."

The first questions were actually easy. What were the basic principles of CS? (All data was binary and all phenomena could be understood by the mind alone. Otherworldly phenomena simply didn't exist.)

Then they were each asked to explain a basic calculation formula.

Nina was asked how Gilles de Rais's crimes compared to Jack

the Ripper's, and she showed how a basic algorithm of viciousness over number of killings, multiplied by age and sex, revealed the Frenchman to be the clear winner.

Kathy Hareton was asked how the slaughter of the firstborn could be calculated to have increased or decreased the political chances of King Herod Antippas *vis-a-vis* the Romans in Judea, and she made the mistake of referring in theoretical terms to the divinity of Jesus. There was a collective groan from the audience, and Agatha Danvers banged a gavel from the side of the stage for silence.

Kathy looked like she'd stepped in shit and she knew it. "I-I didn't mean . . ." she stammered. "I didn't mean that's what *I* thought. It was just the Jews . . . they believed . . . well, King Herod did anyway . . . I mean, at least some of them . . . well, it's a factor that has to be considered."

"Not relevant," Professor Hermes said, sighing, "and scarcely a computational vector, given the spurious nature of such belief systems in general. I'm afraid, Miss Hareton, that I'm going to have to dismiss you from this competition."

There was much spontaneous *aww*ing and *boo*ing as Miss Hareton left the stage, her face red and tears running down her cheeks. Nina swallowed—there were clear pitfalls she'd have to remember. But at least she'd survived this round.

Professor Hermes nodded to the rest of them and said, "Very good. Simone, I particularly liked your use of fractal geometry to explain the Lisbon earthquake of 1755 and the subsequent loss of 90,000 lives. It was a good use of chaos theory. Now, everyone. Points?"

The faculty scribbled numbers on cards and held them up. Not surprisingly, Simone won that round on points, although Nina came in second. Armand and the owl-boy shot her dirty looks, and she ducked her head. Professor Hermes smiled and said, "Thank you. Now I'd like to turn the next portion of the contest over to Professor Threet."

The nervous little Sky Geographer came up and asked them various questions about the constellations, but they were all softballs and easily answered. Nina noticed Professor Danvers shutting his eyes, barely stifling a yawn. No one was disqualified during that round, or during the next one, which covered basic Hygiene. Then they moved on to Professor Mwindo and Skin Eater Literature.

Bella excused himself and sidled along his row and then ran into the main building.

Nina figured his bowels must be acting up.

Professor Mwindo gave them each a short piece of poetry and asked them to explain it. Armand got "Crow" by Ted Hughes, and explained how the line, "Who is stronger than Death? Me, evidently," encapsulated a pure statement of Skin Eater philosophy. Owl-boy drew a blank on Shakespeare's sonnet, "My mistress's eyes are nothing like the sun." He wailed, "I don't know! She's not that pretty, I guess! Maybe he wants to break up with her!" and retired from the stage heaped in scorn. Nina felt guilty at being relieved, but she'd been worried about him during the Transformation test. Simone went next.

"Lord Byron's 'Darkness,'" she drawled.

She held up the slip of paper she'd been given and read in a quiet voice:

I had a dream, which was not all a dream.
The bright sun was extinguished, and the stars
Did wander darkling in the eternal space,
Rayless, and pathless, and the icy earth
Swung blind and blackening in the moonless air;
Morn came and went—and came, and brought no day,

And men forgot their passions in the dread
Of this their desolation, and all hearts
Were chilled into a selfish prayer for light . . .

When she finished, no one spoke, and Nina had to admit she'd read the poem beautifully.

Simone broke the spell by saying, "Well, it's obvious, isn't it? That's what the world is. We're all here on a dying planet. Lord Byron is telling us to pull our socks up. What we've got left is our minds and our appetites and our *wills*. That's what's going to save us. Not wringing our hands and feeling sorry for the little guy. Only the strong will survive, and not all of them will, either." She lifted her chin. "The weakest of our kind will be winnowed out as well as the humans and the *jumbies*. Pity's a waste of time, we've got to wise up now before it's too late."

There was a smattering of applause, and Nina found herself saying out loud, "I disagree."

"*What*?" Simone's head swung around so fast she was like a snake striking. For a moment, her beautiful face was contorted with rage and malice, and something almost like fear.

Nina stood up, so angry at the idea that there was *just no hope*—especially for all the poor *jumbies* who weren't even allowed to be there—that her heart was pounding and she thought, *I have to say something, don't I?*

And clearly in her mind, she heard the words, *"Answer her."* She looked at Professor Danvers, but he wasn't looking at her at all. His hooded eyes were contemplating the toe of one of his boots, but she heard his voice in her head nonetheless. *"You can do this. Why do you think you're here? Just think about what's wrong with that whole idea and answer her."*

And just like that, she knew what she had to say.

"I think we all have a choice," she said. "I think that's what the poem is really saying. We have a choice about how to feel about a world that's been plunged into sudden darkness, with the sun extinguished and the stars either snuffed out or gone away. We can accept it. Or we can still *care*. We can still *hope*. And when push comes to shove, that's what people really do in this poem. That's what's really going on here. Men forget their passions and their petty grievances and become focused on one single, solitary thing. The memory of light. And the hope, the desperate hope, that it will come back.

"Yes, yes, I know," she continued against a storm of muttering that had broken out on all sides. "Daylight's not such a great thing for some of you, and being human is something you've all turned your backs on, but you can't have forgotten it entirely. You just can't. The alternative isn't just dying, it isn't just figuring out how to live underground or construct synthetic sunlight and live in caves. It's giving up. It's forgetting there was ever any such thing as light. You know, they say other stars may have other planets, and sometimes those suns explode, and so, this kind of stuff actually happens. And if there are people left on those dying planets, even if they're actually physically dying of the cold, or their crops are failing, what this poem says is that they spend their last minutes trying to call the light *back*. Praying for it to continue.

"Because they don't want to give up. And isn't that true of all of you? You all want to keep existing." She looked around. "I mean, isn't that the point of all the crossing and consuming of lives and so on? And for that, you have to have hope in its most basic form, the idea that living is better than dying. You've got to say, against every argument in the book, that yes, it *does* make sense to get up in the morning. You've got to say even hurting like hell is better than feeling nothing at all. You guys still remember when the sunlight didn't hurt. You remember how good it felt, and there's a part of you that still likes that it's *there*, even if you have to hide from it. The alternative is despair, and that means death, even if you're still standing up and walking around. You're dead inside. And you guys aren't dead." Her voice cracked. "I mean . . . if anybody had a reason to hope against hope, it's people who've already died and come back, right? Isn't that in itself something worth fighting for?"

She waited. *I'm either the biggest fool in the world,* she thought, *or else they're actually going to buy that.*

And after a moment, Professor Mwindo nodded and said, "Hmm, interesting point. So you're saying the Skin Eaters' existential dilemma is to embrace hope, even though there's no objective support for it? Radical, but very compelling. One's reminded of Sartre's 'Man is condemned to be free.' Very good! Full points to Miss Lamb for a very interesting deconstruction!"

Which moved her into a tie for first place with Simone.

The next test was Animal Dominance, and Professor Samson said, "Okay, Roticus, bring 'em up and let's see how they do."

Roticus came forward, digging his heels into the grass with every step as he attempted to hold back the two big wolves who were dragging him across the lawn. Nina recognized Vlad, but Thor, the wolf she had personally befriended, wasn't there. Perhaps they'd considered it cheating to involve him. This other wolf looked, if anything, bigger, gaunter, grayer, and even meaner than the others, with a mad, hungry glint in his eyes that made more than a few students get up and take seats farther away.

Once Roticus had brought the wolves up to just below the stage, Professor Samson blew his whistle and puffed out his chest and said, "All right! Now each of the contestants will have five minutes to put one of these bad boys through his paces, and we'll be judging you on speed, agility, singleness of purpose, and complication of the task selected. Okay? So . . . you want to go first, Miss Freeland? Why don't you show the others how it's done?"

Simone smiled and stepped forward, looking sassy and beautiful in her black clothes, her long hair rippling in the moonlight. Within five minutes, she had Vlad dancing around on his hind legs, pawing the air and howling helplessly as he moved across the grass in a graceful foxtrot . . . or Nina supposed, it should really be called a wolftrot.

"Oh, yeah, baby, that's the stuff, all right . . ." Professor Samson crooned ecstatically, and then, when Professor Danvers shot him a withering glance, "Sorry, I mean, um, well done, Miss Freeland. You certainly know how to dominate. Okay, who's next? How about you?"

He pointed at Armand, who was handsome and blond and as pale as the moon, and who swaggered up and pointed his finger at the bigger wolf. "I'll take him," he said, his expression suggesting he thought Vlad was barely worth his time.

Bella, who had resumed his seat, cut his eyes between Nina and the wolf and then shook his head. Clearly, he thought this wolf was a killer.

"Okay, let's see . . . How about some fireworks?" Armand jumped down from the stage and ran over to the wolf, neatly leapfrogging over him. The wolf turned around and looked at him like he didn't know quite what had happened. Armand laughed—a high, cruel laugh—and ran at him and did it again. The wolf lunged at him this time, but Armand spun around and snapped his fingers, yelling sharply, "Down!"

The wolf stood stock still, ears back, a growl singsonging in its throat. Armand pointed his finger at him and yelled, "Down, you low-slung bastard!" And after that, things happened very quickly.

The wolf leaped forward and swallowed Armand's whole hand,

and there was a sickening crunch of bone. Armand screamed, and the wolf hung on like grim death.

Professor Samson jumped down off the stage and ran toward them, raising a stick and yelling, "Roticus! Hey you! Get your fat ass over here and stop all this!" although the little *jumbie* looked like he wasn't going anywhere near the wolf. In fact, he looked like he was going to faint.

Armand didn't look much better, and after several moments, the wolf let go and trotted away, spitting out Armand's hand as he went. The boy howled, blood spurting from the stump of his arm to spatter the first few rows of students.

Professor Samson looked up at the stage and mumbled, "Um, sorry . . . new . . . you know . . . didn't know his own strength. I assure you, it won't happen again."

Professor Danvers sighed and said, "Aggie, get some thread and bandages. Armand looks like he needs them," and Agatha muttered something under her breath and stalked down from the stage. She picked up the still-twitching hand, holding it by the tips of her fingers, and then shrugged and led the bleeding youth away. Professor Aspidistrus leaned forward and said something in Professor Danvers's ear, and the younger man nodded and stood up.

"Everyone," Danvers said, "your attention, please. In view of this ridiculous . . . I mean in view of this unfortunate event, we shall skip the rest of Professor Samson's portion of the Hadiade and allow him and Roticus to return his charges to their kennels and settle them down. Professor Aspidistrus has agreed to move us forward to our last test of skill, which will be in Advanced Alchemy. Professor?"

He nodded to the little green man, who waddled over to the lectern and said, "Thank you. Now, Miss Freeland . . . Miss Lamb

. . ." He nodded to the two girls, who were the only students left onstage. "This last challenge is deceptively simple. All you have to do is change this coin—" And he held one up in his leafy green fingers "—from lead to gold."

Everyone in the audience drew in their collective breaths, because of course this wasn't "simple" at all. Simone said before she could stop herself, "That's impossible. Nobody can do that!" and Professor Aspidistrus said, "Tut tut, Miss Freeland. Nicolas Flamel and Roger Bacon did it, not to mention Alessandro Cagliostro and Mary the Jewess. Surely, they're not 'nobodies.'"

"I didn't mean . . ." Simone shut up before she did herself any more harm. Nina looked at her and thought, Can *Simone do it?* Right now, Simone was ahead on points. If she could change the coin into gold, she'd win. If she couldn't, and Nina somehow managed to do it . . .

But then she reminded herself that she didn't have the faintest idea how to change lead into gold.

She watched as Simone went first. They had set up a little Bunsen burner on the stage, with a simple array of chemicals, and Simone tried everything she could think of, but the coin was still dark and gray when she handed it back to Professor Aspidistrus with a frown. Her expression wasn't much brighter, and she shot the professor the finger as he turned away. Several people in the audience giggled, although nobody said anything.

"Miss Lamb, you're next." Professor Aspidistrus's tone was mild.

"Just a second." A man sitting among the teachers stood up, a man so completely unremarkable that Nina had trouble even focusing on his face. Was he white? Black? Asian? Fat? Thin? She had no idea. He looked like nothing in particular, just a man. He vaulted up onto the little stage and inspected the table of chemicals, and said, "Hmm, interesting. You don't have any tin here, I see, or silver."

"No, we don't." Professor Aspidistrus wasn't reacting at all—not like he knew this man, but not like he didn't, either. He seemed calm, detached. "Tell us, why is that important?"

"Well, the seven major elements are all parts of the process. Lead we have here." The unknown man held up the coin. "And gold is what we want as an end result. But you also need tin and iron and copper and mercury and silver to complete the working, and as I said, you're missing silver and tin."

"Interesting." Professor Aspidistrus's voice was like dry palm leaves rustling. Nina suddenly realized this might all be part of the test. "So, would you say the deck was stacked?"

"Yes." The man looked at the equipment on the table, and added, "You also need a new vessel to finish the work."

"Really? Why?"

"Well, you've got one vessel here." The man held up a dark glass beaker, its color shiny as onyx. "That's for the black phase of the work—death, destruction. And another one here." He held up a second beaker, made of milky-white glass. "For the white phase—purification. But you need a third vessel, red, for the final change from lead to gold. Red for light, fire, warmth. And for blood. The rebirthing of matter into new life. Black, white, red."

He held up his fingers, one, two, three, and then walked off the stage and disappeared, and it was like a spell being broken. Professor Aspidistrus looked out at the audience and blinked, as though coming back to himself, and a few of the other teachers shifted position like they were waking up. Professor Danvers looked across at Nina and narrowed his eyes, clearly puzzled.

It was Simone who broke the silence, and her voice was angry. "Wait a minute, you never told us this was a trick question. What the hell's going on? Who was that guy?"

"What 'guy,' Miss Freeland?" Professor Aspidistrus seemed to have regained his equanimity. "I have no idea what you're talking about. Much of alchemy involves preparation, and if we've left anything out, I'd expect you to mention it. Your turn, Miss Lamb. What can you tell us about our little experiment? Do you have anything to add?"

I got nothing, she thought. Clearly, the point of this exercise was to notice what was missing, but that still didn't answer the bigger question. Who was the man who'd just interrupted them, and why was everybody else pretending like he'd never been there? As she walked up to the little table, she snuck a glance at Bella and Alastaire, who both appeared to be asleep still, though with their eyes open. Nina wondered, *Are Simone and I the only two people here who even* saw *him?*

She looked down at the array of ingredients, trying to see what else was wrong, what other mistake she could catch, but she couldn't see one. Iron, copper, and mercury were all there, the metals ground fine, the mercury a blob like liquid silver, shimmering in a little bowl. There were the two vessels, black and white, with the third one, red, missing. What had that man said? "You need a third vessel, red, for the final change to occur. Red for light, fire, warmth. And for blood." Was she supposed to shed blood? Was she supposed to demand some from somebody else? She remembered being in the chapel, and the black cup spurting blood all over her hands. She remembered Zoolie, Legs, the kids on Pauline Street, and Sister Aquilina. And she remembered Sally saying, "You've done things far worse and far harder than this dumb-ass Hadiade. And that's just since I've known you."

And Bella: "See if you can get inside my mind and do magic."

Of course. That's it. She turned her mind outward to everybody who was there, the professors and the students alike, and tried to feel her way inside all of them at once.

What came to her gradually was a crescendo of babbling, as people's brains came back online: questions, distractions, *what just happened*, curious voices, thoughts, sensations, *was I asleep*, as well as plans for tomorrow, three erotic daydreams, and four people getting back to doing the sudoku puzzles in their laps. This was her perfect opportunity to sneak inside their minds without their noticing.

See what I want you to see, she thought as she picked up the lead coin. It felt heavy and somehow . . . well, dead in her palm. Lead: the metal of death, darkness. The metal of Saturn, planet of cannibals, planet of the Saturni. The metal whose symbol was the crow—Who is stronger than death? Me, evidently."

And she thought, *See it change.*

And as she thought that, she thought of gold. Sunlight, warmth, yellow, happiness so bright it burned the eye. She thought of gold medals, buttercups, crowns, honey, daffodils, golden arches . . . everything gold that might make you smile or make you happy. And she thought, *I can feel it. I can actually feel them seeing it change.*

She knew it was a cheat: no alchemy was occurring, no arcane process was actually taking place, but still she thought, *See it.* And she suddenly knew that they could.

She held the coin up, and there was a collective gasp. Everyone there saw it shining like a beacon in her hand. A big, round disc. Pure, solid gold.

"What the hell?" Simone snarled, as Alastaire stood up and yelled, "Woo-hoo! You go, girl!" and Bella pumped his fist in the air and let out a raucous, "Yah, baby!" and the rest of the crowd exploded in spontaneous applause. Professor Samson blew helplessly on his whistle, and Professor Mwindo finally gave up pounding his gavel, and Professor Hermes blinked and said, "What? I can't quite make it out," and Professor Aspidistrus said,

"My word, Miss Lamb, I've never seen anything quite like that in my life!"

Professor Danvers was staring at her with a considering look, but he didn't say a word, and everyone else was cheering and yelling, except for Simone, who was shooting daggers at her.

Simone said, "Professor Danvers, I think she cheated. Nina Lamb cheated. She couldn't have changed that lead into gold by any normal means. Professor Danvers, I want her disqualified at once!"

Professor Danvers stood up and crossed the stage to Nina in two strides, his face tight. "Miss Lamb," he murmured, his voice frighteningly low.

"Y-yes?"

"You seem to have a remarkable talent for beating the odds. By fair means or foul. Miss Freeland is very talented and very astute, *and* very capable of making any number of our lives exceedingly miserable if she loses. Are you very, *very* sure you want to continue and show me that coin?"

Nina looked into his eyes, dark tunnels of endless night, and tried to guess what he might be thinking. It was like she was attached to his navel chakra, one cord pulling her to him so strongly she couldn't breathe. *Protect me*, she thought. *Save me,* but she couldn't feel him answering. Perhaps he refused to even hear her. His mouth was a bloodless gash, the thin line of a frown between his eyebrows, and he looked so bleak, so stoic and proudly convinced that only suffering could be real, that her heart broke. *I wish it was real,* she thought miserably. *I wish I could make it be true and make you happy.*

She held out the coin to him instead, and waited for him to see that it was a fake and punish her.

He flinched. Then, after a moment, he said, "Miss Lamb, that's just not possible."

He was staring down at his palm, where he was holding, very plainly, a real gold coin. And she heard his voice in her head, murmuring, *All right, you win. This round.*

And just as he looked up, Agatha screamed from the kitchen door. "Strickland, come quickly! The *jumbies* are gone!"

Chapter Twenty-Five

In the end, it took them only a short time to figure out what had probably happened.

A broken windowpane in the carriage house had allowed someone to reach in and unlock the door to the street while everyone was out on the lawn watching the Hadiade. No one had been guarding the back of the school, where the *jumbies* stayed, since their passivity was well- known. Someone must have rounded them up and taken them away pretty quickly, someone forceful enough to make them move at more than their usual shambling pace. And it seemed fairly clear to everyone who that might have been.

"She's made her move," Agatha spat, shaking her head. "I could kick myself for having been inside stitching up Armand's hand while she was doing it. If only I'd been able to catch her in the act!"

"We all wish we'd been that lucky, dear sister, but unfortunately, what's done is done." Professor Danvers was trying to remain calm. He looked at Professor Samson. "Will the wolves be of any use in finding them?"

"I can try," Samson said, summoning Roticus. "Hey, you, get the pack out and give them some meat to get the scent. We're going hunting."

Nina didn't want to think what kind of meat he was talking about. All the students were huddled in the front hall, where they'd been told to wait once the alarm was raised. Simone was surrounded by a coterie of friends, and she was whispering to them fiercely. Bella and Alastaire had immediately joined Nina, and they were now stuck to her side like bodyguards.

Alastaire was still excited that Nina had won. She kept holding up her index finger at Simone and mouthing, *"We're Number One! We're Number One!"* while Bella had gotten out his polynomial engine and was furiously calculating. Everyone else seemed to be stunned, the transition from excitement to threat too quick for them to process.

"Everyone, please give me your attention," Professor Danvers said, walking up to the first landing, where he could turn and survey them all. His manner was deliberately calm, although Nina noticed his hands were clenched. "Due to this distressing circumstance, we will postpone the crowning of this year's Hadiade champion—" he sketched a slight bow in Nina's direction "—until we have a better idea what kind of a risk we're facing. I would ask you all not to panic, but to treat this as you would any serious emergency. You may all think you have some idea what we're up against, and you may be right. Sister Aquilina may indeed have returned.

"However, and I would ask you to please keep this in mind, we have no proof at this time. That having been said, no one is to enter or leave the school until further notice. We can't protect you if you go off the grounds. That means all of you."

Nina wondered if he was looking directly at her, or if she was just imagining it.

He went on, "Your teachers and I will be in contact with the Saturni to determine the best course of action. I'd suggest that you all try and do some extra studying, but that may be expecting too much." He shrugged. "In any case, please keep calm. I'll be making an announcement once we know more."

He turned, walked up the stairs, and slammed the door to his office, and everyone else let out a collective sigh. No one wanted to stay cooped up inside the school, but no one wanted to go out and be kidnapped either. Simone hissed, "This sucks I tell you, I *saw* somebody—" and the teachers broke into their own murmuring groups. Professor Threet, in particular, looked so nervous she was practically babbling: "The moon . . . you know what time of the month it is . . . It can't be a coincidence . . . The full moon is *tomorrow night . . .*"

Nina turned to Bella and Alastaire and said, "Come on, we need to talk." They headed for the long corridor outside the chapel, where they were fairly certain no one else would follow them. Not for the first time, Nina wondered why they had a chapel at all, since all the Skinnies claimed to be atheists. Were they hedging their bets? Or had some Skinny somewhere had a revelation and told them they had to build a chapel, to at least *suggest* there might be another way of thinking?

"Okay," Nina said, once they were out of earshot, "listen up. Who was that guy who came up in the middle of the test, and what the hell's going on?"

Both friends looked at her blankly.

"Oh come on!" she snapped. "He was right there! This tall guy . . . or . . . or maybe he wasn't, I don't know. He was kind of . . . well, maybe he was short. Or not. But he was definitely there! And he said they were missing tin and silver, and a red vessel to complete the transmutation! And . . . and . . ."

"Nina?" Alastaire put her arm around her. "Are you okay? I've gotta tell you, I have no idea what you're talking about."

"The man I saw! Oh, for God's sake, Simone saw him! She asked who he was, remember? You were both there! Didn't you hear her? She said nobody told her it was a trick question, and she asked who that guy was! He . . . he was sitting with the teachers, and then he came up and said—"

She stopped. Alastaire was still shaking her head, but Bella was staring into space, a muscle tight in his jaw. He finally said, "She's right. I *do* remember something. Only I have no idea what it was."

"You remember some guy being there?" Alastaire sat down on one of the hard wooden benches lining the hallway and blinked at him. "Really? 'Cause I don't. I mean, I don't remember anything like that. I mean, I kind of remember somebody sitting there, and then getting up and walking across the stage, but it's . . . it's like trying to remember a dream."

Nina waited, then Bella got out his polynomial engine again and started typing. She heard him whispering to himself, "A trance net, extended over the whole school. It's the only explanation, but I can't imagine anyone having that kind of power. It would have taken more energy than a hundred Circles of Force—no one person could ever have done it. And why didn't it work on Simone and Nina?"

"Because it wasn't meant to?" Nina asked.

She remembered the man, his face so blank he might have been wearing a stocking mask, looking down at the alchemical instruments and then holding up his fingers, one, two, three, and she tried to remember anything, *any* distinguishing feature about him, but she drew a blank. He had very clean hands, and that was the only thing she could remember specifically. For some reason, she hadn't expected his hands to be so clean. They were . . . beautiful.

She said slowly, "Maybe it wasn't a person at all. Maybe it was something else." "What?"

"I have no idea."

Rubbing her forehead, Nina sat down next to Alastaire on the bench. She only realized now how tired she was. The intense pressure of the Hadiade, the thousands of things she'd been afraid they'd ask her, were finally taking their toll. She watched as Bella continued to fiddle with his PE and finally said, "Do you have to keep doing that? You're driving me crazy."

"I'm trying to figure something out," Bella said between gritted teeth, and then he stopped. "No, none of it makes sense. None of it. There's something seriously wonky here."

Alastaire made a halfhearted gesture of pointing at him, but he ignored it. "Look," he said, holding out the engine. "There's a whole lot of stuff here that's fake, that just can't be true. For one thing, this break-in. Sister Aquilina doesn't need to break windows to get inside the school. She's powerful enough to blast the whole door off the carriage house if she wanted to.

Besides, Nina already saw her inside the grounds the other night," and Nina nodded. "This whole thing looks like a setup."

But why? Nina wondered. *Does somebody want to create a diversion?*

And then she remembered the Four Gifts.

"Bella, how do your calculations look if Sister Aquilina was just trying to throw us off the scent? What if she made us worry about the *jumbies* when she's actually after something else?"

And Bella got it at once. "Well…" He spun some more dials and punched in some more numbers. "In all likelihood, the Four Gifts are still here, somewhere inside the building, because there'd be a hell of a big disturbance in the school's electromagnetic field if they were moved suddenly. We've seen no electrical storms, ball lightning, or anything like that. So I'm guessing she still hasn't gotten to them *yet.*"

"But you think she's planning to?"

"As you'd know, if you'd ever really studied Calculation Science—" he sighed and held up the PE "—this isn't a crystal ball." He shoved the device back into his pocket. "Besides, there's too many other variables. Like this unknown trance-caster, who—"

He broke off and sat looking at the portraits that lined the walls of the hallway. Then he got up and walked over to squint at the nameplates that were inset into the heavy gold frames.

Nina followed him and asked, "What is it? What did you notice?"

"I'm not sure," he said. "Just look at these, though. This is Madame Livaudais, the woman who once owned this place. And this one is . . ." He squinted. "Unknown male, possibly a slave named Christmas, who may have been a part of the Livaudais household, 1810-1820. Um, guys, doesn't he look like somebody we know?"

The portrait showed a beautiful young man with honey-colored skin and long blond curls, worn loose and flowing, in a ruffled white shirt and a long coat, with lace at his throat and wrists. And there was something else.

He was wearing blue sunglasses.

"Jesus!" Nina yelled. "It's Legs! I mean, it's Legba, Crux, Christmas . . . Christ, how many names do these people have anyway?"

"Lemme see, lemme see, lemme see," Alastaire said, hurrying over and pushing in between them. She pointed. "Look. He's even got that same crappy coat! God, you'd think in two centuries he'd have found a tailor."

"Bella," Nina said, "could that be who it was? The guy who just appeared out of nowhere—Legs?"

"I don't know," Bella said, "but it makes more sense than anything else. Which means the *Lwas* wanted you to win." He pointed at Nina. "But that still doesn't explain whether they knew about Sister Aquilina, or whether they were part of her diversion, or even if they knew she was going to be here at all. And you know, I think we're missing a bigger question. Since Legs and Sister Aquilina are on the same side, can we trust *him*? Can we trust *anybody*? I mean, look . . . Sister Aquilina, who's Niobe Danvers, who was once Madame Livaudais, was once in love with a *Lwa*, who may very well have been this guy Christmas. They may *still* be in love. But we don't know that for a fact either. We don't know anything. He may hate her now. He may be looking for her."

Bella shook his head, and suddenly he looked his real age. Just a kid. He burst out, "We don't know *anything*, and it's all coming to a head, and we don't even know whose side anyone's on! It's too hard! Somebody's working toward a goal, some overall plan that's set to culminate in the next couple of days—the numbers all prove that! But they don't prove anything else, and we came in too late in the game, and we're just nobodies, and there's a big variable we haven't even considered yet. And oh, the hell with it. My bowels are acting up again. Nina, I'm really glad you won tonight, but I hate to tell you—that may not mean a thing compared to whatever it is that's coming next."

And he ran away in the direction of a bathroom.

Chapter Twenty-Six

They finally went to bed, because too many mysteries could be more exhausting than too many answers. As Nina lay tossing and turning, she thought, *Isn't it about time some otherworldly being appeared and told me what's going on?* The Skinnies were her friends, her only family, and yet arrayed against them were shadows, spirits, gods . . . what exactly? A spectral force older than the world, a race of extraterrestrials not even from this universe? And were these beings benevolent or evil, truthful or lying, or even concerned with mankind at all? If you were older than the world, didn't the fate of the world cease to matter? And if it didn't matter, then what was left? Design, or simply chaos?

"The Saturni were our brothers and sisters," she remembered Legs saying, "but they coveted. We had no idea of the inherent contradictions. If you mix fire and gasoline, you don't get a steady blaze. You get an explosion."

In a way, I hate them all. I hate the Skin Eaters.

She hated the idea of killing just to feed, to cram everything living into your mouth and to destroy it. To worship the belly, the navel chakra above all else, until all you ended up with was shit. None of them wanted to plant things, to nurture anything, to make a greater abundance. So long as they filled their gullet, the world could become less and less until it finally disappeared. Theirs was the philosophy of *now*, the philosophy of *gimme, gimme . . . mine*, and so long as every whim was satisfied, they were happy. So long as every appetite was sated, they were content, and they could lie down at the end of their lives in comfort, burping up gouts of blood.

She wanted to scream, but instead, she opened her eyes and stared at the high ceiling above her, willing herself to ignore the tears leaking out of her eyes and running down the sides of her face.

Which was when she saw the light.

A wavering light coming up the stairs, moving back and forth in the slit between her bedroom door and the floor, not supernatural at all. In fact, after a moment, she recognized it for what it was—a flashlight. She lay as still as she could on the bed and barely breathed. There were two sets of footsteps accompanying the light—one heavy and deliberate, if slightly off balance; the other, light and reluctant, almost shuffling. It was as if a larger person were dragging a smaller person upstairs. She heard breathing, and the sound of somebody sniveling. And then she heard Professor Danvers's voice, a little slurred, sounding a little less precise than usual, saying, "All right, show me where they were."

"H-here," came a quavering voice, and Nina recognized Roticus, the one remaining *jumbie*.

"You saw them?"

"Yes, they were there. Pistachio shells, a whole pile of them."

"An evening snack of yours, perhaps?"

"No, sir! I never— I mean, I wouldn't dare to steal anything from the kitchen, I swear it!" "Never mind." The flashlight scanned the floor just outside Nina's door, and she had an irrational impulse to say something idiotic like, *"C'mon, I'm trying to sleep in here!"*

The professor continued to press. "They aren't there now, though, are they?"

"No, sir, they . . . the three students must have swept them away."

"But you're sure the pistachio shells *were* there initially?"

"Yes, sir! I saw them! I swear it!"

"Roticus, Roticus . . ." Professor Danvers's voice sounded even less exact than usual, almost . . . teasing. Almost drunk. "You're swearing up down and sideways tonight. One would think you had something to hide."

"I don't . . . please . . . I-I won't . . . I won't say anything you don't like . . ."

"You'd better not."

"I don't know what you—"

"Oh God, I am truly surrounded by louts and fools! Does no one appreciate subtlety? Be *still* you little worm! Be still!"

There was a sudden movement, and a small intake of breath. Almost like a hiccup. And then silence. Nina focused, and she could finally hear soft breathing and the suspicious sound of fabric being torn, and *Oh God, I do* not *want to be hearing this*, she thought, and then there was a small yelp and a plaintive cry of "Sir!"

"Shh," came Professor Danvers's voice, half grunt, half lullaby. "Don't move and don't say a word. I want very much to pretend this isn't happening, and you probably feel the same way. Don't let's spoil it for each other."

Nina knew she very much didn't want to be eavesdropping, and at the same time, lying there in bed with her fingers in her ears wasn't much better. She also felt angry. Didn't anyone even remember she was there? All right, Professor Danvers might be drunk, and he might have brought Roticus up there on the pretext of looking for the pistachio shells, but they sure as hell weren't looking for them now. Did he *want* her to hear this? Was this his way of telling her to keep her distance? She heard a whimper— and suddenly she'd had enough. She was fed up with the fact that Professor Danvers seemed to think he could do anything in front of her and she wouldn't even care.

She got out of bed and ran to the door and yanked it open so hard it banged against the wall.

She stopped short.

The scene that met her eyes had, she supposed, its comic elements. Professor Danvers was sitting on the floor with Roticus cradled in his lap. He held him gently, and the *jumbie* boy seemed to be in a daze, his head lolling to one side. The professor was holding him in the crook of his arm and seemed to be in the act of nuzzling his neck, and then Nina realized what he was actually doing. He was biting him very carefully on the lobe of his ear. A thin piece of skin was held between his teeth, and as she watched, he detached it and let his own head fall back, swallowing the tiny morsel.

And then his eyes met hers.

An instant later, he was up and on his feet, and Roticus was lying unconscious on the floor. A trickle of blood ran from the *jumbie*'s wounded ear, barely a thread, like a fine red line. You would barely have noticed it if you hadn't been looking for it, and it might have come from a pinprick. But of course, for Nina and Professor Danvers both, it might as well have been a severed artery.

"I—" Professor Danvers said in a strangled voice, and then he turned and bolted down the stairs, running for his life as if the hounds of hell were after him. Nina, for her part, slammed the door on Roticus and sank down onto the floor herself. She only realized when she saw how wet her hands were that her whole body was shaking from her desolate sobs.

Chapter Twenty-Seven

"I have to leave. I can't stay here. That's the only answer. I just have to go."

Sally tried to distract Nina by making her a cup of tea and handing her a plate full of freshly baked profiteroles, but even surrounded as she was by the warmth and light of the kitchen, Nina didn't feel like she could do anything except cry and continue to shiver. Her tears had long since exhausted themselves, but her dry sobs reminded her too awfully of Roticus's little hiccup of dread, and she had the feeling she might never be able to eat anything again.

Finally, Sally took the tea away and handed her a glass of clear liquid instead. "What is it?"

"Vodka," Sally said shortly. "Here, down the hatch." She poured herself a finger as well and tossed it back. Nina forced herself to take a sip, and as it warmed her belly, she did find a little comfort returning to her.

"You're not supposed to get us drunk," she pointed out.

"Your teachers aren't supposed to eat you guys, either. Sometimes desperate times call for desperate measures. Ah, good, here's reinforcements." Sally glanced over her shoulder as Alastaire and Bella came into the room, both in their pajamas. Somehow, the sight of Alastaire in her fuzzy, pink bunny slippers made Nina cry fresh tears she hadn't even known she had left.

"Okay, group hug, c'mon, let's get this over with," Sally said, summoning them all together for a cuddle. "Now," she said when she'd released them. "Tell your friends what's up and then let's decide what you're going to do next."

"So, I don't know what to do," Nina said, wiping her eyes, after she'd told them everything. She had no idea how Sally had summoned them there—telepathy?—but Nina was glad she had. "I feel like every time I get a handle on something, everything pulls the rug out from under me again." She sighed, then sipped a little more of her vodka, though she didn't want to drink *too* much. It was making her too relaxed, and she needed to keep her guard up.

"Well, aside from the ick factor, which I grant you is majorly icky, this really doesn't change much," Bella pointed out, sitting down and pushing up the sleeves of his robe. He got out his notebook and started paging through it. "What have we got? We've got the prophecy, which we know a little more about now. 'The Beautiful Hand' is *you*," he said, pointing at Nina, who raised her glass—ironically, just as Sally appeared at her elbow and poured her another shot.

Nina decided she had to watch out for Sally, who was halfway to getting her shit-faced.

"And we've got Zoolie's riddle, which we pretty much understand now," Bella said. "The Four Gifts are the four most powerful *Lwas*, who were imprisoned and hidden away in clay jars, and who symbolize Wisdom and Love and Memory and Destruction."

"And we know they're still here," Alastaire put in, eating a profiterole, "because the school hasn't blown up and experienced a major *Carrie*-style meltdown yet."

"Right. Now all this business with the *jumbies* . . ." Bella waved his hand. "Let's assume it was all just a smoke screen. Who cares who's taken them? It's not like the Skinnies can't find more at the nearest homeless shelter. I know, I know, that sounds cruel, but that doesn't mean it's not true. Which leaves the Gifts, and the fact that there's a full moon coming up tomorrow night. That *can't* just be a coincidence."

"What's up with the moon?" Sally asked, sitting down with them and sipping her own drink. She was dressed in something other than her usual chef's whites, which made her seem younger, more like their contemporary. Her Flaming Lips T-shirt and black jeans were rocking, but her eyes looked older, and Nina experienced a momentary disorientation. *And why doesn't Sally know about the moon if she's a Skinny?*

"The moon is a powerful weapon in the right hands," Bella said thoughtfully. "You could maneuver someone into standing in its rays and cause them great harm. It's like Professor Threet said—everything the light of the full moon touches works backward. A sick Skin Eater could be cured by its light, but a healthy Skin Eater would be killed. Especially if the rays were concentrated enough." He paused thoughtfully.

"Like with a noctoscope," Alastaire said. "See, you think I never pay attention."

"Right! So if we could get Sister Aquilina in line with a direct reflection from the noctoscope's mirror . . ."

"We could kill her." Nina felt a shiver run down her back. She added what she knew they were all thinking. "The question is, do we really want to?"

The other two looked at her, and she was pleased to see that they both looked uncertain. Sally was watching all three of them with a bemused expression, like she was interested in seeing what they'd end up doing. Bella had his lip caught between his teeth, and she could sense the polynomial engine behind his forehead working like crazy. Alastaire, for her part, looked uncharacteristically grave. Nina guessed this was the first time her friend had ever been called upon to really decide whether or not to kill someone.

"I mean . . ." Nina spoke slowly, thinking it through, "Sister

Aquilina is the enemy of the Saturni, who are the worst beings that ever lived. Father Ignatius and Mr. Benway and the Freelands and General Azazel aren't even human. They're evil *Introim*."

"And the Saturni are the ones who control the media, so they can make Sister Aquilina sound like the world's worst devil," Bella said. "They control the narrative."

"Yet, Sister Aquilina is the one who wants the Four Gifts. The Saturni are happy to leave them exactly where they are."

"Well," Sally said very softly. "Maybe you should let her have them." Nina looked up at her, and Sally made a face. "Look, I'm playing catchup here, so don't blame me. But it seems to me that when you don't know who to trust, you have two choices. You can either see what people do and judge by the results, or you can ask them. Of course, the first way's much more preferable, since people can easily lie, but in this case, you can do both. Why don't you try and catch Sister Aquilina in the act of stealing the Four Gifts, and then ask her why she wants them? That way you can hear what she has to say and see what she does at the same time."

Nina turned to Bella and Alastaire, and they looked at her with guarded but hopeful expressions. In fact, this idea seemed to make such perfect sense it took her a moment to figure out what was wrong with it. And then it hit her.

"But, Sally, we still don't know where the Four Gifts are! That's the whole problem. We know *what* they are, and whose they are, and why they're so valuable, but we still don't have any idea where they're hidden."

Sally just looked at her and said, in a way that was oddly reminiscent of Legs, "Are you sure?"

Nina wanted to snap back, "Yes, of course I'm sure," but instead, she thought about it. Had she seen anything in her visions that might give her a clue? Had Legs, or any of the other spirits, said anything? Was there a hidden subtext in Zoolie's riddle they hadn't figured out yet, or some hint in the prophecy, or something in Professor Danvers's book? But she kept drawing a blank.

All she could think was, *Shit, people have asked me too many questions in the last twenty-four hours. I'm so tired.* She'd been practicing, training, drilling for the Hadiade for *weeks*, and she'd even won the damn thing, but there was no letting up! She drank the rest of her drink, even though she knew she shouldn't. *Shit. If only Simone hadn't gotten her panties in a twist, just because we wrote that email to her grandfather, I wouldn't have had to go through with any of this in the first place!*

Which made her realize they'd never really figured out *why* Simone had gotten her panties in such a twist.

She said, "Guys, remember when Simone challenged me? Exactly what did she say?"

Bella shut his eyes to remember. "Well, first, you said, 'We scared him, isn't that what this is all about? He's superstitious enough that he can't quite bring himself to say that those "things" we talked about don't exist?'"

"Meaning the Four Gifts."

"Right. And then Simone said you didn't know what you were talking about."

"And I said, 'He knows, doesn't he?'" Nina pressed her hands to her temples. "I said, 'He knows they exist in the place of the highest honor'—"

"And then Agatha said you should go out for the school Hadiade!" Alastaire said. "God, we were so close. If she hadn't interrupted you, Simone might have actually told us something!"

"That's assuming she does know where the place of the highest honor is." Nina smacked the counter. "God damn it, it's another riddle! What has no feet and always runs? What's black and white and read all over? It's stupid! It's like a stupid cartoon, Bugs Bunny and the goddamn Road Runner and—"

And then she thought of the safe in Professor Danvers's office. And the name written on it in raised letters. Acme Security Company.

She caught her breath. No, it couldn't be. It was too dumb. It was too obvious. It was too *obscure*. Who used "acme" in that sense? As a word meaning the highest point of honor? No one.

No one, that is, unless they were thousands and thousands of years old, and had spoken old languages like Latin and Greek when they were once in general use. No one who wasn't versed in a world where riddles and poetry and puns were the preferred methods of communication. No one who wasn't a really, really "old man,"—someone who might be rattled enough, when asked about the Four Gifts, to make a foolish mistake.

No one, in other words, except General Azazel. *I'll bet Simone caught holy hell from her mother when she read that column in the newspaper.*

She looked at Bella and Alastaire, and Sally, and something in Sally's strange smile made her wonder, as always, if the cook could read her mind. Nina wondered if she'd been following along all the time, like somebody reading subtitles. *Okay . . . so far so good . . . yes, right, just a little bit further . . . that's it . . . by George, she's got it!* Nina wanted to smack her, and she also wanted to hug her again, but she didn't want to embarrass her.

She looked down at her empty glass and thought how, for the first time in she didn't know how long, she felt like they had a chance.

"I think I know where the Four Gifts are," she told her friends, and Bella clapped his hands and Alastaire said, "Outstanding!"

"And I think I know how we can stop Sister Aquilina," she

added. "But God!" She looked at the big clock over the kitchen stove, "It's almost five o'clock in the morning, and we've still got a ton of things to do before tomorrow night."

Chapter Twenty-Eight

The first thing they did was retreat to Nina's room and rest for a few hours. Nina thought she wouldn't be able to sleep, but she ended up falling into a dense unconsciousness the minute her head touched the pillow. When she woke up four hours later, she felt woolly-headed and thick-tongued. *I guess I did drink too much,* she thought, *or else it was just the cumulative effects of . . . everything.*

Sally's behavior the night before had been a little strange—*all right, be honest; she's always strange*—but Nina put off that thought for later. What she needed now was coffee, and some fresh air. She kicked Alastaire to wake her up and stumbled toward the door, where Bella was already trying to brush the creases out of his wrinkled jacket. Together they went downstairs and got mugs of coffee from the kitchen and wandered out into the early summer day.

"Ow!" Alastaire said as the light hit her forehead. "Anymore bright ideas, Miss Rebecca of Sunnybrook Farm?"

"Hide under a tree. I need some Vitamin D." Nina turned her face up to the brightness, which helped to dissipate the persistent feeling that her brain was full of fiberfill. After a few deep breaths, and having drunk the rest of her coffee, she felt ready for action. Bella and Alastaire were huddling in a small crescent of shade by the kitchen door, so she took pity on them and led them back to the Riding Ring, where the doors were open to the hot, humid breeze, but they were still covered. Nobody was there just then, so they had the cavernous straw- and manure-scented place to themselves.

"All right," Nina said, when they had settled themselves on bales of hay, "here's my idea. If I'm right and the Four Gifts are hidden in the safe in the Headmaster's Office, then that's where Sister Aquilina is going to go tonight. It's got to be tonight; Bella's calculations all point to it. She'll figure she's covered, with everybody locked down and nobody out wandering in the garden because of the moonlight.

"So, what I say is, we set the school noctoscope to focus the moon's rays directly through the boarded-up window into that office and then get in there and confront her. We'll see what she has to say, and if we don't like it, we pull the plywood off and fry her ass like a Thanksgiving turkey."

Bella nodded. "What about Professor Danvers?"

"I thought about that." Nina drew them in closer. "Since we don't know how he'll react, I think the best idea is to get him out of the way entirely." She took a quick breath. "I'll take care of that."

"What are you going to do, fuck him?" Alastaire asked. She only realized how much she'd embarrassed Nina when the latter hid her face and said, "Aauuugghh!"

Alastaire tried to explain, "I mean, um . . . well, it would certainly *work*, right? You could keep him busy for, like, the whole time! You heard what Legs said—he's sporting some serious wood for you. Man, it would be like the perfect diversion."

"Stop it!" Nina stuck her fingers in her ears and sang *La-la-la* until Alastaire finally ran out of steam. When the other girl had fallen silent, Nina said, "No, I'm *not* going to f—I mean, sleep with him. What I'm going to do is ask him to tell me the truth."

People can easily lie, and they usually do, she thought, but at this point it didn't matter. Even if he lied, she could still get him to talk to her, and she could still get him to stay put long enough to trap him. She hated that part of her plan, but she couldn't see any way around it. He would be furious. He would be humiliated and possibly, probably, certainly heartbroken at the missed opportunity to see his sister again, but at least, this way, she knew she could keep him safe.

"When he had me do divination, "Nina explained, "he cast a Circle of Force. Professor Hermes explained to me how you do it. It's actually Calculation Science. I'll send Professor Danvers word to meet me in the carriage house after dark, and then I'll cast a Circle and when he comes inside it, I'll trap him there. Then I'll come back to the office and meet you guys. I'll need to borrow one of your polynomial engines, though," she added, and Alastaire glanced at Bella and then handed over her own.

"Here. Wonk-boy would probably have a stroke if he was parted from his for five minutes."

Nina thanked her and stuffed the beautiful little clockwork device into her pocket. "I promise I'll take care of it," she said, because Alastaire's generosity touched her more than she wanted to admit. Bella was looking at her with a considering expression, and she asked, "What?"

"You ought to stay in the carriage house with him."

"Over your dead bodies." She waved aside the obvious joke. "I'm not letting you two run risks on my account. Remember, I'm the one who got you guys into this."

Besides, she thought, *if I'm the subject of the prophecy, I'm the one Sister Aquilina really wants*, but she didn't say that out loud. "You both would have been fine if it hadn't been for me. You could have spent your whole time here without worrying about anything." She picked at the hay bale they were sitting on. "I really screwed you up."

"No, you didn't." Bella's voice sounded reluctant, like he was admitting something that hurt or scared him. Nina glanced at

Alastaire, who was looking away, refusing to meet her eyes. Her hands were gripping the hay, and Nina had the bizarre idea she was going to cry.

"We wouldn't have been 'all right.'" Bella's words were harsh. "We're none of us 'all right' here. You just made it a little clearer, that's all."

"I don't understand." Nina shook her head. "Okay, so you didn't know about . . . well, everything the Skinnies do, but you would have learned about it in time. And you probably would have been okay with it. I mean, these are your people, right? Alastaire said it's your only home."

Alastaire abruptly stood and went off by herself, head down, and Nina watched her kicking clods of earth.

Bella said, "She pretends that sometimes. We all do. It makes it easier if you pretend you don't know. What do they say—denial is more than just a river in Egypt?"

He took in a deep breath and scanned the ceiling, and Nina realized he was trying to put something into words he might never have told anyone before.

"It's just . . . we all *do* remember. Our real families. Oh, not that much, and not like they were that great, but . . ." He stopped. "I think I was like four or five when I was taken. I was Ngo Van Tuan, which means 'intelligent male.'" He shrugged. "Yeah, I know, kind of obvious. Anyway, they . . . I don't know if they gave my father money, or if they threatened him or humiliated him. I just know my mother told me to go with these people, and I remember I didn't want to go. I cried and held on to her." He swallowed. "I wanted her to go with me. I wanted to take my toys. And they slapped me and told me to shut up. And that's the last I saw of them."

He paused and then continued in a flat voice, "Alastaire remembers going to the Rex parade with her real father, where she caught a stuffed cow. Everybody here's got some kind of shit memories like that. Stuff they remember from when they were normal, stuff they remember or dream about from being warm. The thing is, none of us were ever asked if we wanted this, none of us were ever told what was involved. We were all just spirited away. In one way, we felt like we'd won the lottery, but those kinds of lotteries aren't for the lucky ones. They never are. The only lucky ones were the kids who got left behind, the ones the Skin Eaters *didn't* take, because they didn't look cool enough or smart enough or pretty enough to be Skin Eater children. And they didn't look tasty enough to become *jumbies*."

He rubbed his hands over his face and stood up. "So, don't go blaming yourself for fucking us up. We're *all* fucked up here. Now let's stop wasting time and go out to the Sky Geography lab and set up that noctoscope."

They worked with the scope all afternoon, trying out various formulas for determining depth of field, height, focus, weather conditions, and the azimuth of the moon's orbit, which Nina couldn't understand in the least, but she trusted Bella to know what he was doing. The trick was to set everything up ahead of time, so it would only take her a moment to flip the switch and begin the countdown before she left to join them back in the Headmaster's Office. Bella figured he could give them two hours. More than that, and the moon's own movement would put it out of range.

"You'll have to wait here till ten o'clock and then engage this mechanism here—" Bella showed her "—and then head on over to the office. If she shows up ahead of time, we'll just have to stall her. But it's vital you don't start the countdown before ten p.m."

She nodded, memorizing the switch she had to throw (among several knobs, buttons, toggles, and levers) to start the noctoscope. Bella looked at her, and his eyes had darkened.

"Nina, you know, this could actually work."

"Yes, I know."

"Are you sure you—"

"Yes, yes, yes," she said impatiently. "Ten o'clock. That switch. I get it."

"No, I meant . . ." He hesitated. "Are you sure you really want to kill her?"

"No," Nina admitted after a moment. "I told you both, I'm not sure at all." She studied her two friends, who studied her, looking a little relieved, and she realized they didn't want to kill her either.

"I want to believe Sister Aquilina isn't what we've been led to believe," Nina said slowly. "I want to believe she's something different, something . . . else. That magic, real magic, exists, and it isn't evil. I want to believe all that. I just . . ." She smiled ruefully. "In case I'm wrong, I'd like a little technology to back me up."

They left the carriage house around seven and went inside and ate dinner, even though none of them could eat much. Nina had gone upstairs ahead of time and slipped a note under Professor Danvers's door: "Urgent I speak to you. Meet me at nine p.m. where we had our divination lesson. Please come alone. This isn't about last night. Trust me."

She'd also added, in a last-ditch effort to convince him to come, "I know where she is." Which wasn't an out-and-out lie, was it? After all, she'd been to Sister Aquilina's house. What if Sister Aquilina wasn't going to be there tonight?

After dinner, she couldn't sit still, so she wandered down the long corridor to the chapel, looking at the portraits again. Who were all these people? Would she ever know all their secrets? Here was a man in soft lace and a foppish feathered hat like one of the Three Musketeers. He was blond and handsome and had brilliant white teeth, and he reminded her of someone, although she couldn't for the moment think who. Here was a monk, sallow and hollow-cheeked: surely he looked a lot like Father Ignatius Ragoczy? Here was a man with wavy dark hair, dressed as a naval officer. She read the brass plaque under his portrait: Admiral William Claiborne Benway, Commander of the Garrison at Haiti, 1912. And here was his wife: Isadora Benway, who looked an awful lot like Dr. Freeland.

Nina tore herself away from the portraits, realizing their ominous presence was making her slightly sick, and also realizing with a start that it was almost nine o'clock. Smoothing her suddenly shaking hands over her hair, she thought, *How do I look? How do I look compared to* her? Squaring her shoulders, she hurried out to the carriage house. The night was warm, and the lawn was already brightly lit by the rising moon. She spared a moment to hope Professor Danvers had been able to get outside without too much difficulty. She wondered if he would come at all. Would the chance of finding his sister tempt him, even if he no longer wanted to see *her*?

And with that terrible thought, she turned the knob on the carriage house door and opened it to see a faint, pale light. Nothing like the red illumination in the headmaster's cup. This was more like the light of a single candle, a wavering lesser darkness at the top of the stairs.

She went upstairs and opened the door to the Sky Geography Room, stepping inside.

She could barely see him.

"Miss Lamb." His voice was precise. "I come upon my appointed hour."

"Yes, er . . . thanks." She swallowed. "I-I'm glad we're both on time." *I sound pathetic.* She edged toward him, seeing, as her eyes adjusted to the candlelight, how he was standing far over on the other side of the room from her, his arms crossed tightly over his chest, a posture that said No Trespassing as clearly as a sign. He looked cold and detached, his pale, sculpted face as expressionless as if it were made of wax.

She sighed. "I'm sorry, really sorry I interrupted you last night with . . . with Roticus."

He barked a harsh laugh. "Miss Lamb, there are any number of responses appropriate to finding your professor eating a student's ear, but apologizing is surely the most original. Emily Post would be proud of you."

She decided to let it drop. "I invited you here because, there are a lot of things I think we need to discuss."

"Please enlighten me."

"Well, for one thing, the Hadiade. I have no idea how I did that lead-into-gold thing."

"Clearly. The fact that you're not drowning in wealth right this minute should make that obvious. Your instincts, however, are . . . powerful. If somewhat saccharine."

"What do you mean?"

"You wanted to make me *happy*?"

She flinched, because his voice held nothing gentle in it at all. It was sharp and cutting.

She should have expected he'd react that way to pity. "It wasn't like that, sir. I didn't mean it to be insulting or . . . or anything. I panicked, okay? I was just winging the whole thing."

"So you said. And I agree. I'm not sure I should even let your victory stand. However, the opportunity to tick off Isolde and Archer Freeland may be just too enticing to resist. But that's neither here nor there. You didn't bring me here to discuss the Hadiade, did you?"

He still hadn't moved from his defensive posture on the other side of the room, and she said, "Please come over here into the light a little. I can barely see you."

"A calculation on my part." His eyes narrowed. "What are you, Nina?"

She shook her head. "I told you, I don't know."

"You came to Daedalus. You intruded yourself on my peace of mind, my thoughts, my sanity, my past, my dreams, and you made yourself and your friends the instruments of disruption and upset at every turn. I know you're not doing it on purpose—you couldn't be that perverse—but has it occurred to you to just stop being such a pest?"

"You can't say that!" she burst out, knowing he was doing everything in his power to push her away. "You're the one who keeps dragging me into things! You and your damn family! I didn't want to compete in the Hadiade at all, but your sister made me! I didn't want to find you and Roticus doing . . . well, you know, and right outside my door! I didn't want to know Sister Aquilina was your sister! You think I *like* being part of your damn prophecy, and being the one with no past who'll best the pelican and the Beautiful Hand who'll be revealed?"

"Someone's been talking out of turn," Professor Danvers murmured, and his quiet voice was more menacing than any threat. "May one assume Miss Roget or Mr. Chopin—presumably the latter—has been giving you extracurricular lessons?"

"What if they have? *You* haven't told me jack shit, Professor." She stopped to catch her breath. She saw the momentary leap of fire in his eyes, as if the candle flame had suddenly found its reflection, and she shivered, feeling his anger hot against her skin. *All right, maybe insulting him wasn't a good idea.* She said in a softer voice, "I haven't asked for any of this, you know."

"I know." He seemed to be forcing down some strong emotion as well. She watched him lower his arms and flex his hands, and then he walked over to her and stood a few feet away from her.

"Why don't we consider it a draw, then?" He looked younger again, more like her age.

How could he be so icy and mean one minute, and then make her want to cry, with his quiet face and sad eyes, the next? How could she feel this yearning for him, at the same time his snarky mouth was telling her to get lost? How could she long to comfort him, when she also wanted to smack him upside the head?

"Let's just admit you're trouble for me, and I'm trouble for you, Nina." He sighed. "You don't want someone whose every kindness and emotion were burned out of him decades ago, whose deepest soul is ice and whose heart is stone, and I don't want a silly, warm girl who'll only prompt me to hurt her. I'm not a monster, Nina. I don't particularly enjoy being hateful. If I had my way, I'd wish you were a million miles from here, a figure in sunlight, dancing with a joy I gave up centuries ago. I'd see you surrounded with the love I once glimpsed and squandered. And I'd especially wish you were somewhere where evil isn't triumphant. I'd see you safe, or at least ignorant of your ultimate fate. Maybe that's all any of us can hope for: oblivion, until the butcher sticks in the knife.

"And instead," he went on, almost bemused, "I'm here with you in the dark, in a ruined building, neglecting my work to argue with you." All the fury had drained out of his face. He splayed his arms. "Nina, why did you bring me out here?"

"Because you're wrong," she said quietly. Sometimes things needed to be said, despite all the arguments to the contrary. "I *do* want you, in spite of everything you just told me. I know it's all true. I mean, I know you don't want *me* . . . and I know you're bitter and dark and mean and twisted, and yes, you're a goddamn pain in the ass sometimes, but none of that counts. Because somehow we belong together." She took a desperate chance, stepping up to him and touching his hands, which he'd folded once more into tight fists in front of his chest. "I'm not saying you have to like me. I'm not expecting miracles. It's just that you're stuck with me, at least for the time being. It's like we've been given this assignment, to . . . to put up with each other, at least for a while. I don't like it any more than you do, but still . . ."

"That's where you're wrong," he said, and lowered his mouth to hers, in a gesture that was halfway between surrender and an attack. "I like it far too much."

His kiss was something she'd never expected, because, for all his violence, his lips were gentle. Almost . . . careful. He seemed to be memorizing every line and texture of her mouth, the way a blind man would if, against all sense, he were going to draw it. She heard a low moan which seemed to come from her own throat, and an answering sound like a growl from his, and then she was drowning in the pure electricity of his tongue against her tongue.

Oh God, I never want this to end and I never, ever want to kiss anyone else because it's going to be such a letdown after this, as his hands came up and clasped her skull, his fingers digging into her hair and holding her in place. His mouth was all she could feel, even as it left hers, and he trailed his lips down over her chin, her throat, and into the hollow at the base of her neck. She could feel his breath against her skin, and his hands slipped down over her back to cup her ass. She was warm putty, nothing solid, everything melting in the cold, cold touch of his body all along her, and she felt his voice inside her mind like a shivering pulse beat as he asked, *"Where is she?"*

She broke away from him so sharply they both stumbled, his weight almost making him fall forward against her as she screamed, *"What?"*

"You asked me . . . you said . . . your note."

"I wrote that to get you to come out here! I wrote that so you'd talk to me! I—" She abruptly remembered why she *had* written it and pushed hard against his chest. He leaned back, thinking she was just trying to hit him, and she pushed him again, until he stumbled back farther away from her . . . and then she felt him falling away from her hands, and falling *through* something . . . like he was falling through a thick sheet of plastic.

"You little shit!" he yelled, as he realized what had just happened. He was sealed inside the Circle of Force, which she'd cast that afternoon, caught like a mouse in a trap, and if she'd been in the mood to laugh just then, she would have found his expression comical.

Unfortunately, she was every bit as outraged as he was.

"It's for your own good!" she yelled. "Although why I should give a damn about that right now is beyond me! You only give a damn about her, her, *her*! Well, for your information, Professor, I *do* know where she is, and in other circumstances, I might even tell you, but you hugged me and you kissed me and you didn't even mean it! It was all a lie! It was all one big dirty trick!"

"You have no idea what kinds of tricks I'm capable of, Nina, if you don't let me out of here this instant," Professor Danvers ground out. "Let's just say they'd beggar the imagination of Nero and Hannibal Lecter. Now move it!"

"No way, sir. I've got somewhere else to go right now, and you aren't invited!"

"Dissolve this circle right now, do you hear me?"

"No, sir I can't. I-I really can't."

"Let me go, you little fool! You have no idea what you're doing. You're going to get yourself killed!"

"Probably," she said, trying to keep the traitorous tears from falling, because she didn't want to cry, did she? She was furious at him—she wasn't disappointed, she wasn't heartbroken at his rejection. Was she?

"I'm really sorry I tricked you, sir, and I actually do know where she is, and I'll tell you after this is all over, but right now, you've just got to trust me, okay? I'll be back as soon as I can. I'm not . . . well, I don't know if I'm really mad at you or not, but that doesn't matter, because this is more important. This is like life and death and . . . other things. Maybe more important things, actually."

"Come back here and let me out. Nina, please."

"I can't," she said, running to the noctoscope and throwing the switch. She hoped it was ten o'clock; it had to be close enough. "I-I really am sorry, sir." She took a quick breath, unable to keep looking at his stricken face, his pale skin and blazing black eyes, and the sneer of derision on his lips—actually, something more than derision. He had the bereft look of a man caught against his own cross purposes, wishing things hadn't turned out the way they had. She couldn't bear to see that anymore. She had to leave.

"I'm sorry, sir," she said one last time, and then she ran down the steps and out across the lawn, and the moon was shining like a wash of silver light, cold and colorless, across the gray shadows of the grass. The school was looming up in front of her with its tall windows all closed up in plywood. The silence was everywhere and ringing in her ears like an inaudible bell, and she didn't stop until she was inside and racing up the stairs, the stained-glass windows dark above her, the black coffered wood of the walls gleaming like polished stone, and she reached the Headmaster's Office and knocked on the door three times, and then three times again, and waited. And then she turned the doorknob and quietly entered.

And the first person she saw was Agatha Danvers.

"Ah, Miss Lamb," the older woman remarked. "Glad you could join us. I think you know everybody else here. Now, if you're quite ready, let's begin."

Chapter Twenty-Nine

Nina looked all around her in a panic, but it still took her a moment to realize what she was seeing. There was no tall, dark woman there in black robes, no terrible Sister Aquilina. Instead, there was a stylishly dressed woman in ivory pants and a white shirt, with a red scarf tied around her throat and her white-blond hair pulled back in a French twist. She was standing next to a man with bright white teeth and the vacuous smile of a male model, and standing next to them was a priest in a long cassock, his white hands clasped before him in a parody of prayer.

Finally, at the far end of the room, stood a jowly man in a business suit, with wavy black hair and a five-o'-clock shadow darkening his face.

The four Saturni.

Nina looked at them and then at Agatha, who was standing there with her usual frown twisted into a far more sinister smile.

"Thanks for getting rid of Strickland," Agatha said. "He's so annoying. Sometimes I wonder how he ever became my brother. Of course, blood doesn't run any thicker than sense, and Strickland never had any more sense than God gave a goose."

Nina felt as if someone had shot her tongue full of novocaine. Finally, she managed to stammer, "W-what are you all doing here?"

"We could ask you the same thing," Father Ignatius said in his whispery voice. "But then we'd have to pretend we didn't know, wouldn't we?"

"You came here to protect the Four Gifts," Dr. Freeland said, coming forward to sit on the edge of Professor Danvers's desk. She looked as detached as if she were seeing a patient. "Very heroic of you, but also rather unnecessary. The Gifts are perfectly safe where they are, which is, after all, the problem. We had to get you here so *you* could get them for *us*."

"You see, we need them," Archer Freeland said. "And the real pisser is, we can't just reach in there and take them. The headmaster, in his infinite idiocy, shut us out. Magic." He made a face. "As if anyone did *that* anymore. We certainly don't."

"You don't do anything, dear," Dr. Freeland said. She waved her hand at him dismissively. "You see, the headmaster, wherever he is, or was, is a remarkably suspicious character when you get right down to it, and he's set up a rather clever trick. It's a variant on the old 'only the pure of heart can touch something' idea. If you want to destroy the Four Gifts, as we do, you can't take them. You can't even take them if you want to protect them and put them someplace else. Only someone who's stupid enough to want to *free* them can get them out of the safe. Which is, quite naturally, where you come in."

"I don't understand . . ." Nina said. She thought it was a good idea to keep them talking, at least until she found out where Bella and Alastaire were. She had no intention of getting the Four Gifts out of the safe for anybody. But she didn't want to tell them that.

"If you don't believe in magic, why do you want the Four Gifts?"

"Oh, for God's sake, don't you ever give it a rest?" Mr. Benway sighed. "All right, let's spell it out. There's a war on. It's older than the cosmos, this cosmos at any rate, and it's between us, the powers who control things, and the forces of . . . ah, nature, for want of a better word. Chaos. Magic. The great undifferentiated muck of existence. The universe is our proper food, but the imposition of our will on it is thwarted at every turn by the spirits that inhabit that muck. Love. Memory. The collective oceans. The collective trees. The spirits that call out to every mole and every worm and every other pitiful lower life form from humans to orangutans, and say, 'Live! Continue! Exist! Be fruitful and multiply!' How stubborn is that collective will?

"It's really quite a mystery, actually. How something as undifferentiated as a collective soul can still have the strength to resist us, but there you are. That's why we needed to pursue our more tenderhearted brethren ages ago and strip them of their powers. We simply had no other choice. It was us against them, and we were determined not to be the ones who lost their power."

Nina felt as if her head was spinning. She knew she had to keep him on a roll while she figured all this out.

"You don't think much of the *Lwas*, do you? But aren't they the same kind of unearthly forces as you are? All right, you hate the earth—although you don't mind eating it and every worm and human being on it—but why go after your own? Aren't they the same kind of beings as you are?"

Benway snorted. "In your dreams. We've evolved far beyond them. We destroyed the Haitian forests, and the great pods of whales that swam in the seas are now just fairy tales. The elemental powers of ice and oceans are trembling. The *Lwas* still refuse to give up on this futile little planet. I gather you met some of them the other night on Pauline Street; Agatha informed us of your visit. You've seen the degradation to which we've brought them. Up to a point, of course. Only up to a point."

He wrinkled his nose. "There's always a few, stubborn holdouts with whom you have to use force. Which is why we're here now."

He looked at the safe. "Inside that simple black box lay the Four *Lwas* we could never beat. Until now. Our strength was always limited, and their power too great. We had to bide our time, keeping them contained, while we grew fat. Our Skin Eaters helped us, of course." He smiled. "It's always nice to have tame animals."

What was he saying? That he doesn't care about the Skinnies? That they are expendable? She wondered if the Skinnies knew about that, although she suspected Strickland did.

"She's finally putting two and two together," Dr. Freeland said, chuckling. "How charming. It's like watching a puppy wag its tail for the first time."

Nina whirled on her and said, "So, you ruined their lives for nothing? Just because you needed them?"

"Got it in one," Father Ignatius drawled. "What a mind. Only we don't use words like 'ruin' and 'save.' They carry such a taint of moral absolutism. 'Powerful' and 'impotent' are much more accurate. The Saturni were sent into creation to serve it, but instead, we've become its masters."

"But how? How exactly do you do that?"

Mr. Benway sighed again. "As I said, beings of all types—mortal and immortal, plants, animal, non-terrestrial, even rocks—all have their collective soul. It's what allows ants to follow a single direction; it's what allows trees to know when it's time to leaf and bear fruit, without each tree having to be told individually. And that's our true food. Eating one thing at a time would be intolerably time-consuming. It's far better to eat them all at once. I suppose if you wanted to be poetic, you could say the Saturni eat worlds."

Nina shook her head. "That . . . that's not possible. Nobody could eat every ant in the world, or every tree, or every everything. Even you guys." She bit her lip. "Um . . . could you?"

"Not individually." Benway's eyes were pensive. "But if you cause a whole species to die out, you release their collective souls all at once. The Saturni have dined on dodos and passenger pigeons, infinite species of algae, human Neanderthals, and the life chains of lizards and fish going back before the dinosaurs. Do you realize how much poorer the world has become just in the last century? Species and air and water and land masses have all been eaten by us, thoughts and philosophies, and we've grown strong. Now we can achieve our final goal and break those who once opposed us. With your help, of course." He inclined his head. "I have no idea why, but Agatha seems to think you can actually help us."

Nina took a quick glance at Agatha, who was studying her fingernails. Had Professor Danvers's sister told them everything? Had she held back Nina's connection to the prophecy? And if so, why? Where were her loyalties?

Nina said slowly, "So, you don't believe in magic, but you still think I can do it, and help you guys out? Is that about it?"

"Baldly, yes," Dr. Freeland said. "I suspect you'd like to hear our terms."

Nina nodded.

"Okay." The blond woman was brisk. "I'll summarize. You get to live, first of all. Three score and ten, or whatever. A normal human lifespan. You get to see your little friends again, who'll be presented to you safe and sound when this is all over. Miss . . . who are they again? Miss Roget and Mr. Chopin? That's right. The two annoying children I found in here, and sent over with Professor Samson so he could lock them up in the carriage house."

The carriage house? Nina thought. *But I was just there.* She realized she must have just missed them. Were they still there? Had Professor Samson seen what was going on and disarmed the noctoscope? Had he freed Professor Danvers and then hung around to make sure no one else disturbed school property? Nina tried to pretend it was no big deal.

"Actually, I sent them ahead, because I figured if they got

caught, who cared?" She shrugged, trying to convince Agatha it made no difference. "They're not my friends; they're just a couple of spiritual strivers."

Nina knew Agatha wasn't buying this, but she wasn't sure about the others.

Dr. Freeland seemed to consider her words, then said, "Fine. We'll kill them, shall we? Save you the trouble? But I think there *is* someone here you might care about, hmm?" She raised her eyebrows. "A schoolgirl crush? But those things can be *so* painful, especially when they're unrequited? Or have you realized our esteemed assistant headmaster simply has a taste for fresh cherries? In any case, it's all academic now."

She abruptly turned and nodded to her husband, who walked to the door and opened it, yelling, "Hey, Sam. Get your butt in here, and bring our friend."

And a moment later, Professor Samson shouldered his way into the room, his muscles bulging, dragging a tall, dark, furious figure with his hands tied behind his back and a huge gash on his forehead.

Professor Danvers.

"Well, well," Agatha said, "look who the cat dragged in."

"Aggie," the professor said, "your attempts at humor are pitiful even at the best of times, which frankly, this isn't." He shut his eyes. "Please confine yourself to rude gestures. We'd all be grateful."

She obliged by giving him the finger, then went and sat down in one of the comfortable armchairs on the other side of the desk, leaving the four Saturni in charge. Professor Danvers looked around him and contrived, even bound and bleeding, to regard everyone with near-perfect disdain.

"Your methods are improving, Jack," he told Benway. "When we first met, you used to stalk your prey yourself. Now you get other people to trap it and fetch it for you."

"Strickland, please don't waste our time," Dr. Freeland said. "You're here for one reason and one reason only, which is to bleed. You'll do it either until this idiot girl gives up and does what we want her to do, or until you bleed to death, which shouldn't take long. Especially if, as Aggie says, you haven't been eating much. We'll be sorry to lose you, but we can always make plenty more of you where you came from. Do you understand me? Please nod."

Professor Danvers's nod was so ironic it was a joy to behold. Nina, however, couldn't take any pleasure in it, because she was thinking furiously. Assuming the noctoscope was still engaged, she had a weapon. If she just ripped the plywood down right now, she could probably take out Agatha and Professor Samson, but she might take out Professor Danvers as well.

Besides, who knew if the Saturni even cared about the moon's rays? Better to bide her time. "Isolde," Professor Danvers said, "you're slipping. This girl—" he cut his eyes toward Nina "—doesn't give a damn about me. In fact, she trapped me."

I didn't mean it, Nina thought. *I swear I didn't. I only wanted to keep you safe.*

"If you're relying on her tenderheartedness," the assistant headmaster went on, "I wouldn't bank on it. Besides, I'm tougher than I look. And I loathe screaming."

Mr. Benway was staring at him with unblinking eyes. "Oh, I think you'll scream, Strickland. I really do, and you know why? Because we've brought an old friend here. Someone you met ages ago, back in the bad old days when we were all brave and young and foolhardy, or at least you were. He has a score to settle with you, and I'm sure you remember why. It can't have escaped you. General?"

Nina started. It seemed like a low, squat shadow was detaching itself from the darkness in the farthest corner of the room and moving forward, squeaking, into the light. As whatever it was moved toward them, she saw it was an incredibly aged man in a wheelchair, his grunts of breath accompanying the movements of his gnarled, arthritic hands on the chair, the squeaking, the sound of its wheels. He was thin and hunched over, one shoulder higher than the other with his chin twisted down almost to his chest, but he had dark hair, although it was significantly longer than it was in his photographs. His face looked lean and set, his skin leathery as though, once, he'd spent a lot of time outdoors, and his eyes were bright with cruelty.

General Azazel.

"Strickland Danvers," he said, in a surprisingly strong voice. "What a treat. I haven't seen you since your *pet voodoo god* put me in this chair."

There was someone helping the general forward, and as they came into the light, Nina wasn't entirely surprised to see Simone. The black girl didn't look at her but, in fact, kept her eyes fixed on the carpet beneath her feet.

"Daddy," Dr. Freeland said, after Simone had stopped the chair in front of the desk where he could see everyone. "I hope you didn't mind waiting. I wanted it to be a surprise."

"It is, dearest; it certainly is. Time recaptured is time gained. I almost feel young again, as I was before Crux wounded me."

Crux, Nina thought. Her mind flew back to that horrible dinner party when they'd all eaten *jumbie* meat, and Professor Danvers's drawling voice, "No lingering ill effects from facing a *Lwa*?" So, Legs had been there all those years ago, when whatever war they'd been talking about had taken place.

She tried to keep her expression blank. *Don't panic*, she told herself. There had to be some other way out of this. She tried to cast around in her mind for some solution that would save Professor Danvers's life and still placate the Saturni. Her thoughts were banging around inside her head like somebody in a locked room, pounding on every door, while on the outside, it almost looked like she didn't care.

Strickland turned to Professor Samson and inquired politely, "You couldn't loosen these ropes, could you?"

"Nope. Sorry, sir. Orders." Professor Samson looked honestly uncomfortable as he grabbed the slighter man by the shoulders and held him steady. Dr. Freeland leaned down to her father and said, "Daddy, are you sure you want to do this? You don't have to, you know. There are other ways."

"No." The old man shook his head. "Are you kidding? This delicacy is one I've been waiting ages to sample. The sweeter the meat, the colder the revenge, and a Skin Eater's body is such a rare treat, like brandy, the distillate of all that eaten flesh. I'd be eager to taste it even if I didn't hate this man with every cell in my immortal body. Which I do. And since I do—" he licked his ancient teeth "—I intend to enjoy myself thoroughly. Now hurry up, please. It's time."

He struggled to his feet. He was badly crippled, but with Simone's help, he could stand, and she moved him over to Professor Danvers's side. General Azazel gazed up at the younger man with loathing and then stood on tiptoe and bit him on the cheek.

It was pathetic, and it was also awful. Nina looked away, hearing the wet, slobbering sound, the pitiful little grunts and whimpers with which the old man chewed on the younger one's face, that sounded like nothing so much as a dog worrying a bone. She couldn't watch. She was going to throw up.

Professor Danvers was making a keening sound in his throat, not screaming, exactly, it almost sounded like he was speaking an unknown tongue. She had never imagined anything so utterly, completely unromantic as this gross hunger, and she thought, people who think vampires are sexy are idiots.

She knew she had to stop it, and she was speaking before she'd even quite formulated her plan.

"All right," she said. "All right, I'll do it! I'll do it if you just stop! If you don't stop right now, you can take your damn safe and shove it up your collective assholes! I am *not* standing here and watching this!"

General Azazel let go of Professor Danvers with a sigh that suggested either satisfaction or else sheer exhaustion and fell back into his chair, licking the blood from around his mouth with weak little laps of his tongue. Simone bent down and wiped his chin for him, letting him lick the rest of the blood off her fingers.

I'm so glad I don't have grandparents right now, Nina thought. She moved forward, wondering what time it was.

The big clock on Professor Danvers's desk said it was ten of midnight, which meant there wasn't much time left. Now it all depended on whether or not Professor Samson had disabled the noctoscope, and what he'd done to her friends. She sent Bella a quick, desperate thought, *I know you can't read minds, but if you can, please,* please *get your eyes glued to that scope right now and sit tight.*

She approached Professor Danvers, whose head was lolling to one side, and whose face was deeply gashed and pouring out blood at an alarming rate. He looked like he was unconscious. *God, I hope so, because he's going to hate me enough for this later on as it is.*

"First, you have to bandage him up somehow," she said, amazed that she could make what sounded like demands. "Or else I'm not going to do it."

"I'm afraid that's impossible," Dr. Freeland said. She tucked her father back into his chair and dusted her hands off. "Don't they teach you anything in this school? Skin Eaters are still earthly. We Saturni are not. You mix Skin Eater saliva with human DNA, and you get more little baby Skin Eaters, but the spit of the gods is a little more . . . unstable. He's bleeding out, Nina. He's dying."

"What? He's *dying*? You . . . General Azazel poisoned him?" Nina felt like she'd been punched in the stomach, and all she could add was, "That's not fair!"

Father Ignatius laughed a whispery laugh and said, "My, my, you really are young, aren't you? Do you hear that, General, she's actually shocked that you cheated."

Mr. Benway snapped, "Okay, quit fooling around. Open the goddamn safe and let's get out of here. Enough of this kid stuff."

Nina approached the safe slowly, her mind racing. She had no idea if the noctoscope was ready. At the same time, if she moved too slowly, she risked Professor Danvers bleeding to death. She touched the safe, feeling it hum faintly under her fingertips, and there was power there, no doubt about that.

How can I do what I need to do without any of these douchebags seeing it coming? She envisioned sudden moves, bold jumps, but in the end, the simplest answer seemed like the best.

"Okay," she said, stepping back, "now I want the rest of you guys to give me some room, because when this thing opens, there's going to be one hell of a bang."

She had no idea if that was true, but it sounded good. "Why don't you all . . . um . . . go over on the other side of the room and stand by that window? Take Professor Danvers with you; he's bleeding all over the place. It's distracting."

They don't believe in magic. I can tell them any damn thing I want.

"Get over there as close to the window as you can," she continued. "Right. Okay. Now I'm going to start. Get ready to grab the Four Gifts the first chance you get."

She was counting on their greed, she realized, to make them

stupid. They were so excited at the idea of getting their hands on their prize that they weren't paying attention to the ridiculous gestures she was making, and the strange, singsong chant of nonsense words coming out of her mouth. Meanwhile, she centered herself and felt true magic tingle in her hands.

"Abracadabra, kowabunga, jockimo-fi-na-hey . . ."

I changed lead into gold, with love, true love. I made the wind blow with my anger. I don't know who I am, but I'm the one with no past who'll best the pelican. And I know what I'm doing now is right. I know. I know.

"Abracadabra, one ring to rule them all, there's no place like home, Aslan is on the move . . ."

Feel me, plywood. Feel me, glass. Feel me, vines. Do my will.

She was gradually moving around the desk, glancing back to make sure the Saturni were in the right place, and when they were, she thought, *All right. Here we go.*

"Bibbity-bobbity, May the Force be with you, Whop-bob-aloo-bop-alop-bam-boom!"

She raised her arms and spun around, grabbing all her magical power and pushing it away from her as hard as she possibly could. The plywood exploded outward, and the glass shattered into dust, and the vines were blasted away, whipping and flapping, but none of it was as strong as the bright, cold, blinding light pouring into the room—brighter than sunlight, brighter than silver, as bright as a searchlight searing across the carpet to catch all of the people standing there.

Who predictably jumped out of the way.

All except for two of them.

Professor Danvers stood for an instant after Professor Samson let him go, his tall, graceful, black-clad figure drawn up as if by a wire, hanging in space like a rag doll, as the light went through and through him.

Nina had a moment to see how the rays pierced him in a dozen places, the shafts of light tearing him apart before he fell. She screamed, but it felt like it made no sound.

And there was also a terrible, sizzling, roaring, *squooshing* sound filling the room that seemed to suck every smaller sound out of existence, and it seemed to be coming from the figure in the wheelchair.

It goes backward, she thought, *doesn't it? The moon kills life and heals death, but that doesn't seem to be working here.* As she watched in horror, General Azazel seemed to melt into a shapeless mass, bubbling and getting redder and redder, until he was nothing but a huge, engorged, beating, blood-filled bag—a stomach, a gut, without mind or heart or brain or anything else besides itself— and then he exploded.

Blood spattered everywhere, and Nina felt herself drenched with it. She stumbled back. And at that moment, the door of the safe clicked open.

Chapter Thirty

fterward, Nina wasn't sure exactly in what sequence things had happened.

There was a gradually strengthening breeze, which quickly became a stiff wind, bringing with it rain and the freshness of moisture on new leaves. There was a whispering rustle, like birds and lizards and small animals and insects all moving around at once, and the steadier beating of a great, unhurried heart. There was the sound of running water, and plants seemed suddenly to be growing up everywhere she looked: vast juicy stalks sprouting up through the floor and furling down from the ceiling in huge, shaggy fronds, and the vines were swaying in the wind, which was growing stronger every minute, blowing with a constant hum like air across a wire. The Saturni were backed up in the farthest corner of the room, and Agatha and Simone and Professor Samson had disappeared completely. She couldn't see Professor Danvers at all.

She saw, or thought she saw, an enormous albino snake emerge from the confines of the safe and slowly pour itself out across the room, its muscular coils moving in great, solemn waves, as its square snout rose and its pale moon eyes turned this way and that, its tongue flicking out to taste the unaccustomed air. The wind howled and seemed to draw power from its own strength, swirling around the room in a rage as it knocked over furniture and smashed pictures to bits, crashing the orrery and the pendulum to the floor. The wind almost seemed to be sobbing, while the plants and leaves sighed in pleasure, their rich scents seeming to grow stronger every moment, as though someone had opened the door to a greenhouse.

The snake and the wind and the trees all seemed to be forces of nature and distinct entities at the same time, vast powers and vast beings released to fill up the room till they exploded and spread across the world . . . and Nina was terrified. Just when she was about to scream, she saw a familiar sight.

Zoolie. The little black girl in the short dress. The little girl she'd first met up in her attic.

Smiling and waving to her.

Zoolie, but how changed, how utterly different! Because Zoolie was shining, Zoolie was glowing . . . Zoolie was utterly radiant! And Zoolie was growing and becoming bigger and bigger with every second, until she was a huge, full-bodied, wide-hipped, unbelievably beautiful woman, mahogany brown, pale rose, sculpted ivory, and golden bronze all at once. She had long hair that ran over her lush, naked body like a river, and her eyes were remote, kind, warm, loving, and grateful. She smiled, and Nina wanted to fall to her knees and hide her face. She felt it was an insult to be looking at someone so alien, so powerful, and so lovely.

Zoolie spoke and said, "I am Erzuli, who is called Dantor, who fights for her children, and Freda, who causes them to be born. I am the goddess of sex and motherhood and creation and lost dreams, and dreams that can never be lost. I am the one who kindles loins and hearts, and brings forth life, and commands devotion. I am what cannot be quenched, cannot be stopped, and cannot be killed, for I am Love. You have done well, my child. I bless you."

Nina felt a warm rain falling all around her, and she did cover her face then.

She heard the snake hiss, "I am Damballa, who is called

wisdom. I carry the ancestors on my back to *Guinee*, the land of our begetting. I am what cannot be unlearned, for I am the knowledge we all carry in our bones, and as we shed our skins, we acquire it. I am what spoke to Moses through the crucified serpent. You have done well, my child. I bless you."

The wind rattled the window frame and sent storms of papers flying around her and seemed to scream in her ear, "I am Oya, goddess of destruction. I would tear the world to pieces if I could. I will never forgive what was done to us, never! But you have done well, my child, and so I bless you."

And as Nina felt the wind tear her hair and drive bits of trash from the shattered room into her exposed skin—wood shards, nails, pieces of broken glass—she felt the leaves from all the strange trees and vines in the room close over her, protecting protect her and dripping cool water onto the back of her neck.

And she heard a voice that sounded immensely old and scratchy whisper into her ear, "I am Grand Bois, god of the woods and god of memory. I promise you, child, one day you will know who you are. One day you will know everything, and everything will make sense, and there will be no more sadness. Until then, I bless you. Sleep. You have done well. We must go now, but we will always remember you."

It seemed like there was a long, deep well, and she was falling into it, even though she didn't want to. She wanted to stay and fight. She wanted to take revenge against the awful beings who had killed Professor Danvers. She wanted to make sure Bella and Alastaire were okay, but she was sinking, down, down, down, and through her head was running the silliest song, *Sleep, little one, sleep, if you don't sleep, the crab will eat you, dodo titit, crab in okra gumbo . . .*

When Nina woke up, the first thing she noticed was that she was in a strange bed. "Where am I?" she asked, blinking up at the ceiling. She was lying on an old-fashioned iron bedstead, in a room filled with light. There was a dresser, a desk, and an armoire, all very utilitarian, but still less beat-up than her attic furniture. And most surprisingly of all, there was no plywood over the windows. She could see the green light of the garden shining through a break in the heavy dark curtains that covered the glass. And by the height of the trees, she knew she was down on the second floor of the Daedalus School. She must be in one of the dormitories.

She felt a warm presence on the pillow next to her, and turning her head, she saw Mercy, who opened his bright yellow eyes and meowed. She looked down and realized there were also two people sitting on the bed facing her. Alastaire and Bella.

"Well, you took your sweet time," Alastaire said, pulling her legs up to sit Indian style. "We've been in here for, like, *days*. The next time you pass out, give us some warning, and we'll know to go to the movies or something."

"What . . . what am I doing here?" Nina asked, still groggy. "How long have I been out? And you two—are you all right? What happened?"

"Okay, I see *some*body's got to be the one to explain everything." Bella sighed. "First of all, you've been out for almost three days, very religio-symbolic. Second of all, you've been reassigned to the general population. I guess they felt badly keeping you up in the attic like Oliver Twist after you saved the assistant headmaster."

"The assistant— Is Professor Danvers alive? Is he okay?"

"He's fine," Alastaire grinned. "Snarky as ever. He's been in here to check on you, like, every hour—which is kind of romantic if you ask me, even if he is kind of weird. Every time he caught us in here, he was, like, 'Don't you children have any traffic to go play in?' Not *too* possessive."

"Well, um, he's probably just worried about me," Nina said,

blushing. "I mean, the last time he saw me, we were in the middle of sort of a mini hurricane."

"That's another thing," Bella said. "Not a stick of furniture is out of place in the Headmaster's Office. I mean seriously, it's like something out of *Architectural Digest*. I saw what was going on in there through the noctoscope . . . and you're right, it was seriously Cat-5 in there. But now it's like nothing happened. Alastaire and I sort of *accidentally on purpose* peeked in there, and it's perfect. Even the plywood's back."

"I guess they had to replace it so people could go inside," Nina said, frowning. "They can't risk people getting stuck in there with the sun on them, which reminds me . . ." She nodded toward her own windows. "How come I get to have sunlight?"

"Because you're this week's Chosen One," Alastaire said, bursting out laughing. "God, you're such a dork. You just beat the four biggest Saturni to their knees, and you think the school's going to deny you anything? You could probably keep a pony up here!"

"So . . ." Nina sat up straighter. After a three-day nap, she was feeling pretty much like her old self, although she suspected she had some serious bruises. "So you guys were able to aim the noctoscope, right, and see what was going on? What happened?"

"Well," Bella said, picking up the story again, "it was really Agatha Danvers who's responsible, although Professor Samson was in on it. At least up to a point. Agatha's got stones," he added, shaking his head. "I'll give her that much. She knew the Saturni were the ones who were really after the Gifts, so she let us do our thing and make them think their plan was working, knowing when the chips were down you could really beat them. At least that's what I figure she thought. She risked her brother's life, of course, and yours, and she had to make it look like the Danverses were on the Saturni's side all along, but the Danvers family has been against the Saturni for ages. Professor Danvers told us that. He referred to General Azazel as 'the late General Blood-Bag,' so, of course, he had to explain what he meant by that."

"General Azazel is really gone?"

"Yep! You blew him up real good!" Alastaire laughed and then said, when Bella made a face, "What? Are you telling me *you* didn't go 'Whoo-hoo!' too when she did it?"

"That's true," Bella said, allowing himself a small smile. "We were able to watch the whole thing. See, when Professor Samson brought us into the carriage house, he just told us to stay there and didn't tie us up or anything. Then he released Professor Danvers from the Circle of Force, and the professor immediately made a beeline for the stairs, so Professor Samson had to kind of knock him out to make him go quietly.

"Which . . . I think he kind of liked that," Bella added. "I think he must have been wanting to punch Professor Danvers in the face for a long time, and he finally had an excuse. So, anyway, he brought him over to the Headmaster's Office, and meanwhile, we're back in the carriage house. So, we're, like, uh . . . we're just going to be left here on our own? Alastaire wanted to run right back over there and save you, but fortunately, cooler heads prevailed."

Bella ducked as Alastaire threw a pillow at him, then continued, "We got the noctoscope set back on 'manual,' so we were ready to go whenever we saw the window open, and then the next thing we knew, all hell broke loose! What a show! Wind and explosions and snakes and huge naked women! It was like Mardi Gras! We saw the guy in the wheelchair go splat, and then Professor Danvers did this strange kind of levitating thing, but I'm guessing that was the moon healing him. It's really true, isn't it, that the moon works both ways? If I hadn't seen it myself, I wouldn't have believed it, but I guess that's what Agatha was counting on by letting you do your stuff. Like I said, she's got brass ones, or whatever else you want to say."

"So, um, are the Saturni like . . . gone?"

"No, unfortunately. They just vanished. General Azazel couldn't move fast enough, but the rest of them just split. And just for the record, I don't think the general was ever really Isolde Freeland's father, at least not in the biological sense. I'm guessing it was more of a term of affection, like calling somebody 'uncle.' But there's still a lot I don't know."

"And Simone?" Nina felt a stab of fear as she asked this. If Simone Freeland and her parents had hated her before, how much more were they going to hate her now that she'd blown up the general? She decided to put that thought out of her mind until she could decide how she wanted to deal with it.

"She's fine," Bella said. "Still acting like it was no big deal, although I think she was seriously freaked. I mean, how often do you get to see something like that?"

"Something like that." Nina lay in her new bed and thought about it. The little girl she'd met, the frightened child she'd befriended—Zoolie—was actually a being of immense age and power, locked in a titanic struggle for the world. The Four Gifts, the four spirits who had blessed her, were four things she couldn't even imagine. Much less trust.

But they were real, and that was something. She remembered her dream of the tall, dark woman telling her, *I exist,* and she felt an odd sort of ache.

"So, Sister Aquilina was never really here at all?" Nina asked. "She was just a red herring?"

"I don't know . . ." Bella shook his head. "There's still too many loose ends. The *jumbies* are still gone, for one thing. Yep, even Roticus. He took off. And there's still the business of the woman you saw wrestling with Agatha. Or else hugging her. We still don't know who that was."

"My guess is the *jumbies* are all down in the Bywater," Alastaire said, moving over on the bed so she could escape the encroaching sunlight, which was creeping across the sheets. She patted Nina's hand. "On Pauline Street. Don't forget, we did learn a lot about Sister Aquilina.

She's down there, and she's Professor Danvers's sister, and I guess we can now say she's pretty much on the side of the good guys. So, who knows? Maybe she'll just show up here someday."

"Yeah, maybe." Nina felt suddenly tired, with a weariness that was not just physical, but emotional. *I learned a lot, but I still don't know anything. I don't know who I am. I don't know what's the real deal with the prophecy. I don't know what's happening with Professor Danvers. And I don't know what's really up with the headmaster.* She felt as if her head was bursting with too many ideas, and they were doing nothing but making her sick. She lay back down flat on the bed and said, "I've got to rest a little now, okay? I'll see you guys later."

She came down for dinner that night. There was a moment when she stood in the doorway to the Common Room and everyone turned to look at her, and then the whole room erupted in cheering. There were some notable exceptions. Simone was there, looking daggers at her, and her girlfriends looked equally furious. But everyone else seemed pleased with her having faced down five large-scale authority figures, and Nina thought, *I guess it's the same everywhere. You kick power in the nuts, you get applause.*

She made her way over to the seat Alastaire and Bella had saved for her, and she sat down, saying, "I feel ridiculous."

And Alastaire said, "Oh, you'll get over it. Right now, hand me the mashed potatoes. I'm starving."

They had roast chicken and gravy, peas, carrots, and mashed potatoes, and everything was wonderful. As they ate, Nina snuck a glance up at the teachers' table, where Professor Danvers was still playing with his food. *He must just not like to eat,* and she felt a pang of love and pity and protectiveness and tenderness toward him that went right through her, even though he looked physically all right—and, in fact, perfectly gorgeous as always.

And just as she'd thought that, she heard a voice in her head saying, *"Oh, for God's sake. Please spare me your teenage angst. I'm not some moony seventeen-year-old vampire with perfect skin who glows. Grow up."*

And as she looked at him, she felt his eyes burning into her and saw his beautiful lips curve in just the faintest, most dangerous smile, and she thought, *Okay. I can do this. You want me to grow up, I will. Just watch me.*

They ate everything in sight, and it was all great, delicious and perfectly cooked, but as they finished the last bites, they realized something was missing. No dessert. Agatha sighed a put-upon sigh and pushed back from the table and stalked into the kitchen, and everyone else waited for the apple pie or brown betty or caramel sundaes or upside-down cake that presumably would follow.

Instead, there was an enormous bang from the kitchen, and plumes of smoke came wreathing out into the room.

Of course, everyone ran to see what had happened. In fact, there was such a rush to the door that for a while, nobody could get inside, except for Professor Danvers, who moved through them like a sharp knife, went into the kitchen, and shut the door behind him. There was a pause, and then they could hear his voice saying, unmistakably, "Shit!"

Nina, Bella, and Alastaire, fearing for Sally, pushed their way to the front, where Professor Danvers and Agatha both met them as they came back out.

Professor Danvers turned aside, and Nina noticed there were tears on his cheeks.

Agatha looked a little smug. She said, "Well, Miss Lamb, you're Johnny on the spot as always, aren't you? Just the person I wanted to see."

"Miss Danvers, what . . . what happened?" Nina asked, trembling. The whole room behind the older woman was black with soot. It appeared as if some sort of terrible fire had taken place, a gas leak, a disaster, but there was no sign of the cook at all, nobody in a chef's jacket and checkered pants, no blood on the floor, no nothing. It was as if Sally Bowman had disappeared.

"Our cook seems to have set a delayed-action fuse and blown up dessert, using that as a cover to disappear. Unfortunately, my brother—" Agatha sniffed, rolling her eyes "—has always had disdain for the physical facts of life that keep us going, and I've told him for years it was a mistake. He could have met Miss Bowman at any time, but he declined, which is why he's rather annoyed right now. I, however, have always made it my business to know everything that goes on here, so, of course, none of this surprised me. By the way, Sally wanted me to give you this. God knows why, but it appears she's sentimental about you."

She held out a sheet of paper which she, and presumably Professor Danvers, had both already read. There were numerous sooty fingerprints all over it. Nina unfolded it with shaking hands and read in Sally's well-remembered handwriting,

Dear Nina,

I told you I was obvious. Not entirely honest always, but obvious. Sir Gareth in the kitchen was called Beau Mains, the Beautiful

Hands, and that's where I misdirected you. You thought you were the Beautiful Hands, when, in fact, it was me.

Don't go looking for me on Pauline Street, because we've already moved. I'll find you as soon as it seems necessary. You were very brave, and very good, and you always appreciated my cooking, which is more than I can say for my brother.

Tell Strickland I still love him, but you can have him with my blessings.

Your friend,
Sally Bowman,
otherwise known to my enemies as "Sister Aquilina"

Nina felt as if she couldn't breathe for a moment. Agatha was looking at her with narrowed eyes and seemed to be expecting some response, so she said, "Uh . . . thanks." Professor Danvers still wouldn't turn around and look at her or anyone else, and she figured that was probably for the best right then. Folding up the letter and tucking it into her pocket, she told Alastaire and Bella, "Let's get out of here."

"So, what are you going to do?" Bella asked.

"Well . . ." Nina picked at a loose thread on her skirt, "I think I'm going to stay here, at least for a while anyway." She looked around the chapel, which as always, they had to themselves. "I mean, I know it sounds ridiculous, but I'm used to it here. Where else am I going to go? Tulsa?"

"I have to go to Europe for the next three months," Alastaire groaned. "My parents had it set up for ages. It's a way for us all to 'bond' after the storm. We're going to visit every catacomb and crypt and tomb and mausoleum from Madrid to Moscow while they're fixing up my parents' house in Lakeside, and my mom's going to be all, like, 'Oh we just have to get some of those sweet little souvenir guillotines and have our pictures taken at the chopping block in the Tower of London.' *Boring*."

"Cheer up—you'll be back in time for Halloween."

"Don't remind me. Five hundred kids wandering around the Garden District dressed as Harry Potter. Great."

"What are you going to do, Bella?" Nina asked to distract Alastaire from her bitching.

He frowned and said, "Actually, I'm going away too."

The way he said it made her stomach plummet. *He's leaving,* she thought. *He's learned enough, he's way smarter than us, his parents have decided to pull him out early, and they'll just have the teachers finish up his crossings and make him a full-fledged Skinny right now.*

He saw her expression, and something almost of wonder touched his lips, pulling them up in a smile. "You really would mind it if I left, wouldn't you?"

"Well . . ." She didn't want to embarrass him. "I've gotten to depend on you two," she said defensively. "You're like my posse. Simone Freeland's got hers. You're mine."

"Well, don't worry about it," he said, looking away. "I didn't mean it like that. I'll be back in a few months too. It's just that my parents are taking me away to Washington."

She knew at once he didn't mean the state. "And you're bummed why?" she asked him, trying to draw him out.

"Oh, I don't know! Who wouldn't be thrilled to be going to the epicenter of Saturni power? Benway and Father Ignatius and the Freelands have way more connections there than they do here! Half of Congress is on the menu!"

She was sorry she'd asked.

He subsided and said, "At least I'll be able to get some research done. The Library of Congress has to have more information about the Livaudais family. I'll let you know what I find out."

"Great." She meant it, but the revelation that both of her friends would be leaving New Orleans for the summer still made Nina realize just how lonely she was going to be. With Sally gone, she'd have nobody at Daedalus to talk to anymore. Sister Aquilina had said she'd contact her "when it seemed necessary," which to a Skinny might be anything from next week to twenty years from now. *I guess I'll get a lot of reading done.*

"Oh, I almost forgot, here's your polynomial engine back," she said, handing Alastaire the little computing machine.

Alastaire just shrugged and said, "Why don't you keep it?"

"You're kidding. Don't you want it?"

"I never use it, to tell you the truth. Fact is, I hate Calculation Science. I hate the idea of the world just being data. It leaves out all the important stuff like love and sex and loyalty and how it feels to eat bread pudding with whiskey sauce. Now *that's* something you just can't quantify."

Nina smiled and looked at the beautiful little device in her hands, resting in its ornately carved box. *I really do have to learn how one of these things works.* She could cast a Circle of Force, but Alastaire had said they could provide the answers to everything. She turned to Bella. "Can you do something for me?"

"Of course, if I'm able."

"Ask it what I should do next."

He looked at her, a little bemused, and then took it and fiddled with the numbers, and then pressed his fingertips to the two metal plates. He raised his eyebrows, loaded in some more numbers, adjusted several dials, and then gave it a good quick shake.

"This thing must be busted. It says you should go outside."

They looked at one another and shrugged, then stood up and made their way out to the corridor, and from there out into the garden. It was now twilight, with the world fading into a beautiful, limpid, late spring evening with soft, puffy, gray clouds looking lighter against the darkening sky. The garden was full of the scents of gardenias, jasmine, roses, and freshly cut grass, and the banana leaves were rustling, and the ghostly Spanish moss was swaying in the breeze.

The sun had set, but then suddenly, once again, there was radiance, the afterglow, as the gold sprang back up into the sky and ran from pale pink edges to pale blue, storm-gray and rose to flame striations in the center, a hallelujah of bruised color up and up to the distant and impossible clouds, a climax of indirect light already gone. Ribbons, estuaries of gold and pink fire, rumbles of grayish-blue and lavender ran everywhere, from horizon to horizon, along with frills of yellow and palest white. It was a silent song like a mighty chord of music, a hallelujah punctuated by the writhing limbs of the trees, with a sky so filled with color it almost hurt to look at it. And its taste would have been like a sick-ripe fruit exploding on the tongue.

And then it faded, as they watched, and the light was gone and the moon rose, waning now, a warm yellow crescent hanging low in the sky. It was a friendly moon, no harm to anyone, and Bella stood transfixed by it, his dark face yearning upward, while Alastaire stretched out her hands as if she would touch it and hold it still in its flight.

Nina wanted to cry because she loved them both so much, and she loved this place, this perverse, strange place where she had found herself and where people did horrible things and lovely things, and horribly lovely things at the same time, and sometimes the lovely things and the horrible things were almost the same, and impossible to tell apart.

Everything was fluid here, life and death and spirit and matter combined, and what had Legs said? Mankind worshipped some places as locations where the membranes between the worlds were exceptionally thin, and people could cross back and forth. And he had said New Orleans was such a place. And so it was.

Nina decided she could wait for some of her questions to be answered, and for now, it was enough to be here, in this beautiful garden, breathing in the intoxicating air so thick and heavy with scent it felt like wine, and standing with her brave, loyal friends under the light of the healing moon. At some point, of course, all that would change. If Bella and Alastaire became full-fledged Skin Eaters, the moon could eventually kill them. If she, Nina, didn't change, she would eventually grow old and die. No resolution was absolutely possible between the needy flesh and the impatient spirit, the flesh that hungered and the spirit that longed to fly free, and Legs had also said that all hungers involved a sacrifice, and Love would lie stillborn if we couldn't ignore the fact that it hurt so much.

Nina knew she had to figure out how she felt about all of these things someday, but not tonight. Her foot crunched against something just then, and she looked down and realized with a start what it was.

It was a small pile, placed very deliberately in the middle of the gravel path, of pistachio nut shells.

$\mathcal{A}$BOUT THE $\mathcal{A}$UTHOR

Photo Credit: Breton Littlehales, photographer

The enigmatic A.V. (Adrienne) Parks has written an exceptional four-book series, The Saturni, based in New Orleans, where there is no shortage of captivating lore. Think southern gothic, dark fantasy, magical realism . . . Adrienne has created a masterpiece quartet.

From the prestigious halls of Princeton University, where she graduated summa cum laude, to the late-night horror movie shows she hosted in Scranton, PA, she has led a life as enchanting as the stories she tells.

Born to a stockbroker and a swing musician, and the granddaughter of a Catholic priest, Adrienne's roots are as diverse as her experiences. She grew up in the bustling New York City metro area, where she and her late husband created mesmerizing music videos and documentaries. Twenty years ago, she ran away to New Orleans, where she now owns a charming (haunted?) guesthouse in the historic Garden District.